ALPHA
AND
OMEGA

ALPHA
AND
OMEGA

Harry
Turtledove

DEL REY

NEW YORK

2020 Del Rey Trade Paperback Edition

Copyright © 2019 by Harry Turtledove

Published in the United States by Del Rey, an imprint of Random House, a division of Penguin Random House LLC, New York.

DEL REY and the HOUSE colophon are registered trademarks of Penguin Random House LLC.

Originally published in hardcover in the United States by Del Rey, an imprint of Random House, a division of Penguin Random House LLC, in 2019.

LIBRARY OF CONGRESS CATALOGING-IN-PUBLICATION DATA
Names: Turtledove, Harry, author.
Title: Alpha and omega / Harry Turtledove.
Description: First edition. | New York: Del Rey, [2019]
Identifiers: LCCN 2019003078 | ISBN 9780399181511 (paperback) |
ISBN 9780399181504 (ebook)
Subjects: | BISAC: FICTION / Alternative History. | FICTION / Suspense. |
FICTION / Action & Adventure.
Classification: LCC PS3570.U76 A79 2019 | DDC 813/.54—dc23
LC record available at lccn.loc.gov/2019003078

Printed in the United States of America on acid-free paper

randomhousebooks.com

2 4 6 8 9 7 5 3 1

Book design by Jo Anne Metsch

ACKNOWLEDGMENTS

With thanks to Alan Abbey, who caught some places where I was stupid. The ones still here are my own.

ALPHA
AND
OMEGA

I

Eric Katz poked the ground with his trowel. A clod the size of his fist came away. He tapped it with the side of the trowel. It broke into several chunks. He tapped each of them in turn. They were all just . . . dirt. At a dig, you went through lots of dirt.

Doing it almost in the Temple Mount's shadow, though, added a kick you couldn't get anywhere else.

Almost in the shadow . . . Not many shadows here. He was glad for his broad-brimmed floppy hat. Without it, his bald head would have cooked. There were things worse than a sunburned, peeling scalp, but not many.

He swigged from a water bottle. It had been ice-cold when he took it out of the refrigerator this morning. It was still cool—and wet. You had to stay hydrated.

"Heavens to Betsy, Eric, how do you go on like that in this heat?" Barb Taylor asked. She really said things like *Heavens to Betsy!* She was an evangelical Protestant from Pawtucket, Rhode

Island, and would no more have taken the Lord's name in vain than she would have danced naked halfway up the Mount of Olives.

Dancing naked wouldn't have been a good idea for her here. She could burn under a fluorescent lamp, let alone the Holy Land's ferocious sun. She slathered herself with sunscreen, but she really needed something industrial-strength.

But she had the money to come to Israel, and she wanted to work at a dig, so here she was. The heat and sun took it out of her, but she was a trouper. She did everything she could.

Eric grinned crookedly. "I live in the Valley in L.A. As far as the weather goes, I hardly left home."

"And you tan, too," Barb said mournfully.

He nodded. "Guilty." He turned very dark after a few weeks in the sun. Barb burned and peeled and burned and peeled. If she wasn't white, she was red.

"As far as the weather goes." Orly Binur's accent turned English into music. "I've been to Los Angeles." The grad student's shudder said what she thought of it. "It isn't like this."

Eric couldn't deny it. A glance west showed him the glorious gilded Dome of the Rock: a Muslim shrine built to rival the Church of the Holy Sepulcher and placed over the stone from which Muhammad was said to have ascended to heaven—and on which, if archaeological speculation was right, the Ark of the Covenant had rested in the Holy of Holies in Solomon's Temple.

A little bit going on there, Eric thought. *The Angelus Temple doesn't measure up.* He laughed at himself. Next to this lineup of holy heavy hitters, the Vatican didn't measure up.

"I didn't know you were ever in L.A.," he said to Orly. "What for?"

"That conference three years ago." She wore a floppy hat, too—with more style than Eric did. When those big brown eyes looked at him from under the brim, his heart turned to Silly Putty. "We might have met then."

He grimaced. "Good thing we didn't. You wouldn't've wanted anything to do with me." His divorce was laceratingly new in those days. Archaeologists, he'd discovered the hard way, shouldn't marry marketing consultants. For a long time afterwards, he'd thought one particular archaeologist shouldn't marry anybody. Now he'd started wondering.

He wondered harder when Orly sent him another smoky look. "It might have worked out," she said, which proved she'd never dated anybody just coming off a divorce.

Barb Taylor sipped from a bottle of water like Eric's and smiled. Eric wasn't sure whether she thought they were cute or that they were fornicating sinners who'd sizzle side by side on a giant George Foreman Grill forevermore.

He switched to Hebrew to say, "Not a chance." He'd lost most of what he'd learned for his bar mitzvah, but working in Israel revived it. He was fluent these days. And Barb spoke and understood next to none. He knew she knew he'd changed languages so she couldn't follow, but he didn't care. He didn't like putting himself on display.

Later, he had occasion to remember that. Sometimes it made him want to laugh. More often, he felt like screaming. Much good either one did him.

"So should I run now, while I still can?" Orly asked. "What do you think?"

"Your call, babe." That came out in English. Eric returned to Hebrew: "I can't make you stay."

"You can make me want to. Or you can worry about everything till you drive me crazy."

"C'mon. If I didn't worry, I never would've got into this racket." Eric dug out another trowelful of earth. He sifted through it. And earth was what it was . . . except for a blackened *something* half the size of his little fingernail. He pounced.

"What is it?" For business, Orly came back to English.

"Coin," he answered. He took a hand lens from the breast pocket of his shirt to get a better look. It looked like a magnified blackened *something*. "Have to clean it up."

"A widow's mite?" Barb asked. "That'd be exciting."

"It'd be weird," Eric said. This was a Persian level, from centuries before the time of Christ. Hasmonean and Herodian coins didn't belong here.

Besides, to him they were dull. You could get them in carload lots. Dealers and shopkeepers sold them at ridiculous markups to people like Barb who wanted a connection to Jesus. *Maybe He handled this coin,* they'd think. *Maybe it belonged to a money changer He chased from the Temple.* Maybe, but you'd never prove it. Even if you did, so what?

Coins from Persian-ruled Judaea were more interesting—to Eric, anyway. The local issues imitated Athenian money, down to the owl on the reverse. Would the Jews have done that if they knew Pallas Athena was a goddess and the owl her symbol? Not likely. But they didn't. They just knew the originals were good silver, so they made knockoffs.

Only the inscription on the reverse—YHD in Aramaic or Hebrew letters—admitted where the coin came from. Sometimes it would be YHDH. The difference helped show when the coin was struck. He put the close-up lens on his iPhone to immortalize it in digits.

"Anything good?" Munir al-Nuwayhi asked around one of his endless stream of Marlboros. The Israeli Arab archaeologist's English held only a light accent. He smoked like a steel mill. At that academic conference in Los Angeles, he'd ducked outside after every panel to grab a coffin nail before the next one started. Rules were looser here.

Rules about smoking were, anyhow. Munir was a highly capable man, but had only an interim appointment at the Israeli equivalent of a junior college in Nitzana, a small desert town right on the

Egyptian border. He was probably lucky to have that. Like blacks in the USA, Arabs in Israel had to be twice as good to get half as far.

"Little coin," Eric said. "Persian period."

"I still think it's a widow's mite," Barb said. "Plenty of signs of the Last Days lately."

Munir puffed on his cigarette. He was Muslim but secular; he'd done his share of drinking and maybe a little more at that conference in California. He didn't tell Barb she was nuts, even if he thought so.

Eric held his tongue, too. Whatever he might've said wasn't worth the squabble. You couldn't convince people like Barb. They had their faith, period. Where faith didn't impinge, lots of them—Barb included—were surprisingly nice.

Orly snorted. Israelis wasted less time on politeness than Americans—or, Eric often thought, anyone else. And she wasn't used to, or was less resigned to, literal-minded Protestants than Eric. "Like what?" she said, plainly not expecting an answer.

But Barb had one: "Like the red heifer. I saw in the *Chronicle* how they're looking for it."

"Oy," Eric muttered. The *Jerusalem Chronicle* was the city's biggest English-language paper. Its politics lay well to the right. Compared to the the people who sought the red heifer, though, the *Chronicle* fell somewhere between Nancy Pelosi and Leon Trotsky.

"There won't be any Third Temple." Orly pointed at the Dome of the Rock. "That's been there longer than the First and Second Temples put together. It isn't going anywhere, no matter what some zealots say."

Eric wished she hadn't used that word. *Zealots* was what Josephus called the Jews who touched off the rebellion against Rome that led to the destruction of the Second Temple.

Maybe Barb didn't know about Josephus. "God will find a way," she said serenely.

"What can you do with people like that?" Orly snarled—but in Hebrew.

"Not much," Eric answered in the same language. "But every faith has fanatics . . . or nobody would look for a red heifer."

She winced. That hit home. She said, "People wouldn't blow themselves up in God's name, either"—which made Eric scowl. Things had been quiet the past few months. But he looked around warily whenever he went into a crowded restaurant or boarded a bus. A murderous maniac sure a vest full of explosives and nails bought him a one-way ticket to eternity full of wine and houris could ruin your whole life, not just your day.

"You're working hard, aren't you?" Yoram Louvish had one of the more sardonic baritones Eric knew. The chief archaeologist was dangerous in English, worse in Hebrew and Arabic. He dipped his head to Munir, whom he'd also hired. "You, too."

"Piss and moan, piss and moan," Munir said. He was as fluent in Hebrew as Yoram was in Arabic. Like the Jew, he stuck to English, though. English was foreign to them both. Using it didn't say anything about which of them held the power and which didn't.

As usual, sarcasm sailed over Barb's head. "Eric found a widow's mite!" she exclaimed.

"Did *he* say that?" Louvish gave Eric a hooded look, as if to ask if he could be so dumb.

"From the stratigraphy, it's probably Persian." Eric held up the plastic bag where he'd stashed the coin. "Have to clean it to make sure."

"That can wait," Yoram said, which surprised Eric. The Israeli fell into Hebrew to ask, "How'd you and Orly like to come along on something different—something bigger?" He returned to English to address Munir again: "You, too."

"What is it?" Eric asked.

"You'll see." Behind bifocals, Yoram smiled.

* * *

Yitzhak Avigad drove a rented Ford north and west from Little Rock. His nephew Chaim sat in the other bucket seat. Yitzhak, a solid, stocky man in his early forties, kept his eyes on I-40. Chaim had just turned thirteen. He tried to look every which way at once.

"What do you think?" Yitzhak asked.

"It's so *big*!" Chaim exclaimed. They both spoke English. Neither used any Hebrew since the El Al flight touched down at DFW and they changed planes for the hop to Little Rock. "And it's so sticky, too."

"Well, yes." Yitzhak's grin was crooked. When he'd stepped out of the air-conditioned terminal to take the bus to the rental-car center, his glasses steamed up. That wouldn't happen in Jerusalem.

Chaim's enthusiastic wave almost smacked his uncle in the face. "Everything's green!" They rolled past stands of pine and oak. In front of the trees, closer to the Interstate, grew shrubs and knee-high grass. Israel made the desert bloom, but you could always tell there *was* desert underneath. This seemed halfway to jungle.

By the way Americans reckoned things, Arkansas was a medium-sized state. It would have been nothing much by itself, but it added to the country. Yet it was more than six times the size of the nation the Avigads came from.

Americans didn't understand what that meant. Trouble in Arkansas rarely made the national news. Nobody in Indiana or Vermont cared what went on here. But it wasn't a long spit from the Jordan to the Mediterranean. Trouble anywhere in Israel meant trouble everywhere.

A crested streak of red shot across the highway. "Wow!" Chaim said. "What's that?"

"I think it's a cardinal," Yitzhak answered.

His nephew looked confused. "It's Catholic?"

"No. Cardinal's a color, too—kind of red."

"Oh." Chaim considered. "English is weird."

"No kidding," Yitzhak said. "Now hush—we're getting close to where we turn off."

They turned out to be farther than he thought. He was used to kilometers, and the road signs showed miles. But Russellville came up soon enough. Yitzhak turned north onto Highway 7. When he got off the Interstate, he seemed to fall back in time fifty years. No more McDonald's and Burger King, Walmart and Target, Office Depot and Staples. No more multimultiplexes with lousy movies. No more of the chains that made one strip mall in America look like the next.

No more prosperity, either. Russellville, on the Interstate, thrived. Dover, not far north, didn't. The downtown business district, two blocks long, was almost deserted. Shops were dark, with pathetic FOR LEASE signs in dusty windows.

A man walking a mean-looking dog eyed the Ford. What were strangers—especially swarthy strangers in *kippot* (or even yarmulkes, the more usual word for the same thing in the States)—doing in his town? He might have been a Druze villager in the Carmel Mountains, except the Druzes were used to tourists wearing peculiar clothes.

"I don't think he liked us," Chaim said.

"Neither do I." Yitzhak hoped the car wouldn't break down. Maybe the locals would be friendly and helpful. Or maybe not.

Getting out of town was a relief. The wooded Ozark Mountains rose ahead. Where was the little road that bent left? Yitzhak had been here before, but even with GPS he always worried about missing the turnoff.

"There!" His nephew pointed.

"Uh-huh." Yitzhak flipped on the turn signal even though nothing was coming south down 7. The side road was twisty, and only a car and a half wide. He passed a farm where razorback hogs rooted in a wallow. Chaim stared at them in fascinated horror. He sure wouldn't have seen the like back home. He wouldn't have seen the sagging rail fence or the muddy entranceway or the beat-up buildings in Israel, either. The Palestinian territories? Yitzhak's lip curled under his beard and mustache. That was different.

The next farm was different, too. Its new-looking chain-link and barbed-wire fences glittered in the sun. The driveway was neatly graveled. A satellite dish perched on the farmhouse roof. HENDERSON CATTLE, a neat sign declared.

Gravel rattled off the Ford's undercarriage as Yitzhak drove up. He killed the engine, stepped off the brake, unhooked his seat belt, and got out. Chaim did, too. He scanned the fruit trees near the farmhouse. "There's one!" he said. Another cardinal brightened a branch.

"*Pichew! Pichew!*" it sang: a clear, sweet whistle. Chaim listened, entranced. Yitzhak smiled. He also liked the bird. It was different from anything in *Eretz Yisrael*.

The farmhouse opened. A big, fair man in a polo shirt and khakis came out. "Mornin', Mr. Avigad," he said, holding out his hand. "Good to see you again."

Yitzhak shook. "And you, Mr. Henderson."

"Bill," the farmer said. "I'm Bill. We do this every time you're here."

"All right—okay—Bill." Yitzhak used the slang not too self-consciously. Henderson grinned. The Israeli went on, "This is my nephew, Chaim."

"Hello, son." Henderson extended his hand again. The big, square paw swallowed Chaim's. "Praise the Lord, I've heard a lot about you. You're a special young fella, you know?"

Yitzhak knew Chaim had heard that as long as he could remember. Right now, he looked more jet-lagged than special. "It wasn't anything *I* did, Mr. Henderson," he said. "My father and mother—"

"Like I told your uncle, I'm Bill," Henderson broke in. His drawl turned English into something slower and more musical than what Israelis learned in school. "And what your folks did, they did for you."

"It was weird," Chaim muttered. Yitzhak knew he hadn't thought so when he was smaller. Then he'd taken everything for granted, as kids do. He'd been born in a room raised above the ground on columns. He'd lived his whole life in an upper-story apartment. Even his playground was aboveground. He and half a dozen other boys about the same age went through the same thing.

"Ritual purity matters," Yitzhak said.

"If you reckon it does, then it does for you," Henderson answered easily. "I figure Jesus made it so we don't have to worry about that stuff, but you've got to do what you've got to do."

His friendly eyes slid for a moment to Chaim's shoes. They had clunky platform soles, straight from the 1970s. The rabbis had decided that, with enough prayer, those would insulate the boy from ritual pollution on this trip. That was what his unusual upbringing was about.

"One reason we're dealing with you, Bill, is your animals," Yitzhak said. "But you're not the only farmer with fine stock. The other reason is, your farm was never an Indian burial ground or anything."

"I told your friends so," Henderson said.

"Sure." Yitzhak let it go. His friends in the States and back in Israel had investigated Henderson every legal way and several illegal ones. Bill had no idea how they'd scrutinized his acres. Odds were he'd be furious if he found out. But nobody could afford a mistake on something this important. As far as anyone could tell, nobody'd ever been buried here.

"You'll want to give Rosie another once-over," the cattleman said.

"Right." Yitzhak was resigned to the chance of disappointment. His comrades had been disappointed before, more than once. It could happen again. There were other possibilities. But Rosie was the best.

"She's in the back forty," Henderson said. "Why don't y'all come with me?"

"Y'all?" Chaim whispered.

"More than one of us," Yitzhak whispered back: another thing English classes didn't teach.

He watched the pleasure his nephew took in walking on gravel, then on dirt, then on grass. Chaim had even enjoyed walking through vast, soulless DFW. He looked like a fish raised in a bowl that suddenly found itself in a lake instead. So much to the big world!

Then Chaim stopped, staring. "Cows!"

Bill Henderson grinned. "You betcha. Mind where you walk." Now he didn't look at those funky shoes.

Yitzhak had eyes for only one cow. Most of them were ordinary Holsteins, black and white and uninteresting. But Rosie was brick red all over, which made her the most important cow in the world.

"She's beautiful," Chaim breathed. Yitzhak wasn't sure his nephew knew he'd spoken out loud.

"She's the herald of the End of Days," Henderson said. "She'd be beautiful even if she was ugly, y'know?"

"She's beautiful," Chaim repeated, louder. "I didn't know she'd be beautiful." He pelted across the field toward Rosie. She paid no attention. Her jaw went back and forth as she grazed.

Yitzhak and Henderson followed more sedately. "He likes Rosie too much, that be a problem?" the farmer asked.

"No. He's a good kid. He was raised right," Yitzhak answered, which was true in more ways than Bill Henderson, *goy* that he was, understood. "When the time comes, he'll do what needs doing."

But he wondered when he watched Chaim throw his arms around the cow's neck. Rosie eyed him with that blank bovine stare. She was a good-natured creature; Yitzhak had seen that before.

The farmer said, "Check her out. You won't find anything different."

"That's why I'm here." Yitzhak pulled a jeweler's loupe from his pocket. A few years earlier, a red heifer born in *Eretz Yisrael* raised everyone's hopes, only to dash them by sprouting a white patch on her jaw before she turned three. One white hair was acceptable. More than one . . . *More than one, we look somewhere else,* Yitzhak thought. *What can you do?*

Chaim looked up at him. "I hope you find white," the boy said. "She's too nice."

"They call it a sacrifice because you're willing to give it up to God. God's more important," Yitzhak said. "Abraham would give up Isaac, you know. His own son." The English version of his name sounded odd to him. "After a son, how can you hold back a cow?"

"I guess." Chaim frowned. "But I don't like it."

"Don't get yourself in an uproar yet." Yitzhak examined Rosie along the edges of her jaws, at the base of her tail, on her fetlocks: the places where white hairs that would make her ritually unacceptable were likeliest to sprout.

He hadn't found any the last time he was here. His heart beat faster when he found none now. Rosie was three. She'd never been yoked. She seemed flawless. He examined her flanks and back and belly. He found not one white hair. He got manure on his trousers, but so what?

His eyes shone when he turned to Bill Henderson. "They'll inspect her again in Israel, but I think she'll do. I'll buy her." Once sacrificed and burned on a pyre, Rosie—or rather, her ashes— would make whatever they touched ritually pure in the ancient sense, the sense lost since the destruction of the Second Temple almost 2,000 years before.

"Praise the Lord!" Henderson said again.

One red heifer—so much money, Yitzhak thought. *Shipping her to* Eretz Yisrael—*so much more. The coming of the Messiah? Price-less.*

No one threw a chair—or a punch—but people were screaming at one another when the show ended. The audience howled like wolves in a butcher's shop. *This one went pretty well,* Gabriela Sandoval thought with an odd mixture of satisfaction and shame.

The cross-dressing, meth-dealing armed robber (currently out on parole) and his three girlfriends (who hadn't known about one another till taping time) didn't want to settle down. Gabriela guessed Paddy Bergeron would lose all three of them, and maybe his *cojones,* too. Once a woman realized she wasn't *it,* the writing was on the wall.

Gabriela wasn't sorry she'd put Brandon Nesbitt between her and their charming interview subjects. She also wasn't sorry three or four burly stagehands strolled out where those subjects could see them. No homicides here! *Gabriela and Brandon* already spent too much money on lawyers.

Things quieted down. Paddy shook Brandon's hand, then Gabriela's. He did something with his middle finger in her palm. She jerked her hand away and wiped it on her skirt. His grin showed bad teeth. She wanted to smack him.

One of his girlfriends was coming on to Brandon. She didn't drop her thong and assume the position, but she didn't miss by much. Gabriela thought—hoped—Brandon had the sense to stay away. He wasn't always fussy about where he found pussy. But if that gal wasn't a total skank, the word had no meaning.

As the audience filed out and a guest-relations assistant eased the losers off the set, the producer came over. "Good one, guys," he said with a big smile.

Brandon nodded. He soaked up any kind of praise like a sponge, and believed it all. "Thanks, Saul," Gabriela said. If she sounded weary, it was only because she was.

Saul Buchbinder persisted: "No, really. This was hot. I think we save it for the next sweeps month."

That told Gabriela he meant it. "Okay," she said—making your producer unhappy wasn't smart.

"Outstanding!" Brandon's happy smile showed off his mouthful of capped, almost mirror-bright teeth—nothing like Paddy's mottled snags. Yes, he got off on having his vanity stroked. He wished the show were called *Brandon and Gabriela,* even if he hadn't had the nerve to say so out loud.

"We'll do this forever," Saul crowed, visions of adding on to his Maui estate dancing in his head. "Know why? 'Cause we'll never run out of slime."

"Saul, I'm going on back to my dressing room to get the TV makeup off." Gabriela escaped. She really didn't like so much pore-clogging junk on her skin. But that wasn't the only reason she didn't feel like listening to Saul blow smoke. Let Brandon soak up the bullshit. She needed to get away. Some days . . .

Some days were tough. Lots of people had rotgut in a drawer to help them through days like that. Gabriela could afford better. She stashed a bottle of artisanal mescal in there. She swigged. It went down smooth and warm as a mother's kiss. The kick made her smile as she put the squat bottle away. She held it. It didn't hold her.

But she slammed the drawer shut. A good show, good enough for sweeps month. Freaks and geeks, freakier and geekier than usual. And wasn't that scary? Scary enough to make her want to take another knock to keep the first one company.

She didn't. "*Mierda,*" she muttered. Her family had been in

Texas since before it joined the Union, but she'd learned most of her Spanish in school and from her ex. Not that, though. It sounded so much more ladylike than the harsh Anglo *shit*. Her *abuela* used to say it all the time, and no one even blinked.

She did hope Brandon had the sense to stay away from the hard-eyed loser who'd been screwing Paddy Bergeron. With his looks and money, he could do better in the ICU, let alone in his sleep. But when a dick got hard, nothing else mattered. Her ex had taught her that, for sure. Hadn't he just!

After one more sigh, she made as if to reach for the drawer again after all, then sternly checked the motion. Brandon wanted top billing on *Gabriela and Brandon*. Gabriela wanted to get back inside the big tent again, next to the lions and the trapeze, not stay stuck in Sideshowland with the bearded lady and the sword swallower.

MSNBC, she thought wistfully. She'd been a star reporter there for a while. Everyone said they'd pull her out of the field pretty soon and give her her own show. She had the smarts, she had the looks, she had the ethnicity. She was heading for the top. Everyone knew it—especially her.

Then she ran headlong into everything that made being a woman in the professions such a joy and a delight. While she was on her second trip to Iraq, her husband filed for divorce. César was an IT guy at a pharmaceutical firm in New Jersey. He worked ten minutes from home when he wasn't working out of the living room. His lawyer used that to get a judge to grant him sole custody of Heather, who'd been three then.

Was he jealous of Gabriela's growing acclaim? Was he just sick of talking to her by e-mail? Had he already started messing with his new squeeze? Try as they would, Gabriela's lawyers hadn't been able to prove that, which was bound to be why the custody arrangement worked out the way it did.

Going through a divorce made you crazy. Going through one

by long distance made you crazier. One of the key features of the craziness was that you had no idea how crazy you were. To Gabriela, getting ahead in her career by any means possible suddenly seemed the most important thing in the world. With her family blown up behind her, what else did she have to hold on to?

She said some things that made her seem to have come a lot closer to flying Kalashnikov rounds and RPG blasts than she really was. And, after a few weeks, she got caught. A man telling that kind of lie might have been suspended or reassigned. They canned Gabriela. *That's what you get, you uppity bitch,* they might have been saying.

So there she was, out on the street. She thought about suing, but it wasn't as if the bastards didn't have cause. She still needed to make a living. She still had her looks, her presence, her skills in front of a camera. She still had her—tarnished—name recognition, notoriety, whatever the hell it was.

And so *Gabriela and Brandon* was born. It made money. It kept her on, or at least close to, the fringes of real journalism. Days like today, though, showed just how fringy those fringes could get. She longed for the real thing the way a methadone junkie longed for heroin.

She eyed the drawer she'd slammed. Enough mescal and she could forget Paddy Bergeron and his unlovely loves. But, though she eyed that drawer, she didn't open it.

Not even a saved-by-the-bell feeling when someone knocked on the dressing-room door. "Yes?" Gabriela said.

"The limo's ready to take you home, Ms. Sandoval," a young assistant said through the plywood. Sophia thought Gabriela was a wonderful role model. She'd said so, many times. It would have been flattering as hell if it didn't hurt so much

"Thank you." Gabriela squared her shoulders. "I'm coming." Out she went, ready to face the world again.

2

"Your limo's ready, Mr. Nesbitt," Sophia said.

"Coming," Brandon Nesbitt answered.

Sophia's smile when he emerged from his dressing room showed blond good looks, expensive contacts—*nobody's* eyes were that blue—and steely ambition. She was heading up in this world, and God help anybody who got in her way. She put Brandon in mind of a younger, more Aryan version of Gabriela.

Calculation glinted behind those contacts. If throwing a fast fuck at Brandon helped her get where she was going, she'd do it. If he thought it meant more than that, he'd be a bigger fool than any of the jerks who populated *Gabriela and Brandon.*

Next to Sophia, Paddy's girlfriend seemed . . . honest, anyhow.

The doorman nodded to Brandon as he slid out of the stretch Lincoln. He nodded back, and smiled his most sincere TV smile. He tipped the guy plenty, and made sure he acted friendly all the time. If you didn't keep the help happy, they had all kinds of ways to make you miserable.

His apartment was spacious, but none too clean. He wasn't a

swine of a bachelor, but he wasn't a neat freak, either. Life was too short. He looked in the fridge. Nothing seemed interesting, or even edible.

Head for a restaurant, then? He didn't feel like it—he was tired, and he'd put himself on display enough today. So takeout Chinese? Or maybe Thai?

A call to the Seafood Garden made sure he wouldn't starve. While he waited for the doorman's assistant to bring up his food— God forbid the doorman himself should leave his post—he checked his Galaxy for the latest.

Twitter, Instagram, Facebook, e-mail. Public addresses first. They were the ones from which he drew guests. Some people were so desperate to expose themselves. . . .

Nothing juicy, dammit. He checked his most private e-mail. Only his agent, his producer and director, and his first ex-wife knew it. It held nothing but spam for a stock "guaranteed to triple." He swore as he deleted that. All the secrecy in the world only slowed the tide of crap.

He was about to start the news feeds when the bell rang. His phone said he'd spent half an hour online. The virtual world could swallow your life.

Before opening up, he peered through the security spy-eye. Getting robbed and pistol-whipped made him check every time now. But this was just François with cardboard cartons from the Seafood Garden.

Brandon gave the Haitian three bucks and took his supper. No, nothing came free. And if the staff decided you were a cheapskate, you could pack it in. Nothing would go right after that.

He shoveled in the food—a shame, because it was great. What the Seafood Garden did with shrimp should have been illegal. And jellyfish, which he'd never dreamt of eating while he was growing up, were even better. But he'd spotted something he wanted to go back to. Never could tell who else was looking. . . .

Leftovers plopped into Tupperware. Maybe he'd remember them before they went bad, maybe not. He gave the phone his attention. He read. He took a few notes. Then he made a call.

"Saul? Brandon. What do you know about a red heifer? What do you mean, nothing? You're Jewish, for crying out loud. . . . Yes, I know you're not Orthodox." Saul liked jellyfish even more than Brandon did. He also liked bacon double cheeseburgers, and you couldn't get any *treyfer* than that.

Brandon checked his notes. "These guys in Israel want to build the Third Temple. One thing you need to do to make it ritually pure is sacrifice a red heifer. . . . It's a cow, Saul. A rare cow—like a purple cow, almost. There've only been nine since the beginning of time, except now they've found number ten. In Arkansas, no less."

By the noises Saul made, he didn't give a shit about cows. Maybe he was eating dinner himself. *Well, too bad,* Brandon thought.

"Listen," Brandon said. "The fundamentalists are creaming their jeans about this. It's all over Twitter and Facebook. They think it's the start of the Last Days and the Second Coming." Raised Lutheran, Brandon believed in Brandon, period. No. He believed in ratings, too. "There's a hell of a lot of fundies, Saul. And they watch TV. I see a *Gabriela and Brandon Special* coming on."

They didn't just do *Gabriela and Brandon.* Their Specials played on the credibility Gabriela'd built up when she really was an investigative reporter. Sometimes they used it up. They'd had a couple of fizzles. And if Brandon's own rep hadn't had some spots on it, he wouldn't have needed to work with Her Chicana Majesty. But there you were. And here he was.

Saul pissed and moaned. He always did when he started facing a new project. Brandon let him. TV shows weren't one-man bands. You needed a team, and you had to know everybody's moves.

When the producer slowed down, Brandon said, "C'mon. Think about it, man. Israel. The Palestinians. Jerusalem. The Apocalypse. If people won't watch that, what *will* they watch? 'Mixed Martial

Arts Fight Night 319'? Funny, Saul. But I'm serious. We can make this fly."

"Have you pitched it to Gabriela yet?" Buchbinder asked: the first cogent thing he'd said.

"No. I was hoping you'd do it," Brandon answered. "If she knows it's from me, she'll think I'm trying to upstage her." She'd have good reason to think that, too, because he was. He went on, "If you put it to her, she'll figure you saw the red heifer stories yourself. She'll be able to look at the idea without looking for a knife in the back. And this is gold. You know it's gold."

"Maybe." Saul held his cards close to his chest.

"Think it over, okay? If you don't see a way to make it work, call me back, that's all. Sound good?" When Saul didn't tell him *no* right away, Brandon said, "Thanks, man," and broke the connection. He waited to see if the producer would call back.

Saul didn't. Brandon smiled a predatory smile, there where no one could see it. Yeah, this just might work out pretty well.

"Wow!" Eric said. "I didn't know you could do this." The LED light on his hard hat let him pick his way through the tunnel under the Temple Mount.

Yoram Louvish chuckled wickedly. "Technically, you can't. We aren't. This isn't happening."

Behind Eric, Orly added, "And if the Waqf finds out—"

"Bite your tongue," Eric said in English. Orly laughed.

But it wasn't funny. When the Israelis conquered East Jerusalem and the Old City in 1967, they had to decide what to do with the Temple Mount. For the first time since Roman days, the holiest site in Judaism was in Jewish hands.

Only it wasn't *just* a Jewish holy site. The Muslims had held the ground for the past 1,300 years. So Moshe Dyan imposed a compromise. Jews could go up on the Temple Mount to look around, but not to worship; they prayed at the Western Wall below. Israel provided security, at a distance. The Waqf—the Muslim religious foundation—administered the Temple Mount, as before.

You couldn't make everybody happy, not in the Middle East. The Muslims resented the Jews for holding the Temple Mount. Some right-wing rabbis said the Messiah would have come in 1967 if the Israelis had dynamited the Dome of the Rock and started building the Third Temple then.

A lot of the time, you couldn't make *anybody* happy in the Middle East. Archaeology in and under the Temple Mount proved that. The Muslims denied that the Mount was ever a Jewish holy place. They hated the idea of excavations that might prove they were full of it. And they'd brawl if they heard about Israeli incursions. It had happened before. This was life and death—no, heaven and hell—to everybody on both sides . . . and, to complicate things even more, to all the different flavors of Christianity.

A triangle, Eric thought, *but a hate triangle—no love.*

He had a mineralogist's hammer on his belt, a tool every archaeologist carried. That was as close as he came to a weapon. He wasn't sure he could use it even if some Muslim fanatic screaming *"Allahu akbar!"* tried to rearrange his cranium. He hoped he didn't have to find out.

Munir al-Nuwayhi was along, armed with the same not-quite-weapons the other archaeologists carried. He kept his face expressionless as a stone. He didn't like what Yoram was doing. But he had enough intellectual curiosity to want to be in on it in case it turned up something good. And Louvish had chosen him to come, which meant he trusted him.

About the combat skills Orly and Yoram owned, Eric had no doubts. Louvish had seen real combat. And Orly had gone through the Israeli Defense Forces. Even when she was at her frilliest and girliest, Eric never forgot that. There was a certain . . . he didn't know what . . . about a girlfriend who could beat him up.

Not that Orly ever had or anything. But the thing was still there. Every once in a while, it surfaced in Eric's mind in the bedroom. Whether he was on top or underneath didn't matter. Was it a turn-on? *Can I take the Fifth?* he asked himself.

Himself let him off the hook by asking Yoram, "We're looking for artifacts from the period of the First Temple?"

"Yeah. Let's see those *mamzrim* from the Waqf say we weren't here when we bring out something like that."

Modern Hebrew borrowed its swear words from Arabic and Turkish and Russian—the revived language originally hadn't had its own. But Louvish could call the Arabs *bastards* with a word that came straight from the Bible. Munir would know what it meant. But he didn't say anything, regardless of what he thought.

"How did this tunnel get dug without them knowing?" he asked.

"Carefully." That wasn't Yoram. That was Orly. She laughed again. Eric might be sweating bullets down here, but she was having a great time.

And she was kidding on the square. The tunnel took off from a passageway that let Jews reach the Western Wall without running an Arab gauntlet. Then it dove like a submarine. They were far below the Herodian level. Anything they did find would be *old*. Were they *too* deep? Eric wondered, but he hadn't done the calculating.

Who had? Yoram? Maybe, but Eric wasn't sure his boss had the clout to set this in motion. There would be hell to pay if the Waqf found Jews poaching on, or under, its territory.

"Here we are," Louvish said. The tunnel stopped and widened into a space that reminded Eric of the bulb on the end of an old-fashioned thermometer. He turned his head this way and that, so his headlamp showed everything there was to see: yellowish rock, mostly.

What was the last light that shone down here? A torch? The flame from a handheld olive-oil lamp? Had light *ever* shone down here? Or was this a subterranean wild-goose chase? If it was, some people up top would be unhappy. But that was their worry, not Eric's.

The archaeologists played their lights around the chamber. The shifting shadows exposed anything out of the ordinary. They were old hands at spotting things by their shadows. Usually, the sun cast them, but lamps could, too.

"There!" Eric and Orly said, he in English, she in Hebrew. They both pointed to one stretch of the wall.

"What have you got?" Yoram was looking the other way when they called out. He turned toward them.

"Don't know. But something." Eric sounded sheepish. He couldn't make out what had caught his eye before; the light wasn't right now. But he knew he'd spotted something worth checking out.

Like a bird dog, Orly kept pointing so they wouldn't lose it. "Well, let's see," Yoram said. He and Munir advanced on the wall. After a moment, the Jewish archaeologist grunted. He stopped and nodded. "Yeah, that's something. Old stonework—really old."

"Uh-huh." Now Eric could consciously see what he'd noticed instinctively before. When layfolk thought about archaeology and didn't think about Indiana Jones and his goddamn fedora, they thought about Schliemann at Troy and Mycenae, about Howard Carter and Tut's tomb, about gold and treasure and spectacular artworks. *Wonderful things,* Carter said when he first looked into the tomb.

They didn't think about potsherds, let alone bricks and stonework. But broken pots and the remains of walls were what an archaeologist dealt with every day. Most stone blocks from Herod's day had a low, flat, smooth raised boss in the center. Where the stonework would be below ground level and out of sight, Herodian masons didn't bother smoothing the bosses at all.

The Hasmoneans—the Maccabees' descendants, who predated

Herod—also used rough bosses, but less so than the ones on concealed Herodian stonework. There wasn't any surviving Hellenistic stonework on the Temple Mount. The Maccabees had made sure of that. Persian masonry, which was older still, had bun-shaped bosses.

This . . . The bosses were rough, but they didn't look like Herodian foundation stones. This style was borrowed from the Phoenicians farther north. The blocks were long and narrow, laid alternately in groups of two and three stretchers and headers.

"It's from before the Babylonian conquest!" Munir exclaimed. From the Kingdom of Judah, in other words. When these stones were laid, Solomon's Temple still stood atop the Mount. That pushed things back 2,600 years, maybe further. Now Eric knew the pattern of headers and stretchers—blocks facing out and facing sideways—was what had drawn his eye.

"But the Jews weren't on the Temple Mount. Never, no sir." A scornful rasp filled Yoram's voice. "Ask the Waqf." He took his phone from his pocket and photographed the building stones.

"Let it go, Yoram," Munir said quietly, and, for a wonder, Yoram did.

Orly came up beside Eric. His arm slid around her waist. She snuggled against him, but her mind stayed on the masonry. "What's on the other side of that? How do we see without driving the Arabs bugfuck?" The last word came out in English.

In any language, it was a goddamn good question. Eric wished he had a goddamn good answer for it.

Kibbutz Nair Tamid lay a few kilometers inland from Tel Aviv. When Chaim Avigad went to see Rosie in the field there, platform shoes weren't enough. Unlike Arkansas' wide open spaces, almost every square centimeter of *Eretz Yisrael* had seen death and burial. So the rabbis said, and he couldn't argue with them. He didn't try.

To avoid religious pollution, then, he had to stay off the ground. But he wanted to see the heifer. People at the kibbutz went out of their way to accommodate him. Even by their standards, he lived an austere life. What fun he could have, they wanted to give him.

They laid down a roll of indoor-outdoor carpet from his house to the field. Contact with the ground polluted the carpet. But on top of it they laid a roll of bubble wrap—a new one whenever he went out. The rabbis said that gave him enough protection.

The bubble wrap made just going out fun. It popped under Chaim's feet. If he jumped up and down . . . But he didn't, for fear of going all the way through. He was a good kid.

When he got near the edge of the bubble wrap—but not too near—he called, "Come here, Rosie!" Her name came out in English, because she understood it that way. *Rose* in Hebrew was *shoshanah*. Chaim knew that, but Rose didn't.

She knew *Rosie*—and that Chaim had a treat for her. She stopped pulling up grass and ambled over to him. She even *smelled* grassy. A fly landed on her ear. When the ear twitched, the fly buzzed away.

"Here you go." Chaim pulled a carrot from his pocket. The carrot was special, from another kibbutz in the Negev. It wasn't pulled from the ground and meticulously cleaned to make sure no polluting dirt remained. No dirt had ever touched it: it was hydroponically grown, raised in a sterile vat from water and chemicals and nothing else. If you were going to be ritually pure, you had to *be* ritually pure.

Rosie didn't care. It was a carrot—that was all that mattered to her. Her mouth took it from Chaim's hand with surprising delicacy. But then her lower jaw went back and forth, back and forth, turning it to orange mush. A swallow, and it was gone.

She nuzzled Chaim's hand, hoping for more. "Eww!" he said, not sure whether that was cow spit or snot. Whatever it was, it was wet and slimy. He gave her a second carrot. A happy rumble came from deep in her throat. Chaim grinned—he liked making her happy.

But the grin slipped. She was a red heifer, the first in 2,000 years. They'd sacrifice her—the first sacrifice in more than 1,900 years—so her ashes could make other things, and people, ritually pure. Chaim *was* a good kid. He saw the need . . . but his eyes stung whenever he thought about it. He liked Rosie alive.

She nuzzled him again—sometimes he was good for three carrots. Not today. He threw his arms around her neck. She stared in mild bovine surprise. His mother and Uncle Yitzhak said she was just a cow, but they didn't understand. "I do," Chaim murmured.

"Chaim!" As if thinking of Uncle Yitzhak had brought him to life, he let out a yell now. "You've got a phone call!"

"Tell him to get lost." Chaim didn't want to let go of Rosie.

"Can't. And it's not a him, it's a her. A TV reporter from America. Ever hear of Gabriela Sandoval?"

"No." If Chaim hadn't heard of her, maybe he wouldn't have to talk with her.

But he did. "Come on anyway," his uncle said. "She—her production company—they—want to do a story about how we're getting ready to rebuild the Temple."

Thinking about that made Chaim think about sacrificing Rosie. He clung to the heifer. "Is she Jewish? Is she *frum*?" The word meant *observant*.

Uncle Yitzhak laughed. "No way. But she'll aim the story at the Christians in the USA. If it weren't for Henderson Cattle, we wouldn't have Rosie, remember." He said her name in English, too.

"Okay." It wasn't, but Chaim knew he was stuck. Sighing, he let go of Rosie and retreated along the bubble wrap. It kept popping, but he didn't enjoy it the way he usually did.

"Here he is," his mother said—in English—into the landline when he walked up the steps and inside the house. He took its being raised off the ground for granted, though lots of the buildings in Kibbutz Nair Tamid sat on concrete slabs. She handed him the phone, continuing, "It's Ms. Gabriela Sandoval, from the USA."

"Hello, Ms. Sandoval," Chaim said. Americans liked you to use those titles. Chaim thought it was dumb, but that didn't change anything.

"Hello, Chaim." Gabriela Sandoval sounded like somebody who belonged on TV or the radio, sure enough. Everything she said was very clear. "You're the young man who isn't allowed to get dirty, aren't you?"

"I'm one of them, uh-huh. I'm not supposed to," Chaim said.

"A lot of the time, people *do* do things they're not supposed to. I guess you know that." Gabriela Sandoval sounded sure of herself, the way TV people usually did. And she wasn't wrong. A couple of boys who'd been born ritually pure hadn't stayed that way. They and their parents weren't at the kibbutz any more. If a boy did something like that, it disgraced his whole family. The American woman went on, "You want to see the Temple come again, don't you?"

"Sure," Chaim said. Didn't she have any clue?

"What do you think about the Dome of the Rock and Al-Aqsa Mosque and everything else on the Temple Mount?" she asked.

"What about it?" Chaim said. "It doesn't belong there." Smiling, his mom set a hand on his shoulder.

"It's been there longer than the Temple was," Gabriela Sandoval said. "How will you get rid of it?"

"*I* don't know." Chaim rolled his eyes. Didn't she remember he was only thirteen years old? Worrying about that stuff was for grown-ups, and they were welcome to it. He added, "When God wants it gone, He'll take care of it."

"Just like that?" the American woman asked.

"Sure. He's God. He can do it." Chaim had no doubts.

"When will it happen, then?" She was full of questions.

"I don't know, but I think soon. We have the red heifer now and everything, and that's got to be a sign." Chaim's hand still smelled like Rosie. Grief stabbed him—they would kill his friend to restore ritual cleanliness to the world. Chaim wished God could have figured out some other way to arrange it.

Gabriela Sandoval changed tacks: "How would you like to be on TV with this red heifer?" She was only a cow to the woman. Chaim could tell.

He had to remind himself they needed publicity in the USA. "That would be all right, Ms. Sandoval," he said carefully.

"Great!" She had enthusiasm, anyhow, like so many people from the States. "Call me Gabriela. Everybody does."

Now that they'd talked for five minutes, it was okay. Chaim didn't think he'd ever understand Americans. "Okay . . . Gabriela," he said.

"We'll see you soon," she said. The line went dead.

Chaim hung up, too. "What do they want?" Uncle Yitzhak asked.

After explaining, Chaim added, "People from the United States are weird."

"They sure are," his uncle agreed. "But we can use them."

The Reverend Lester Stark had a long, craggy face; piercing gray eyes; an expressive baritone that was almost a bass; and a four-inch pompadour held in place by lots of hair spray. He also had two dozen buttery-soft Savile Row suits tailored to look as if they came from Walmart five years ago, twice that many neckties (a little too wide, a little too loud), and a drawl that was, unlike much of the rest of him, genuine.

His Birmingham church was also his studio. Six thousand people saw him live every week. Satellite feeds and the Gethsemane Network took him across North America, into the UK and Europe, into Mexico and Brazil, and, subtitled, to Korea and Taiwan. Lester Stark was a televangelical institution.

He'd preached on TV for twenty-five years, and not a whiff of scandal had touched him. He was married to his high-school sweetheart. Plenty of girls had thrown themselves at him since, and they'd all bounced off. Some boys had, too, but he was boringly straight. He didn't seduce secretaries; he didn't pay hookers to do things he couldn't get from Rhonda.

He lived well. He dressed well. His financial statements and his tax forms spelled out what he took and what he didn't. No matter how well he lived and dressed, his church threw money at poverty and what it reckoned injustice. Donations came in from half the world, after all.

"The Last Days are coming!" he thundered. "They are close at hand." When you heard him preach, you wanted to believe. He had that kind of voice, and that kind of confidence. The reason was simple: he didn't say anything he didn't believe.

"Signs multiply every day," he went on. "We will come to the Tribulation, and we will pass through, and we will prevail, for God is on our side!"

"Amen!" people called. "Preach it!" Most of the well-dressed men and women in the pews were white—most, not all. Nobody'd accused Lester Stark of being a racist, not even when he was starting out in Alexandria, Louisiana. He agreed with Martin Luther King that God cared more about the color of a heart than the color of a skin. People in his organization who didn't feel that way suddenly found they didn't work for it any more, and it did fine without them.

"We will prevail," he repeated, "but it won't be easy. The Antichrist is coming. He will lure many away from the true path, the path of righteousness. You won't let *your*selves be fooled, will you?"

"No!" the congregation shouted, and, "No way, Reverend!" and even, "Hell, no!" The sound engineers would have to scrub that before the sermon aired. *The Lester Stark Hour* stayed clean. Stark occasionally swore in private, but never in public. He didn't think that was hypocrisy; he called it good manners.

"Here are ways you can tell the hour is approaching," he said. "Before long, I'm sure, the Temple in Jerusalem *will* be rebuilt. The Rapture *will* come. The Antichrist *will* be loosed upon the world. And he *will* be a great trickster, like Satan, his master, who dwells below. Beware, lest you follow him and stumble into eternal damnation."

Many preachers these days got nervous talking about damnation. Not Lester Stark. He didn't shy away from it. It was nice to think everybody would go to heaven and see God face-to-face, but it wasn't in the cards, not from what the Good Book said. You could make people happy, or God. Stark knew which was more important to him—and to the people who listened to him.

"For those with eyes to see, the signs have been here for a lifetime," he said. "Israel was reestablished in 1948, for the first time since Roman days—fulfilling prophecy. It took the Temple Mount in 1967—fulfilling prophecy. When the Temple rises again—fulfilling prophecy . . ."

He left it there. Sometimes what you didn't say was as important as what you did. If you could make your listeners form pictures in their minds, you had them. If they did some of the work themselves, the ideas seemed their own. And people clung tighter to what was theirs than to what you handed them.

"The other day I heard from Rabbi Kupferman at the Reconstruction Alliance in Jerusalem," he said. "These Israeli patriots have been preparing for the appointed hour since the Six-Day War. They've made vestments for the priests and sacrificial vessels and musical instruments and hangings for the Temple. . . ."

He paused again. The TV screen would show the Reconstruction Alliance's address and URL. If his listeners could speed the Temple's rising by sending a contribution, that helped God's path.

Not that God needed help. When He wanted something, He made sure it happened. "If you're like Doubting Thomas, here's another sign for you," Stark said. "In the history of the world, there were only nine red heifers, the animals whose ashes brought sanctity and purity to priests in the First and Second Temples. Now a tenth has been born—here in the United States, I'm proud to say. As some of you will have seen, it's been brought to Israel, where it can sanctify and purify priests in the coming Third Temple.

"But do you need so many portents if you have faith? Remember our Lord's words to Thomas after He rose from the dead. 'Jesus saith unto him, Thomas, because thou hast seen me, thou hast believed: blessed are they that have not seen, and yet have believed.'"

He looked out over the congregation. He looked straight at the camera, out to the much larger congregation he couldn't see. "Believe," he said. "Believe with me. If you don't, nothing is possible. If you do, everything is. Thanks, and God bless you."

He stepped away from the pulpit, and dipped his head when the congregation broke into applause. The choir sang "A Mighty Fortress Is Our God." The light on the camera went out. On the air, the announcer would be asking people to tune in to *The Lester Stark Hour* next week, and to send contributions to. . . . Fundraising embarrassed Stark, but you couldn't do God's work without it.

A few people came up to shake his hand, to tell him or ask him something. He took his time with them. This was part of his job, too, sometimes the most rewarding part. Too many preachers scanted it once they got too big for their britches. Not Lester Stark.

Rhonda waited when he managed to get away. "You were good today, hon," she said, and kissed him.

She made him smile. She always did. To him, she looked as good as she had in her cheerleader days. If she was a little wider through the hips now, so what? She hadn't had four kids then. He wasn't the same, either, but she put up with him.

He squeezed her. "Thanks," he said, knowing she meant it. She always leveled with him, which kept his head on straight. "Let me clean off the TV makeup, and then shall we head for home?"

"Sounds good," she answered.

He drove their Navigator. They went past the statue of Vulcan up on Red Mountain. The iron statue's torch glowed red, not green. That meant someone had died in a traffic accident the day before. Lester Stark prayed for the victim's soul and drove on.

3

People said the United States was full of guns. People who talked that way had never been to Israel. Soldiers going on leave or returning to duty took their assault rifles with them. Security also toted Galils, and were ready to use them.

Eric Katz had stayed in Israel enough to take lethal hardware for granted. But the men outside the Reconstruction Alliance's museum weren't playing. They didn't just carry rifles. They wore helmets and body armor and khaki outfits that weren't . . . quite . . . Israeli Army uniform. Their eyes said they would shoot in a second.

They had reason to be jumpy. Around the corner from the Reconstruction Alliance building in the Jewish quarter of the Old City stood the Burnt House. A priestly family had lived there when the Romans sacked Jerusalem and destroyed the Second Temple in 70 AD (or CE, depending on your attitude toward such things). One man died reaching for a spear. *Plus ça change . . .*

Even from a block and a half, the guards creeped Eric out. "I don't know why Yoram sent us here," he grumbled.

Orly shrugged. Since she wore a tight T-shirt and jeans, Eric would've given that his undivided attention most of the time. Not everybody male in the Jewish quarter appreciated Orly's outfit. Two Orthodox men sweating in long black coats out of *The Matrix* and broad-brimmed black hats yelled unpleasantries.

"It's for the artifacts, not the politics," she said.

"No shit!" Eric exclaimed in English. The Reconstruction Alliance was a feather on the tip of the Israeli right wing. The people here had never stopped being mad that the Army hadn't blasted the Dome of the Rock after the Six-Day War. If they'd had their way, the Temple would have risen then—and every Muslim country in the world would have hated Israel forever. So would every archaeologist and art historian.

Orly shrugged again. "Nobody would notice them if not for ISIS and Hezbollah and our other friends." Eric grunted. The Israeli right was strong because the country had neighbors dedicated to wiping it off the earth. Once, people thought the neighbors were dedicated to wiping Israel off the earth because the right was strong. But the Palestinians hadn't made a deal even with the Israeli left. So . . .

So those guards gave Eric a fishy stare as he came up. They gave Orly a once-over, too, but a less demanding one. The Arabs didn't use provocatively dressed women as distractions to help guys with bombs. *Death before immodesty,* Eric thought.

When he and Orly passed and started to go into the building, a guard said, "Everything out of your pockets and into a tray. Same with your purse, lady." His Hebrew had an American accent like Eric's. He couldn't have made *aliyah* to Israel long before.

They went through an airport-style metal detector and X-ray inspection. "Okay?" Eric asked.

"I guess," an attendant answered. *His* Galil was slung, but he could grab it in a second.

After all that *tsuris,* they had to pay admission—adding insult to injury. Eric didn't like giving these people money, either. But he couldn't walk out now.

The first thing he saw inside was a model of the Temple. There was another that had been on the grounds of the Holyland Hotel and now lived in the Israel Museum, but this one was larger and more ornate. It was based on Herod's rebuilding of the Second Temple: half classical, half bulkily Semitic, and over the top with gold leaf.

"Wow!" Eric said. "How'd you like to have *that* on the skyline?" An Alliance functionary stood by to explain and comment. Her disapproval stuck out like spines. The air-conditioned room suddenly seemed thirty degrees colder.

One of these days, I will keep my foot out of my mouth, Eric thought. *Don't know when, though.* But Orly, bless her, said, "It's pretty tacky."

"Why did you come if you make fun of us?" the attendant asked.

"We're archaeologists," Eric answered. Let her figure that out.

Her feathers unruffled—partway. "Then you'll want to see the sacrificial implements," she said. "Come down the corridor."

Eric and Orly came. They saw a seven-branched menorah nearly as tall as a man. The sign, in Hebrew and English (no Arabic here—surprise), said it was fit to be kindled in the Third Temple. It was the first gold menorah since the days of the Second Temple.

"That's a *lot* of gold," Eric murmured.

Also on display were golden pitchers for filling the menorah with purified oil, and a vessel with a brush and tongs for cleaning the cups that held the oil. The precious metal . . . This was Fort Knox's gussied-up cousin.

The table for the twelve loaves of showbread—one for each tribe of ancient Israel—was larger and more impressive than the menorah. It wasn't solid gold, but only—only!—wood overlain with gold. It still weighed several hundred kilos. Golden censers that would be filled with frankincense stood nearby.

"They don't think small, do they?" Eric had trouble staying flippant.

"It's splendid," Orly agreed. "It's also—pointless."

"*We* don't think so," the attendant snapped. "What we have here is only a fraction of what the Temple once boasted."

Herod had squeezed his kingdom till its eyes popped to pay for rebuilding the Second Temple. Maybe he thought that would make his subjects forget he was a foreigner, and barely a Jew. Having Roman backing didn't hurt, though.

Like the table, the incense altar was of gold-plated wood. It was ready for the Temple. With it stood an incense chalice and a golden shovel for coals and ashes.

Two *mizrakim*—one silver, the other gold—rested on wooden bases. The vessels looked like cups with pointed bases and long handles. They were for spilling blood from slaughtered animals onto the altar.

Blood sacrifice had vanished from Judaism for more than 1,900 years. Eric didn't miss it. "What would the SPCA have to say about this?" he wondered.

He didn't expect the Reconstruction Alliance girl to follow him, but she did. "All animals will be killed humanely, of course," she said.

"Of course," he echoed. In the fourth century, they'd called the Roman Emperor Julian the Bull-Burner because of his sacrifices. The fourth century was much more used to gore than the twenty-first. Did these people think about the public reaction if they started killing cattle and sheep and goats and doves for the glory of God?

Of course—not, he thought. Why would they? The Third Temple had two chances of going up—slim and none. It would take . . . He didn't know what it would take to make that happen. *The end of the world?* Even that might not do it.

There was another shovel for ashes, this one bigger and made of silver. Its place was at the southwestern corner of the sacrificial altar. With it went a three-pronged fork for turning offerings or rearranging the woodpile.

There was a wheeled copper cart for hauling ashes (Eric didn't smile). There were copper vessels for meal-offerings and silver measuring cups. There was a copper laver with six faucets to hold the water the priests would use to purify their feet and hands. There were stone vessels for preparing the red heifer's ashes. (A placard said they'd been made years before a red heifer was found. These people might be out there, but they were thorough.)

There was a lottery box to choose which of two goats would be sacrificed each Yom Kippur and which made the scapegoat for the people's sins. It came with two sets of lots. One was wooden, as in the First Temple, and one golden, as in the Second. *Thorough— yeah,* Eric thought.

There was a harp and a lyre. There were long, straight silver trumpets. There were *shofars,* the ram's-horn trumpets overlain with gold (for Rosh Hashanah) and silver (for fast days). *Really thorough.*

There were priestly robes, woven in one piece without any seams except the ones joining the sleeves to the robe. There was a crown for the high priest, and a breastplate, too, with precious stones bearing the twelve tribes' names. Verses in Exodus told which stone went where. There were golden bells to alternate with woven pomegranates on the hem of the high priest's robe.

And there was the Ark of the Covenant. Its placard warned it was only a model, which made Eric think of Monty Python. The golden cherubim on top didn't look like the cute little cherubs on Valentine's cards. They had wings, but the resemblance ended there. They reminded Eric of spirits from Mesopotamian mythology, which was about what they were.

Seeing the Ark gleaming in gold, seeing the gold-plated carrying poles, brought Indiana Jones to mind again. Eric imagined himself in a fedora, brandishing a bullwhip. He shook his head. Only Harrison Ford could bring it off. A bald, bearded, fortyish Jewish archaeologist needed to stick to floppy hats and whisk brooms.

Well, Harrison Ford would look the fool at a real dig. Since Harrison Ford had more money than Carter had Little Liver Pills and all the starlets he could eat, that was imperfect consolation.

There was a jar for donations as they left. Eric and Orly looked at each other. The Reconstruction Alliance people were crazy as bedbugs and had poisonous politics, but their artisans did wonderful work. Eric threw in a 10-NIS coin. Ten New Israeli shekels—between two and three bucks—wouldn't let the Reconstruction Alliance ship the Dome of the Rock to Hoboken.

Orly put in one of those fat, two-toned coins, too. She looked no happier about it, but . . . *Conscience does make cowards of us all,* he thought.

After the AC and the fluorescent lights, the street was like walking into an oven. Eric looked for a falafel stand. Deep-fried smashed-up garbanzo beans didn't sound like much, but he'd got addicted to Israeli fast food. It had to be better for you than a Big Mac.

"What did you think?" Orly asked.

"It's the fanciest goldwork I've seen outside the British Museum and Cairo," he said slowly. "But it's so pointless. Do *you* think they'll build the Third Temple?"

She shook her head. "No way."

"Okay. We're on the same page," Eric said. And Orly voted Labor but wasn't part of the peace movement even before the second Intifada. The Arab uprising made its goals painfully naive. (The right was no better. Israeli politics were, amazingly, even uglier than the USA's.) He went on, "Why'd Yoram wanted us to see it, though?"

"Maybe he thinks more's hidden under the Temple Mount," Orly said.

Eric laughed. "Whatever he's smoking, I want some, too." Orly grinned. If you wanted pot or Lebanese hashish, you could always get some. Eric had the munchies without weed. Where *was* a falafel stand?

Gabriela and Brandon swept into Israel on a wave of publicity . . . aimed at the States. The Israelis were much less overwhelmed. Gabriela had discovered that as soon as she checked in with El Al for the flight from JFK. The United States talked the talk about airline security. Israel walked the walk. Her luggage, and Brandon's, and everyone else's, got inspected with microscopic thoroughness. She herself got grilled like a Coney Island frank.

Finally, she lost patience and complained, "Do you know who I am?"

The man questioning her was handsome in a tough-cop way. He was also quite grim. "No," he said in Winter-Is-Coming tones. "Purpose of your visit to Israel . . . ?"

Sometimes you could cut through crap by pulling rank and blustering. Sometimes—less often, Gabriela had found—bluster brought more crap down on you. This looked like one of those times. "Journalism," she answered mildly.

"Tell me more," the security guy said, so she did. Brandon and Saul Buchbinder chimed in here and there. When they finished, the Israeli shook his head. "Those people . . ."

"It will make an interesting story," Gabriela said, hoping she was right. "People in America care about what's happening with the red heifer."

"They should find something more important," the man said. But he passed Gabriela through. The rest of the entourage also endured the kind of security nobody'd done since the *Vopos* quit trying to keep people from getting out of East Berlin. They all passed and were grudgingly allowed on to the 747.

"Jesus!" Brandon said with feeling.

"Not on this flight," Saul said. Gabriela gave the joke the small laugh it deserved. Brandon scowled. He liked to top other people's lines. When they did it to him? Not so much.

One more flight. Gabriela'd long since lost track of how many she'd taken. The rest of the crew were also veterans. Business class made travel easier to endure, but *easier* wasn't *easy*.

Ben Gurion Airport lay twelve miles east of Tel Aviv. The kibbutz where Rosie the red heifer of the apocalypse—*Apocalypse Cow,* Gabriela thought, as if ruining a movie title with one letter on Twitter—and Chaim Avigad lived was closer to the airport than the city was. She didn't want to live on a kibbutz, though, even if *Gabriela and Brandon* had to film one. She'd grown up poor, but once was enough.

She and her mob collected their luggage. They had enough to intrigue and even alarm the Israeli customs officers. Brandon's jet-lagged temper frayed. "Good God!" he exclaimed. "Didn't you hear we were coming?"

"Easy," Gabriela said softly. "Easy." The scene back at JFK had warned her how prickly Israelis could be.

"We didn't expect all—this." The customs official waved at the nylon sacks full of video gear.

"You get *Gabriela and Brandon,* you get what goes with them." Saul Buchbinder sounded proud. The customs man grabbed his phone and spoke in Hebrew. Gabriela glanced at Saul—did he follow? By his blank look, no. That was a shame.

A supervisor ambled over. He needed a shave. His deodorant had quit for the day. He and the other customs officer yakked incomprehensibly. Then he switched to English: "You can go through once we make an inventory. You have to take everything out again, not sell it here."

"That's fine." Gabriela hid her exasperation. Brandon looked affronted at the idea that they'd part with anything. Without this stuff, he forgot he existed. Gabriela felt that way, too, but less than she had when she was younger.

She would have been more exasperated if she'd known the inventory would take two hours. A production assistant had to call the two limo drivers waiting outside to make sure they stuck around. They wanted more money for sitting there. They'd have to get it, too.

At last, the procession started. They were staying at the Alexander, on Havakook Street. Gabriela got the Superior Suite. The guests in the lobby gaped as she and her colleagues strode in. Those guests were a nebbishy-looking lot. Gabriela wasn't the only one who thought so; Brandon asked the desk clerk, "Is a dentists' convention in town or something?"

"No," she answered. "The Alexander caters to the diamond trade."

"Oh." Brandon sounded nonplused. Gabriela knew she was. Those bad haircuts and off-the-rack suits were probably protective coloration. If you looked as if you made your living doing root canals, who'd knock you over the head and run for the closest fence with your briefcase?

The Superior Suite boasted satin sheets. Gabriela's mouth twisted. She'd had those on her wedding night—or were they silk then? Whatever they were, they'd kept her and César from getting much traction.

She yawned. Lack of traction wouldn't worry her now. It was still early evening, but she aimed to hit the sack anyway. Even flying business class, go seven time zones and someone might as well have hit you over the head with a rock. If she woke up too soon tomorrow, she'd go out and see what Tel Aviv looked like these days. She hadn't been here for a long time.

She closed the curtains, used the bathroom, and went to bed.

Even with the curtains closed, the room wasn't quite dark. That annoyed her—for about fifteen seconds. Then she forgot about it, and about everything else.

Several floors below Gabriela, Brandon Nesbitt fumed. The bitch with the top billing got the Superior Suite. The second banana got . . . a hotel room. By American standards, it was on the crowded side and a little old-fashioned. He'd stayed in plenty of worse places—a tent in Somalia, for instance—but he didn't feel like remembering that. He had resentments that needed nursing.

Old-fashioned room or not, the WiFi worked and his phone had bars. He called Kibbutz Nair Tamid to let them know *Gabriela and Brandon* had arrived. Gabriela didn't bother with that, no. She'd left it for him. What else was he but a hewer of wood and a drawer of water?

Maybe the people at the kibbutz were too naive to understand that. They sounded happy to get some publicity. Yes, the show could film Chaim and Rosie tomorrow.

"Maybe the day after," Brandon said, yawning. "I want to lose some of my jet lag first." Jet lag was the correspondent's occupational disease, the way black lung was with coal miners. People kept coming up with what they claimed were cures. Brandon had tried them all. The next one that worked would be the first.

"That will be all right, too," Chaim's uncle told him, and hung up. The uncle was Yitzhak . . . Avigad. Brandon beamed at remembering the last name. He was the guy who'd decided Rosie was red enough and holy enough to die for religion. *Gotta interview him, too,* Brandon reminded himself. *Maybe in front of the barn or wherever they keep the cow. Good visuals that way.*

But that could wait. Even thinking about it could wait. He wanted food, he wanted to wind down a little, and he wanted sleep. He checked the room service menu. No bacon and eggs for breakfast. No sausage or ham and eggs, either. Damn! Now he wanted dinner, though. He ordered lamb and eggplant. It felt Biblical, or maybe just Mediterranean.

While he waited for it to come up, he turned on the TV. The laminated channel guide was in Hebrew and English. The local channels were in Hebrew, too, of course. But the international ones were in English, sometimes with Hebrew subtitles or crawl, sometimes not. Feeling worn out and brainless, Brandon went to ESPN.

It turned out to be ESPN Europe, full of soccer news and highlights even if the Brit doing the broadcasting called it football. Brandon cared more about soccer than he did about suicide, but not a whole lot more. He was also so brain-damaged from the flight, he watched the guys in short pants run around till room service knocked on his door.

The little fellow who wheeled in the cart was a Thai, not an Israeli. Like most developed countries, they used cheap Third World labor for scut work here. He spoke just about enough English to get by. Brandon tipped him—American money, because he hadn't changed any yet—and sent him on his way.

He ate. The lamb and eggplant was pretty good. Not great, but you couldn't expect great from room-service cooking. When Brandon finished, he wheeled the cart out into the hall. A maybe diamond merchant was doing the same thing a few doors down. They nodded to each other and disappeared back into their rooms.

Brandon left the TV on. It gave him something to look up at every so often when he wasn't staring at his phone. He remembered how things had been before you could carry the whole world in your pocket, but only distantly. The generation coming up behind him wouldn't remember at all.

North Korea was acting stupid. So was Iran. So was the President. That was how things went these days. With everything else so crazy, wouldn't the red heifer and the dream of rebuilding the Temple seem more like comic relief than real news?

That Brit talked about the Mexican wave. It just looked like the wave to Brandon. He noted differences between British and American English. That was a new one for him. *The driving seat* was another, and so was *the finishing line*. They were close to American usage, but differed from it. *Fixtures* and *ties* had to do with the *schedule,* and the Brit said *table* when he meant *standings*. But Brandon needed to Google *breaking your duck* to learn it meant the same as *getting off the schneid.*

After a while, he couldn't stay interested in either the dumb sport or the funny phrases. The TV made a faint popping noise when he killed power with the remote. He dug a plastic vial of pills and a pill cutter out of his Dopp kit. He cut one of the small round white tablets in half. After a moment's thought, he cut one of the halves in half again.

He nodded to himself as he washed down the quarter-pill with water from the bathroom sink. You had to be careful with roofies. A whole one would leave you out of it for almost a day. He couldn't afford that now. He judged even a half here would be too much. A quarter, though . . . A quarter and he'd turn off, sleep deeply till morning, and be ready to do whatever needed doing then.

Walking back to bed, he nodded again. Roofies had other uses, too. He'd never done that with them, but he knew how. He had done some other things, things he wished now he hadn't, not because they weren't fun but because people remembered them too well. In this age of Weinstein and Lauer, Wynn and Ailes, that wasn't so good. He'd drawn too much of the wrong kind of gossip.

He muttered as he pulled back the sheet. He would have been a much bigger deal in the business if not for that stupid goddamn chatter. He wouldn't have been junior partner to a Mexican bitch who'd blown her own shot at glory, that was for sure.

He slid into bed. The mattress was squishy. He hated squishy mattresses—one more reason to take some Rohypnol. Out went the light. The smoke detector's little red eye glared down at him from the ceiling. He glared up at it till the quarter-pill started to kick in. Then he rolled from his back to his side and floated away.

Gabriela woke in darkness. She looked at the glowing digits of the clock on the nightstand. The clock said it was 4:28. *"Mierda,"* she said, not that she was really surprised. She'd sacked out early, so of course she'd get up early. Much as you wished you could, you didn't slot into a distant time zone right away.

She thought about sleeping some more, but not for long. She'd got eight hours and then some. She was *awake,* even if out of phase. She turned on the bedside lamp, then checked her phone. There was a text from Brandon saying they'd film at Kibbutz Nair Tamid the next day. He'd dealt with it. That was good. And they'd all be happier and able to work better after an adjustment day.

Her stomach growled. It wanted breakfast, or possibly lunch. She checked the little hotel guide on the dresser. It told her room service went into action at 0630. *"Mierda,"* she said again, louder this time.

She jumped in the shower. Then she put on jeans, a knit cotton top, and Adidases and went downstairs. Her footfalls echoed in the deserted lobby. She got some local money at an ATM, then went to the front desk. The clerk behind it was yawning as she walked up.

"Where can I get some breakfast?" Gabriela asked—beating around the bush had never been her style.

The clerk frowned. "It's so late, it's early," she said, which was either bad English or very good, depending. She went on, "All the clubs are closed, and the morning things, they aren't open yet."

"But I'm hungry now," Gabriela said. Her body might not know what time it was, but it was sure she needed food.

"Let me think." The clerk didn't yawn again, but plainly needed an effort not to. After a moment, she brightened. "You can try down by the bus station. That's open all the time. I think you can get something inside, and places around it may be up, too."

"How do I get there?" Gabriela demanded.

The clerk reached under the desktop and pulled out a city map. "We're here; it's *here*." The hotel was almost on the beach; the station lay farther inland and a bit south. "It's a couple of kilometers, more or less. You can take a taxi, or it's not even a half-hour walk."

"Is it safe to walk alone in the dark?"

"Oh, yes. All the thieves, they are asleep at this time. And Tel Aviv is a pretty safe place anyway."

"Okay. Thanks." Gabriela had the map. She had her phone. The bus station looked big and important. She figured she could find it.

But she hadn't gone far before she wondered if this was a good idea. Tel Aviv was muggier than Los Angeles, but at least as warm. And, like L.A., it had homeless people sleeping or shooting up wherever they could. No one bothered her, but she didn't feel safe, either.

The bus station was in a pretty gritty part of town. Gabriela had to clear security to get inside. More druggies found odd corners to nod off in. Hookers—Asians, Africans, blondes who came from Russia or Poland—strutted along the corridors, looking for business even before sunup.

Even before sunup, the huge terminal bustled. Signs in Hebrew, English, and (in smaller letters) Arabic directed travelers where they needed to go. Almost all of the people ignored both prostitutes and homeless folk. Gabriela made her way to a food court. Stores that sold clothes or books or tchotchkes were closed, but not the restaurants. There was always a demand for coffee and food.

Gabriela gulped two espressos from paper cups and got some *fuul* beans, which seemed to be the preferred Israeli breakfast. They weren't quite Tex-Mex refried beans, but they came close. She ate them at a small, beat-up plastic table with something in Hebrew scratched onto the top.

No one paid her any special attention. Her black hair, brown eyes, and light-brown skin made her look more normal here than she would have in, say, Wichita or Des Moines or St. Paul. She blended in. Her looks would have let her do the same thing in Iraq and Afghanistan, but the cultural divide was far wider in places like those.

She chucked the cardboard bowl and plastic spoon, grabbed another slug of espresso for the road, and headed out. Hebrew, Arabic, Russian, English, and other languages in the background reminded her of every international airport she'd ever walked through. So did the bland coolness of the air-conditioning.

Then it was out into muggy reality again. She glanced at the security men and women screening people before they let them in. They looked like combat soldiers, not ordinary guards. They had helmets and body armor and rifles. You saw a lot of rifles in Israel, more than you did in the States. People here didn't shoot each other nearly so much, though. It made you wonder.

It was getting light outside. A star still shone in the east. Venus? Jupiter? Something bright, anyway. Not bright enough to be the Star of Bethlehem, though. Bethlehem, these days, lay in the West Bank, in territory Israel had occupied years longer than Gabriela'd been alive.

She walked a couple of blocks west, toward the Mediterranean, then turned right to go north. Traffic was picking up. Israelis drove with the suicidal machismo that prevailed everywhere in the Middle East. Even so early, car and truck horns played a cacophonous symphony. Lanes and traffic lights were matters of opinion, not the gospel they would have been most places in the States.

A big van roared past on the wrong side of the road and made a screeching left as it raced toward the station Gabriela had left a few minutes before. She turned around to stare after it. Even by Israeli standards, that was insane driving.

Unless . . . Hardly thinking why, Gabriela spun 'round and started back the way she'd come. The story-detector light every good re-porter needed came on inside her head. Something wasn't right.

She hadn't got to the corner when she heard the sharp stutter of automatic weapons. Gunfire never sounded like anything else, not after you'd heard it a few times. She'd just had time to realize that when the world blew up.

The office building she hadn't rounded shielded her from the worst of the blast. *Car bomb,* she thought dizzily. *Big fucking car bomb.* She didn't realize she was picking herself up off the sidewalk till she'd already done it. Her palms were all scraped. Her jeans were out at the knees. One knee and one palm bled with some en-thusiasm. Pain reached her a little at a time. Her butt hurt along with everything else. She must have landed on it before rolling or being blown over.

She'd worry about all that later. She dug her phone out of her pocket, then swore. Protective case or no protective case, the screen was smashed. She held a useless piece of electronic junk.

But she still had her eyes and her ears. She knew how to take notes, a skill younger reporters had mostly lost. And she was on the spot for something big. She wouldn't let it go to waste. She hur-ried back around the corner, and straight into a vision of hell.

The worst thing was, it was an all too familiar hell. She'd seen such things before in Baghdad and Falluja, in Kabul and Kandahar. She'd smelled them, too: gasoline and explosives and charred paint and charred flesh that reminded her too much of a pork roast for-gotten in the oven. Razor-like glass shards had scrunched under her shoes before, as well. Her disgrace and exile to the safety of the USA had let her forget things like this existed. But here they were again, as if they'd never gone away. And they hadn't. She had. She was back with them again, though.

Also far too familiar were the bodies and pieces of bodies and blood of the dead and wounded splashed across streets and sidewalks and walls, burning cars sending pyres of filthy black smoke into the sky, buildings on fire or in rubble or leaning crazily, and all the people who hadn't been killed outright shrieking and screaming and ululating at the tops of their lungs.

Men and women who hadn't got badly hurt rushed to help those who had. The Israelis handled that better than Gabriela remembered from her days in Iraq and Afghanistan. Most of them had gone through the military and knew how to give first aid. But the disaster and the toll were plainly enormous. The front of the bus terminal was a crumpled, shattered mess. How many inside the building had flying glass and metal fragments scythed down?

Ice tingled along Gabriela's spine. If she'd lingered in the shower or at her breakfast, she might have still been in there when the car bomb went off. If she had been, they might have had to clean her out with a push broom—or with a hose.

You couldn't think about things like that, not if you wanted to keep doing your job. But you couldn't *not* think about them, not when the iron stink of blood clogged your nostrils, not when you were bleeding yourself, not when the howls of police and ambulance sirens threw new notes into the chaos all around.

A man grabbed her arm and pulled her toward the carnage, shouting in Hebrew. "I don't understand," she said. When he heard English, odds were he'd leave her alone.

Only he didn't. He shifted to that language himself, saying, "Come on. We have to do what we can." He had a cut under one eye. His left ear had been half Van Goghed, and dripped blood onto his powder-blue polo shirt. He had other damage, too—about like Gabriela's, maybe a little worse. He didn't seem to realize he'd been hurt.

Gabriela followed him. They hadn't gone more than ten feet before they came to a man thrashing and bleeding on the sidewalk. He was clutching his belly and making noises human ears weren't meant to hear for long. The man who'd grabbed Gabriela pulled his torn clothes aside and examined the wound in his flank. "You have a handkerchief?" he barked.

"I . . . may." Fumbling in her purse hurt Gabriela's hands, but she was damned if she'd show it. She gave the Israeli a square of blue felted cloth—not a hankie, but what she used to clean her glasses.

With a grunt, he wadded it up and stuffed it into the wound. His own handkerchief followed it a moment later. "Gotta slow down the bleeding," he said.

"I suppose so." Gabriela's stomach lurched. She didn't want to give back the *fuul* beans, but she wasn't sure she could keep them down.

"Americans. You aren't used to this." Scorn edged the Israeli's voice.

"I'm a journalist. God help me, I've seen it before. I only wish I hadn't," Gabriela said. "Who do you think did . . . this?"

"Arabs, of course," the man said coldly. "ISIS? Hezbollah? Hamas? You know what? I don't care. Whoever it is, we'll make them sorry. You hit us, you get hit back harder." A certain cold, fierce anticipation filled his voice.

What happened to Turn the other cheek? Gabriela wondered. But Jesus had given that admonition a long time ago. Hardly anyone listened to Him then. No one in the Middle East gave a damn about Him now.

The Israeli hopped up and stopped an ambulance by jumping in front of it and daring it to run him over. Gabriela thought of the Chinese man holding back tanks in Tienanmen Square in 1989. The ambulance driver yelled furiously. The Israeli yelled back and pointed at the man he'd just plugged up. An attendant jumped out of the back of the ambulance. He had a pistol on his belt along with his aid kit. He and the fellow who'd dragooned Gabriela got the badly wounded man into the ambulance. It backed up, turned around, and squealed away.

"Something," the Israeli said, and then, "What's your number?"

She gaped at him. He stood there, smiling and confident, ready to tap it into his phone. Israeli men were sure they were God's gift to women. No hesitation, no doubt—if it looked good to them, they went for it.

No luck, either. "None of your damn business," Gabriela snapped.

The guy shrugged, not a bit put out. He'd swung, he'd missed, he'd swing again as soon as he could. "Your loss," he said, and trotted toward the next closest injured person. That was a woman. Gabriela wondered if he'd come on to her while he was trying to patch her up. She wouldn't have been a bit surprised.

Brandon Nesbitt woke up in morning twilight. He was wide awake, too; the quarter of a roofie'd totally worn off. *Should've taken half after all,* he thought. He knew he'd be hammered by the time he finally got some sleep tonight.

He dialed room service. A recorded message told him they'd go to work at 0630, half an hour from now. He said something foul. Food might wait, but he needed caffeine. A coffeemaker sat on the dresser. He went over to fix himself some brain cells in a cup.

He was about to pour water into the reservoir when the floor shook under him and a roar filled the world. The windows rattled. He thought they'd blow in, but they didn't—quite.

Earthquake? No; he'd been through some. This was too big a boom to come and go that quick. Which left? *Plane crash,* he thought, then shook his head, remembering where he was. *Car bomb! Goddamn big one, too!*

And we're on the spot! He grabbed his phone and called Gabriela. He got her voicemail. "The fuck?" he muttered. Then he said, "Big bomb. Big story. Call me back!" Where the hell was she, anyway?

Before he could put the phone down, it rang. Not Gabriela—

Saul. "Come to my room—427," the producer said when he answered. "You can see it from here. And how come Gabriela's not answering?"

"I dunno. I was wondering the same thing. But I'm on my way. Get the rest of the gang, too." Brandon threw on jeans and New Balances. He didn't bother with socks or with changing the old T-shirt he used for a pajama top.

No elevators. Some kind of emergency stop. He ran down the hall and down two flights of stairs. No one complained about his getup. A nerdy diamond merchant in PJ's had a companion who looked like a Victoria's Secret model and dressed the part. Maybe they *were* a girl's best friend. Brandon hurried past her, ran down the fourth-floor corridor, and banged on Saul's door.

Saul let him in, then pointed east, toward the center of town. "There."

"Jesus!" Brandon said. "That's one fuck of a bomb." He judged partly by the smoke rising above and behind a mall in the foreground, partly by the bite the explosion had taken from a medium-sized skyscraper. "What's that building?" He didn't know his way around Tel Aviv for hell. And Saul was a Jew. He ought to have this figured out.

And he did. "It's the new bus station they put up around the turn of the century."

Brandon grunted and nodded. "Makes sense if you're a terrorist. Banks hold money. Bus stations hold people, and that's what they're after. But where's Gabriela? It's not like her to stay off the phone."

Saul only shrugged. "I dunno. I had the hotel operator ring her room phone. Zilch there, too."

"Damn!" *If she can't do the story, it's mine,* Brandon thought. He stared out the window at the smoke. Not much wind; the cloud hung above where the bomb had gone off. Faintly, through the glass, he heard siren after siren scream. More thuds against the door startled him. Then he relaxed—he'd told Saul to get the rest of the crew. The producer let them in.

"Turn on the TV!" Brandon exclaimed.

"What for?" somebody said. "It's right in front of us."

"I want to find out what's going on," Brandon said with more patience than he felt. "The locals can tell us. And I want to see if the world press is in town. We may have a beat. It's not what we came to cover, but we sure can."

"Where's Gabriela?" two guys asked at the same time.

"We don't know. All we know is, she's not picking up," Saul said.

When Brandon punched the remote, he found the locals were already at the site, gabbling in Hebrew. Things looked like hell, or slightly worse. Big chunks of the bus station had fallen in, or maybe gone up in smoke. Another building close by had taken a bad hit, too. Bodies and body parts lay in the street. The Israelis didn't blur them the way American TV would have. Dazed, bleeding survivors staggered around. People were screeching. Cars blazed like tiki torches.

"Anybody understand any of what's going on?" Brandon asked.

"Believed to be a van . . ." a cameraman said. Brandon hadn't known Danny was Jewish—he was a freckled redhead. "Believed to have two men in it . . . Hundreds trapped in the wreckage."

"Arabs?" Brandon asked. "The perps, I mean."

Danny waved for him to quiet down. "When you talk, I can't follow. Somebody's calling for people to go to hospitals and give . . . something."

"Blood." Brandon and three others said it together. Brandon went on, "Let's get ready to roll. What we look like doesn't mean shit right now. CNN, eat your heart out."

An Israeli with a look only too familiar—the kind of top firefighter or cop who took charge in disasters—snatched the mike out of a reporter's hands. He shouted into it with desperate urgency.

"Oh, Lord!" Danny went white—or maybe green.

"What?" Saul wanted to get clued in.

"He said something about radiation. I wish I knew the language better."

"Dirty bomb!" Brandon got it out first. People had dreaded one for years. *Someday,* they'd said. Well, it looked as if *someday* was here. And, with Gabriela silent, he was Johnny on the spot. "Come on!" he said, his voice crackling. "We'll get as close as they let us."

Half the people crowding Saul Buchbinder's room looked at him as if he'd gone nuts. "What if that's too close?" a cameraman said. "I don't want to glow in the dark."

Saul came through. "Double hazardous-duty pay," he said.

"Snag gas masks if you want," Brandon added. "A country like this, the hotel'll have some. And get cracking, okay? Nobody's gonna go anywhere I don't. Who's game?"

In twelve minutes, the whole crew was rolling toward the disaster. Sure as hell, the Israelis were trying to put a perimeter around the bombing, and a wide one, too. Well, with radiation involved you could understand that. But Brandon browbeat one set of cops into letting them go through, and Saul bribed another. Brandon thought so, anyway—*no* suddenly turned into *okay,* and the producer looked smug.

They set up right at the ragged edge of catastrophe. Somebody handed Brandon a gas mask. Clumsily, he put it on. The light under the camera lens went red. Gas mask or not, he was on. "This is Brandon Nesbitt, in the bleeding heart of dirty-bombed Tel Aviv!" he said, and hoped his voice would get out.

Eric Katz thought he'd got numbed to disasters. Suicide bombers, mass murderers, zealots flying planes into skyscrapers, earthquakes, tsunamis, hurricanes . . . The world had taken some tough knocks lately, and he'd seen most of them.

Now this new one. Israel had seen its fair share and more, but this felt different. This felt worse. The crowd in the little Jerusalem café sat silent, staring at the TV. You couldn't hear yourself think here most of the time, but events had outrun arguments about them.

Somehow, an American reporter was in the middle of the blast zone. "This is Brandon Nesbitt, in the bleeding heart of dirty-bombed Tel Aviv!" he exclaimed, his pig-snouted gas mask muffling some—but only some—of his excitement. There was a Hebrew voiceover for anyone who needed it, but Eric could get the English through it.

He and Orly were as stunned as everyone else in the café. The look on her face scared him. He'd been shellshocked after 9/11, but he was a continent away from New York City. Tel Aviv lay next door to Jerusalem. Everything in Israel lay next door to everything else. This wasn't a country, it was a family—one that had just had somebody murdered.

"Brandon Nesbitt, live from Tel Aviv!" the reporter repeated. The name rang a vague bell for Eric. Hadn't Nesbitt lost a job somewhere because of something unsavory? The details wouldn't come. The day felt too weird. Disasters were like that. 9/11, for older people the day JFK got shot . . . As Nesbitt had said, a whole city got its heart ripped out today.

"An hour ago, two—the authorities think two—men exploded a van outside the new bus station here in Tel Aviv," Brandon Nesbitt said. "I hurried to the scene, or as close as I could get."

"Why was he there? Did he know ahead of time?" The ferocity in Orly's voice made the hair on the back of Eric's neck try to stand up. It was scarier than her eyes, which was saying something.

He thought she was paranoid. Then Nesbitt said, "With me is my colleague and friend, Gabriela Sandoval, who was slightly injured in the blast. Tell people how you happened to get caught in it, Gabriela." Eric started wondering about conspiracy theories himself. Wasn't that *too* pat?

Ms. Sandoval also wore a gas mask. Her hands were bandaged; blood splashed her top. "You'll know, but the world won't, that *Gabriela and Brandon* came to Israel to cover the red heifer and the possible rebuilding of the Temple," she said. Orly snorted softly. A few people in the café jeered, but only a few. Disaster even trumped woo-woo. Gabriela Sandoval went on, "I had an early breakfast at the bus station, and I was on my way back to our hotel when the bomb went off. I did what I could to help hurt people till I saw you and the crew. That was when I found out it was a dirty bomb." One of her battered hands went to the gas mask.

"We were stopped from getting within half a mile of the station by Israeli security personnel," Brandon said. "They'd already started cordoning off the area. Here is Captain Mordechai Yehoshua. Captain, why did you suspect this was something worse than an ordinary explosion?"

Yehoshua didn't bother with a mask. He was filthy and blood-spattered. He'd got a lot closer than half a mile. "We brought Geiger counters. We always fear the possibility," he said, his English accented but more precise than that of many native speakers. "We fear it, and now we have it. What the people who did this will have . . ." He shook his head. "It is not for me to say."

Fuul beans, bread, and cups of espresso sat forgotten in front of Eric and Orly. Hardly anyone in the café was eating much. How could you, after this?

"Do you know what the radioactive substance is?" Brandon asked.

"Not yet," Yehoshua answered. "We will soon. The explosion spread it wider than we would have liked. The wind, thank God, is calm, or it would have gone farther yet."

"How wide an area is contaminated?" Gabriela Sandoval inquired, and then, "How radioactive are *you*, Captain?"

"Me?" The Israeli looked surprised. "I haven't had time to worry about me. How wide an area? We're finding out." He eyed the

American reporters. "You are likely inside it here. I wouldn't be surprised."

"Chance we take." That was Nesbitt, brave, foolhardy, or sure he lived a charmed life. Eric thought Gabriela was older, though with the masks he couldn't be sure. She made no blithe comments, anyway. Eric would have got the hell out himself. Nesbitt went on, "Is there any estimate of casualties?"

"Not yet. With a bus station, with people going in and out, it's hard to say," Yehoshua replied. "Dead will be close to four figures, if not in them. This is from the explosion, you understand. The radiation . . . I have no idea."

"Has anyone claimed responsibility?"

"Not that I know of," Yehoshua said. "There are obvious candidates, though. They should think twice before they celebrate. Our reach is long, and they *will* pay. Oh, yes." His voice sounded even scarier than Orly's.

"Every Ahmed in the world better run," said a man with hairy ears two tables over from the archaeologists. Certain kinds of Israelis called all Arabs Ahmeds, the way some Americans in MAGA caps called all blacks Rastuses. People nodded and shushed the man with the hairy ears at the same time. But chances were he wasn't wrong.

Somebody handed Brandon Nesbitt a note. He glanced down at it through the mask's portholes or whatever their right name was. "The Security Minister has resigned. The Prime Minister has accepted the resignation," he said.

"That *mamzer* better run, too," said the man with the ears. "Screw up like this and quitting isn't good enough."

"Whole government should resign," someone else said. "They let us down."

"Everybody did, everybody in the world," the hairy-eared man agreed. "And now? Now it's payback time."

4

lick. Click. Click, click. Yitzhak Avigad was no expert on Geiger counters. He hadn't known Kibbutz Nair Tamid owned one. He wished he still didn't. That would mean nobody'd had to pull it out of storage.

"Come on!" He shouted as loud as he could through his gas mask. Almost everybody wore one. Yitzhak wished they had a mask for Rosie. *Wish for the moon,* he thought. Two men led her in from the fields toward a horse trailer hitched to a Toyota pickup.

"Hose her down!" Yitzhak yelled.

Somebody had already turned on a hose. Rosie snorted in surprise and what sounded like pleasure. The day was warm. The water probably felt good. But that wasn't why Yitzhak gave the order. If anything radioactive had landed on the red heifer, he wanted to wash it off.

He glanced west, toward Tel Aviv. The dirt on the portholes wasn't the only thing blurring his vision. So did tears of mourning and fury, and the smoke pall hanging over the city.

There were moments you always feared. When you found yourself in one of them, you commonly discovered it was as bad as you'd thought it would be.

This nightmare moment was worse. Not just a truck bomb but a dirty bomb! The dead, the maimed, the wreckage—and who could say when people'd be able to go back into downtown Tel Aviv? Even after the experts declared it safe, how many ordinary people would believe them? How many tourists would?

It was worse than a disaster. What could be worse than a disaster? A catastrophe, and this was one.

"Get her into the trailer," Yitzhak told Rosie's handlers. Dripping, the cow went up the ramp. She *was* a good-natured beast. They'd put feed in the manger inside the trailer. Rosie'd started eating when the men locked the gate behind her.

"Uncle Yitzhak!" Chaim called from the closest building. They'd have to get him and the other ritually pure kids out, too. That would be more complicated than moving Rosie. Plenty of kibbutzim could care for a cow. Keeping the boys ritually pure till she was sacrificed . . . They had to do it.

"What?" Yitzhak asked.

"Come see what's on Al Jazeera!"

Yitzhak said something foul. But he came. Word about the dirty bomb was all over the world. That crazy American who wanted to do a story about the red heifer and Chaim ended up in the right place at the right time—unless he ended up dead of radiation poisoning, anyhow.

What would the Arab satellite channel's take be? Yitzhak remembered men in *kaffiyehs* and women in *hijabs* dancing in the streets of Palestine after 9/11. He remembered how fast the Palestinians suppressed those pictures after they realized—too late—they weren't winning friends but were influencing people. Surely they wouldn't . . .

But they would. There was a cheering crowd in Hebron. "Death to Israel!" people chanted. "Death to America!" others cried.

Yitzhak spoke fluent Arabic. A scraggly-bearded kid struck his face in the camera and screamed, "An Arab A-bomb! *Allahu akbar!*"

"Makes you want to throw a rock through the screen," Chaim's mother said.

"Oh, a little," Yitzhak answered.

The picture cut to Cairo. The crowd there was bigger and more excited. Egyptian Arabic differed from Palestinian, but Yitzhak followed well enough. The Egyptians yelled "Death to Israel!" too. Cops stood by, looking stern but doing nothing.

"Although the President of Egypt has deplored the attack, here is the popular response," a reporter said.

Chaim understood Arabic, too. What he said after that startled Yitzhak.

"Here is Riyadh," the Al Jazeera newsman said. Fewer people in Riyadh wore Western dress—no women did. But it was party time there, too, and in battered Baghdad as well. Then the feed cut to Teheran. That was an even bigger, even louder demonstration. The ayatollahs must have organized it, but the people shouting and pumping their fists were having a great time.

Yitzhak noticed he was grinding his teeth. He made himself stop. His dentist kept telling him he'd be sorry later on if he didn't. Then he started again. He had other things to be sorry about now.

"Nice to know everybody loves us," his sister-in-law said.

"It doesn't matter," Yitzhak said. Rivka Avigad looked at him in surprise. So did Chaim. Yitzhak went on, "We've spent too much time caring whether people love us, and look what we got." The TV switched to more shots of the Tel Aviv ruins, then to people in hazmat suits with Geiger counters. Yitzhak quit grinding his teeth again—briefly. "Look what we got," he repeated. "From now on, we do what *we* need to do, and that's it."

"We've always thought that, here at Nair Tamid," Chaim's mother said, and Yitzhak nodded. She continued, "But what will the government do? I wish more people saw things like us, but—"

"They will now," Yitzhak predicted. "How can they help it?"

A shout from outside: "We're ready to move the kids!"

"Get going!" Yitzhak told Chaim. The boy put on his gas mask. Behind the glass panes, his eyes were enormous. Yitzhak set a hand on his shoulder. Then he wondered if he should have. Was *he* radioactive? The counter hadn't chattered *much* here. He hoped he was okay.

Chaim's Nikes popped bubble wrap as he hurried to a waiting minivan. He carefully didn't step off the strip of purity. The other kids who'd been born into ritual cleanliness followed. The wagon rolled off to the south, away from the prevailing winds.

The truck pulling Rosie's trailer had already left. Was a red heifer more important than the children? Harder to come by, anyhow.

Now they were all heading to safety. Yitzhak laughed at himself. They'd still be in *Eretz Yisrael*. Those shots of contaminated Tel Aviv, and of the Arab world and Iran celebrating, reminded him nobody here was safe.

No one would be, either, till the Messiah came. That was what everyone at the kibbutz was working toward. When the Temple rose, when the heifer was sacrificed, the time would be ripe for His coming.

If the Muslims didn't care about wrecking an Israeli city, why should Israel care about the Dome of the Rock or anything else on the Temple Mount? The smile that stretched across Yitzhak's face was predatory. Those terrorists might have played into his hands.

No. Into God's hands.

Gabriela Sandoval wished for a ham sandwich. Pork wasn't against *her* religion. It was, however, almost as deeply underground here as porn in Saudi Arabia.

She was so tired, she couldn't see straight. Her voice was shot, too; she'd been on the air for hours and hours. She sipped from another little cup of sweet, highly caffeinated mud. So far, she hadn't used anything stronger. She would if she had to, though. Uppers were easy to come by everywhere. She'd never joined the Boy Scouts, but *Be prepared* still made a good motto.

For a while, she could watch TV instead of being on it. CNN, MSNBC, Fox, and the BBC had crews in town. So did CBS, ABC, and NBC, though they'd taken longer. But tiny little independent *Gabriela and Brandon* had got the beat! "Hurray for that red heifer!" she said wearily.

"Yeah." Saul Buchbinder had a martini. Gabriela wished for one, but coffee was a better idea. The networks and news channels wanted to talk to her and Brandon because they'd been too close to ground zero.

She wasn't *very* radioactive. The Israeli doctor who'd checked her out had assured her of that. But what if the stuff got into her bones and started eating her up from the inside out? What could you do about that? You could die of it, that was what.

CNN was on in the hotel bar, rerunning the President's speech. "This shows how hard it is to fight freedom's enemies," he said. "We've got to stop them *all* the time. If they win even once, they can brag about that. Or they think so. They haven't dreamt of the punishment this atrocity will bring down on them."

He went on and on. He wasn't the world's greatest speaker, especially if you owned an IQ above room temperature. But the message he needed to get across today was pretty simple.

"Open season on anybody whose uncle's pool guy knew somebody who heard of terrorists once upon a time," Buchbinder remarked.

"Just what the Israelis need—a hunting license," Gabriela said. "They do plenty without one."

"They'll do more with," Saul predicted.

"Uh-huh. What would we do if somebody got off a dirty bomb in San Francisco?" she wondered.

Gulping the martini, Saul pointed at the President's fleshy face on the TV screen. "Way things are these days, *he'd* give the guys a fucking medal."

Gabriela snorted, but Buchbinder wasn't kidding. "You know what I mean," she said. "We'd go after those guys—they might hit Dallas next, or somewhere else important."

"Meow, pussycat," the producer said. Gabriela stuck out her tongue at him. That hurt; she'd bitten it when the bomb knocked her down. Saul went on, "Yeah, you're right—we'd smash them if we figured out who they were. The way the FBI and the CIA are these days, we might not even manage that. Who do *you* think pulled this one off?"

"Maybe ISIS, maybe al-Qaeda, maybe Hezbollah," she answered. "Not Hamas or Fatah—they couldn't do this kind of job."

An hour and a half later, she was saying the same thing on Fox News, sitting across from Forrest Charleston. His haircut had to cost three times as much as hers; his politics lay a little to the right of Attila the Hun's. Unlike several former senior Fox people, though, he did keep his hands to himself.

Charleston was sure the dirty bomb had to be an ISIS operation. "They're trying to unite the Muslim world against the West," he insisted. "They're doing a good job, too."

"It could be." Gabriela didn't want to push back too hard on someone else's show. She did say, "They aren't the only terrorist group with a grudge against Israel, though."

That made Forrest Charleston pounce: "Where would they get the radioactives?"

"Where would ISIS?" Gabriela returned. "There are four places I can see: renegade Russians, Iran if it was Hezbollah and not ISIS, Pakistan, and North Korea."

"What about France?" Charleston came from the Freedom Fries school of Francophobia.

"Oh, come on, Forrest." Gabriela wasn't usually the sedate one in a pairing, but she could roll with it. "If France passed that stuff to terrorists going after Tel Aviv, there isn't a big enough hole for them to hide in. Whoever did this doesn't count the cost."

"All the French need is plausible deniability." Charleston wouldn't get off his hobby horse.

Gabriela knew she'd sound like a contradicting bitch if she told him he was full of it, but she'd look like an idiot if she didn't. So she said, "If they mess with the Israelis, they need more than that. So does everybody else. Talk about holes to hide in, I bet some terrorist big shots are in them now."

Just for a second, Forrest Charleston looked as if he'd bitten down hard on a lemon. But he pulled himself together; no matter how far to the right he sat, he was a pro. "You were on the spot," he allowed. "You and your partner got closer to the scene than any other American journalists. Do you think this was a professional job?"

"I got *much* closer than I wanted to," Gabriela said, wondering about her long-term health again. "With the radioactives, it almost has to be professional. And it was a big bomb, and they blew themselves up where it would hurt most. So yes, they were pros."

"How will this impact Tel Aviv? Will it ever be the same?"

"That's hard to say." Gabriela had to hide an ironic grin. Yes, this was TV. Something had just happened, and Charleston was talking about *will it ever?* as if the moment were eternity, world without end, amen. She made herself go on: "Let's see how well the Israelis can clean it up and how the people who live in Tel Aviv handle it. Maybe this is one thing more, and they go on. Or maybe it breaks the camel's back. We'll find out."

"Will the Security Minister's resignation keep the government in power?" Charleston asked.

He comes to Israel and he wants me to play prophet? Gabriela thought wryly. Shrugging, she answered, "I don't know for sure, but I doubt it. Public anger's just starting to boil here."

"I think you're right." Forrest Charleston sounded disappointed at thinking anyone besides his own infallible self could have something straight. Gabriela didn't blame him. No one got noticed or controversial or rich by agreeing with other people on-camera. Charleston went on, "So you look for a hard right turn in Israeli politics?"

"I'm afraid I do," Gabriela said. *And I wonder how the red-heifer people are managing. If anything will make the country pay attention to them, it's this.*

She said nothing to Charleston about why she was in Israel. If the commentator with the fancy haircut wanted contacts with people like that, he could damn well roll his own.

The red lights died. Forrest Charleston leaned back in his chair, far enough to make it creak. "Thanks, Gabriela," he said, and then, "Hell of a thing to do a show about! What a Charlie Foxtrot!"

"I know." Gabriela held up a bandaged hand. "Do I ever."

An aide threw a note in front of Charleston. When he read it, he scowled and clicked his tongue between his teeth. Somehow, Gabriela knew what he'd say before he said it: "They just found the Security Minister's body. He left a note—and a wife, and five kids."

"Oh, Lord!" Gabriela reflexively crossed herself, but she wasn't much surprised. If you took your work seriously, and if it was important, and if you failed that badly, what was left? Not much. You'd always be *the guy who* . . . The Security Minister was still *the guy who* . . . , but he couldn't hear about it any more.

"That's the first collateral damage," Forrest Charleston said. "How much more?"

Gabriela didn't know. Who could? But her answer came close enough for government work: "Lots." Charleston nodded.

When the camera went on, the Reverend Lester Stark said, "Let us pray for the children of Israel in their trial and tribulation."

And the men, women, and children of his comfortable congregation, far from danger, bowed their heads and prayed for people killed and maimed and poisoned in Tel Aviv. Whether they would have been so charitable toward closer Jews . . . few thought to wonder. Nor did Lester Stark.

To give him his due, he didn't focus on things close to home. He was trying to look ahead, the most dangerous thing a preacher could do. How many had made jackasses of themselves by prophesying things that didn't happen? Far too many. Stark didn't want to join them.

But he didn't want to sit silent, either. That seemed safe, but the seemingly safe was the most unsafe. You had to stand up. God said so in Revelation 3:15–16: *I know thy works, that thou art neither cold nor hot: I would thou wert cold or hot. So then because thou art lukewarm, and neither cold nor hot, I will spew thee out of my mouth.*

"I take my text today from the Book of Revelation," Stark said, which was why those verses were so much on his mind. "I do this with no small fear, for Revelation has led many bold ministers astray."

In the pews, people smiled as if he were joking. The imperfectly godly consensus at his seminary was that St. John the Divine chewed morning-glory seeds or magic mushrooms or whatever other first-century hallucinogens he could find on Patmos. Revelation was the word of God, but it was that word seen, in sober Paul's phrase, through a glass, darkly. You sought certainty in Revelation at your peril.

If the text stood before you, though, you couldn't ignore it, not without being lukewarm. "Consider Revelation 6, verses 2–10." He read the King James version, which he preferred to more recent translations. Some wag said the King James version was itself a miracle: the only great literary work produced by a committee.

"Now consider the meaning of the Four Horsemen of the Apocalypse, and how those verses may apply to the present situation," Stark said. "Might not the first Horseman, the one riding a white horse who goes forth conquering, signify Israel and its astonishing victories in 1967?

"And might not the second, who rides a red horse and takes peace from the earth, stand for the Muslim terrorists who have wreaked so much havoc since? Now, the third rider had a black horse—and I'm not talking about the Nazgûl from *The Lord of the Rings*." Stark let the people who would laugh do it. Better to break the tension now than when he'd be coming to his important points. "That third rider carried scales in his hand. Couldn't that be another way of saying the struggle in the Middle East has been deadlocked for a long time?"

He looked at the congregation and at the people who would see him on TV. "I know you know your Scriptures. The fourth rider had a pale horse, and his name was Death. Do I need to draw you a picture of what the Lord was telling us with that image? Not after the horror that was visited upon Tel Aviv, and upon people who'd done nobody any harm.

"Everyone knows the Four Horsemen. But you should also notice the last part of verse 9 and verse 10 in Revelation 5. I'll read them again: 'I saw under the altar the souls of them that were slain for the word of God, and for the testimony which they held: And they cried out with a loud voice, saying, How long, O Lord, holy and true, dost thou not judge and avenge our blood on them that dwell on the earth?'"

He looked out at the people hanging on his every word. It was a heady feeling. He'd drunk liquor in his younger, wilder days. He knew the high you got from alcohol. He got a bigger one from preaching. (He also knew his television audience would follow him Bible in hand. If he made a mistake in text or interpretation, he would hear about it. That was the other side of being listened to attentively.)

"Vengeance is coming," he said softly. "Those souls who were martyred in this attack *will* see vengeance, and soon. For God cannot abide those who do such things, and their victims take His cause into their hands with righteousness. I believe that's what those verses mean.

"You should take them together with Daniel 5, where Daniel speaks of the downfall of Nebuchadnezzar and Belshazzar, the Kings of Babylon—Babylon being the ancient name for Iraq, and how can we deny that Saddam Hussein was the Nebuchadnezzar of our age?

"I call your attention particularly to verse 27, where Daniel tells Belshazzar, 'Thou art weighed in the balances, and art found wanting.' Perhaps this also connects to the third rider. I don't know— I say *perhaps*. God knows His own patterns. All of us mortals, no matter what codes we think we find, we're guessing."

People who listened to him read *The Da Vinci Code* and books about vast cryptograms running through the Bible. Some people believed them. Stark didn't; he thought they were pure heresy. But if you said that right out, you lost part of your audience. Better to slide around it. You caught more flies with honey than vinegar.

"Now Daniel prophesied the end of an empire. And he prophesied truly, for Belshazzar died that night, and Darius the Persian took his lands. As the Last Days approach, everything takes on a larger scale. Not just an empire will pass away, but the world we've always known. And my other point is that even atrocities like the one we've witnessed can work toward good, if the Lord wills they should. That's the message I want to leave with you today. I want you to think about it till we meet again. Thanks, and God bless you."

Organ music swelled. The choir sang "Rock of Ages." The camera lights went out. Now Lester Stark was just a minister with his congregation. He felt smaller without the world's eye on him. But that wasn't all bad. He could think about things more immediate than the Last Days. Vern Neugebauer's daughter was getting married. Ethel Harris had lost her mother. Sam Anderson had won a prize in the state lottery—not millions, but Sam wouldn't turn down thousands. Lester congratulated him.

"Thank you, Reverend," Sam said. "Your church'll see some—I promise."

"Mighty kind of you. Take care of what *you* need, too." Unlike some ministers with enormous flocks, Lester didn't insist on tithing. If you didn't want to give, you were welcome here anyway.

But Sam only smiled. "I cast my bread upon the waters, and it came back. You'll get some, and I'll send some straight to those poor, sorry folks in Tel Aviv."

"That's a good thing to do," Stark said. "There's a lot of trouble and distress in the world—"

"There always is," Sam broke in.

"Yes. But that seems to be where the hurt's sharpest right now," Lester said.

"Not only that, it connects up with the Last Days, like you said." Anderson nodded, more to himself than to the preacher. "I've been studying the Scriptures myself. I believe you've fit the pieces together the way they should go."

"We'll see," Stark said. "I wasn't joking. The Book of Revelation has made fools of other men of God. It may make one of me, too. At least God gave me the humility to see that's possible." *I don't want to look like a jackass in front of the world. But if You want me to . . . Your will be done.*

"Such a dreadful thing," Barb Taylor said. "Really dreadful."

"Yeah." Eric frowned at the woman. He knew she meant well. Thoughts of the road to hell, though, and its paving, came to mind. The bastards in the van with the dirty bomb meant well, too—by their standards.

When Eric didn't say anything more, Barb tried again: "Things *will* get better in a while."

Eric Katz didn't answer that. He was an American, too, but he was also a Jew, and partially immunized against Pollyanna-flavored optimism. He frowned harder.

Orly said something poisonous in Hebrew—in sweet tones, so Barb never suspected. Then she ran another shovelful of dirt through the screens. Anything larger than a couple of millimeters across would get trapped.

Yeah? And so? Eric didn't say that, either. The dig on the side of the Mount of Olives was dead on its feet. Barb seemed the only one who didn't realize it. She worked as hard as she always had. Nobody else gave a shit. They wouldn't find anything exciting. And if they did, so what? Next to what had happened in Tel Aviv, archaeology seemed small potatoes.

This archaeology did, anyway. Yoram Louvish hardly showed up here. Munir al-Nuwayhi decided whatever needed deciding. It wasn't much. If Yoram was digging under the Temple Mount, he was doing it without Eric and Orly. Why would he have brought them to the edge of something interesting (at least by pre-dirty bomb standards), and then left them in the lurch? It made no sense.

What did, these days? *The blood-dimmed tide is loosed. . . .*

Eric shivered in the heat. Born-agains were baying about the Second Coming like dogs howling at the moon, and he had to come up with that line from Yeats? Sometimes a subconscious worked in mysterious ways.

And the zealots connected with the Reconstruction Alliance hustling their precious red heifer away before much radioactivity from the dirty bomb reached the kibbutz? And the ritually pure children, too, but only after the holy hamburger on the hoof?

You don't have to be a goy *to be crazy,* Eric thought.

"Anything?" he asked Orly.

She looked at the screen. "Dirt. Some seeds. Something that may be a sherd. I'm going to cream my jeans."

She wanted to shock Barb. It didn't work. The American tourist just beamed at her. Plenty of evangelicals would have plotzed. Eric didn't know which flavor of Christianity Barb embraced. Whichever, it was more nearly shockproof—or Barb was—than most.

Yoram suddenly appeared, as if a wizard had conjured him up. One second, he was nowhere around. The next—here he was. Yoram had a gift for silent movement. He was an ex-*rav-seren*— a major—in the Israeli Army who'd commanded a battalion in the Gaza Strip. *Not* a good man to mess with.

Eric blinked—Louvish was wearing khakis and a blue blazer. No tie, but there were limits to everything. Seeing the archaeologist in anything but a shirt with lots of pockets and cargo shorts wasn't just wrong; it was unnatural.

"You okay, Yoram?" Orly asked, so she was thinking the same thing.

When the head of the dig smiled, Eric felt like grabbing the children and running for the tall timber. You'd smile that way with an enemy in your sights. When Yoram was in the IDF, he probably had smiled that way—right before he fired. To an academic who'd lost his childhood fights and hadn't had one since he started shaving, that was doubly alarming.

"Okay?" Louvish echoed. "I'm fine. They are delivered into our hands."

"Who?" Orly suddenly got serious. "The ones who helped bomb Tel Aviv?"

"No. Not yet." Yoram caught her eye, and Eric's. He jerked his head: he wanted to talk where Barb couldn't overhear. They would wonder if the Jews headed off to chat among themselves. And it would be rude—which bothered Eric more than Yoram or Orly.

So they drifted off one by one. Maybe that made Barb feel better, maybe not. They made the effort. When Munir joined them, Louvish didn't shoo him away. "*Nu?*" Eric asked.

Yoram grimaced. To him, Yiddish was the ghetto language Jews had escaped. To Eric, it was childhood memories of his folks saying things they didn't want him to understand. What better incentive to learn a language? And, ironically, he'd grasped much more after taking German in college.

"I have it from the Interior Ministry—we can do what we want under the Temple Mount. The Waqf won't be allowed to interfere. Won't," Yoram repeated with somber satisfaction.

"What we want?" By the pronoun Munir chose, he wanted to be included. But he didn't sound delighted.

"What if they send their thugs down?" Orly asked. That had happened to earlier Israeli excavations under the Mount. The Muslim trust was territorial as a mean dog.

"They'll end up dead," Yoram answered. "Not in jail, not in the hospital. Dead. Word's been passed. If the Waqf plays rough, we're ready. The gloves are off. Nobody fucks with us."

Eric whistled. "What happens when the ayatollahs and the Saudis and the Egyptians and the Palestinians pitch fits?" he inquired.

"I don't know, and I don't care. Ask somebody who gives a damn." Louvish lit a cigarette. He offered Munir the pack. The Israeli Arab took one. Yoram gave him a light, then took the question in a different direction: "Ask how much the ayatollahs and the Saudis and the Egyptians and the Palestinians worried when those assholes brought their shit to Tel Aviv. That's how much I'll worry now."

"They *were* Palestinians," Orly said. "I heard that today. One from Hebron, one from Janin."

Eric nodded unhappily, though he looked downright gleeful next to Munir al-Nuwayhi. The only way they wouldn't have been Palestinians was if ISIS or al-Qaeda had imported specialists. He started to ask if Orly knew which faction they belonged to, but didn't. What was the point? All over the Muslim world, people cheered when the bomb went off. Governments deplored, most of them. Even the Palestinian National Authority sent a statement of concern—coupled with worry lest radioactivity reach the West Bank. But Israel would be a long time forgetting the smiling faces and dancing bodies on Al Jazeera.

"They were lice on the balls of mankind," Yoram said in Hebrew. It wasn't the best language to swear in, but he knew better insults in English than most who grew up speaking it. "But they showed us where we stand, who stands with us—and who doesn't."

"They showed us what being nice all those years was worth." Orly snapped her fingers: "This."

"This attitude will not make it better, either," Munir said. "In the occupied territories, they do not say Jewish Israelis are nice."

Eric knew that, too. They had good reason for not saying so. Orly knew the same thing—or would when she calmed down. But it wasn't as if Israel hadn't had provocation.

He sighed. It wasn't as if everybody here hadn't thrown torches into the gasoline drum. Now there was a big fire, and everybody was sorry. But it was too late for that.

"Anyway, we start work under the Temple Mount tomorrow," Yoram said. "You three want to be a part of it?"

"Oh, yes!" Orly said. Eric nodded more slowly, but he did nod. Even more slowly, so did Munir al-Nuwayhi. They all wanted to see what was under there. Muslim obstruction had blocked that for generations. If it didn't . . .

"You handle an assault rifle, Eric?" Yoram asked casually.

5

Chaim felt closed in. Raised as he was, always indoors except when he got out on bubble wrap, he'd known that feeling his whole life. It was worse at Kibbutz Ha-Minsarah. They'd run up a special tent with a raised floor of planks for him and the other ritually pure kids from Kibbutz Nair Tamid.

He wanted to get out and look around. The Negev was desert like nothing he'd seen before. The Dead Sea lay to the east. To the west was the lunar mountainscape of Sinai. How Moses could have wandered there for forty years with the children of Israel . . .

The joke at Kibbutz Nair Tamid was that Moses didn't have GPS. When Chaim told the joke to somebody at Kibbutz Ha-Minsarah, the man left in a hurry. He came back with Uncle Yitzhak.

"Don't make jokes," Yitzhak said.

"I didn't mean anything," Chaim said.

His uncle nodded. "You and I know that. These people . . . don't. They haven't got much of a sense of humor."

"Why not?" Chaim was curious. "What's wrong with them?"

"Nothing." Yitzhak Avigad spoke firmly, as if to convince himself and Chaim. "But they're more *frum* than we are—"

"Wow!" Chaim hadn't thought anybody could be more pious than the people among whom he'd grown up.

"Well, they are," his uncle insisted. "We smile about things sometimes—they don't. They've got close connections to the Reconstruction Alliance. Some of their people are goldsmiths, some weavers, things like that. For us, the Third Temple is coming before long. For them, it's already here. That's simplified, but it's pretty much true. With me so far?"

"I guess." Chaim still thought getting in a fuss about a joke was dumb. He kept quiet—he could see he'd lose that argument.

"And most of the visitors here are *goyim*, and they don't like company," his uncle went on.

"Dumb *goyim*," Chaim said. Uncle Yitzhak didn't tell him to be nice or anything. *Ha-Minsarah* meant *The Carpentry*, so lots of Christians figured it must have to do with Jesus. They were wrong. Chaim thought they were wrong about lots of things, but he knew they were wrong about that.

Kibbutz Ha-Minsarah lay a few kilometers from a rock formation also called Ha-Minsarah, from which the kibbutz drew its name. Piles of prism-like rock there looked like a carpenter's tools—if you had imagination. On the same hiking trail was the Ammonite Wall. It drew the occasional disappointed amateur archaeologist. The ammonites in the name weren't the ancient, extinct Semitic tribe but the far older extinct sea creatures whose fossils were easy to find there.

"You wouldn't want company, either, if the company you got was people who wanted you to be something you weren't," Yitzhak said.

"I guess," Chaim repeated. "But people from Kibbutz Nair Tamid aren't like that."

"Nooo." His uncle answered more slowly than he might have.

"We're not!" Chaim exclaimed in some alarm.

"No," Yitzhak said again. "But we're the cousins whose house burned down, and we've got nowhere else to stay. We're welcome and everything, but they feel they're stuck with us."

"I feel like I'm stuck with them, too. I feel like I'm stuck here"—Chaim patted the raised tent floor—"and I am!"

"Sorry. Nothing to be done about it right away," Uncle Yitzhak said. Chaim sighed. That was grown-up for, *You're stuck with it.* Chaim already knew he was.

He didn't have to stay stuck with it. If he jumped down and ran around and did things regular kids did, he wouldn't be ritually pure any more. He could have a normal life and go anywhere he chose, and nobody could do anything about it.

But he'd have wasted his life till now. He'd forever be tormented by thinking he could have done all that cool stuff sooner. He'd also be forever disappointed in himself. And everyone else—everyone who mattered to him—would be forever disappointed in him, too.

He'd played by the rules so far. He supposed he could a while longer. He didn't want to let people down. He would've been offended if anybody said so, but he *was* a good kid.

There was a roar, and then something streaking almost straight up. He'd watched a million jets land and take off at Ben Gurion. But those were partridges compared to the hawks that roosted near Kibbutz Ha-Minsarah. The *Heyl Ha-Avir,* the Israeli Air Force, had a base close by.

"I wonder where they're going," he said.

"Maybe it's practice," his uncle answered. "Or maybe we start getting our own back."

"That would be great," Chaim said.

Haji Ibrahim ibn Abd al-Rahman was not a happy man. The head of the Waqf felt pulled too many ways at once. He had to keep the

Saudis happy: they gave the most money. God had given Arabia the Prophet and all that oil, too. So many riches lavished on a barren land seemed unfair, but the world was the way it was.

And Ibrahim had to keep the Palestinians happy. Only he couldn't. Nobody could. They were only happy when they were being unhappy. He saw it that way, and he was one. The Grand Mufti of Jerusalem, who'd been appointed by the Palestinian National Authority, was convinced God meant to destroy Israel.

The ranting made it no easier for Haji Ibrahim to keep the Israelis . . . if not happy, then below boiling. He *really* had to do that. If they wanted to throw him out and administer the Temple Mount themselves, they had the muscle. He knew it. All that held them back was the outrage the move would provoke in Muslims everywhere.

After the dirty bomb, how much did they care about Muslim outrage?

Then again, how much had they ever cared? He'd been a boy when they overran this half of Jerusalem and the West Bank in what Arabs called the Setback and most of the world knew as the Six-Day War. An Israeli soldier, crazy with ferocity and fear, had almost shot him then, before realizing he was just a kid and jerking his rifle to one side. Haji Ibrahim had never forgotten how black the inside of the rifle barrel was when he looked down it. He'd wanted to pay the Israelis back for that terror ever since, and he'd wound up having to work with them instead. Life gave you what it gave you, not what you wanted.

And now, the Jews cared about Muslim feelings a lot less than they ever had before. The hulking Israeli colonel in Ibrahim's office said as much, loud and clear. The Waqf's head had always got on well enough with the Jerusalem police. He'd even got on well enough—unofficially—with the people who ran the Israeli Antiquities Authority.

The Waqf's official view was that the Jews had never built a

Temple on the Mount. It was holy because Muhammad went to heaven here. If you looked at the stone inside the Dome of the Rock, you could see the Prophet's footprints and the imprints of Gabriel's fingers where the angel held the rock down so it wouldn't head heavenwards, too.

When Ibrahim looked out the window from his office, he saw the Dome of the Rock, brilliant sunshine gleaming off the gilded dome. It had been anodized aluminum till 1994, when King Hussein of Jordan paid for the gold sheathing. That gold was microscopically thin, but it was there. It enhanced the magnificence of one of the most nearly perfect buildings anywhere.

Haji Ibrahim gave his attention back to Colonel Shaul Shragai. Shragai wasn't remotely perfect. He had a wrestler's shoulders, a bulldog's underslung jaw, and gray eyes full of don't-mess-with-me. He'd been vague about his affiliation, vague in a way that made Ibrahim fear he belonged to the Mossad, the Israeli CIA.

"You know we're doing more excavating under the Mount," he rumbled in accentless Palestinian Arabic.

"I've heard rumors," Ibrahim said. "Under the agreements in place since the Setback, you have no right to do that. We will resist."

"Don't," Colonel Shragai said. "That's why I'm here. If your people interfere, even a little bit, they're dead. Not arrested, not rubber bullets or tear gas. Dead. Got it?"

"You may threaten, Colonel," Haji Ibrahim said. "But when the fury of the Arab people is aroused—"

"Get a new script," Shragai snapped. He was even blunter and ruder than the rest of his countrymen. "That one went out the window with Tel Aviv. If there's trouble, we'll line up tanks around the Temple Mount. If anyone hiccups after we do that, we'll open fire. You hear? I hope so, because things have changed bigtime." He dropped the English word into his Arabic, waited to see whether Ibrahim got it, and nodded on finding he did.

"This is not your land. It never was," the head of the Waqf said. "I don't know why you want it. You never had a Temple here." He stuck to the official stand. He was well read in several languages. He knew Western opinion differed from the official stand. His own . . . was influenced more than he cared to admit by his reading.

"I told you, get a new script," Shragai growled. "That's crap. Even you don't believe it."

"I do," Ibrahim said with dignity. Truth? What was truth? Pilate had asked the same question not far from here.

"Okay, fine. You've got a line to toe," the Israeli colonel said, which also held too much truth, whatever truth was. "But you need to understand something. You make us any angrier than we are already, the Al-Aqsa Mosque is gone. The Dome of the Rock, too. If you *want* to see the Third Temple go up, just piss us off."

"The people who want to make this so-called new Temple are madmen," the head of the Waqf said. That was the Muslim line, too. It had been the official Israeli line. If it wasn't any more . . . Ibrahim's hand found worry beads in his pocket. They clicked as he began to finger them.

Colonel Shragai nodded. "They sure are," he said. "And do you know what the dogs who blew plutonium oxide all over downtown Tel Aviv did? They drove the country into their arms."

"Is that why you bombed Damascus yesterday?" Haji Ibrahim asked.

"It's one reason," Shragai answered calmly. "After all he's done, even you can't tell me anybody'll miss the President of Syria."

Still dignified, Ibrahim replied, "Assassination is not statecraft."

"No? You think the ayatollahs in Teheran and Qom aren't paying attention? You think Syria's going to screw with anybody now?"

Ibrahim didn't answer. The late President was an Alawite, from a sect small even inside Syria. His father and predecessor had been brutal and highly capable. The just-slain ruler was only half the man his father had been—he was only brutal. He'd mostly won his civil war, but he had no obvious successor. All the factions he'd been fighting and all his friends would go mad trying to grab as much as they could and murder one another.

And Iran . . . Since the President of Iran had called the Holocaust a hoax and said Israel ought to be wiped off the map—and since he'd backed the deceased Syrian leader—he and the religious leaders behind him probably were deepening their bomb shelters now.

"So that's how things are," Shragai said. "We aim to excavate under the Temple Mount. Anybody who gives us grief will be sorry, but not for long."

"You cannot speak to me that way," Haji Ibrahim cried. "This is the third most holy spot in Islam. Of course we will protect it."

"I don't know how often I've heard that—the third most holy spot in Islam," the colonel mused.

"It's true!" No hesitation in Ibrahim's voice now.

"Okay, fine. Know what? I don't care. If you're a Jew, it's *the* most holy spot. You bastards forget about that. Time you remembered."

"You have the, uh, Western Wall." Ibrahim almost called it the Wailing Wall, but the Israelis didn't like the name. They said that, since Jerusalem was theirs again, they didn't have to wail. They would burn in hell for their effrontery!

"Some people are okay with that. The government has been—it makes less trouble about the top of the Temple Mount," the colonel replied. "But now we're thinking, *We've* got *plenty of trouble. What's some more?*"

"I cannot decide this myself, and I cannot speak for the young Arabs who will be outraged. The Intifada can begin again, you know." Haji Ibrahim played for time, and played the highest card he had. The longer he alarmed the Jews into waiting, the more things would have a chance to settle down, and the better the odds the leaders would come to their senses.

Colonel Shragai snorted. "Cut the crap—I already told you that.

We'll smash it—smash it flat, however we have to, however many we kill. I'm letting you know to warn you not to mess around with us. You and your 'young Arabs'"—he laced the words with scorn—"can do whatever you want. If you get in the way, you'll get run over. *Shalom*."

Out he went. Like the Arabic *salaam, shalom* could mean *hello* or *goodbye* or *peace*. Ibrahim had never heard it used as a threat before, but that was what it was now.

So the Jews thought they could get away with doing as they pleased under the Temple Mount? Plenty of Arabs didn't fear ascending to Paradise while young.

Ibrahim reached for his phone. Then he stopped. The Americans could tap cell-phone calls. The Israelis surely could, too. He had ways of getting out the word without pointing to himself.

"This is Gabriela Sandoval. I'm speaking from Tel Aviv's radioactive heart." Gabriela hadn't come here for the dirty bomb, but she was making the most of it. "The hazardous conditions are why I look like a carrot with a piggy nose."

She wore an Israeli hazmat suit. It smelled like dirty socks inside. She'd had to do some pleading to get it, but she had. The local authorities wanted the world to see what the terrorists had done. If that meant putting up with a reporter who didn't mind dressing up in orange plastic-impregnated coveralls and a respirator, then it did.

Gabriela's cameraman wore a hazmat suit, too, but he wouldn't show up on TV. Only the person on the screen was real. Nobody cared about how a shot got made, only that it did.

"With me is Ari Eitan, head of the decontamination effort. Thanks for talking with us, Dr. Eitan," Gabriela said.

"You're welcome." Eitan wore the same gear as Gabriela. On camera, they weren't even two talking heads—they were two talk-

ing gas masks. But Gabriela didn't feel like inhaling any more plutonium oxide, and the gutted bus station behind them spoke louder
than anything she and the Israeli would say.

More people in orange suits and masks scurried over the bus
station and the wreckage of nearby buildings. "Will you explain
what your crews are doing?" Gabriela passed Eitan the wireless
mike.

"Yes, certainly." The decontamination expert spoke good if
stilted English. "When we discovered this was a radiological dis-
persal device—"

"A what?" Gabriela broke in—that was too stilted for most listeners to get.

"A, uh, dirty bomb." Eitan grudgingly edited himself. "When we
learned it was, we began spraying all the surfaces within a ten-
block area with a sticky substance."

"Why did you do that?" Gabriela asked.

You dummy, Eitan had to be thinking. But Gabriela remembered the people on the other side of the screen. Sighing, the decontamination maven answered, "To keep the radioactive material
from spreading with the wind. The smaller the area we deal with,
the better. Much radioactive material will adhere to the coating
when we remove it, which we are doing now."

"I see." Gabriela nodded. Inside the suit, sweat rivered down her
back, and she was just standing here holding a mike. "How can
your people work in those things without keeling over? They're
really hot."

"They are, yes," Eitan agreed. "We work one-hour shifts, then an
hour in the shade to cool down. We've had only a few heat casualties."

"That's good. Now, the coating gets up a lot of the radioactive
stuff?" Gabriela kept it as basic as she could. "Not all?"

"No, unfortunately. Our next step, which we will begin soon, is to use water-based gels. These are like the ones in disposable diapers, only with nanoparticles that soak up more contaminants and take them out of circulation."

"And will you be finished then?" Gabriela asked.

Eitan shook his head. "We have chemicals that also go after the radioactives. We want to capture as many as we can, to keep them from spreading in our country and from entering the Mediterranean, as they would if we simply hosed everything down. People would blame Israel for the contamination, even if those Arab murderers brought the poison here. We've already had warnings from France."

"What's your opinion of that?" Gabriela tried to sound innocent. She was also glad Forrest Charleston wasn't within earshot.

"My opinion is not fit to repeat on camera," Ari Eitan said.

Too bad, Gabriela thought. She wasn't Charleston, but she also wasn't allergic to poking France for higher ratings. How many Frenchmen watched *Gabriela and Brandon,* after all? She asked, "When you're finished, Tel Aviv will be clean?"

"Absolutely," the decontamination expert answered.

"You'd live here yourself? Even where the bomb went off?"

"Yes," the Israeli said firmly.

"Do you think other people here will feel the same?"

"If they have sense, they will."

"They won't be anxious there's still radioactivity around?"

"Why should they, if Geiger counters say there isn't?"

Gabriela let that hang. She could think of lots of reasons. Ari Eitan might be good with plutonium, but what did he know about human nature? Not so much. In the States, there'd be environmental-impact studies and lawsuits before people moved back. The first time somebody came down with cancer, there'd be more lawsuits, even if the person who got it smoked twelve packs a day. Things worked like that back home. Which brought another question, perhaps partly prompted by memories of the Marathon bombing: "If a dirty bomb went off in, say, Boston, how well would America handle it?"

"Our chemicals come from the United States," Eitan replied. "But you don't stockpile them the way we do. You might have more trouble in an emergency—you aren't so ready to move fast."

Thinking of Harvey and Irma and Katrina and the last couple of California earthquakes, Gabriela judged that an understatement. The USA was too mired in bureaucracy to respond quickly to almost anything. That seemed a good place to leave it, so Gabriela did. "Thank you, Dr. Eitan. I'll let you get back to work."

"Thanks." The Israeli walked out of the shot.

"Something to think about," Gabriela said to her listeners. "If we had to clean up a dirty bomb, how well would we do? That question has to be on officials' minds from Rio to Riyadh. They're wondering about their countries—and about us. In the light of what's happened here, they need to. Gabriela Sandoval, signing off from Tel Aviv."

"That was awesome, Ms. Sandoval," the cameraman said.

"Thanks, Danny," she answered—praise always felt good, especially when she'd earned it. "Wanna do some pans for voiceover later?"

"Sure thing," Danny said. The red light came on again. He filmed the battered ruins of the bus station—it looked a lot like Oklahoma City a generation earlier. He filmed the decontamination crews taking one kind of goop off and putting another on. He filmed a woman (Gabriela thought) in a hazmat suit eyeing instruments and shaking her head. "Enough?" he asked.

"Should do it," Gabriela said. "Let's clean up."

Even that was complicated. The Israelis had their perimeter up to make sure nobody tracked plutonium outside the area already contaminated. At the edge, they applied their glop to Gabriela's and Danny's suits, then cleaned them. After that, the Americans stood under a portable shower. And after *that,* another Israeli ran a Geiger counter over them. Only then could they peel off the suits and masks and breathe hot, humid, unfiltered Tel Aviv air. It felt wonderful.

"Do you think this city will ever be the same?" Gabriela asked a soldier patrolling the perimeter.

"The same? No," the young man said in halting English. "Can we live again here? Yes. We do it." He sounded confident.

"What about the people who did this? What about the people who helped them?"

"We fix." The guard hefted his Galil.

Yoram Louvish wasn't kidding when he asked Eric if he knew how to handle an assault rifle. He showed up with one, and a full magazine, a few days later. "When we go, take this along," he said.

"You gotta be kidding," Eric blurted.

The Israeli soldier-turned-archaeologist—a surprisingly common combo here—shook his head. "You may need it." He didn't sound like somebody who was joking. Eric wished he did.

"I'm liable to be more dangerous to our side," the American protested.

Yoram barely hid his scorn. "Look at Tel Aviv. These are not nice people. They'll kill you if they can. One way to make sure they don't is kill them first if you have to. Nobody will be happier than me if you don't shoot. But if you need to, you need to, that's all. And you may."

"*I'll* be happier than you if I don't use it," Eric said.

"I doubt it, because I've seen combat and you haven't," Yoram answered. "I know what you'll be missing. If you have to use your weapon, know how. Orly will show you."

"Okay, okay." Eric knew when to quit arguing. He did ask, "You going to give one to Munir, too?"

Louvish didn't even blink. "Damn right. I wouldn't have asked him in on this if I worried about him shooting us in the back or ratting on us." The American shut up.

Orly trained Eric with a seriousness she seldom gave to less urgent matters. If anything was weirder than learning to shoot from a woman you were thinking about marrying, he hadn't met it. She walked him through the Galil's care and feeding. He learned how to attach the clip, how to chamber a round, and how to clean the weapon and strip and reassemble it.

"In the Army, we would do this blindfolded," Orly said. "If the drill sergeant felt mean, he'd take away a piece and make us figure out what was missing."

That didn't sound mean to Eric—it sounded sadistic. "Why?"

"So we knew what we were doing." She touched the rifle's metal-and-plastic stock. "You carry this, you go places where you can't try again. You have to be right the first time. Everything has to work. So you make sure it happens."

Eric understood that intellectually. And, intellectually, he understood intellectual understanding wouldn't do him any good if he had to shoot somebody. "I'd almost rather bail out," he muttered.

"You can," Orly said. *You can bail out on me if you do.* She didn't say it, but it hung in the air between them.

Did he have the courage of his uncourageous convictions? Or did he want to see what lay under the Temple Mount enough to shoot anybody who got in his way? Archaeologists joked about things like that. If it wasn't a joke . . . ? "I said *almost.*"

"Okay," Orly told him. Then she showed him that, to her, it was better than okay. He didn't like to think that thinking about violence got him hot, but . . . "Maybe I should give you a gun more often," Orly purred afterwards.

"Full-metal-jacket Viagra," Eric said. They both giggled. Eric almost forgot about the Galil.

If he'd had his druthers, he would have. But Orly made sure he didn't. She borrowed Yoram's beat-up Nissan and drove Eric to an Army training center twenty minutes southwest of Jerusalem. There, under her watchful eye and the contemptuous glare of an Israeli noncom, he fired a clip's worth of ammo on a range.

"Maybe you'll scare them," the noncom said—a dubious recommendation. "How come you can't shoot straighter?"

"This is the first time I tried." Eric's ears rang, though he wore protective covering. Gunfire was *loud*. His shoulder ached, but he didn't rub. The Galil kicked, all right.

The Israeli looked incredulous. Eric spoke Hebrew well enough to pass for a local—and plenty of Israelis had accents, too. "He's an American," Orly explained.

"Oh," the noncom said. *Softy.* He didn't say that, but Eric heard it. The Israeli did ask, "What are you doing with a weapon, then?"

"In case there's trouble under the Temple Mount," Eric answered. "I'm an archaeologist."

"Oh, yeah? You sure don't look like Indy," the noncom said.

"Uh-huh," Eric said. "Orly's an archaeologist, too. She doesn't look like him, either, thank God."

"Thank God is right." The noncom eyed her. Israelis were subtle as a battering ram. "She's okay with me, though. Can I give you my number, babe?"

"I've got plenty of toilet paper." Orly put up with BS from nobody. The noncom laughed—he came from the *If you strike out, keep swinging, 'cause you'll hit something sooner or later* school.

Driving back to Jerusalem, Eric asked, "What would you have done if he got mad?"

"Something." It hadn't happened, so she didn't worry about it. Eric wished he could be like that. He wasn't Woody Allen, either, but he came closer to angst than to a fedora.

There was a traffic jam up ahead as they neared the city. There shouldn't have been, not at two P.M. "What's up?" Eric said. "Looks like the 405 at rush hour." He'd often wished he carried a rifle when he got stuck on the freeway. Now he had one, but opening up didn't seem smart.

Orly leaned on the horn. She was a *sabra*, all right; half the people stuck on the road were honking. Eric's head, which ached from the gunfire, hurt even more. He couldn't close the window—the car had no AC. He turned on the radio to find out what was wrong. That proved *he* was from L.A. Nowhere was the urge to know why you were getting screwed stronger.

"—in Jerusalem," an announcer said. "Police hope to control the unrest, but some streets remain closed. Repeat—there is rioting in Jerusalem. Police hope to control the unrest soon."

"Why now?" Eric didn't like feeling paranoid, but in the Middle East you often couldn't help it. Somebody really might be out to get you.

"Probably the Palestinians saying they don't want Yoram digging," Orly said.

Eric started to tell her she was more paranoid than he was. Paranoid or not, she was likely to be right. The Arabs were trying this instead of fighting. "They know how to get their message across," he said.

"Maybe—but maybe not," Orly answered. "We won't put up with much nonsense in Jerusalem, not after what they did in Tel Aviv. If we're looking for an excuse to crack down, they just handed us one."

Again, that made sense. Eric wanted people to get along. He was an American; when he disagreed with someone, his impulse was to sit down and talk. Here, opening up with an assault rifle was more common. Both sides scoffed at negotiation. Beating each other over the head for a lifetime didn't seem to have done anybody much good, though. When you wanted everything and couldn't give up anything for fear of seeming to yield it all . . . you were screwed. And the Middle East was.

Traffic snailed forward. Eric sneaked glances at the temperature gauge. Several overheated cars made the jam worse, but the Nissan seemed okay.

A cop at a checkpoint looked inside. In the States, he would have had a cow about the Galil. Here, he just made sure Orly was an Israeli and Eric an American. He checked her service discharge papers. "You know what to do if you have to," he said. "I hope you don't."

"How bad is it?" Orly asked.

"Not good," the cop answered. "They brought extra trouble-makers from the West Bank." The Palestinians would have said *from the rest of the West Bank.* And they would have talked about holy warriors, not troublemakers. The cop didn't give a shit. He went on, "We'll squash 'em. You folks can pass on." He had no doubts. Eric . . . did, not that that changed things.

6

Haji Ibrahim wept in an upstairs room near the Souq al-Lahamin: the meat market in the Old City's Muslim quarter. Some tears were outrage at what the Israelis were doing to his people and to the Haram al-Sharif, the Noble Sanctuary—the Arabic name for the Temple Mount. Some would have flowed anyway; one thing the Israelis were doing was firing tear gas to bring the rioters outside under control.

His refuge was supposed to be airtight. Lots of things that were supposed to be something didn't live up to the promise. This was one; gas leaked into the room.

So the Grand Mufti of Jerusalem was crying, too. Haji Jamal Ashrawi was close to seventy, with bushy sideburns and thick glasses that magnified his eyes. He wagged a forefinger at Ibrahim. "Do you see?" he demanded, his accent Egyptian. "*Do* you see? You spend all these years kissing the dogs' behinds, and they pay you back this way. God is just, for you deserve it."

"Easy for you to say." The director of the Waqf tried not to get angry, but he did. "You never had responsibility. If we talked to the

Zionists as you speak to the faithful, do you know what would have happened?"

"They would have respected and feared you," Ashrawi said. "They understand nothing but a clenched fist."

"Ha!" Ibrahim laughed bitterly. Ashrawi looked shocked— when had anyone last laughed at him? *Too long ago*, Ibrahim thought. "They would have booted the Waqf out of the Haram al-Sharif and taken it over for themselves."

"And it would have been war with the Muslim world!" Haji Jamal exclaimed.

"That wouldn't have helped the Noble Sanctuary," Ibrahim said. "How many plots have the Jews made to blow up the Dome of the Rock and Al-Aqsa? Israeli authorities stopped them. We didn't. We couldn't. If the authorities stood back, that would all be gone, and the Jews would build their miserable Third Temple."

"Not one Temple was ever there before, let alone two," Ashrawi said. "Besides, they are going to do it anyway."

"God prevent it!" Ibrahim said. But the talk he'd had with Colonel Shragai made him fear the Grand Mufti was right. If he hadn't, he wouldn't have kindled the unrest in Jerusalem.

"God will do as He wills," Jamal Ashrawi said. "Don't you see? The Final Days draw near. The prophet Jesus, peace be upon Him, and the Mahdi will put down the False Prophet's army. The prophet and the Mahdi will kill every pig there is and break every cross, and Islam will be the only faith in the world."

"So may it be." Ibrahim didn't like the way Ashrawi preached in ordinary conversation. Did the Grand Mufti think him ignorant? Ibrahim was too caught up in the flow of events to worry about the Final Days, but he knew what would happen then.

Was that time near? Till the dirty bomb went off, Ibrahim wouldn't have believed it. Now . . . Who could say? Events were taking on their own momentum—or God's.

Outside, in the *souq*, somebody fired an AK-47. That *buda-*

buda-buda was unmistakable. Harsher Israeli Galils returned fire. A bullet punched a hole in the wall. Somebody shrieked, whether in Arabic or Hebrew Ibrahim couldn't tell—pain had its own vocabulary.

The Souq al-Lahamin usually displayed meat, from chops to sheep's heads with staring eyes. Now there was torn human flesh down there, human blood on the cobbles.

"Send the Zionists to hell," the Grand Mufti said. "Let Satan give them filth to eat and fire to drink."

"What if that's one of ours crying out?" Ibrahim asked.

"Then he rises to Paradise, like the martyrs who died to strike the infidels in Tel Aviv," Ashrawi replied. "He rises to Paradise, and he shall have joy in the rivers of milk and wine, in the arms of the houris there, and in the presence of God forever."

"May it be so," Ibrahim said.

Someone banged on the front door. A frightened teenager rushed in. "The Israelis!" he exclaimed. The bangs got louder and more insistent. The soldiers would break in whether anyone let them in or not.

"Time to go," Ashrawi said. He and the teenager and Ibrahim hurried away. There was another way out, one Islam's enemies wouldn't find soon enough. This struggle had gone on a long time. The Israelis had made their preparations, the Palestinians theirs. The duel wouldn't end . . . *until the Final Days,* Haji Ibrahim thought as he hurried down a narrow, dark, dusty stairway.

Ibrahim uneasily remembered the Grand Mufti's words. How far off *were* those days? Maybe they lay closer than the head of the Waqf had believed.

A plump, pale, middle-aged woman in a wide-brimmed hat got out of a little Nissan at the administration building in Kibbutz Ha-Minsarah. If she wasn't a tourist, Yitzhak Avigad had never seen one. Sure enough, she nodded to him and said, "*Shalom!* Sorry—that's most of my Hebrew. D'you speak English?"

She sounded sure he would. And he nodded back. "Yes. What is it?" Then, sharply: "Did the guards check you?" She looked harmless. She sounded American. But you never could tell.

"Heavens to Betsy, I should say so!" she exclaimed. "Went over the car like you wouldn't believe, and this girl patted me down." She blushed. "I told 'em I was on Professor Louvish's dig at the Mount of Olives, and dang if they didn't call him and try and make me out a liar."

If she was working with Yoram Louvish, she wouldn't blow anything up. *Heavens to Betsy? Dang?* Yitzhak knew the expressions, but sure didn't hear them much. "Who are you?" he asked. "Why are you here?"

"My name's Barbara Taylor, but everybody calls me Barb," she said. "And I came down here because I wanted to see the red heifer."

"Oh," Yitzhak said heavily. Would this place turn into a tourist Mecca—he winced at the comparison—despite everything? "Why is that?"

"Because the Last Days are coming. The Antichrist and the Tribulation and all." She sounded surprised he needed to ask. "But the heifer's here now. It's like it's part of prophecy you can reach out and touch, or look at, anyway."

"Oh," Yitzhak said again, this time with only apprehension in his voice. The last thing he wanted—well, this side of a car bomb—was swarms of born-agains (she couldn't be anything else) descending on Kibbutz Ha-Minsarah.

His first impulse was to tell her to get lost. But, standing there toasting in the sun, she was plainly less dangerous than the cats that prowled around the kibbutz. Dumpy and ditzy as she was, she brought out a soft streak he hadn't known he had.

"I'll make you a deal," he said. "All right?" Barb Taylor nodded. He went on, "You can see Rosie—*Shoshanah*, we're calling her—if you promise you won't tell anybody—*anybody*—you did. We don't want her on display."

"Cross my heart," Barb said at once, and damned if she didn't sketch a cross there. "What I promise, I deliver, too."

Yitzhak believed her. He'd got to know enough people with beliefs like hers to see most of them were uncommonly reliable. If they said they would do something, they meant it. "Come on," he told her. "The heifer's in the barn."

She came. She was pathetically eager. People stared as she went by. A few folks on the kibbutz were almost as fair, but her skin wasn't what set her apart. The eagerness did. It shone from her—*like shook foil*, Yitzhak thought, recalling the line from some English poet but unable to remember which one.

"This is so exciting!" She leaned forward as she walked—the barn, or the heifer, might have been pulling her like a lodestone.

"Don't expect anything special," Yitzhak warned. "Rosie looks like, acts like, well, a cow. She *is*."

"But she's not any old cow," Barb Taylor answered. "She's the cow God sent so the Temple could rise again." She beamed at Yitzhak, as if sure they knew the same thing.

He said, "Well, yes," but he wasn't so sure. Yes, God had sent the red heifer. What would happen afterwards . . . Jews thought one thing, Christians another, and Muslims something else. Each group was the hero in its own story, and the villain in the outsiders'. *But we're right*, Yitzhak thought as they reached the barn.

Barb Taylor wrinkled her nose. If Yitzhak hadn't guessed she was a city woman, that would have told him. He preferred barnyard smells to smoke and diesel fumes. No accounting for taste, though.

"She's in this stall," Yitzhak said, leading Barb past a man shoveling what would become fertilizer but was now definitely and unmistakably cowshit.

"She's so beautiful!" the American gasped.

Yitzhak thought Shoshanah was beautiful, too, but not like *that*. Barb Taylor saw the Second Coming in a cow's hindquarters and switching tail. To the Israeli, she was a means to an end: sanctifying the priests who'd serve the Third Temple. To Barb, she was—what? A harbinger. Yitzhak hadn't thought he knew that English word, but it seemed to fit.

"May I . . . touch her?" Barb asked.

No. The word automatically came to Yitzhak's lips, but didn't pass them. Rosie was a good-natured creature, and so, obviously, was Barb Taylor. "All right," he said, "but only for a second."

"Thank you!" she breathed.

He stepped into the stall and turned the red heifer away from the manger. He led her to the gate. "Go ahead," he told Barb.

Eyes wide, the American woman stroked the heifer's velvet muzzle. "Oh," she said. She stared at her hand—she might have been a teenager who'd touched a rock star and was telling herself she'd never wash it again. Shoshanah snorted in mild confusion. People often perplexed her. Barb didn't look perplexed—she looked exalted. "You don't know what this means to me," she told Yitzhak.

That might well be true. "Now it's done," Yitzhak said. He let the red heifer go back to her feed. Yitzhak left the stall and closed the gate. "You did what you came to do."

"Yes. Thanks. You were very kind," Barb said. No one had accused Yitzhak of that lately. The American woman started out. He followed. The kibbutznik shoveling shit gave them a curious look, but for a wonder kept quiet. Barb Taylor blinked in the sun outside. She might have been coming back to herself. "Touching history is wonderful—that's why I enjoyed the dig with Professor Louvish so much. But touching prophecy's even better. It's touching history before the history happens."

"I guess so." Of course Yitzhak believed in prophecy—would he have put so much of his life into the Third Temple if he didn't? But he thought about what the Scriptures said. To him, that was what led to understanding.

Not to Barb, not if he read her right. She grabbed an idea and hung on tight, and that was it. He thought that made her likely to be wrong, but he knew plenty of people, including some Jews, who would disagree.

She got back into the car. "Thanks again," she said. "I'll remember you in my prayers."

"All right," he replied. What else could you say? He figured God listened to *goyim* when He felt like it, but did He listen to foolish *goyim*? Rosie wasn't the Golden Calf.

Barb drove off. By the way she shifted, Yitzhak could tell she was used to an automatic transmission. Most Americans were.

He shook his head, wryly amused. If God listened to foolish Jews, why wouldn't He listen to foolish *goyim* sometimes, too?

"I want you to pray," the Reverend Lester Stark said. "Pray for peace in the world, and especially in the Middle East." He looked solemn. "Some ministers seem to pray for war, hoping war now will usher in the Antichrist and the Last Days. I don't know how they can do that in good conscience. I'm sorry, friends, but I don't."

He thought some of his colleagues had embarrassed the whole Christian movement in the United States. When you said God struck down a fat old Israeli politician because he'd removed settlers from Palestinian land, who'd take you seriously? Nobody in his right mind, not so far as Stark could see. If the other minister was sincere . . . Even if he was, he was so far out in left field, he was up in the bleachers.

But Jesus said, *Judge not, lest ye be judged.* Sometimes Stark thought that required superhuman forbearance.

Sighing, he went on, "War *will* come, if that's what God wants. But *hoping* for war, *praying* for war, seems to be doing the work of

Satan and the Antichrist. If you have no peace at the bottom of your heart, how can you hope to enter the Kingdom of Heaven? Pray for peace. Work for peace. If war comes anyhow, fight hard, fight clean, fight fair. And when it's over, work for peace again."

He looked out at the congregation. Some people were nodding. But he saw more frowns and scowls than usual. Some people wanted, needed, to hate their enemies. When someone they respected told them that wasn't a good idea, they didn't like it.

"Remember what the Book of Luke says in chapter 23, verse 46. Jesus was up on the cross then, His human flesh dying in such slow, painful agony that few people today can even imagine it. And what did He say? 'Father, forgive them; for they know not what they do.'

"Take that lesson to heart. It was the last one Jesus had for us before His Resurrection, and He gave up the ghost right afterwards. He was dying, and He still forgave. Now you, who I hope are blessed by good health and will remain so for many years, you could do worse than to think on that. Revenge and recrimination aren't worth the torment they inflict on your soul."

Some scowls turned to thoughtful frowns. Some frowns smoothed out. But not all. After the cameras went out, a man asked, "What about the Israelis? Don't they have a right to get their own back after what those no-good . . . you-know-whats did to Tel Aviv?"

"That's not easy to answer," Stark said carefully. "Judaism does not follow the New Testament. There is a case for *An eye for an eye and a tooth for a tooth* in the Old Testament. Not all Jews live by that, but some do. If they judge it necessary to preserve their state from further attacks . . . You would have to be a bold man to tell them they were wrong."

"You've got something there." The man bobbed his head. "Thanks, Reverend."

"You're welcome." Stark was unfailingly polite. His friends applauded him for that; it unnerved his foes. You couldn't slam him as you could so many preachers who guided huge flocks on television. If you did, chances were you'd look petty yourself.

Even now, part of him wished he had an ordinary church with a congregation of ordinary size. You got to know people then, and know all their problems. Hearing about troubles by letters and e-mails and desperate phone calls wasn't the same. If you *knew* people, you could—sometimes—deal with troubles before they got catastrophically bad.

But, even if the good he did was less concentrated this way, he did more when you added it up. He brought in more money for good works than he would have with an ordinary church and congregation. He had more overhead, too, but, again, what he accomplished justified it.

"Good sermon!" somebody called as he headed back toward privacy. "I hope people listen. We'd be better off if they did."

"Thanks," Lester Stark said. "They don't have to listen to me, necessarily. They just need to listen, period. Plenty of people are saying sensible things. But if those in power don't want to do sensible things . . ."

In that case, we get wars any which way. We get one step closer to the Last Days, to the Antichrist. One step closer, certainly, but how many remained? Some ministers were shouting that the Last Days were coming day after tomorrow, as if Armageddon were a summer blockbuster. There was a terrific way to look idiotic if you proved wrong. All the signs said soon, and Lester Stark had preached on that, but he was too cautious to think he knew the day or hour.

He *prayed* the Last Days were coming soon. But he recognized the difference between hoping and praying and *knowing*. And he was convinced some of his colleagues wouldn't recognize that difference if it piddled against their leg.

"How do we get the Third Temple built, Reverend?" a woman asked.

Another question waiting to blow the Middle East sky-high. "*We* don't," Stark said, which was true, no matter how it disappointed this lady. He explained why, since she couldn't see for herself: "The Jews do, when and as God moves them to. We encourage them and we support them with resources. We aren't the only evangelical group that does. But the building is up to them."

"Why don't they get on with it, then?" By the way she said it, she thought they couldn't find a contractor they liked.

"Political issues are involved, you know." Stark wouldn't have bet she did, but he always gave people the benefit of the doubt. That worked for him more often than against him.

The woman said, "Politics? After Tel Aviv?" So she had some idea of what was going on. No, you couldn't tell ahead of time.

"Even after Tel Aviv. Deciding to rebuild the Temple is a mighty step. If Israel takes it, her neighbors won't be happy with her." Lester Stark discovered in himself a talent for understatement.

The woman only sniffed. "After Tel Aviv, why should she care?" Since a friend of Stark's in the Reconstruction Alliance had sent him a text saying the same thing that morning, he could only spread his hands. The woman sniffed again, and walked away. Sometimes you just couldn't make people happy.

Yoram Louvish inspected his troops. And that was what it amounted to, because everybody going under the Temple Mount carried a Galil. "Ready?" the Israeli archaeologist demanded. "Ready to learn if we can, and for trouble if that's what happens?"

Beside Eric Katz, Orly said, "Yes!" without the least hesitation. Eric said, "Yes," too—they would throw him out if he said no, and he did want to see what hid under there. Did he want it enough to shoot somebody for the privilege? He wasn't so sure about that.

But the guys on the other side were willing—no, eager—to shoot Jewish archaeologists . . . or blow them up, or, if they could get hold of more powdered plutonium, to make them glow in the dark. If you didn't stand up to those people, they won by default. If you did . . . maybe you had to shoot sometimes.

Maybe. Eric hoped not.

"Don't do anything stupid," Yoram said. "Stupid includes shooting people on your side—and not shooting the bastards on the other side if they're shooting at you. We hope the Army has the Temple Mount sealed off. We hope, but we don't know—and the Army's been wrong before. People have tunneled here for more than three thousand years. Maybe the Muslims have some burrows the Army doesn't know about. Let's find out. Follow me."

"Wait." One of the other archaeologists—his name was Shmuel Something-or-other—pointed at the Galil Munir al-Nuwayhi was holding. "What's he doing armed?"

"Same thing you are." Yoram's voice went harsh and flat.

Shmuel didn't want to listen. "What if he shoots me in the back?"

"Fuck you," Munir said evenly, in English.

Yoram nodded. "Yeah. Fuck you." He used English, too. "You don't like it, you can leave right now. Otherwise, you can shut up and soldier. Are you coming or not?"

Shmuel hesitated, but only for a moment. "Yeah, I'm coming." The snake from the Tree of Knowledge had bitten him as hard as Munir.

Anybody who went first, showing no fear, could pull other people along by force of will. Force of chutzpah, Eric thought, which didn't keep him from going into the tunnel under the Temple Mount with everybody else.

He flipped on the LED light in his hard hat. Without lights, they would have been blind as cave salamanders. After the outside world got behind him, he felt more weight on his shoulders than Atlas could have handled. Atlas just had to hold up the heavens.

Eric felt the stifling, crushing, overwhelming weight of years and history. Jebusites, Jews, Babylonians, Persians, Alexander, Antigonids, Ptolemies, Seleucids, Jews again, Romans, Byzantines, Arabs, Fatimids, Seljuk Turks, Crusaders, Ayyubids, Mamluks, Ottoman Turks, British, Jews *again* . . . He knew he'd left some peoples out of his mental catalogue, but they pressed on him anyhow.

Jerusalem had been quiet the last couple of days. It didn't feel like peace to Eric, not even the peace of exhaustion. It felt more like a little girl who was really, really mad at somebody saving up more spit.

The tunnel sloped steeply downward. Eric's ears popped and hurt a little, the way they had the last time he did this. Maybe the weight wasn't just the burden of history. Maybe part of it was increasing air pressure.

"Allahu akbar!" The cry almost made him piss his pants. A moment later, automatic-weapons fire broke out.

But the Arabic battle cry and the gunfire weren't close. Yoram Louvish laughed softly. "Sometimes," he remarked, "it's better to send rumors through the *souqs* than soldiers."

"What's that mean?" Eric asked.

"Rumors say we're going to dig in a different tunnel this time, on the east side of the Mount," Yoram answered. "People who went in there wore what archaeologists usually wear. . . ."

Eric looked at himself. He had on an old Pete Yorn T-shirt, battered Levi's, and Nikes. He didn't stand out a bit. Yoram's T-shirt asked, in Hebrew, *If all men were brothers, would you let one marry your sister?* Eric wondered what that meant.

Louvish went on, "No matter what they look like, they're really top Army people. So the Arabs who went over there to make trouble will find it instead."

More gunfire erupted. "Those are Galils, all right," said somebody behind Eric—Shmuel, he thought. He sounded delighted.

"How can we hear all the ruckus?" Orly asked. "The guns, maybe, but people yelling? There aren't supposed to be any connections between that tunnel and this one."

"No, there aren't," Yoram agreed. "But it's like I said—nobody knows everything under the Temple Mount. If we already knew everything, we wouldn't need to dig, would we?"

With the racket of combat echoing in their ears, they came to the wall of stones whose bosses proclaimed them to be more ancient than almost any masonry aboveground on the Temple Mount. All these years, all those peoples, pressed on Eric harder than ever. "How many battles have they fought here?" he wondered, staring at the stonework in the shifting beams of the archaeologists' headlamps.

"Oh, a few." Yoram sounded positively gay. "When something's worth fighting over, people fight. And Jerusalem and the Temple Mount have been worth fighting over for a *lonnng* time. We didn't come for that, though. We came to work." He started chipping at the mortar between two stones with a mineralogist's hammer.

Eric had one on his belt, too. He'd used it more often and in more ways than he could remember. Maybe the continuing gunfire in the distance was what made him think, *Something like that killed Trotsky*. An ice axe wasn't the same critter—but pretty close.

As he reached for his hammer, he asked Yoram, "What do you think we'll find on the other side of this wall?"

"Wonderful things," the Israeli answered in deadpan English.

Everybody laughed. "Well, hush my mouth," Eric said, also in English. Back in the 1920s, that was what Howard Carter replied when somebody asked him what he saw inside Tutankhamen's tomb. Returning to Hebrew, Eric went on, "We'll have to go some to beat Howard."

"Yup," Yoram agreed, and went back to attacking the wall. A chunk of the mortar he knocked loose clicked on the stone floor.

He doesn't think small—that's for sure, Eric thought. To him, that was all to the good. Most of the action in modern archaeology was sifting sand and dust through ever-finer screens to see what got left behind. You learned important things that way, but it was as exciting as Jimmy Carter's sanctimonious speeches. If you didn't dream of shining the first light in millennia on gold in an unplundered pharaoh's tomb, weren't you in the wrong racket?

If chipping mortar wasn't the dullest thing this side of working at McDonald's, Eric didn't know what was. Two burly Israeli archaeologists attacked the masonry with short-handled sledgehammers. It made a hell of a racket. You couldn't usually do stuff like this, because people from the Waqf would spit rivets—and bullets.

They *were* spitting rivets—and bullets—but not here. And after Tel Aviv, would things ever be usual? Eric doubted it.

He was bent into an uncomfortable position, which seemed a universal constant of archaeology. Nothing was ever at a convenient height or angle. You had to bend or stretch or twist, or else reach farther than your arms were designed for.

If they'd brought along a jackhammer, the work would have gone faster. Running a compressed-air line under the Temple Mount might've given the Waqf a wee hint about where the archaeologists would dig, though. And it would've torn up lots of interesting evidence. But damn! It would have saved work.

"Hold on," Yoram said presently. "Let's get some pictures."

He leaned a meter stick against the wall to give scale. It was a special model available only at archaeologists' secret supply shops, with alternating centimeters painted white and black. The camera had better optics than a phone and, with a thirty-two-gig memory card, held a slew of photos. Photography had come a long way since Howard Carter's time.

While the flash brought milliseconds of daylight to the tunnel, Eric twisted, working kinks from his arms and shoulders. He'd feel like an old man tomorrow. Some of the Israelis were doing the same. That made him happier—he didn't want to look like a flabby American to them.

He shone his headlamp onto the palms of his hands. "Blisters?" Orly asked.

"I'm getting there," he answered. "How about you?"

"The same," she said. "If I wanted pick-and-shovel work, I could have joined a road crew. They're honest about what you're getting into."

"Yeah." Eric swigged from a plastic water bottle. It wasn't so hot down here as it was in the sunshine, but he'd worked up a sweat.

"That should do it." Yoram stowed the camera. "Back to it, *khaverim*."

As people started chipping and pounding again, Munir al-Nuwayhi said, "You only call us *friends* when you want something from us."

Yoram nodded. "This surprises you because . . . ?" Everybody laughed again, Eric included. When you looked at it that way, it wasn't man bites dog.

Whack, whack, whack. Sooner or later, they'd pry out a block or two. And then? Somebody would take off his hard hat and use the lamp to peer into whatever the wall had hidden for the past 2,600-odd years. And what would that be? Eric guessed it would be an empty chamber, as exciting as Geraldo's tour of Al Capone's cellar.

When he said so, Orly shook her head. "I think you're wrong. They wouldn't have gone to all this trouble to build a wall to hide nothing."

"Maybe," Eric said. "Bet you a shekel, though. Hell, bet you ten." The extravagant life of an archaeologist. Almost a three-buck bet!

"You're on." She stuck out her hand. They shook. The clasp hurt—Eric's blisters were developing nicely. Orly winced, too, so hers also had to be coming along.

A soldier brought down the Israeli equivalent of MREs. They

were kosher, which didn't keep them from being as bad as the U.S. versions. Eric inhaled his anyhow. Sometimes quantity counted more than quality.

A stone grated when Yoram prodded it. The archaeologists cheered . . . wearily. Little by little, Yoram wiggled it out. Eric helped grab it and ease it to the ground. The square black hole in the wall reminded him of a missing front tooth.

The two men looked at each other. Eric stepped back and waved at the hole. "Go ahead," he said. "It's your baby."

"Thanks." Yoram stooped so he could look in. He gasped. He stiffened. One hand went up to clutch at his chest as he staggered back. Orly caught him, or he would have fetched up against the tunnel's far wall. "My God!" he said. "I hoped, but I never really thought, I never really dreamt—"

Half the people down there asked, "Are you okay?" The other half asked, "What?"

"It's—" Yoram fought for breath, and to get the words out: "It's— the Ark!"

Pandemonium. In the midst of it, Orly said, "Pay me!"

Eric scarcely heard her. He stood next closest to the hole, which meant he got the second look. As he bent to peer in, he wondered whether Yoram was kidding. Would he start laughing because he'd fooled his colleagues? Would they kill him afterwards?

But no. There it was, dazzling in the headlamp's beam. It looked a lot like the museum model. Not quite, though: the cherubim weren't the same. They looked more Mesopotamian, more primitive—and more menacing. There was one other difference, too, though Eric needed a moment to notice it. *The Ark floated two or three inches above the floor of the chamber.*

7

From Tel Aviv to Jerusalem was thirty-five miles. As the rented car that held Gabriela and Brandon rolled southeast along Israel's Highway 1, she kept seeing 100 on the speedometer and wondering why they weren't there yet. Then she remembered those were kilometers an hour, not miles. They were doing 60.

And then they were doing zero. Israel was a little country with big traffic jams. Given the terrifying way everybody drove, it was no wonder there were accidents all the time.

From the Nissan's cramped back seat, Brandon asked the driver, "Can we get off the highway and use side roads?"

"We could maybe try," the local said. "But they're narrow, and plenty of other people will try them, too. Chances are we'll do just as well sticking with 1."

"You know best," Gabriela said, thinking *I hope.* "Flying here for the red heifer has really worked out well for us."

"Glad you think so." He inflated his chest like a puffer fish; modest, he was not. "We've been on the spot for two of the biggest stories in years."

The driver gave Gabriela a look—not come-hither, but disgusted scorn. She would have bet he'd've done the same thing at full speed. "You came to *Eretz Yisrael* for that stupid cow?" the Israeli asked.

"That's right," Gabriela said. "Lots of Americans are interested in it."

"Jerks," the driver declared.

"You say that even after they found the Ark?" Brandon answered. "Doesn't it seem like the pieces in Somebody's plan are fitting together?"

"Who knows what they found?" the driver said. "Most likely, nothing. There are stories about big waddayacallems—finds in archaeology—every week. They all turn out to be shit."

He was right, but Gabriela cared very little and knew Brandon cared even less. If there was enough to the Ark story to get *Gabriela and Brandon* a special, she'd be happy. And if the guys with the thick glasses decided later that it wasn't the Ark from the First Temple, she wouldn't get upset. Retractions never caught up with stories.

"You gotta know it's bogus," the Israeli went on. "All the talk about how it's floating above the ground. How's it gonna do that?"

"Beats me." Brandon Nesbitt sounded positively cheerful. "But I want to check it out. How cool would it be if it *was* true?"

"I've seen *Raiders*, too," the driver said. "Doesn't mean I believe crap like that."

Gabriela thought he had a point, but Brandon said, "Suppose it does turn out to be true. What would you think then?"

The Israeli jerked a thumb back at him. "Like you said, man, beats me. I'll worry about it when it happens."

When Americans thought about Israelis, they thought about

pious Jews. But more Israeli Jews were secular like this guy than Orthodox like Chaim Avigad and the others raising and cherishing Rosie the red heifer . . . till they cut her throat.

"If it is true, will that make you start believing?" Gabriela asked.

"Maybe." The driver sounded as if he didn't want to admit it. "I've got *frum* cousins. They're welcome to all that. If God wants to step in now, why didn't He do it when the Nazis were shoving people into gas chambers?"

People had been asking that since 1945. To Gabriela, there was no good answer. Well, maybe one: there was no God, which made it a stupid question. She wasn't a very observant Catholic, but she didn't want to believe that. If this *was* the Ark, though, and if it *was* doing something science couldn't explain, then the possible good answer wasn't any more. Which left . . . ?

Nothing Gabriela could think of. Except a God with a sick sense of humor. So odds were the Ark wasn't doing anything miraculous. If it was . . . *If it is, we'll get it on TV,* she thought.

They finally crawled past the wreck, which was as nasty as anything on the New Jersey Turnpike or the 405 in L.A. As soon as they got by it, the driver put the pedal to the metal.

The Sheraton Plaza in Jerusalem was . . . a Sheraton. Gabriela knew she could have got the same perfect, calibrated comfort in any of several hundred cities around the world. As the driver extracted luggage from the trunk, Brandon said, "Gotta film the model of old-time Jerusalem and the Temple at the Israel Museum."

"It's the wrong Temple, though," the driver said. "It's Herod's, the one where Jesus came. The Ark was in the First Temple, and disappeared before Nebuchadnezzar captured it." He might be secular, but he knew his onions.

Gabriela knew hers, too. "Nobody who watches American TV will care one bit. It's a Temple—that's all they'll care about."

"You should get it right." The driver proved he'd never worked in television.

"Does anybody have a model of the First Temple?" Brandon asked.

"I don't think there is one," the driver said. "Herod's is a lot fancier."

"Okay. The visuals are what matter in our business." Brandon looked up and up at the glass front of the high-rise hotel. "I guess this will be good enough."

"It'll be fine," Gabriela said quickly. How could you go seriously wrong at a Sheraton? She also had the sense to understand when she was well off. She'd slept rolled in a blanket between American and Afghan soldiers. The Yanks worried more about their alleged allies than they did about the *mujahidin* they were fighting. *Mujahidin* were enemies all the time, while government troops might open up without warning.

"You're a trouper, Gabriela," Brandon said. Sarcasm? She sent him a sharp look, but his expression was too bland to let her read anything from it.

"Thanks. You, too," she said, remembering her *abuela*'s advice: always repay one compliment with another, so you left the other person owing you. She went on, "After we check in, I'm going to go straight up to my room and start calling archaeologists."

Eric had a sleeping bag on the floor of the tunnel leading to the Ark. Orly had another, a couple of feet away. Neither bag was big enough for two, and there was no privacy anyway—they weren't the only people who wouldn't leave. Munir was still there, either because he wanted to see the Ark come forth or to give the Muslim world a qualified observer.

Israeli soldiers had brought down a Porta-Potty. The air was getting high, but nobody complained. Eric needed a shower, too.

So did everybody else. But they'd all been on digs where showers were scarce. He'd survive. If Orly started holding her nose . . . he'd worry about it.

No more blocks had come out of the wall since removing the first showed what lay beyond. Yoram was playing it as cool as liquid oxygen. Fair enough, when what lay beyond the wall was as explosive as LOX.

"From now on, we do nothing we don't photograph or video," Yoram declared. "Nobody will say we planted the Ark or any of the other bullshit you can expect. We won't let them or give them any excuse." He stuck out his chin, looking more like the combat commander he'd been than the scholar he was.

Nobody argued. Eric didn't try. When you were sitting on a discovery that matched Tut's tomb and the Dead Sea Scrolls put together, you did things by the book. If people had any reason to think you weren't legit, plenty would.

Plenty would anyhow. The soldiers brought news along with food, water, coffee, cigarettes, and that outhouse on wheels. Eric had known Gabriela and Brandon were in Israel since the dirty bomb hit Tel Aviv. Now they'd come to Jerusalem. If anybody could whip hysteria into frenzy, they were the ones.

Eric wasn't sure the Israelis understood that. If Yoram didn't, it wasn't because Eric didn't tell him. Yoram shrugged. "What? You don't think a miracle should be on television?" he said. "The more people who see, who know, the better."

"A miracle." The word, in English or in Hebrew, made Eric want to run.

After Yoram's first astonishment, he took it in stride. "What do you call it?" he asked. "If you've got a rational explanation for how the Ark's been floating for the past 2,600 years, I'd like to hear it."

"We don't know it was floating all that time," Eric said.

Yoram raised an eyebrow. "Of course not. Maybe it sat there till we got that stone out, then jumped in the air to confuse us."

"Right." Eric's ears burned. It wasn't any less a miracle if it happened a second before that stone came out than if the Ark had floated there since before the Babylonians took Jerusalem and wrecked the First Temple. "Yoram . . . what are the rabbis saying?"

"Everything—depending on who you listen to. What else are rabbis for?" Louvish said. "Some say wait and see. They remember Sabbetai Zevi, I suppose."

"I hope so," Eric said. Sabbetai Zevi was a seventeenth-century Sephardic Jew, born in the Ottoman Empire, who'd proclaimed himself the Messiah and attracted a large following, Christians and Muslims with Jews. He grew prominent enough to alarm the Sultan, who threatened to make him a head shorter if he didn't convert to Islam. He did, whereupon his movement collapsed—though a stubborn handful still believed he'd been genuine. For most people, he was an object lesson: you shouldn't commit too soon.

Yoram wasn't finished: "Some want to start building the Third Temple yesterday."

"Like the Reconstruction Alliance," Eric said.

"Yes, like them," Yoram agreed.

The Reconstruction Alliance gave Eric the willies. It bothered Yoram less. Eric snapped his fingers. "You had Orly and me visit their museum. How come?"

"To see what Temple implements are like," Yoram answered.

"They have a model of the Ark there." Eric waited. The Israeli nodded, his face a poker player's mask. Eric plowed ahead: "You wanted us to see that stuff because you expected the real Ark was down here."

"Expected? No." Yoram shook his head. "You never expect . . . this. I hoped. I prayed, too. But when it happened . . . No, you don't expect such things."

"Okay. But you thought there was a chance. Why? Stories put the Ark everywhere from Chartres to Ethiopia. So why'd you think it was still here?"

"Because this is the logical place. No one found it and took it away after it got hidden in Josiah's reign. It's so big and fancy, there'd be a record if somebody carried it away. I thought it would be around, if we could find it." Yoram hesitated. "Rabbi Kupferman felt the same way."

"Kupferman?" After the way the other archaeologist had sneered at rabbis a moment before, Eric blinked to hear him praise one now. Then the name registered. "Oh. Him." Shlomo Kupferman was the leading theologian connected with the Reconstruction Alliance. He headed the Pious Bloc, one of the little religious parties in the Israeli Knesset.

Yoram Louvish looked embarrassed. "I don't care whether you like his politics. He's a learned man, and he's spent years researching the Ark."

"If you say so." Eric sounded uncomfortable. He felt uncomfortable. Rabbi Kupferman gave him the willies. Kupferman had black eyes, a fierce expression, and a long, tangled white beard. If he'd worn a turban, not a *kippah,* he would have looked like an ayatollah.

"I do," Yoram answered. "Have you seen any of Nechshat's articles?"

"Sure," Eric said. "He's a sharp guy. But what's he got to do with . . . ?" His voice trailed away. *Nechshat* was Hebrew for *copper.* *Kupferman* was *Copperman* in German or Yiddish. "Oy!"

"See? You're not as smart as you think," Yoram said. Eric was thinking the same thing. He liked it less when the Israeli spelled it out. He'd always felt Nechshat—whose first initial was Sh. (one character in Hebrew)—knew his business. Did that mean Rabbi Kupferman knew his religious business? Eric still didn't believe it.

He didn't want to quarrel with Yoram, so he sidestepped: "Why did he think the Ark was still under the Temple Mount?"

"There's no evidence it ever left Jerusalem," Yoram answered. "Some hints in the Talmud imply it stayed here, too. Nobody knows more about those than Shlomo."

Eric knew *he* didn't. You had to be a rabbi to fight through the Talmud and the Gemara—the commentaries—that had accreted around it like nacre 'round irritating grit.

"Does he know how it's floating above the ground?" Eric asked.

"Nobody does." Yoram spread his hands. "The physicists say they don't understand it. Those are the honest ones. The others say it isn't floating, no matter what they see."

"Ha!" Eric said. Cautious probing with a long, thin pole had proved no wires held the Ark up. He asked, "Is there anything in the Talmud about *that?*"

"Not that I know," Yoram answered. "Some Freemasons are saying they knew it all along. Maybe. Or maybe they're crazy."

"Or maybe they did *and* they're crazy," Eric said. "When it comes to that thing"—he nodded toward what lay behind the wall—"crazy is all that makes any sense."

"Now that you mention it," Yoram said, "yes."

Cleaning out Rosie's stall was an honor. It was one Chaim Avigad couldn't win, because it would have left him ritually impure. He'd put up with so much. Somehow, that seemed the crowning insult.

"They'll kill her, and I can't even take care of her!" he complained to his mother.

"It's part of God's plan," she answered. "Everything is happening the way He intended. Look how the Ark is found at last, so it can go in the Holy of Holies after they rebuild the Temple."

"Yeah." Chaim showed less enthusiasm. Everybody at Kibbutz Ha-Minsarah was excited about the rediscovery of the Ark. Chaim wasn't. Finding it made the Third Temple likelier to go up. To him, that wasn't all good. Before they rebuilt the Temple, they'd sacrifice the red heifer so its ashes could make everything ritually pure.

They'd slaughter Rosie!

Most boys Chaim's age fixed on sports stars. A few had already started mooning over girls. What about him? *What about me?* he thought. The most important thing in his life that wasn't family was a cow from America. If that wasn't weird . . .

They'd always been bound together. He'd been kept away from religious pollution so he would be fit to serve in the Temple from the start. And Rosie could confer purity on others—but only dead. It felt wrong. What was God thinking?

"Now that we have the Ark, too, I don't see how the Knesset can do anything but let us rebuild—especially the Knesset coming after the new elections," his mother said.

"We don't have the Ark yet," Chaim said. "It's in that room behind the wall." It could stay there, for all of him. If it didn't come out, nobody would do anything to the red heifer.

Rivka Avigad smiled. "You'll make a fine rabbi someday, the way you can split hairs."

He didn't want to be a rabbi. Being a farmer looked great. So did ditch digger. Anything that let him mess around in the dirt. He'd never had the chance to get dirty. What kind of life was that? On TV, he'd watched kids grinning from mud puddles. It looked wonderful. He was probably the only boy in *Eretz Yisrael* who didn't know what playing in the mud was like.

Well, not quite. There were others like him here at the kibbutz, here in this miserable tent. But they were the way they were for the same reason he was. They had to stay ritually unpolluted, too. It didn't seem right.

And he'd found something he cared about, and what would happen? Rosie'd be sacrificed. All the signs pointed toward it. The horrible bombing in Tel Aviv. The rediscovery of the Ark. His mother was right. How could the Third Temple *not* go forward now?

No wonder everybody at the kibbutz was so pumped. Chaim had never felt this out of step. He'd seen plenty of ordinary animals slaughtered. He had no trouble imagining that happening to Rosie. The blood would spurt, her legs would get wobbly, and she'd fall.

She wouldn't understand why the people who'd been nice were cutting her throat. How could she? She was a special cow, but she was only a cow.

Why the ashes of a red heifer? Because it was in the Bible. But what was God thinking of when He made the rule? Chaim didn't ask his mother. She'd tell him not to worry, or she'd say that wasn't the right question to ask. She'd say people shouldn't ask about why God did things.

She'd said that before. And Chaim asked, "What about Job?"

He remembered the odd look his mother gave him. He didn't understand why. If the Book of Job wasn't one long scream of, *Why are You doing this to me?*—what was it?

Chaim had asked Uncle Yitzhak the same thing—Uncle Yitzhak knew the Bible with his head, not with the heart like Mom. Talking about Job made his uncle nervous, too. "Job is . . . a special case," was as much as Yitzhak Avigad wanted to say.

"Why?" Chaim asked. "What about Psalm 8: 'What is man, that Thou art mindful of him?' Wasn't Job asking that, too?"

"It's a good question." Uncle Yitzhak looked uncomfortable. "It makes people think about what the answer should be."

"Well? What should it be?"

"God should be mindful of you because you do what He says and follow His commandments."

"Job did all that. Look what happened to him."

"Because he kept following the commandments, it worked out for him in the end."

"But God let Satan kill Job's sons and daughters. He had more in the end, but he'd never get back the ones he lost. It didn't work out all right for them, and Satan killed them to make Job sorry. They didn't do anything to deserve it."

Uncle Yitzhak didn't want to talk about the Book of Job after that. Everybody quoted the Bible when it suited his purpose. When it didn't . . . you were an annoying little kid.

There were times when he resented his family more than he knew how to say. They'd made him so different from everybody else, and on purpose, too! But they'd also explained why, and their teaching made him believe they were doing the right thing. How could you usher in the Messiah without the Temple or have the Temple without people to serve it?

He was, in short, a messed-up kid. But how many kids his age weren't messed up? Damn few, especially if you asked them.

Gabriela had done interviews that seemed tougher than Rabbi Shlomo Kupferman. She'd talked with men who could incinerate the world by touching a button. A couple of them looked eager to do it while the cameras rolled. *That* would have made a ratings coup, but not one she could have enjoyed long.

Kupferman owned the most intimidating eyebrows Gabriela'd seen, and she'd interviewed Russians. Maybe the difference was that the Russians disapproved of her for being a prominent American. The rabbi disapproved of everything and everybody.

"The excavators are right to be careful with the Ark. Anyone not properly pious would throw away his life if he touched it," Kupferman said. "Are you acquainted with the sad fate of Uzzah son of Abinadab?"

"As a matter of fact," Gabriela answered, "no."

Rabbi Kupferman's sniff said he'd expected no better from a *goy* like Gabriela, who also had the presumption to be of the female persuasion. "This is in Second Samuel, the sixth chapter," he said. "The Ark was placed on a cart, and the oxen shook it. Uzzah son of Abinadab put his hand on the Ark to steady it. The Lord struck him dead."

"Do you believe that?"

This time, Shlomo Kupferman looked at her as if she were road-kill. "Of course," he said. "It is in the Holy Scriptures, and they are

God's word. If they weren't true, how would we have found the Ark, which is described in great detail there, after so long?"

Since Gabriela had no answer, she tried something else: "What other things is the Ark supposed to be able to do, Rabbi?" As soon as she asked the question, she wished she had it back. That *supposed to be* would tick Kupferman off.

She got another scorching glare from the old rabbi, but he just said, "Do you know of the time when the Philistines captured the Ark?"

"No, and many of my listeners won't, either. Please tell us." Gabriela knew about Goliath. She knew the Philistines gave Palestine their name, though they'd long since vanished. Past that? Not very much.

"They captured the Ark and brought it to Ashdod, their city," Shlomo Kupferman said. "This is in First Samuel, chapters five and six. They put it in the house of Dagon, their idol. And Dagon's statue fell on its face before the Ark. The Philistines set it up again. The next night, its head and hands were cut off: the Lord was mightier than any idol. He smote Ashdod with emerods, and many died."

"What are emerods?" Gabriela asked—the people who watched would wonder at the archaic word.

"Hemorrhoids, you would say in modern English," Kupferman replied, his face perfectly straight. "And the Philistines moved the Ark to Gath, and the plague followed it. Then they moved it to Ekron, and the same thing happened—and they were also plagued with mice."

"I see." Gabriela fought back the urge to giggle. "That's . . . quite a plague."

"The Philistines thought so." Kupferman sounded grave as a tomb. No, he wasn't swallowing laughter. "They made golden images of the mice and others of their emerods, and sent them back with the Ark to the children of Israel—and their plagues ceased."

"Golden . . . emerods?" Gabriela had trouble imagining that. "Are they still in that chamber with the Ark?"

After considering, the rabbi shook his head. "I doubt it. The Babylonians took the gold associated with the Temple, and the emerods and mice would have been part of that."

"So everything was all right from then on?" Gabriela persisted.

"No," Kupferman said. "The Ark came to the town of Bethshemesh. The people there dared look inside. And the Lord slew some 50,070. And the people there lamented—"

"I'll bet they did!" she broke in.

She might as well have saved her breath. "—and the men of Bethshemesh said, 'Who is able to stand before this holy Lord God?'" Shlomo Kupferman sent his ferocious stare Gabriela's way once more. "So you see, this Ark is not just a very holy thing. It is a very potent thing, one that deserves respect."

"You believe this happened because it's written in the Bible?"

"Yes," Kupferman said simply. An Alabama fundamentalist preacher or a mullah from Qom would have sounded the same way. He went on, "All these years ago, the scribes wrote of the Ark, and now we see it as they wrote of it, and undamaged. Why should I *not* believe?"

"But you believed the same things *before* the Ark was found." Gabriela made that sound like an accusation.

"It's called faith," Rabbi Kupferman said. "You might try it one day."

Enough screwy things had happened lately to make Gabriela wonder about that herself. She'd never admit it on the air, though. She asked, "How does the Ark keep floating?"

"By the will of God," Kupferman answered. "Nothing may be accomplished any other way."

"But *why* is it God's will that the Ark should float?"

"I have no idea," Shlomo Kupferman said placidly. "Ask Him, in prayer. He may tell you."

"Thank you very much, Rabbi Kupferman," Gabriela said. They were out of time—not soon enough for her.

Ibrahim ibn Abd al-Rahman poked the remote's power button. Gabriela Sandoval and Shlomo Kupferman disappeared. The screen went black, but less black than his mood.

Jamal Ashrawi scowled at the TV, too, for a different reason. "That Jew was born lying, and he's got better at it since," the Grand Mufti said.

"What if he's not?" Haji Ibrahim said. "Harder to lie when you quote from the holy books."

"Not for Jews or Christians," Ashrawi said. "Their books are distorted. Only the Qur'an tells all of God's truth."

"Of course." The head of the Waqf didn't like Haji Jamal telling him things he already knew. The two fugitives had shared tight accommodations ever since they escaped from the room above the *souq*. Ibrahim ibn Abd al-Rahman was sick of it.

"What are you worrying about, then?" Ashrawi said.

"Why would the people who wrote the Jews' and Christians' holy books falsify things that have to do with the Ark?" Ibrahim asked. "It was long lost. The scribes had to think it would never be seen again. They had no reason to distort what it could do. And if it *is* that strong, the Jews have a new weapon!"

"God wouldn't allow it." But the Grand Mufti sounded less certain now.

"God has allowed so many things we never dreamt of," Haji Ibrahim said gloomily. "That the Western infidels should learn so many things Muslims did not grasp. That they should defeat us whenever we fought. That the Jews should beat Syria, Jordan, *and* Egypt again and again. That they should take Jerusalem and the Haram al-Sharif. Who could have imagined God would allow that?"

"We need a new Saladin," Jamal Ashrawi said, "to sweep them into the sea the way he beat the Crusaders so long ago."

"We need him, but where is he?" Ibrahim asked. "We had such hopes for Arafat. . . ." He left it there. Jamal Ashrawi had been Arafat's creature once. But the old PLO warhorse was years dead, Palestine split, and the Jews strong as ever.

"God will find another man, or make one. He is God," Ashrawi said.

"May you be right. May He hear our prayers," Haji Ibrahim said. "But I would be easier if you could tell me how the Ark floats."

"I can," the Grand Mufti said. "By trick photography, that's how."

"May you be right," Ibrahim ibn Abd al-Rahman repeated. "But I wish Kupferman did not sound so sure." The rabbi reminded *him* of a mullah who'd memorized the Qur'an. He asked, "What do we do if . . . if this turns out not to be true?" He'd said it.

"We had two *shahidin,* two martyrs, and look what they did to the Jews' city," Haji Jamal answered. "If we need more, God will provide them."

Ibrahim felt better; that was plainly true. Young men who'd martyr themselves for eternity in Paradise were never scarce among the Palestinians. Young women as willing were less scarce than they had been, if rarer than men.

"We should beat them without martyrs," he said. "Millions of Arabs against a handful of Jews?"

"We can't all get into the fight," Jamal Ashrawi replied. "The Israelis have Western weapons, and Satan behind them. Only God's power is stronger than Satan's."

"But surely the Ark isn't a thing of Satan's," Ibrahim ibn Abd al-Rahman said.

Haji Jamal shrugged. "It is what it is. But whatever the Jews touch, nothing good is likely to come from it. This struggle is just beginning!"

"May you be right," Haji Ibrahim said once more.

8

Yitzhak Avigad scowled across the desk at Shlomo Kupferman. "You've seen it?" Yitzhak demanded.

"Officially, no," the rabbi answered. "I'm not supposed to go down there. It would provoke the Arabs, God forbid." He rolled his eyes. "But Sh. Nechshat, the archaeologist, he's been there. A fairly sound man, Professor Nechshat."

"Heh." Yitzhak grudged the laugh. Kupferman's alias was an open secret to people who wanted the Third Temple to rise. "What does the professor think?"

"That it is the Ark of the Covenant." Rabbi Kupferman's voice went soft. "Louvish is a very sound man, but with something like that you have to see for yourself before you believe it's true. I've seen—and I believe."

"Good. That's what I wanted to hear." Yitzhak came to the point: "When do we deal with the Dome of the Rock and Al-Aqsa Mosque? When do we start building?"

"If it were up to me, we would've done that when we took the Temple Mount in the Six-Day War," Kupferman answered. "But it's not. It's up to the government. They have soldiers and tanks around the Mount to keep the Arabs away—and our people, too."

"What do those idiots want?" Yitzhak made a fist. "I hate to wait till after the election. After what the Arabs did to Tel Aviv, they've got no business pissing and moaning if we do what we need to on the Temple Mount."

"They will anyway. They're Arabs." Kupferman didn't hide his contempt.

Neither did Yitzhak. "Sure. But we don't have to pay attention to them any more because of Tel Aviv. *And* we've got the Ark! Twenty-five hundred years gone, and we found it! So what's the government waiting for with the Temple? An engraved invitation from On High, brought down by an angel?"

"You're preaching to the choir," Kupferman said in English. Grimly amused, Yitzhak nodded. In Hebrew again, the rabbi went on, "I'll tell you what. They're waiting for the votes to get counted. Till they're sure which way the wind blows, nothing important will happen."

Yitzhak snorted. "Don't they know? If they don't, they have to be blind. From now on, we take care of ourselves, and the hell with the rest of the world . . . mm, except America." Israel couldn't last a year without U.S. backing. Nobody liked to talk or think about it, but everybody knew it.

"America isn't the problem," Kupferman said. Yitzhak Avigad nodded. The problem was Israeli pols who couldn't see how much things had changed the past few weeks. "After the votes get counted, lots of people here will lose their cushy places. Mark my words. And wait till you see what the Pious Bloc does!"

A certain secular gleam lit his features. He couldn't imagine himself as Prime Minister . . . could he? If there was a new Cabinet, though, he was bound to have one ministry or another.

"*Alevai!*" Yitzhak liked that idea. Once the Ark came up from under the Temple Mount, even the most irreligious Israelis would have to think hard about what being a Jew meant.

"*Alevai omayn,*" Kupferman agreed. "We have to believe in our cause as strongly as the Arabs do, don't we? If they believe and we don't, won't they win in the end? That's my biggest fear."

"Yes." Yitzhak's mouth tightened. You could call suicide bombers fanatics. But they were brave fanatics, and the other side had an unending supply of them, and of other people who would do anything to defeat Israel.

His thoughts must have shown on his face, for Kupferman said, "Don't despair. We have believers, too. Would you be talking with me if we didn't? Would your nephew be a boy raised in ritual purity—and raised to understand why he was—if we didn't?"

"Well . . . no." Looking at it that way made Yitzhak feel better. "Ask you something else, Rabbi?"

"Of course." Kupferman made you feel he had the answers if anybody did. That was just what Yitzhak was looking for.

"Why does the Ark float?" he blurted.

"I haven't the faintest idea." The rabbi's smile was startlingly sweet. "If you need to know something like that, ask God—I said the same thing to that Gabriela woman. Maybe He'll tell you. He hasn't told me yet—but I don't worry about it. It floats because He wants it to float. But that isn't what you wanted to hear, is it?"

"I hoped for something a little more, uh, detailed," Yitzhak admitted. Kupferman spread his hands—he had no more to give.

He knows the answer if anybody does, Yitzhak thought again. What could you do when nobody knew the answers? You could ask God. The rabbi was right. Yitzhak intended to do it. He didn't know what kind of answer he'd get from the Lord, either.

* * *

Eric Katz blinked and wished for the sunglasses he wore above-ground. Television lights turned the tunnel under the Temple Mount brighter than daylight. Looking into a spot was like looking at . . .

He shook his head. The first thing that sprang to mind was *like looking at an atomic bomb*. He knew a dirty bomb wasn't the same as a real nuke. It was bad enough, though.

They were working like madmen to decontaminate downtown Tel Aviv. How long would that take? How much would people trust it after the authorities said it was done? Anyone who'd been within a hundred miles of Tel Aviv and got diagnosed with cancer—or even housemaid's knee—would blame the dirty bomb for it. How could you expect somebody in a mess like that to do anything different?

A voice floated down the tunnel: "May I please come observe the removal of the Ark?"

"When was the last time Brandon Nesbitt said please?" Orly asked, amusement in her eyes.

"The last time somebody told him no and made it stick," Eric answered. "Maybe 2009."

"No," Yoram Louvish yelled up toward the tunnel mouth. "You're getting the feed like CNN and Fox and the BBC and Gethsemane and our own TV channels. Nobody has a reporter down here, so you're staying where you are, too."

"Gabriela and I came to Israel to talk to the people who've got the red heifer," Brandon said plaintively. "This ties in so well!"

"No, it doesn't," Orly said. "That's religion. This is archaeology." But she couldn't make that sound convincing, even to herself. "This is *religious* archaeology," she amended.

"You bet," Eric agreed. "How many evangelicals are watching the Gethsemane Network now? And how many who aren't are watching Fox instead? If this were an ordinary dig and we found something spectacular, we'd get one minute on the news and maybe a *National Geographic* documentary two years from now. But we're live all over the world."

Thou shalt not take the name of the Lord thy God in vain. He couldn't remember the last time he'd thought about the First Commandment or about letting it affect how he behaved. If you were only a wall away from the Ark of the Covenant, though, and if the Ark was doing things science couldn't explain, who could blame you if you reexamined your options?

And what else did Exodus say before the Decalogue? *For I the Lord thy God am a jealous God visiting the iniquity of the fathers upon the children unto the third and fourth generation of them that hate me; And shewing mercy unto thousands of them that love me, and keep my commandments.*

Eric hadn't killed anybody. He'd—mostly—honored his father and mother. He hadn't stolen (much) or committed adultery (more than a couple of times). He hadn't coveted his neighbor's ass. His neighbor's wife's ass . . . That was how the adultery happened. He was a typical upper-middle-class twenty-first-century guy.

A typical upper-middle-class twenty-first-century guy, suddenly remembering that the God of Abraham, Isaac, and Jacob, the God of his ancestors in Whom he halfheartedly believed, was Not Amused to a degree that made Queen Victoria seem giddy by comparison.

Not the most reassuring thought he'd had. And that *visiting the iniquity of the fathers upon the children unto the third and fourth generation* . . . Not just his own bad karma, but his folks', too. Brrr!

Yoram Louvish coughed. Everybody's eyes swung his way. He had that knack. Maybe it came from commanding troops. Maybe he got to command troops because people paid attention to him. The chicken or the egg? Eric didn't know. He knew he looked toward Yoram, too. So did the camera.

"We're ready to get down to business now." Yoram used English.

A lot of Israelis understood it. There'd be translators for those who didn't.

Yoram needed a shave. He hadn't combed his hair for a few days. The TV lights reflected from his glasses. He looked as much like Indy as a warthog looked like Miss July. He had presence all the same.

"We're doing things differently here," he said into the camera. "Most of the time, we'd chip through this wall one stone at a time." Nobody'd straightened his teeth, which made his grin more disarming. "Because we've got something interesting on the other side, we'll take direct action instead."

He slipped on goggles that fit over his specs. Another archaeologist lugged up a chainsaw with 'roid rage. Orly said it reminded her of a gasoline-powered sawfish. *How does she do that?* Eric wondered. *It's my language . . . isn't it?*

"Thanks to Dov Ben Zakkai of Ben Zakkai Quarrying for lending us the fancy saw," Yoram said, which might bring Mr. Ben Zakkai extra business. The archaeologist grinned again. "The quarrymen who cut these stones before the Babylonian invasion would be jealous of how easy it makes things."

"Jealous, my ass," Orly whispered. "The noise that *mamzer* makes would scare anybody way back when shitless."

"It scares me shitless," Eric said, also quietly. He didn't like regular chainsaws. This thing? It was made for cutting the golden limestone that helped Jerusalem look so marvelous in the early morning and late afternoon. If an arm or leg got in the way, the saw wouldn't notice.

Yoram put on a surgical mask, then pushed the red starter button. The stonecutting saw roared to life. Eric longed for ear plugs, the way he would have at a concert. It wouldn't be anything on TV, though—they'd smooth it out. Not even gunfire was loud on TV.

Fumes made him cough. It was like getting stuck behind a

jalopy on the freeway in Friday-afternoon rush hour. He didn't head for fresh air, though.

The noise redoubled when the blade bit into a stone just below the one Eric and Yoram had removed. It reminded Eric of the noise the Jolly Green Giant's dentist's drill would make during a root canal. He set his teeth—carefully—and tried not to think about dentistry or the racket.

Dust and grit spurted. Yoram had to be glad for that mask. The saw had a built-in water dribbler to cool it. Without that, the teeth would have glowed red in nothing flat.

Flying grit stung Eric's forehead. Even with goggles and mask, he wouldn't have wanted to be as close to the action as Yoram. But the Israeli had faced worse things flying through the air than little chunks of stone.

He took the cut down to ground level. When he killed the motor, silence slammed down. Looking like a demented doctor, he smiled into the camera. "One down," he said. "I'm not used to working this fast. None of us are."

Most of the time, they would have worried about what they might miss. It would have been chip, chip, pick, pick. It would have taken days or weeks. Banging straight ahead had its charms.

Gabriela and Brandon weren't the only ones waiting at the top of the tunnel. Unlike the broadcasters, Shlomo Kupferman got to come down. Eric didn't like him for hell. That didn't mean he'd tell Kupferman to get lost. Why shouldn't a rabbi come to look at the Ark? And Kupferman, alias Nechshat, was an archaeologist, too.

"*Shalom*," Yoram called cheerfully. Several other Israeli archaeologists nodded to the rabbi. The rest—Orly among them—pretended he wasn't there. Eric followed their lead.

Munir al-Nuwayhi didn't look or act any different from his colleagues. They'd come to take him for granted. Shlomo Kupferman made a point of ignoring him. Munir didn't seem to mind.

Eric more than half wished the Ark had stayed undiscovered. It would pour gasoline over a religious situation already inflammable. So many Muslims denied the Temple Mount had ever had anything to do with Jews. How could they keep doing that after the chief artifact of the First Temple came up from under it?

He saw a couple of ways. They could call it a lie and a trick. Preventing that was one reason everything that happened was getting filmed. Or they could try to destroy the Ark once it came up. Anything was possible.

"Hello, all," Kupferman said, pretending not to see that half the archaeologists wanted nothing to do with him. "I want to say *mazel tov*! for your work here. What you've found confirms the truth of the Holy Scriptures. You will help the Temple rise again. I hope you are proud. I know God is proud of you."

How do you know? Did you ask Him? Did He send you a text? The fight between pious and secular Jews was coming, too. Eric could see it as plainly as he could see the one between Jews and Muslims. But it would have to wait its turn.

Yoram got a drill. More grit flew as he bored a hole in the wall. He screwed in a stout metal peg with a ring on the unthreaded end. Then he said, "Now back to peace and quiet," and fired up the stonecutting saw.

The noise was as horrible as it had been before. Maybe it was worse—this time, Yoram didn't slice straight down. He carved out a gentle curve, so the blade was traveling almost horizontally when it got down to the tunnel floor. It ground through sandstone and ancient mortar toward the cut he'd made before.

A sharp *snick*! announced that the new cut met the old. Yoram turned off the saw. Into the sudden silence that followed, he said, "Now we're in business."

He threaded a nylon rope through the eyebolt, then waved Eric forward. "Me?" Eric said in surprise.

Yoram nodded. "Why not? We got the first block out of the way.

Only fair we should bring down the rest. Besides, you're a big, strong guy."

"Yeah, right." Eric was fairly tall. Till now, nobody'd accused him of being strong. There were good reasons for that, too. But he couldn't resist being part of history.

Yoram shooed the other archaeologists and camera crew away from the space in front of the wall. That made excellent sense. Eric wouldn't have wanted those blocks crashing down on him. He stood to one side, Yoram to the other.

"Ready?" the Israeli asked.

"I guess," Eric answered.

"Okay. On three, pull like anything. One . . . Two . . . *Now!*"

It wasn't *three*, but Eric pulled anyway. He wondered if the eye-bolt would pop out, but Yoram had seated it well. It took the strain they put on it. The chunk of wall Yoram had sliced through stood . . . swayed a little . . . swayed more . . . and crashed forward down onto the floor of the tunnel.

The ground shook under Eric's New Balances. With the strain off, he staggered. He might have fallen if Orly hadn't caught him. "Thanks," he said.

"Any time—you big, strong guy." She winked. Was that love or mockery or some of each? He feared the best he could hope for was the last.

Coughing from the dust of ages the falling masonry kicked up saved him from needing a snappy comeback. And Yoram hadn't staggered—unlike Eric, he was braced for the wall to come tumbling down. *Him and Joshua,* Eric thought.

"Shine your lights in there," Yoram told the camera crew. "Now the rest of the world can see what we've got."

The rest of the world had to wait. Eric and Orly and the other archaeologists crowded forward for their own looks. They shoved and jostled. Eric hadn't been in a scrum like that since a pickup football game before his doctoral orals.

"Move it!" yelled the guys handling the lights. "Out of the way!"

Nobody wanted to. Not much light got through between the people, but enough to glint off gold. This was more dramatic than peering through an opening one building stone wide by the light of a single headlamp. Eric stared.

Two archaeologists started to go into the chamber behind the wall. "Stay back if you value your lives!" Kupferman shouted, in English and Hebrew. "The Ark will not let itself be touched by profane hands!"

Eric wasn't sure he believed that. Not long ago, he would have said he didn't. But the Ark *was* floating above the ground. If it could do that, what else could it do?

God knows, he thought. And maybe that didn't mean *Nobody knows* this time. Maybe it meant what it said.

Wasn't that scary?

"Are those the poles people carried it by all those years ago?" Orly asked.

"What else?" Eric said. "Not likely anybody went in there and changed them."

She nodded. "What happens if somebody picks up the Ark by them now?"

"Good question," Eric told her. "If there are no other questions, class dismissed." She gave him a dirty look. He said, "Hon, how do I know? Maybe they break. But maybe they don't. Look at it. It's floating there. How much does it weigh? Anything?"

Orly blinked. "That's a good question, too." She frowned. "It has to weigh *something.*"

"Beats me. Last time I worried about physics was in high school, and Mr. Goldberg didn't give any exceptions for miracles," Eric answered. Sounding flip when he talked about miracles was the ironic, detached, twenty-first-century way to deal with them.

The other was just to believe in them. That was how Kupferman dealt with them. To Eric, it was also how the bastards who'd dirty-bombed Tel Aviv dealt with them, to say nothing of the televange-lists back home. He didn't want to be like them.

What if they're right? Every time he looked at the Ark, floating there with no visible means of support, the question got louder inside his head.

"Move back!" Yoram shouted. "Give the cameras a chance!"

Reluctantly, the archaeologists obeyed. When Yoram told you to do something, you did it first and wondered why later. It *had* to have something to do with yelling in battle. Eric wished he could make people listen that way, but not enough to wish he'd been a combat soldier.

When bathed in the TV lights, the gold sheathing the Ark re-flected so much that details were hard to make out. The only excep-tions were the cherubim on the lid. Eric could see those better than he had before.

The better he saw them, the more they alarmed him. It wasn't that they weren't splendidly worked; they were. He could make out every vane on every feather in their wings, every detail on their faces. But those faces . . .

Inhuman was the first word that sprang to mind, but it wasn't right. The cherubim looked out toward him and the other archae-ologists. Those two golden visages peered toward them, through them, past them, toward . . . something else, something people weren't meant to see. Whatever it was, it filled them with savage, terrible joy. Their eyes were wide, nostrils distended, lips slightly parted, and teeth longer and sharper than teeth had any business being.

Next to Eric, Orly shivered; he felt it against his shoulder. When he slipped an arm around her, she nodded and drew close. If she wasn't seeing the same thing he was, he would have been surprised.

Not everybody noticed, or cared. Shlomo Kupferman leaned forward, his eyes as wide as those of the cherubim. *The better to see you, my dear,* Eric thought. "Beautiful," the rabbi whispered.

"How do we get it up into the city?" someone asked.

That brought Kupferman back to himself. "I have Levites wait-ing at the top of the tunnel," he answered. "As they did in David's day, they will bring the Ark into Jerusalem."

Eric swallowed a giggle. If you walked into an Orthodox *shul,* the *shammes* asked you, "Cohen or Levite?" Most people answered, "*Yisrael,*" and went in. Like most Katzes, Eric was a cohen, a de-scendant of the priestly class—and, from what the DNA guys said, that was a genetically traceable clan. In the days of the Temples, the Levites were priests' assistants and singers and musicians and gate-keepers and guards. They and the *cohanim* got precedence in read-ing the Torah, but that was it. Thinking the old distinctions mattered for anything more was crazy.

A lot of what had happened in the Holy Land lately was crazy. If God wasn't pulling the strings . . . it looked even crazier.

Which means what? Eric wondered. Thinking God *was* pulling the strings struck him as crazy, too. It meant Rabbi Kupferman might be right: a terrifying thought. Or it meant the Grand Mufti of Jerusalem was, or a TV preacher like Pat Robertson or—less obnoxiously—Lester Stark.

God's most passionate advocates made atheism looked good to Eric. Looking good to him, though, didn't make it true. Adjusting to that notion was harder than adjusting to a stick shift after driv-ing an automatic.

"The Ark isn't going anywhere now," Yoram declared. "First we finish the *in situ* photography. God won't mind. The Ark is holy, but it's also the most important find in—well, forever. No one will forgive us if we don't learn everything we can before we move it."

Would Kupferman forgive? Eric waited for him to swell up and turn purple at delaying by even a millisecond. The rabbi didn't. Eric thought it was because Kupferman had his own archaeolo-gist's hat on. But he proved wrong.

"It will go into Jerusalem and into the new Temple when God is ready," Kupferman said. "It waited outside the city till David took Jerusalem from the Jebusites. It waited in a tent in Jerusalem till God found Solomon worthy of building His Temple. And it waited here till He found us worthy of recovering it. Take your pictures, Yoram. God wouldn't have let you find it if He didn't mean for you to."

"I don't know what He means me to do. I only know what I mean to do." Yoram snapped away.

Brandon Nesbitt wanted to punch somebody. The soldiers who kept Gabriela and him from going into the Temple Mount and getting a firsthand look at the Ark would have done nicely. But they had Galils and watchful expressions. Brandon didn't think he could get away with slugging one of them. He didn't think even Oprah could, not with these dudes. And if Oprah couldn't, it was serious.

He wouldn't have minded popping one of the Levites, either. They looked like weirdos. Nobody'd worn those turban-like hats, tunics, and baggy pants—all white linen—with a long, multicolored sash around the waist for two thousand years. The Levites didn't carry rifles. But they looked as serious as the soldiers. Chances were they'd been through the IDF and would clobber him if he took his frustrations out on them. Too bad!

There was the Ark on the monitors. It floated like a special effect, but it wasn't. It was real. If the scientists figured out how to bottle that, what would it mean? Would it put the airlines out of business? Or automakers? Or Saudi Arabia? With antigravity, why would you need a 747 or a Cadillac Escalade or the fuel to run them?

Brandon pointed a mike at the nearest Levite. "What's your name?"

"I am Avraham Moser," the man answered in careful English.

"When you're not a Levite, what do you do?"

"I am always a Levite. It is part of my . . . inheritance. I make my living as a graphic designer, if you mean that."

"What do you think of the Ark?"

"It is wonderful. What can anyone think?"

"Do you believe it can strike people dead?"

"If the Bible says it, how can I not?"

For Brandon, not believing the Bible was easy. The same held true for most of the Western world. The principal exceptions were American evangelicals. He wanted them to watch Gabriela and him. Otherwise, his opinion of them couldn't have been lower.

What they meant by the Bible wasn't what this Levite meant. They had an extra Testament bolted on. Muslims believed in the literal truth of the Qur'an. How would this guy like getting lumped with them? He'd give you lumps for suggesting it.

True believers of any stripe—Muslims, Jews, evangelicals, Nazis, PC people—horrified Brandon. You couldn't reason with them. They had assumptions where reasoning should have lived.

But what if this crowd was right? "How do you suppose the Ark floats, Mr., uh, Moser?"

"God lets it, so it does," the Israeli answered. Shlomo Kupferman had said practically the same thing. It didn't explain anything, not to Brandon. But it seemed to satisfy Avraham Moser completely.

Brandon tried a different question: "Where do you get your regalia?" Moser looked blank. *Doesn't know what regalia means,* Brandon realized. "Your clothes. Your, um, Levite's uniform."

"Oh. The Reconstruction Alliance. They . . . weave them."

"That's Rabbi Kupferman's outfit, right?" Brandon knew it was. But the lip-movers in TV land couldn't remember their own names without checking their driver's licenses, let alone the handle for a bearded Hebe's religious movement.

"Yes, of course." Avraham Moser had no doubts. Kupferman was a much bigger deal in Israel than in the USA. He couldn't very well be a smaller deal here than in the States. Even here, he counted for a right-wing nut . . . or he had till the Arabs dirty-bombed Tel Aviv and till the archaeologists found the Ark.

Now? Brandon didn't think anybody knew anything now.

Someone shouted in Hebrew. Brandon would have had trouble understanding English from down a big, deep hole. This way . . . "What's up?" he asked the Levite.

"He says it isn't coming up now." Moser couldn't hide his disappointment. "He says they aren't ready."

"Oh. Crap." Brandon passed the word to Gabriela. She said exactly the same thing. They both hated standing and waiting for something that wouldn't happen. What reporter didn't? Brandon forced a laugh. Hate it or not, he'd done it often enough—too often. Maybe he could get a quote before he headed back to the hotel. "Do you think everything that's going on means the Messiah will show up soon?"

"I don't know," Avraham Moser said. "But if we work for the Messiah's coming, that makes it more likely, yes?"

Brandon Nesbitt shrugged. He didn't worry about it, except that he wanted an interview if the Messiah *did* come around. He wanted something else, too . . . "Are the tablets God gave to Moses on Mount Sinai inside the Ark?"

The Levite's eyes widened. "How can anyone know? Only the High Priest went into the Holy of Holies with the Ark, and only on Yom Kippur—one day a year."

"Wouldn't it be something if they were?" Brandon persisted.

"I don't think anyone will find out, not for certain," Moser said. "To touch the Ark is to die."

"Yeah, the rabbi told Gabriela the same thing," Brandon replied. "You don't think that works after so long, do you?" He figured that, if the Ark *had* killed people—or given them emerods!—it put the whammy on them because they believed it could. If you didn't buy into a curse, how could it bite you?

Moser's eyes got wider. He sidled away from Brandon as if he didn't care to stand too close when the lightning crashed down. "I don't want to find out. If you are smart, you don't, either."

Keep talking. Scare off the competition, Brandon thought.

9

Time to vote. Yitzhak Avigad marked his ballot for the Pious Bloc's slate and watched while it went into the box. Of course, as an American remarked long ago, one on the tally sheet was worth two in the box. Every party would have observers to make sure nobody got creative counting.

He nodded to Chaim's mother as they left the polling place. "We've done what *we* can," he said. "Now it's up to the fools everywhere else."

"How can they not give the government to people who know what to do with it?" Rivka Avigad said, adding, "People who know what God wants them to do?"

"How?" Yitzhak raised an eyebrow. He liked his ex-sister-in-law: more than he'd ever said, in fact. Talking about it would have felt like poaching on Tzvi Avigad, even though his brother was long out of the picture. But no denying Rivka could be naive. "They've kept us out of the government since Israel was founded. Why should they change now?"

She took him literally. "Because of everything that's happened," she answered.

"Sure," Yitzhak said, and then, "Hope so, anyway."

The polls were good—better than he ever remembered. If the results lived up to them . . . Israel would have a new direction. And if it didn't, the pollsters would look like fools. One way or the other, they would know tonight.

"Will they let us go home to Nair Tamid soon?" Rivka asked. "It would be nice to get back where we belong."

"I'm tired of it here, too." Yitzhak shrugged. "But if it's still radioactive there . . ."

She said something about the Arabs who'd bombed Tel Aviv that should have turned the ground here radioactive or melted it under her feet. Yitzhak nodded. He didn't think Israel had taken enough reprisals. If the government changed, if they got people with sense running things, he could hope that would be different, too.

But reprisals might be secondary. If they rebuilt the Temple and did God's work, revenge would take care of itself. "Almost two thousand years," he murmured.

Rivka nodded. "We've waited so long," she said. "*Alevai*, we won't have to much more."

"*Alevai omayn*," Yitzhak echoed.

"Do you want to come to supper tonight?" she asked.

He shook his head. "Thanks, but I'll fix something for myself." He didn't feel sociable. His brother's wife knew better than to push him.

His apartment was as bare as if he were an officer on occupation duty. That wasn't because he'd been forced out of Kibbutz Nair Tamid; his flat there had been just as empty. The only decorations were two photos of a woman with dark, curly hair. Sarah'd been shopping in Jerusalem with some girlfriends, and they'd paused for lunch in a crowded café . . . minutes before a suicide bomber turned it into a slaughterhouse.

One of the girlfriends lived. She identified what was left of Sarah. Nobody let Yitzhak see the remains before they went into the coffin. The Jewish custom of quick burial was a mercy—as with surgery in the days before anesthesia, the worst was over in a hurry.

As with surgery of that sort, the pain didn't go away once the cutting stopped. Much lingered yet; a big part would linger till the day when Yitzhak went into his own coffin. One of these days, he might get up the nerve to tell Rivka that pain shared was pain lessened. Or, of course, he might not. He hadn't yet.

He threw a frozen dinner into the microwave. Americans called that nuking their food. After Tel Aviv, Yitzhak didn't want to think of it that way. While the dinner spun, he poured himself a slug of local brandy. It was a savage hangover-maker if you drank too much. Imports were better—and more expensive. The cheap, nasty stuff would do.

The microwave dinged. Yitzhak ate mechanically. He was still hungry when he finished, so he had an orange and another knock of brandy. He chucked the trash and washed his silverware. Then he turned on the TV. The polls would close any minute. They were doing news to lead up to the results.

A bomber in Beersheba tried to disrupt the voting there, but blew himself up on the street, and no one else got hurt. If the one in Jerusalem had been that clumsy . . .

Another American saying popped into his mind. *If pigs had wings* . . . He didn't know much about pigs, but he got the idea.

Eight o'clock came. The polls closed. Results started showing up right away. The count was electronic; once ballots were verified, no more waiting for polling officials to mark tallies and total them.

"It appears preelection polls did foretell which way the new government would lean, but not how far it would go," a newsman said. "The Likud and religious parties will have a large majority in the next Knesset. Labor and the centrist Kadima Party have lost many more seats than expected. Even with the Arab parties, they won't be able to block or delay measures the new government proposes."

"Thank God!" Yitzhak had prayed things would go this way. But you couldn't be sure till you saw the numbers.

Cheers from other apartments said he wasn't the only one watching. Somebody started singing "Hatikvah," the Israeli anthem, loudly and off-key. The bellowing patriot would have got tossed from any karaoke bar from Metulla to Eilat.

In the distance, an assault rifle emptied a clip in nothing flat. Another answered, and another. They all sounded like Galils. Yitzhak hoped they belonged to exuberant Israelis celebrating. If they didn't, a small war had started.

He didn't hear screams or alarm sirens. So it was kibbutzniks going nuts. Yitzhak felt like squeezing off a few bursts himself.

Instead, he turned back to the TV. Returns flooded in now, and the look of the new Knesset was firming up. Likud and the religious parties would grab more than two-thirds of the seats. That wasn't a sea change; it was a tsunami.

And the Pious Bloc looked to be the second-biggest party on the right. Yitzhak pumped a fist in the air. Maybe Kupferman's TV appearances from under the Temple Mount made a difference. Maybe finding the Ark did. Or maybe people were wising up.

The TV cut to Likud headquarters. Party officials and campaign workers there seemed half-jubilant, half-stunned—*they* hadn't looked for such a huge win. The leader came to the microphone. He acted more like an American pol than an Israeli; he'd been educated in the States and lived there for years.

"This is a new day!" he shouted. "The people have spoken, and we are proud they've spoken of us!" He couldn't go on, because everybody else in the crowded room started yelling. When he could make himself heard, he said, "We'll do what's right for *Eretz Yisrael*. Nobody else looks out for our country, so we have to take care of ourselves. Right?"

"Right!" the crowd roared.

"I have to think that after all we've been through, God wants it to be this way, and I thank Him, too." The Prime Minister was as pious as a telephone pole, but he knew his constituency. "The first appointment for the new Cabinet I want to announce is the Minister for Religious Affairs, Rabbi Shlomo Kupferman."

Yitzhak shouted. He wasn't the only one. The apartment block rocked with whoops and pounding feet. More gunfire split the night.

Kupferman wasn't at the headquarters of the Pious Bloc. He was still supervising the excavations. That didn't stop TV from sending his image around the country. "We've been waiting two thousand years to rebuild the Temple," he said, his eyes flashing. "We won't wait any more."

Yitzhak yelled even louder. He jumped up and down. The guy who lived above him was jumping up and down, too, sending dust and acoustic cottage cheese floating onto the sofa and into his hair.

Then the television shifted to Labor headquarters. The mood there was grim. Labor supporters might have been sitting *shiva* after their hopes died. Labor ran Israel for more than a generation after independence, and still seemed amazed it didn't any more. The party couldn't have expected to do well. But what Labor faced was a disaster.

A cruel reporter thrust a microphone in the Labor leader's face. "What are your plans now?" he asked.

Had things gone differently, the politician would have been Prime Minister. Now he looked like a man whose puppy had just been run over by a Merkava tank. "We have to reevaluate our message," he said glumly, and added, "And we will be a voice of reason in the new Knesset. Someone has to."

Yitzhak sent the screen an obscene gesture. "*Cus ummak!*" he shouted. Arabic had wonderful curses in it. Yelling *Your mother's cunt!* at somebody you despised had to make you feel better.

The results show cut to the headquarters of the biggest Israeli Arab party. A plump man with glasses spoke guttural Hebrew: "If anyone interferes with the *Haram al-Sharif,* there will be trouble. I do not intend to cause trouble. But it will come. This shrine is holy to Muslims. They will let it be profaned."

"*Cus ummak!*" Yitzhak yelled again. He wasn't the only one shouting at the screen. The Arabs had held the Temple Mount more than 1,300 years. Wasn't it time to let the Jews have another turn, especially since the Ark had shown itself at last?

The reporter asked the Israeli Arab politician that question. The man shrugged sadly. "You will do whatever you do," he said. "You will, and so will the world's Muslims. They are many and strong. If you go out of your way to make them hate you, they will avenge. Look what happened when *Charlie Hebdo* lampooned the Prophet, peace be upon him."

"Fool!" Yitzhak said, and cursed him again.

Orly sat on a blanket under the Temple Mount. They had a TV there turned to the election results. She looked up every so often and shook her head, as you would when you passed an accident so horrible, it drew your eye whether you wanted it to or not. She followed Labor, and Labor was getting trounced.

Eric put his arm around her. She sat rigid, then slumped against him. She needed whatever comfort she could find. "I knew it would be bad," she said sotfly, "but not *this* bad."

More Israeli archaeologists there belonged to some party on the other side. They were having a fine time. Eric swigged from a bottle of licorice-flavored lightning when it came his way. Orly drank, too, to numb the pain. So did Munir al-Nuwayhi. He might be a secular Muslim, but he knew the triumph of the Israeli religious right wasn't good news for his people.

"I don't think I want to live here any more," Orly said. "This isn't the country I grew up in." Democrats in the States said the same thing as the Republicans kept hold of the White House.

"The world doesn't end. You just wish it could." Eric spoke from experience.

Orly looked toward the Ark, still shining and still floating. "Are you sure?" she asked.

Suddenly, Eric *wasn't* sure. The Ark broke too many rules. "You can always come back to California with me," he said.

"Live in Los Angeles?" Orly sounded as if he'd asked her for something kinky she didn't much fancy. Then she sighed. "Maybe. You have some sane people there."

That had to be one of the few times anybody had leveled such an accusation against L.A. Eric defended his home town: "We do, but we keep them locked up."

His girlfriend's smile didn't last long. "The crazies here are running the asylum. Those people at the mouth of the tunnel . . ."

"You mean Brandon? He's pretty bad."

"Not him. He's only an . . . ordinary troublemaker. But the Levites, and those costumes out of the museum . . . They want to turn Israel into Iran." She whispered in his ear, which would have been sexy if she hadn't said, "So does Kupferman."

The same thought had crossed Eric's mind. "It won't be that bad," he said.

"No. It'll be worse," Orly predicted.

Eric would have told her she was crazy, but Yoram Louvish said, "We don't have to blow up the Dome of the Rock. If we move it someplace, that should keep the Arabs happy."

"There you go. Better than they deserve, too," another Israeli archaeologist said. In his journal articles, he was pure scholarly detachment. When detachment bumped into real life . . . he wasn't.

"It would not be a good idea," Munir said—in Hebrew, one of the few times Eric had heard him use the Jews' language.

"Yeah, you'd say that, wouldn't you?" the other archaeologist snapped. He got to his feet, hands bunching into fists. So did Munir.

"Knock it off, both of you!" Yoram had the command bark in his voice again. He stepped between the two angry men. "We're all working here together, and we're going to keep on doing that. You hear? You have trouble with anybody, come to me. Taking care of trouble is my job, not yours." The Israeli Jew and Munir both slowly settled back onto their haunches. Whatever leadership took, Yoram had it and then some.

"You see?" Orly said. Eric didn't answer. He saw trouble ahead, the same way Munir al-Nuwayhi did. But this was the Middle East. When didn't you?

Yoram didn't. He went on, "We'll move the Dome to the Arab quarter or somewhere," he said. "Once they get used to it, they won't care."

"There you go," the other archaeologist repeated, as if it were that simple.

"No," Munir said, in English, and not another word.

That was too much for Eric, too. "They'll care," he said. "It's the Temple Mount. When somebody does something up there, everybody cares."

Yoram looked at him. "It's not your worry," he said, perhaps more gently than he felt. "It's not your country, your land. This is a dig for you. Here's something you can dig or not—it's more than a dig for us. This is our life."

"There you go." That other Israeli might have had a one-phrase sound chip.

"It's also my land, my life." Munir stuck to English, and to holding himself in as best he can. That was what you did when you were a minority working in the majority's bailiwick—if you wanted to keep working there, anyhow.

Eric's ears heated. As an American, he could say things Munir couldn't, and he did: "Maybe I see the big picture better than you— I'm not in the middle of it."

"He's right," Orly said.

Yoram looked through her. He had some Middle Eastern machismo: women were fine for decoration, but not for taking seriously. "Of course you say that," he told her. "It's what he says."

"I belonged to Labor before I met him," Orly retorted.

"The more fool you," Yoram said. Orly said something that would have curled Hammurabi's beard. Yoram laughed. "And I love you, sweetie," he answered.

"We can't stop them," Munir said gloomily.

"I noticed, thanks." Eric stated the obvious: "They have the bit between their teeth, and they'll run."

Orly shook her head. "One thing wrong—you're mistaking a horse's ass for the whole horse." She won the last word, but not, he feared, the argument.

"They have—the Ark of the Covenant! They'll enshrine it in the rebuilt Temple." Lester Stark wasn't preaching a sermon. He didn't have millions hanging on his every word. He was at home in bed, reading for a while before he went to sleep.

"It's nothing you haven't talked about for years." His wife was reading, too: a Tony Hillerman mystery on her Kindle.

"I know." Lester set the copy of Edersheim in his lap. In the 1870s, the author had put together everything known about the Temple and its services during Christ's time. Lester had read it before, but now he felt he needed to grasp what was in it. "You can *see* the day coming closer. I think it may happen in our lifetimes."

Rhonda also put down her device. She smiled from the other

twin bed. "That would be wonderful," she said. "But even if it doesn't work that way, we'll be resurrected, won't we?"

"Of course," he answered. "Still, to know the Rapture in the flesh . . ."

He knew the look she gave him. They'd both known rapture in the flesh many times, as ordinary human beings could if they found a partner they loved and who loved them back. It wasn't the same. He would have been shocked if she'd suggested it was. She knew better. Nothing could match going to heaven, not even that. But it was also special in its own way.

After a moment, Rhonda asked, "Will you go to Israel, to be there when it happens?"

"Maybe," he said. "I get tired of secular reporters explaining things they don't believe in or understand. Gabriela Sandoval and Brandon Nesbitt . . ." He shook his head. "Anyone would handle it better than they do."

"Then you *should* go," Rhonda said.

"Not yet." Lester shook his head again. "When the Israelis rebuild the Temple, maybe. If I went now, I might have to stay for years. I don't want to. I have too many things to tend to here."

"It may happen faster than you think," his wife said. "Look what's already happened." She picked up the Kindle again, and went back to the Arizona Navajo reservation.

Stark returned to nineteenth-century prose on long-vanished Jerusalem. Nothing in the Middle East disappeared forever. Jerusalem was again the capital of a Jewish state. Hebrew was again the language of the Holy Land, though even in Jesus' time Aramaic had ousted it there—and pockets of Aramaic-speakers persisted now in Lebanon and Syria. The few hundred Samaritans who survived and clung to their faith still offered sacrifice on Mount Gerezim, near Nablus in Palestinian territory. They still thought they were the true children of Israel, too.

And who could tell them they were wrong? History had passed them by, but maybe their hour *would* come 'round at last. Stranger things were happening.

Stark shivered, there in the air-conditioned bedroom. The Yeats poem was bad doctrine, but it made the razor-cut hair on his neck stand up whenever he read or thought about it.

What rough beast slouched toward Bethlehem to be born now? This might not be the Second Coming, but the birth of the Antichrist, of the Tribulation, of troubles worse than any the world had known. God had foretold it, but people hadn't listened. A lot still didn't.

No one had any guarantee that the Antichrist's blandishments wouldn't take him in. *That means me, too. I have no guarantee,* Stark thought. He shivered again, this time in earnest.

Haji Ibrahim ibn Abd al-Rahman should have despised cell phones. They came from the West, from Kafirstan—the land of disbelief. But they were *useful*. They could trigger bombs, as U.S. soldiers had learned in Iraq and Afghanistan. And they could keep a running man in touch with his allies.

"You cannot let them profane the Noble Sanctuary. *We* cannot let them profane it." The man he was talking to spoke elegant Arabic with a slight Iranian accent.

"I can't stop them," Ibrahim said. "They're after the Grand Mufti and me. They blame us for the uprising in Jerusalem." The Israelis had excellent reasons, too. At least the two of them had separated, so Ibrahim didn't have to listen to the Grand Mufti any more.

"If they tamper with our holy site, they will pay," the other man said. "We have ways to make them. They need to remember that. Make it plain to them. We shall do the same."

"Right," the head of the Waqf said. What did the Shiite expect him to do? Write a warning in fiery letters with his nose? The Islamic Republic could handle warnings . . . couldn't it?

"All Muslims, regardless of creed, stand together against Jews," the ayatollah said. "When we show this solidarity, they'll retreat like the cowards they are."

Iran was hundreds of kilometers away. It had never had to deal with the Zionists up close. "They are evil, yes," Haji Ibrahim said. "But they are not cowards, and don't retreat unless they see some advantage."

"Do you want our backing?" the other man asked. "You have to show you deserve it."

You have to show you are our puppet. Ibrahim ibn Abd al-Rahman had no trouble following. You didn't get something for nothing from an Iranian. Iran's armies had fought Islam's in early days. The Iranians still resented losing. Even after accepting the true faith, they'd changed it.

But they had oil money—more than anyone but the Saudis—and missiles, and maybe bombs bigger and stronger than the one in Tel Aviv. "I will do as you say," Ibrahim answered. "There is no God but God, and Muhammad is the Prophet of God."

"And Ali is the Friend of God," the Iranian finished. The addition to the *shahada*, the profession of faith, irked Ibrahim. He couldn't say anything, not if he wanted this man's help.

He did say, "I'd better go. The Jews may be tracing this call. Peace be unto you."

"And to you also peace." The farewell was so ingrained, neither thought anything of wishing each other peace after a talk full of violence.

Ibrahim turned off the phone. It was a burner, bought in a *souq*. The Israelis would find it—and him—harder to track . . . he hoped.

At least Iran cared. Nice somebody did. Everyone else had forgotten Jerusalem and the Palestinian cause. Egypt and Jordan kept relations with the Zionist entity. With Syria in ruins, Lebanon was going mad. Hezbollah was too busy closer to home to strike hard because of the desecration of the Noble Sanctuary.

Up to me, Haji Ibrahim thought. *And to the Grand Mufti,* he added, grudgingly.

A knock. The code was right—one, three, one. He opened up. "You've got to get out!" someone yelled in his face. "Zionist security forces are coming!"

Ibrahim said something foul. He scrambled out the escape door and slammed and barred it behind him. He was sick of running through black tunnels with hounds baying after him. But he didn't want them catching him, either.

As he ran, thumps turned to thuds behind him. They were breaking down the door. It was stout; that would take a while. If a driver waited at the other end of the tunnel . . .

If one didn't, he could scramble through this ancient maze and find another hideout. If the Israelis came after him, they'd have a riot on their hands. But they might not care.

He found the other door by running into it. Recoiling, he threw it open and dashed out. A battered Renault sat in the alley. Ibrahim jumped in. "Away!" he said. "Quick!"

"Okay, okay." The driver was eighteen or so. He drove like a madman. Haji Ibrahim wondered if the Israelis would have been a better bargain.

They raced up Highway 60, past Bet El. When they passed Bir Zeit, too, he breathed easier. The driver still scared him, but they were the only car on the road. Unless the kid blew a tire or flipped, they should be fine.

The Renault's engine noise obscured the buzz of a smaller, better-tuned motor high in the sky. A car whizzing out of Ramallah after a raid drew the notice of the people controlling the drone. They didn't need long to decide it held their man. The drone dove.

"Slow down a little," Ibrahim urged the driver.

"What?" he said around a cigarette.

"Slow down," Ibrahim repeated. "Don't drive like that."

"Don't you want to get away?" But the driver eased off . . . a little.

"What's that noise?" Ibrahim ibn Abd al-Rahman asked.

"What noise?" But the kid heard it, too. "Sounds like it's—over there?" He pointed up and to the right.

Haji Ibrahim peered from the dirty window. He saw nothing but night. Then he did—a lance of flame in the sky, heading for the car. He shrieked. Fast as he could, he prayed: "There is no God but God, and Muhammad is—"

A fireball swallowed the Renault. He never finished his prayer.

Rabbi Kupferman at their head, eight Levites came down the tunnel. They looked like extras from *The Passion of the Christ*. As they stepped into the TV lights, their faces had the half-orgasmic expressions on other men who knew they were doing something great and true and holy.

Eric Katz had seen such expressions before: on Protestant fighters in Northern Ireland, and on videos suicide bombers made before blowing themselves to heaven. He didn't like them on Jewish faces. His own faith was Americanized, assimilated, attenuated. These people meant it, and he was a backslider to them. Some of the archaeologists looked just about as exalted as the Levites. By contrast, Munir al-Nuwayhi's severe frown might have come straight off a relief in an Assyrian palace.

"Don't touch the Ark itself," Kupferman said. "Scripture shows it will slay any man who transgresses on its sanctity."

Yeah, right. Eric had worn a NATIONAL SARCASM SOCIETY—LIKE WE NEED YOUR SUPPORT T-shirt till it fell apart. The Bible said lots of things that ranged from unlikely to impossible.

Then his gaze slid to the Ark, which had yet to touch the ground. Was that impossible or just unlikely? And what did it mean? Anything?

He didn't know. He didn't want to think about it, either. It alarmed him. If God was real, and alive in the world, a lot of people had a whole bunch to answer for.

Orly's mind went in a different direction: "I wonder if the poles will hold? I know they're wrapped in gold, but they've been there a *long* time. What will Kupferman do if they don't?"

"Stay tuned," Eric said. "We'll find out—after these commercial messages." She glowered.

They found out with no commercials. The Levites ducked through the opening Yoram had cut—*the opening I helped start,* Eric thought in pride and fear. Kupferman stayed outside in the tunnel, praying. He was media-savvy enough not to block the TV lights shining into the ancient chamber.

The Levites were praying, too. *They* took the Ark seriously. Eric could see only two of them as they stooped.

"Ready?" Kupferman called.

"Yes, *Reb* Shlomo!" they chorused.

"Then, blessing the holy Name—*lift!*"

They lifted, and the Ark rose. "It doesn't weigh any more than my little boy!" one exclaimed in wonder. He had a right to marvel. There was a lot of gold in the Ark. Eric didn't know what it should weigh, but, even divided by eight, *a lot more than a kid* seemed a good bet.

He wondered whether Yoram had cut the opening wide enough to let the Ark come forth. By the Israeli archaeologist's expression, so did he. That would go up there with the biggest anticlimaxes ever.

But he had. Out it came. The Levite bearers looked even more exalted than when they were coming down the tunnel. Eric had a hard time blaming them.

With the other archaeologists, he scrambled out of the way. A mummy coming to life in the Valley of the Kings might have been weirder, but that was movie fare. This was real, not on a screen.

Kupferman winded a *shofar*. The blast from the ram's-horn trumpet filled the tunnel. Then the rabbi started dancing, as II Samuel said David did when he brought the Ark into Jerusalem. Unlike David, Kupferman was no spring chicken. Eric hoped he didn't have a coronary and drop dead. (And a small part of him hoped Kupferman *did*. If anything could quash the craziness surrounding the Ark, that might.)

Regardless of Eric's hope, Kupferman went right on dancing. He pranced along the tunnel, blowing the *shofar* every so often. The Levites followed with the Ark, singing a song of thanksgiving. After them came the archaeologists and media people.

The light at the end of the tunnel might have felt like a train, but it was only light. "Behold!" Kupferman shouted. "The Ark of the Covenant comes forth!" The *shofar* blatted again.

"Get back!" was the first thing Eric heard from outside. The first thing he saw was soldiers. They were imitating King Canute, who came from a different legend. The tide they held back consisted of everybody and his uncle.

Orthodox Jews, people who would've looked ordinary if they weren't screaming, people who'd've looked weird in Amsterdam if they weren't screaming, Gabriela and Brandon and other media big shots who were screaming themselves . . . Everybody tried to rush the Ark, its bearers, and Rabbi Kupferman—and the grubby archaeologists behind it.

Eric's admiration for the IDF swelled over the next few minutes. Nobody got through. He didn't think anyone got killed, either, though he couldn't swear nobody got trampled. And, Kupferman dancing before it, the Ark started through the streets of the Old City.

10

Brandon had figured Shlomo Kupferman for a tough old bird. Turned out he'd had no idea. The rabbi cut capers all the way through the Old City. Maybe he'd run a marathon next.

Watching him boogie through Jerusalem wasn't easy. Nothing was easy that day. Brandon and Gabriela and their crew had their primo location near the mouth of the tunnel. They had it—and they were stuck with it. Once the Ark passed, they couldn't follow.

The town should have been shut down tighter than Stormy Daniels' snatch. Much of it was. Vehicle traffic was banned. Only the helicopter overhead had a camera that showed the progress of the procession. *Heyl Ha-Avir* F-15s screamed above the helicopter to make sure nobody got cute. Their orders were to shoot first.

Despite the top cover, Brandon wondered what would happen if someone smuggled in a drone carrying a bomb or a missile. Those things were hard to spot, and to dodge. Ibrahim ibn Abd al-Rahman would have testified to that. The Palestinians were screaming about the leader of the Waqf, but nobody in the West listened to them these days.

Everyone in town should have been ordered to stay indoors, too. That would have been smart. It would also have been impossible. Jews, Christians, even Muslims—everybody wanted to see the fabulous relic.

What had to be a quarter of the IDF made sure the people who wanted to see the Ark didn't trample the people carrying it. Some had nightsticks. They swung them without hesitation. The rest carried assault rifles with fixed bayonets. They made sure nobody messed with the troops with the nightsticks.

"Just as well we're not along, I guess," Brandon said. "Looking at the monitors is scary enough."

"No kidding," Gabriela agreed. One screen showed a bespectacled, scholarly looking Orthodox man up against the soldiers. His eyes were wide, his mouth open and panting. He looked more like a guy getting a blow job than one having a religious experience. The girl next to him was shrieking and shaking as if she were on the point of coming, too.

Danny—the redheaded, freckled Jewish cameraman—said, "How much you think the Ark weighs?"

"Beats me, but that's a lot of gold," Brandon said. Beside him, Gabriela nodded.

"Yeah." Danny nodded, too. "How come those guys carrying it aren't falling over?"

Sometimes the most obvious questions had the least obvious answers. "Don't know," Brandon said. "But now that you mention it, how come the poles aren't breaking, too? They're old as anything."

"They said it was floating above the ground," Gabriela said. "The photos showed it before they brought it out."

That showed nobody paid much attention to things that went against what everyone knew. And everyone knew nothing floated that way. If you saw it, you didn't want to believe it. Maybe you

ALPHA AND OMEGA | 157

were nuts, maybe it was a special effect . . . or maybe the world was a weirder place than you'd thought.

"The old-time Jews could do shit science can't do now?" No, Brandon didn't want to believe it, even if a similar idea had crossed his mind before. "Tell me another one. If they could manage that, how come everybody's been kicking 'em around for God knows how many thousand years?"

"Beats me," Danny said. "I'm just a camera jock, but I've got eyes. No way that little gang of guys could lug so much gold. No way the poles'd put up with it, either."

"Maybe we should get a physicist," Brandon said. "Or a sci-fi writer. Or a physicist who *is* a sci-fi writer." There were such beasts. Talk about bizarre . . .

"It's going to the Shrine of the Book now, isn't it?" Gabriela asked.

Brandon nodded. "That's right. Along with the Dead Sea Scrolls and everything."

"The Ark makes the Scrolls seem new," she said.

"I guess it does." Brandon hadn't looked at it that way. "From what the Israelis say, they'll keep it there till they rebuild the Temple."

"I still think they have to be crazy to try that," Gabriela said. "What the Arabs will do—"

"We could get ahead of the curve, like," Brandon broke in. "We could go into the West Bank and talk to some Palestinians—"

He got interrupted in turn, by Saul Buchbinder. "*You* could do that," the producer said. "Not me. I'd be as welcome as a Jew on the West Bank."

"I don't want to do it that much," Brandon said. "No drama in it. I want to open up the Ark and see what's inside."

"Are you nuts?" That wasn't Gabriela—it was Danny. "The old rabbi and that Levite both told you the Ark'll kill you if you mess with it."

"Yeah, right," Brandon said. "This religious crap is dripping out of my ears. C'mon—*that's* the real story." He pointed to the monitor. The Ark was passing from the Old City to the New, from antiquity to the twenty-first century. "What's in there? *Does* it hold Moses' tablets?"

"I thought you didn't care about the religious crap," Danny jabbed, grinning.

"For me? No way," Brandon said. "But for ratings? Fuckin' A."

"It *would* make good television, but we'll never get access," Gabriela said. "The Israelis'll keep the Ark buttoned up so tight . . ."

"You already interviewed Kupferman. Now he's Religious Affairs Minister. You should talk to him again, Gabriela." Brandon said it grudgingly, but he did say it. He added, "What's the worst that can happen? He can tell you no. How are we worse off?"

"You're pushing it," Danny warned.

He played into Brandon's hands by putting Gabriela's back up. "We're supposed to push it," she said sharply. "That's our job. And if anybody gets a look inside the Ark, it'll be me." She jabbed a thumb at her own chest. "Hear that? Me!"

Brandon held his face straight. *No, bitch,* he thought. *Me.*

Eric looked around as he traded Old City for New. "This is a different world," he said.

"Sure," Orly answered. "We didn't worry about pissing anybody off when we built here, so we did it right."

"Mostly, anyhow," Yoram said. "Toes we didn't want to step on here, too. Maybe we'll fix some more things now that the rules have changed."

Eric looked around to see what Munir would think of that. He didn't spot him. Somehow or other, the Arab Israeli had dropped out of the procession. The Ark wasn't his talisman. Maybe—

probably—he'd had enough Jewish celebration to last him forever and a day, no matter how secular he felt he was.

Now that we've quit caring about what anyone else thinks, Eric thought Yoram's words meant. He didn't want to argue with Louvish. Being part of the team that found the Ark would make him someone to reckon with at every archaeological conference. It might even land him a tenure-track job. But he wasn't comfortable with any group remaking Jerusalem to its heart's desire. To many Muslims, though not all, anything before Muhammad's lifetime was the *Jahiliyah,* the Time of Ignorance, and not worth taking seriously or preserving. The Israelis looked back further, but they also had their own agenda.

He looked over his shoulder, past the wall, past the Jaffa Gate— through which the procession had come—to the Temple Mount. The Dome of the Rock still shone there. For how much longer? Would the Israelis disassemble it, the way the Egyptians took apart their temples when waters rose behind the Aswan Dam? Would they rebuild it somewhere else? Would they do the same with the nearby mosque?

Al-Aqsa was a Johnny-come-lately—it dated only from the late eighth century. He supposed he should be thankful the Israelis reckoned it worth preserving.

Then his eyes went to Rabbi Kupferman, who was still kicking up his heels ahead of the Ark. Whatever Kupferman put in his coffee this morning, Eric wished he'd got some, too. From one side of Jerusalem to the other wasn't a *long* walk—two miles as the crow flew: a little longer by the roads they used—but he'd been cooped up underground for days. He was old enough to feel it.

He walked past another TV camera peering out past the Israeli soldiers protecting the route. Those pictures were going worldwide. What would people think of the archaeologists trailing the dancing rabbi and the Ark? Probably that, with the exception of

Orly, they made a piss-poor end for the parade. Broad-brimmed hats, wrinkled shirts, jeans or khaki shorts with too many pockets didn't measure up.

Well, too bad.

They went west and north along Ha-Emek to Gershon Agron, then south and west along Gershon Agron, past the Muslim cemetery and Mamila Pool (a scandal to the Orthodox because both sexes swam together) on the right, then past Independence Park.

Shrieking people packed the graveyard, the park, the streets. The din was astonishing. It crashed through Eric's ears and took up residence in the middle of his brain. He would be a little deaf tomorrow, the way he would have after a rock concert. No Marshall stacks here—this was raw lung power.

The ecstatic Jews, Christians, and maybe Muslims, too, drowned out the helicopter circling overhead, and helicopters were loud. They even drowned out the fighters flying top cover, and fighters were *loud*.

Somehow, the soldiers kept the mob from rushing the Ark. Eric had always known the Israeli Defense Force was one of the top militaries around. If it weren't, Israel would have gone down the drain long since. He'd never admired the conscripts more than today. They did what they had to do, and didn't shoot anybody. If that wasn't a miracle . . .

Eric shivered. He was watching a miracle. He was walking right behind one. What else was it? That handful of Levites had no business lifting the Ark, let alone easily carrying it on poles brittle with the age of millennia. Steroid-soaked weightlifters should have had trouble raising it.

But it hadn't been on the ground, had it? It had floated above it. Or maybe it sat on the ground while nothing was going on and gave a discreet hop into the air just before he and Yoram got the first looks at it.

Which was more impossible? Eric had no idea. The world had gone loopy, and he didn't know how to cope.

Beside him, Orly walked along, smiling, looking like someone who enjoyed what was happening. Maybe she did; she lived in the moment. Or maybe she was better at acting than Eric.

And what about Yoram? He deserved all the credit in the world. He'd thought the Ark lay behind that wall, and he'd proved right. His name *would* go into the textbooks and popular histories along with Schliemann's and Howard Carter's.

So why didn't he look happier? He wore the expression of a man who'd hooked Leviathan on a line meant for bluegill. Nobody in his right mind would have imagined any archaeological discovery could touch off . . . this.

Eric saw staring faces pressed against every window of the Sheraton Plaza just west of Independence Park. The tourists and businessmen staying there picked the right place. Would some maniac break a window and fire an RPG at the Ark? How well had Israeli security checked who got access to the hotel?

Well enough, because nobody did anything but stare.

They came to an intersection with five arms like a starfish, and went on west on Ramban. More faces gaped down from the Prima Kings Hotel. When Eric first got to Jerusalem, he thought Ramban was named for Maimonides. But Maimonides was the *Rambam*: the abbreviation for Rabbi Moshe ben Maimon. The *Ramban*—Rabbi Moshe ben Nachman—lived later, and was a lesser scholar. (Ben Maimon Street, which *was* named for Maimonides, ran parallel to Ramban, one block south.)

"I think we're gonna do this!" Eric bawled into Orly's ear.

"What?" she said. He could read her lips, but he couldn't hear her. She couldn't have heard him, either.

Once they crossed into Sacher Park, they left the New City's hubbub behind—and got new hubbub, with swarms trampling the grass. But nobody trampled the IDF troops, who linked arms and held back the crowd.

To the left was the Valley of the Cross—what would Jesus have made of *this*? To the right stood the Knesset, the Israeli Parliament building. It reminded Eric of the Forum in Inglewood, except it was square, not round.

Left of that, a little farther on, stood the Israel Museum and, separate from the main building, the Heikhal Ha-Sefer, the Shrine of the Book. The museum had taken a shell hit during the Six-Day War, but hadn't lost any exhibits.

The Shrine of the Book had a white, pointed dome in the center of the roof that called up the shape of the lids on the jars in which the Dead Sea Scrolls were found. The rest of the square roof was black granite, symbolizing the struggle of the sons of light against the sons of darkness. That struck Eric as a Zoroastrian concept for a Jewish museum. But what better for the Shrine of the Book than black and white together?

They went inside. The Isaiah Scroll, the most important Dead Sea Scroll, held pride of place under the center of the dome. Its case could sink into the ground if war came, a sensible precaution here.

Kupferman left off impersonating John Travolta in front of the broad stairway that led to the Isaiah Scroll's case. He gestured to the Levites, who set the Ark on the ground: or rather, those few inches above the ground. The Ark floated here, too.

Not even breathing hard—what *was* he made of?—Kupferman said, "Here, O Lord, we leave Thy precious Ark until we place it in the Holy of Holies in Thy restored Temple. May that day come soon."

"*Omayn!*" the Levites chorused. So did some archaeologists. No one scowled at Eric for keeping quiet, nor was he the only one who did. Everybody who'd been in the tunnel knew how everybody else felt, and why.

No one seemed surprised Munir al-Nuwayhi hadn't come all

the way, either. Israeli Jews often claimed to understand Israeli Arabs, as Southern whites in the States often claimed to understand Southern blacks. Maybe they were right, maybe . . . not so much.

No matter how you felt about the Third Temple, there was the Ark, shining under rings of fluorescent light set into the inside of the dome. Eric had lived with it under the Temple Mount. He'd walked behind it through Jerusalem. It still drew the gaze like a magnet.

"We made it!" he said to Orly.

Her eyes shone. "Yeah!"

Shlomo Kupferman had a fancy office at the Ministry of Religious Affairs. He didn't use it. He had another fancy office above the Reconstruction Alliance Museum. He didn't use that one, either. He met Gabriela in a cramped cubby at his synagogue.

She wondered what the choice said. Was it *I trust you, so let's meet where I feel most at ease* or *Look at me—I'm just a plain old little rabbi*? Genuine or horseshit? Gabriela had trouble being sure; her handle on Kupferman wasn't as good as she wanted.

If you didn't bet, you couldn't win. "Thanks for talking with me," she said. "You know what I've got in mind."

"Yes. Your show wants to make a television spectacle of the Ark." Kupferman's voice was cold as Winnipeg winter.

But Gabriela nodded. "That's right," she said. "It's an important discovery. People have the right to find out all they can about it."

"True," Kupferman said, which surprised her. Then she remembered the rabbi was archaeologist *and* theologian. Kupferman went on, "But do you remember what I told you? Do you remember the Biblical examples I cited?"

"You said that, if anyone disturbs the Ark and God doesn't like it, that person dies," Gabriela answered.

"Do you believe that?" Kupferman leaned forward, as if to impose the power of his personality on Gabriela. He had a formidable presence. But Gabriela had faced down the great and the notorious for years. Kupferman made no more than a middleweight intimidator.

"I don't know," Gabriela said slowly. "Are you afraid to let me try? If I open it and look inside and nothing happens to me, then what? One of two things, I'd say. Either God means for me to do it, or He's not paying any attention." Or God wasn't there at all. Catholic upbringing or not, that was what Gabriela suspected. But she didn't want to anger Kupferman, so she kept quiet about it.

"You realize you're risking your life?" the rabbi persisted.

"I've done it before," Gabriela said, which was true, even if not so true as she'd made it out to be before she fell from network grace. "I'll do it again if you let me."

"Are you sure you want to? The archaeologists know better. Isn't there an English saying about fools rushing in?"

"I'm no angel, but I'm game," Gabriela said.

The rabbi eyed her. "If I say no, you or your smarmy young associate will try to sneak or bribe your way into the Heikhal Ha-Sefer." He'd nailed Brandon in one, though Gabriela hoped she didn't react to the dig. Shlomo Kupferman didn't sound admiring, the way most people would have. Gabriela would have herself; she relished other people's gall. But Kupferman, a born tightass, seemed revolted at the idea.

Gabriela nodded anyhow. "If I figured out how we could get away with it, we would."

What Kupferman said next made Gabriela doubt her own judgment, something that rarely happened: "'And he softly and silently vanished away,/For the Snark *was* a Boojum, you see.'"

Could a born tightass quote Lewis Carroll? "I'll take the chance," Gabriela said.

"Are you sure, Ms. Sandoval? I am trying to talk you out of this.

I do not want to go on while feeling I have your blood on my hands," the rabbi said.

"You won't. If you like, I'll write a release that says I'm doing this of my own free will, and if anything happens to me I know it's my own fault," Gabriela said.

Rabbi Kupferman still looked dissatisfied. "You say that, but you say it expecting to open the Ark and live. You say it not believing in the power of the Lord, blessed be His holy Name."

Gabriela looked him straight in the eye. "Yes, I do. So what? I'm willing to risk being wrong. Are you willing to risk that I may be right? You gave me old sayings, Rabbi. I'll give you one back—put up or shut up."

Did Kupferman go red? His expression didn't change; he already looked as sour as one man could. "All right," he said. "*All right.*" Jew though he was, he might have been Pilate washing his hands. "Write me your release. Maybe it will ease my conscience later."

Jubilation burst in Gabriela. "Now you're talking!" She took a notebook and a fancy Rotring fountain pen from her handbag. She wrote rapidly, signed *Gabriela Sandoval* in a neater hand than she used for her signature most of the time, tore out the sheet, and handed it to Kupferman. "Here. Are you happy now?"

"Happy? No. If you and your foolish show respected God's power and feared to transgress against the Law, then I would be happy." The rabbi read the release. "But this makes it plain you're committing your folly of your own free will. Would you like a copy for your legal people—and your heirs?"

He really was trying to scare her. How many men had done their best to make her turn green? Regiments of them. How many had had any luck? Damn few, especially the past twenty years. She shook her head. "That's fine. I'll tell Brandon and Saul you have it. If they need it, you can pull it out afterwards. But I'll bet my life they won't."

"That's what I'm trying to tell you, Ms. Sandoval," Kupferman said.

"Dear, you've got to see this!" Rhonda Stark called from the living room.

Lester Stark was muttering at his Mac. Microsoft Word had just unexpectedly quit, taking with it an unsaved page of Sunday's sermon. He thought the program was unsaved, too. When he asked, "See what?" he sounded less forbearing than usual.

"It's Gabriela, from Jerusalem," his wife said.

"I'm coming." Stark would have watched anything in preference to the word-processing program that had done him wrong . . . again. *I was going to save when I finished that paragraph,* he thought. Close only counted in horseshoes and hand grenades.

Gabriela was staring out of the TV when Lester got there. The minister discounted that; she always stared. If she didn't, somebody would have taken her to the doctor to see what was wrong.

"I'll tell you one more time. Next Thursday, at nine o'clock Eastern, six o'clock Pacific—four in the morning on Friday here—I'll open up the Ark of the Covenant, and we'll see what's inside."

"She can't do that!" Lester Stark exclaimed.

As if to contradict him, Gabriela went on, "I have special permission from Rabbi Shlomo Kupferman, the new Israeli Minister of Religious Affairs. He made me sign a release stating that I don't hold him responsible for anything that happens afterwards." She struck a pose. "And I don't. Bringing the news comes first. I'll see you Thursday, with the Ark of the Covenant."

The TV cut to a commercial. "What do you think of that?" Rhonda asked.

"Either she's gone 'round the bend, or Kupferman has." Lester looked at his watch. Half past three here in Birmingham; it would be half past eleven in Jerusalem. He knew Shlomo Kupferman well, and knew he was a night owl. He had the rabbi's number on his own phone. Taking it from his pocket, he made the call.

"Kupferman here. How are you, Lester?"

Stark smiled. Not many people from area code 205 called the Religious Affairs Minister. "I'm fine, thanks. Yourself? Your family?"

"Well enough. You're calling about Gabriela Sandoval, aren't you?"

"What does she think she's doing? What do you think you're doing, letting her try?"

"I'm giving her what she wants. She *does* want it—I made sure of that. She has faith in herself. I have faith in the Lord."

"Yes," Stark said. "But this could be tawdry. A spectacle on TV—"

"People need to know. Television will let them find out." Stark heard the shrug in Kupferman's voice.

"But what if it doesn't turn out the way you want it to?"

"It will turn out as God wants it to, blessed be His holy Name," Rabbi Kupferman said.

"Of course." Stark couldn't disagree with that. "But what if Gabriela takes the lid off and nothing happens? After all your warnings, you won't look good then." He remembered his hesitation over getting too explicit about what Revelation meant. Kupferman hadn't hesitated at all. He'd thrown I and II Samuel in the world's face. Would he pay for it now?

"It will turn out as God wants it to," the rabbi repeated. "I am a man. I have made a fool of myself before—that is part of being a man. There was a girl once—" He broke off. "But that was long ago. I would not be that kind of fool now . . . I hope. If I am some other kind of fool . . . it is because God wants me to be that kind of fool."

Stark hadn't called to debate free will and predestination. "Aren't you afraid being wrong will hurt you?" he asked.

"No." Kupferman's answer was sharp. "The new government is

in place. So is the new Knesset. We will move forward. This is not for publication, but we are going to relocate the structures that clutter up the Temple Mount now."

"The Dome of the Rock? Al-Aqsa Mosque, too?"

"Yes, yes," Kupferman said impatiently: it was as if naming them made them more important than he wanted them to be. "We'll take them down. We won't harm them. If I had my way . . . That's what the Prime Minister wants, and that's what he will get. The Temple Mount will be ours again, as it was in Abraham's day."

"My goodness," Stark said. Kupferman was a friend as well as a colleague. Stark wouldn't violate his confidence—but he was tempted. This was enormous news. "You're sure Gabriela's stupid TV stunt won't hurt your plans?"

"Lester," Kupferman said, "I am positive."

The waiter who led Brandon and Gabriela to a table in the Sheraton's upscale restaurant spoke excellent English. The name on his little breast-pocket badge was PABLO; that and his features made Brandon guess he came from the Philippines. "Can I bring you something to drink?" he asked as he seated them.

"Let me have a St. Pauli Girl," Brandon said. Ordering a German beer in Israel tickled his imp of the perverse.

Gabriela frowned. "I'm not sure I should."

"You've got hours to kill yet," Brandon said, which was nothing but the truth. To reach a big audience in America, the special with the Ark would start in the wee small hours here. He went on, "You can have an extra slug of espresso later if you think you need it, or even a nap."

"Espresso, maybe. I wouldn't sleep now—I'm too keyed up." Gabriela swung her attention back to Pablo. "Let me have a glass of Chablis, please. He's right. One won't hurt."

"Yes, ma'am. Coming right up. And your beer, too, sir." The chubby little black-haired man hurried away.

Brandon eyed the menu. He wanted the best slab of steak he could get here. "Something with pasta," Gabriela murmured to herself. She looked over the top of the menu at Brandon. "This is working out really well, you know? If we hadn't come for the red heifer, we wouldn't have been on the spot when the dirty bomb hit Tel Aviv."

He smiled his most charming smile. "You were a little too much on the spot."

"No kidding!" Gabriela shuddered. "I still don't know what all I breathed in or what it'll do to me. But I was talking about you. You earned the props for pushing me to get Kupferman to let us open up the Ark and see what's inside of it, too. I didn't think he'd let us, but he did."

"What did we have to lose?" Brandon said. He noticed she wasn't giving him the credit he knew damn well he deserved, the credit for being the one who went on-camera and pulled Moses' old laundry list out of the Ark while Kupferman stood there with his thumb up his ass. Oh, no. She kept that for herself. She was the talent; he was the second stringer, the hired help. That was what she figured, anyhow.

Brandon had other ideas.

Pablo came back with a glass of white wine and a bottle of beer. As he set them in front of Gabriela and Brandon, he asked, "You folks ready to order?"

"I am," Brandon said at once. The waiter raised an eyebrow. He went on, "I want the New York strip, rare, and a baked potato. Butter and chives on the potato—no sour cream."

"Okay." Pablo wrote that down, then turned to Gabriela. "And for you, ma'am?"

"I'd like the Sichuan noodles, please, with chicken." She made a wry face at Brandon. "I'd like them with shrimp, but you can't get shrimp here."

"Nope." Brandon nodded. If he was having steak, the butter on his potato was a Jewish no-no, too. But it was one he could get away with.

"Sichuan noodles with chicken." Pablo scribbled again. "How hot you want the sauce?"

"As hot as the kitchen can fix it," Gabriela said, not without pride.

The waiter looked alarmed. "Oh, no, ma'am, you don't want me to say that to the chef. Kittirat, he's from Thailand, from the Isaan country in the northeast, and he burn your tongue off. Americans, you don't know what hot is."

Brandon would have backed off after a warning like that. It just put Gabriela's back up. "As hot as he can fix it," she repeated. "My *abuela* would disown me if I said anything else. I'm Mexican, and I know as much about spicy food as any Thai ever born. You can tell him I said so, too."

"Oh, no. I won't do that. It would only make things worse," Pablo said. "If I say you like it real hot, you get it real hot. I promise." He scurried away, looking back over his shoulder as if to memorize the crazy foreigner's face.

"Sure you know what you're doing?" Brandon sounded sympathetic, but he was chortling inside. He couldn't imagine how this might have worked out better for him. He would have tried it anyway, but now he had a real chance to bring it off.

Pablo came back, not with their dinners but with two huge glasses of ice water. He set them both in front of Gabriela. "Maybe these help put out the fire. Maybe." He paused, then added, "I bring you glass of milk, too, if you want. Milk supposed to be good for hot food. Regular hot food, I mean, not what Kittirat gonna do to you."

"I'll be fine," Gabriela replied. The look on Pablo's face said *It's your funeral, lady* loud and clear. Brandon saw it. If Gabriela didn't—and how couldn't she?—she pretended not to. Shaking his head, Pablo went away again. Once he was gone, her self-assurance slipped a bit. She murmured, "I hope I'll be fine," and sipped from the Chablis.

"You can still back out," Brandon said, hoping he would make her want to do anything but.

"Like hell I will," she snapped, so that worked fine. She went on, "If I fry my tonsils, I do, that's all. It's just chili powder. It won't kill me. It's not like that damn plutonium."

"I hope that doesn't come to anything." Brandon even more or less meant it. He'd been exposed to radioactivity, too, though less than Gabriela had. If it bothered him, he could see how it would scare her. That was about as far as his empathy stretched. Anything that didn't bother him was just somebody else pissing and moaning off in the distance.

Here came Pablo, with a tray on his left shoulder and supported underneath by his left hand. He used his right hand to pluck two plates off the tray and set one in front of Brandon, the other before Gabriela. Even the steam rising from her Sichuan noodles was enough to make Brandon's eyes water. He wished he had a gas mask again, though he couldn't see how he'd eat with it.

"Enjoy your dinners, folks," the waiter said, and beat a hasty retreat. His eyes were bound to be feeling it, too, and maybe the inside of his nose with them.

Brandon tried his steak. It was as rare as he liked, and a fine piece of beef as well. He chewed and swallowed with real appreciation.

Then he watched with clinical detachment as Gabriela twirled noodles onto her fork and raised them to her mouth. "*¡Madre de Dios!*" she whispered. She grabbed one of the glasses of ice water and gulped. When she lowered it, it was half empty. A tear ran down her cheek. The makeup crew at the Shrine of the Book would have some extra work to do.

"How is it?" Brandon asked.

"It tastes good," she said. "It does, honest. But the heat—! Whatever he put in there, it could boil water at the South Pole. I'm going to eat it anyhow." She took another defiant bite.

"You're a better man than I am, Gunga Din." Brandon had never been into hurting himself for the fun of it. He didn't light forest fires in his mouth when he ate dinner. Even in this much-inked age, he wore exactly zero tats. Hurting other people, now . . . Yes, there had been times when he got off on that.

"Oh, my God!" Maybe Gabriela'd got the measure of the noodles now: she exclaimed in English, not Spanish. But exclaim she did. A tear slid down her other cheek. Sweat popped out on her forehead. She drained her first glass of water and started the second. Brandon caught Pablo's eye and pointed at the water glasses. Nodding and grabbing a pitcher, the waiter hurried over to refill them.

"You all right, ma'am?" He truly sounded anxious.

"I . . . think so." Gabriela's voice sounded as raspy as if she'd smoked three packs a day for years. "Tell, uh, Kittirat he's an *hijo de puto.*"

Brandon didn't follow the *español.* By Pablo's scandalized giggle, he did. Away he went, still chuckling.

Gabriela would steel herself, take a bite, wince, and gulp water to extinguish the flames. Before long, that had its inevitable effect. She stood up, murmured, "I'll be right back," and made for the ladies' room at a pace Pablo would have envied.

As soon as her back was turned, Brandon's hand darted into his trouser pocket. It came out with a tiny plastic pill bottle. Fast as he could, he spread a whole roofie, crushed to powder, over Gabriela's noodles. It vanished into the fiery Sichuan sauce and the pill bottle disappeared well before she came back.

She didn't notice anything odd as she started eating again. The peppers masked whatever slight bitterness the Rohypnol added.

Brandon savored his steak. No way in hell she'd go on in the wee smalls. Unless the crack of doom sounded, she'd be out till close to noon, and she wouldn't know what had hit her. She might suspect, but she wouldn't know.

And, by noon tomorrow, it would be too late. She wouldn't be the lead dog in the team any more. He would. Brandon Nesbitt, understudy on the spot, the man who'd opened the Ark of the Covenant, come out with Moses' padded expense accounts, and lived to tell the tale. His name would be all over Twitter and Instagram and Facebook. This was what fame looked like nowadays. He'd have it back, more than he'd ever had before.

He waited with practiced patience, making admiring noises as Gabriela fought down the whole plate of deadly noodles. Pablo brought Kittirat out of the kitchen. The chef bowed to Gabriela: the salute of one fighter to another. He said something in accented Hebrew and carried away her empty plate with his own hands.

"Your dinner is on the house," Pablo said. He turned to Brandon. "Sorry—not yours."

"It's okay," Brandon said, laughing. As the waiter followed the chef, Brandon asked Gabriela, "How are you doing?" Hunter's curiosity hid beneath sympathy.

"I dunno," she said. "I feel like I swallowed a lit Bic, or maybe three of them. And I'm woozy, too. Should I be woozy after I ate all that hot stuff?"

"Beats me," said Brandon, who knew perfectly well. "Want to head back to your room and see if it goes away?"

"I think I'd better," Gabriela said, the words spreading out as if she had to find each one separately. She scowled. "This can't be happening! I've got to go on with the Ark."

"Don't worry. I'll get you there." Brandon knew where her room was—right down the hall from his. She didn't have a fancy suite here, the way she had in Tel Aviv. He tossed enough New Israeli Shekels on the table to cover his steak and to make Pablo happy.

Then he helped Gabriela to her feet. She was out of it, all right—he thought he was supporting more of her weight than she was.

Pablo came back. He smiled as he scooped up the money, then asked, "The lady, sir, she is okay?"

"Oh, yeah," Brandon said easily. "She's just feeling those noodles. The things people do for pride! I didn't even taste them, but I could smell how strong they were."

"I don't believe she ate them all. Kittirat, he don't believe it, either," the waiter said. "You have a pleasant evening, sir, and the lady, too."

"Thanks." Brandon half walked with, half steered Gabriela out of the restaurant and over to the elevators. Up they went. She was almost out on his shoulder by the time the doors opened on the seventeenth floor.

By then, he'd already fished her key card from her handbag. Luckily, the room wasn't far from the elevator. Even more luckily, no one came down the hall to see him just about carrying her to the door. He stuck the card in the slot. The light flashed green. He opened the door, got Gabriela inside, and put out the PRIVACY, PLEASE notice before he let it click shut. As soon as it did, he grinned like a Red Army soldier with Berlin spread out before him. He'd won! He was home free!

Gabriela muttered and stirred a little when he eased her down onto the bed. Her dress gave ground as he did. Her legs were nicer than he'd thought. If he wanted to, he could enjoy himself the way those Red Army men had. She'd be too wasted to know the difference. And if ever a cunt deserved fucking . . .

"Don't be stupid," he said out loud to himself, shaking his head. If she even suspected anything afterwards, DNA would crucify him like Jesus.

And besides, he'd screw her with the Ark story harder than he ever could with his dick. He'd get the glory. He'd be the one who made Shlomo Kupferman look like the superstitious fool he was, and in front of a worldwide audience. Gabriela would be the one who came down sick at exactly the wrong time.

People would talk about her behind her back for the rest of her career, if she had much of a career after this. Maybe he'd be generous and let them go ahead as *Brandon and Gabriela* for a while after this. Or maybe he wouldn't. When you were a rocket taking off, did you want a big old weight attached to your first stage?

He looked at his phone. It wasn't even midnight yet. They'd go live at four A.M. He'd show up as little before then as he possibly could, to give Saul and everybody else less time to ask inconvenient questions. They could ask all they pleased once he'd saved the day and everything was great—and once he'd shown that old Kupferman bastard what a bunch of bullshit the Biblical God was.

The first text came in for Gabriela at a little past one. He heard her phone chirp. Ten minutes later, since she didn't answer, she got another. He didn't want them getting edgy and sending someone to knock on the door. That wouldn't be good. Time for Plan B.

He called Buchbinder. "Brandon! Good to hear from you!" the producer exclaimed. "Where the hell's Gabriela?"

"In her john heaving her guts out, unless I'm crazy." Brandon told Saul how Gabriela had taken on the Sichuan noodles, mentioning Pablo and Kittirat by name. Why not? Everything they'd seen would only back up what he was saying. And he was telling the truth—if you forgot about the smashed roofie, anyhow.

"Oh, for fuck's sake!" Saul Buchbinder burst out when he got done. "And it sounds like her, goddammit. She can't resist the spicy shit, any more than I can with chopped liver. This time she won but she lost, huh?"

"Yeah, I guess." Brandon forcibly held relief from his voice. Saul knew about some of his unsavory past. If the producer tried adding two and two, he might land on four. But he'd gone off on a tangent instead, one that left Brandon out of the equation.

"What are we gonna do now, though?" Buchbinder said. "We've

got the *Gabriela and Brandon Special* ready to rock, only no Gabriela. I don't want to tell Kupferman—or the people we're getting airtime from—that we have to wait a day or two. The rabbi's just itching for a chance to cancel, and that would screw us to the wall bigtime."

"Saul, if you want, I can take it. I know the program as well as she does, and the teleprompter will get me through if I fluff." Brandon worked at sounding the-show-must-go-on, not I'm-jumping-up-and-down-eager. "I can open by saying she's been taken ill, sadly, but I'm here to fill in for her because this really is her big moment and all."

"Could you do that? Would you do that?" Buchbinder sounded like a man splashing in shark-infested waters who'd just spotted a lifeboat he could swim to. "You give her the credit like that, Brandon, you're a hell of a *mensh,* y'know?"

"Least I can do," Brandon replied. The way it looked to him was, nobody would care about or even remember anything he said before he took the lid off the Ark and showed up Shlomo Kupferman. Words on TV mattered only so far. What really carried the weight was what people saw. That was what they took away with them.

"A *mensh,*" Saul said again. "Okay, get your ass over here. You're still at the hotel, right? Won't be a fifteen-minute cab ride."

"Probably not even," Brandon agreed. "No traffic this time of night. See you soon. The makeup crew can slap me around a little, and then I'll be ready to rock. 'Bye." He broke the connection and headed for the lobby.

As soon as the girls put his game face on him, Brandon started checking everything in the Heikhal Ha-Sefer. The lights. The mikes. Their booms. Where the teleprompter was. And the cameras. "If you move that one a few inches to the right—" he began.

"No way." Danny cut him off. "This is how we set it up, and this is where it stays. If I move it, you'll start shoving the other shit around, too. Take an even strain, okay? We'll make it work."

"Sorry. I always get antsy before a big one." Brandon sounded sheepish. There weren't bigger ones than this. But everything looked fine. He wanted to fiddle with the setup to give himself something to do.

The cameraman yawned. "Wish I could be so bouncy. It's the middle of the night, man."

Brandon eyed his phone. Half past three. Half an hour to go. "I'm up for it. If you can't get up for it no matter what time it is, you don't deserve a job in this racket."

"I'm here, man. Don't get on my case," Danny said.

Brandon turned away. "Saul!" he said urgently. "Satellite feed okay?"

"Beautiful, Brandon. Whole board's green," the producer answered. "You're beautiful, too."

"Yeah, yeah." Brandon muttered. Saul was also trying to calm him down. That was one of the things Saul did. Except it didn't work less than half an hour before show time.

Brandon started to unload on Shlomo Kupferman, then hesitated. The rabbi stood where he should have. He didn't have many moves. The ones he did have, he'd blocked out with Gabriela the afternoon before. He would hit his marks. That was all that mattered.

Only it wasn't. He pulled out a release Gabriela had written and signed. "I would like your signature on this document, too, please, Mr. Nesbitt," he said. "In case anything goes wrong, I want it clearly understood you were acting of your own free will."

"In case of an act of God, you mean?" Brandon made a joke of it.

"Yes. In case of an act of God." Rabbi Kupferman didn't.

"Gimme that." Brandon snatched it from the old man's hand. He read it before applying his John Hancock. He'd long since learned not to sign anything he hadn't looked at first. But it was what Kupferman said it was. And he did indeed recognize Gabriela's almost schoolmarmishly precise script. He had a pen in a trouser pocket. Extracting it, he added his signature below Gabriela's. As he gave the release back to Kupferman, he asked, "Happy now?"

"Happy? No." The rabbi shook his head. "I would be happy if you had sense enough to fear the Lord and forget about this foolish, dangerous stunt."

"I'm not afraid, and I don't think it's dangerous," Brandon answered.

"I know," Kupferman said mournfully.

After what seemed a month, Saul called, "Five minutes!" and then, "Two minutes!" and then, "One minute! Places, everybody! We're going live!"

Brandon hit his mark. He suddenly didn't care if it was four in the morning. He was about to go on, to face the world, to remind himself he was real. This was the kickiest high in the world.

The light under the lens went red. Brandon came alive, too. "Welcome to the *Gabriela and Brandon Special*!" he said. "Due to a sudden, unfortunate illness, Gabriela can't be here tonight. I'm Brandon Nesbitt, her longtime colleague, and I'll be standing in for her. We all regret more than we can tell you that she couldn't be here at this vital moment she worked so hard to set up. Thank you for joining the show with us tonight—tomorrow morning here in Jerusalem, of course. Together, we'll explore the mysteries of the newly rediscovered Ark of the Covenant. Before we go on, I want to thank Israel's Minister for Religious Affairs, Rabbi Shlomo Kupferman, who's made the program possible. I'd also like to thank you, Rabbi, for joining me here tonight."

"You are welcome." By the way Kupferman sounded, Brandon was anything but. So what, though? The Religious Affairs Minister was doing this, which was all that counted.

"And I'd like to thank Israel's Department of Antiquities and Museums, which maintains the wonderful Heikhal Ha-Sefer—the Shrine of the Book." Brandon hoped he didn't botch the Hebrew too badly. He went on, "The Dead Sea Scrolls are stored here. Some of you will have watched when they brought the Ark here from under the Temple Mount not long ago."

He paused. A monitor showed the cut to tape. There were the Levites in their funny clothes, carrying the Ark from the tunnel. They couldn't have looked more ecstatic if they'd won $600,000,000 apiece in Powerball. In front of them danced Shlomo Kupferman, as if he were a third his real age.

"Why did you dance before the Ark?" Brandon asked.

"To welcome it back to Jerusalem," Kupferman answered. "David danced before it when it first came into the city. I thought I should do it the same honor."

"You danced all the way across Jerusalem. Forgive me, Rabbi, but you're not a young man. How did you do that?"

"God lent me strength," Shlomo Kupferman said. From most people, it would have been a figure of speech. Kupferman sounded as if he meant it.

Good, Brandon thought. *That'll keep them on the edge of their seats.* "Why is it so important that the Ark is back?" he asked.

"The Ark is the seat of the Lord's power. He proved that power again and again in the time of the Holy Scriptures. You would be wise, Mr. Nesbitt, to heed it."

"I do," Brandon said. *It's the power to draw eyeballs by the million. What bigger power is there?* "That would also be the power that makes the Ark float, right? How does it do that?"

As he had before, Kupferman answered, "It floats because God wills that it should float. What more proof do you need that it is like nothing else in the world?"

Brandon hardly listened to him. He went down his own path: "It's shaped like a chest. What can we expect when we look inside,

Rabbi? Does it hold the tablets of stone that God gave Moses on Mount Sinai, the ones with the Ten Commandments on them?" Whenever he said *Ten Commandments,* he flashed on the fifties movie epic.

"In Exodus 12:19, we read that Moses broke the tablets the Lord gave him," Kupferman replied. "In Chapter 34, verse 1, the Lord said He would write them again. But verse 28 of the same chapter says Moses did the writing. So that is uncertain. And it is uncertain whether these tablets, whoever wrote them, lie within the Ark to this day."

"That's what we're here to find out," Brandon said.

"That is what you are here to find out," Kupferman said, which might have been halfhearted agreement or more handwashing.

Brandon chose to take it for agreement. "In just a few minutes, we'll take the lid off the Ark and find out what's inside. Our worldwide audience will see it at the same time we do. We have lights and a camera overhead to look straight down into the Ark once the lid comes off."

"You made those arrangements, yes." Kupferman wasn't putting his name on anything. But he was here. And he'd let Brandon come, which was the be-all and end-all, the Alpha and the Omega.

"I am going to approach the Ark. I wish Gabriela could be up here to do this." Lying through his teeth with that last sentence, Brandon made himself sound awed and respectful. As he took half a dozen slow steps toward the gleaming chest, the TV light above it came on. So did the downlooking camera. Brandon smiled and nodded. Everything was on track.

He reached out to take the lid off the Ark.

I I

When you wanted to see something that started at four in the morning, you had two bad choices. You could stay up and be a zombie or set your alarm for a little before four—and be a zombie.

After some argument, Eric and Orly set their alarm for twenty to four. Eric killed it when it went off. He didn't jump on it and stomp it into electronic chunks, which proved he had no energy at twenty to four. Instead, he staggered into the kitchen and made espresso.

Orly lay in bed, calling down curses on Whoever'd put North America so many time zones away. She seized the tiny cup Eric brought her like a starving vampire seizing a vein. Once she drank the sweet, scalding caffeine, she started cussing out Kupferman and Gabriela instead.

Eric had already started doing that. "Do *we* get to look inside the bloody Ark?" he said. "Oh, no. All we did was find it. Who does? That fast-talking charlatan. She'd cut her mother's throat for a rating point."

"Somebody ought to cut *her* throat, for making me be awake at this hour." Orly held out the cup. "Is there more?"

"Yeah." Eric had gulped his, too. By the time he came back with refills, he was almost halfway toward life. He got back into bed with her. As if by accident, his hand fell on her thigh. She knocked it away—*she* wasn't that lively yet.

He fired up the TV. It hadn't turned four yet. Smooth pitchmen who could reduce your waistline and your bankroll were as ubiquitous here as back in the States. If that didn't say something depressing about mankind, Eric was damned if he knew what did.

Then he was looking at the inside of the Shrine of the Book, and at the Ark floating above the floor. He was looking at Rabbi Kupferman scowling into the camera. And . . .

It turned out not to be Gabriela. "Welcome to the *Gabriela and Brandon Special*!" Brandon Nesbitt said.

The show came with Hebrew subtitles here, but Eric ignored them. "Yoram isn't invited," he snarled. "How cheesy is that? If not for him, the Ark'd still be missing."

"Yoram didn't want to be there with Gabriela and Brandon," Orly said. "He's not like Kupferman—he doesn't want publicity 24/7."

"Maybe," Eric said. "Hell, *I* want to be there. If anybody gets to see what's in the Ark, it should be a trained archaeologist, not that trained seal. And Kupferman's pimping for him so he can get his own puss on TV."

"It's not just not wanting to be on television," Orly said. "Yoram is more *frum* than he lets on. I think he's worried what will happen on the show."

"If God wants to strike Brandon Nesbitt, He's had excuses before," Eric said. Orly snickered, but he wasn't kidding. Brandon had done some things over the years to make himself tabloid fodder, and to raise the wrath of a God like the one in the Old Testament.

No denying the son of a bitch was smooth, though. "Our worldwide television audience will see it at the same time we do," he said. "We have lights and a camera overhead to look straight into the Ark when the lid comes off."

"You made those arrangements, yes." Kupferman sounded gloomier than usual. Eric thumbed his nose at the TV screen. That wasn't a common Israeli gesture. It made Orly giggle.

"I am going to approach the Ark. I wish Gabriela could be up here to do this." Brandon took six slow strides toward it. The lights overhead came on, bathing him in brilliance. He smiled and nodded at the camera. *See how wonderful I am,* his bearing and expression said.

He reached out to take the lid off the Ark. Eric had always thought the stares of the cherubim were directed outward, far past anything merely human. But when the TV camera focused on the Ark, those golden eyes seemed to be aimed at the spot where Brandon's hand was going. Eric shook his head. He knew enough about camera angles to know how unreliable they could be.

Brandon touched the lid.

His mouth opened. He was going to say something—Eric was sure of that. Instead, the broadcaster looked surprised. His eyes rolled up and he crumpled to the floor in front of the Ark.

"Give me a fucking break!" Eric yelled. "You bum!"

Brandon's eyes were set and staring. "He's . . . not blinking," Orly said. A moment later, she added, "I don't think he's breathing."

Eric also didn't think Brandon's chest rose. That wasn't what made him stop jeering. A large wet stain spread across the broadcaster's crotch. If you suddenly dropped dead, your bladder'd let go. Someone faking it wouldn't pay *that* much attention to detail, would he? No way. Not on worldwide TV. You'd never get anybody to take you even halfway seriously after pretending to piss yourself in front of millions of people.

"I don't think he's going to get up," Orly said.

"Either that's the best-timed coronary or stroke in history, or . . ." Eric's voice trailed off. He and Orly looked at each other. He didn't know what the hair on the back of her neck was doing, but he knew about his. If he were a cat or dog, his tail would have puffed out, too.

The TV cut to a wide shot. Kupferman was staring at Brandon's body. His mouth moved soundlessly.

"What was that?" Eric asked. "I can't read lips in Hebrew."

"I think he said, *I tried to tell him,*" Orly said.

A cameraman in jeans, sneakers, and T-shirt knelt by Brandon. He fumbled for a pulse, than bent over the broadcaster and started CPR. An Israeli guard rushed into the picture. "Want help?" he asked in Hebrew, then in English.

"Yeah. Spell me when I get tired," the cameraman said. "If we can keep him going till he gets to a hospital—"

"If there's anything to keep going," the guard said. But he traded with the cameraman. They crouched only a couple of feet from the Ark—and made sure not to bump into it.

Somebody shouted into a telephone for an ambulance. Sirens outside the Shrine of the Book said one got there a minute later. Paramedics ran in. One tried to start an IV on Brandon. Another used a defibrillator. Brandon jerked at the charge, but that was it. Eric suspected he needed something stronger than human intervention: something like what Lazarus got.

The paramedics wouldn't quit. They put Brandon on a stretcher and carried him out. The siren wailed again, then dopplered away.

The cameraman, the guard, and Shlomo Kupferman looked out at the camera. There floated the Ark of the Covenant. Nobody would open it tonight, no matter how many millions watched. "'Hear, O Israel, the Lord our God, the Lord is One,'" Rabbi Kupferman said in English. "'Blessed be His glorious kingdom for ever and ever'"—both lines of the *Shma*. He nodded to his audience. "This show is over. A man did what he thought he could, and the

Lord willed that he pay for his folly. Is that not more important than anything else you might have learned? Good night."

Somebody behind the scenes pulled the plug. The TV in Eric and Orly's apartment went dark. After a few seconds, a news feed from a hospital ER came on. Brandon Nesbitt was dead on arrival. "Good night!" Eric said.

"Good God!" Orly echoed.

"I am going to approach the Ark. I wish Gabriela could be up here to do this," Brandon said.

Chaim Avigad yawned. He'd had some cappuccino, but he was still sleepy. So were the other ritually pure boys who shared the tent with him. Nobody slept, though. How could you miss this? The Ark! Counting Rosie, there'd been ten red heifers, but only one Ark. Seeing it gleam, Chaim could understand why, too. All that gold! And it wasn't just fancy. It was holy.

"You think Moses' tablets are in there?" a boy asked.

"You think God will let an American *goy* open the Ark and find out?" another said.

Brandon touched the Ark's lid where the cherubim were looking. Before you could blink, the broadcaster lay on the floor of the Heikhal Ha-Sefer.

"Fake!" two kids shouted. "So fake!" one added.

But Brandon lay there. Chaim stopped thinking it was a fake when he saw the American had wet his pants. Some things you wouldn't do, even on TV. Another boy made gross-out noises when he saw the same thing.

"He's dead," Chaim said.

"No way," someone came back.

"Way," Chaim insisted. "Look. He touched it, and he keeled over."

"It's phony. He'll get up," the other boy said.

But he didn't. A guy in ordinary clothes and a guard worked on him. Paramedics came in and worked on him, too. They carted him off like a sack of fertilizer. Then word came that he'd died.

By that time, Chaim wasn't sleepy. "God killed him," he said, wonder and fear in his voice. None of the other boys argued. They stared at the TV.

Chaim's glance strayed toward the barn where Rosie, Shoshanah, slept. If what the Bible said about the Ark was true, what it said about the red heifer was probably true, too. God *did* want people to sacrifice one to make things ritually pure. The only one in the world was over there.

How could you get around that? Did you dare think about trying? Chaim . . . dared.

"I am going to approach the Ark. I wish Gabriela could be up here to do this," Brandon said.

Lester Stark did not admire Brandon Nesbitt the man. He wished anyone but Brandon were covering this fast-changing story. Brandon wasn't just secular. Stark knew secular men he respected, men who believed what they believed for reasons they found good but recognized others might think differently. To Brandon, religion was hooey; he made scant effort to hide his opinion.

But Brandon the broadcaster was a pro's pro. A pro himself, Stark admired the control Brandon had over his audience, even when he'd had to do this at the last minute. You couldn't take your eyes off him. He made you want, *need,* to know what happened next. Being able to do that was a gift.

He touched the Ark. Stark leaned forward in his chair. He wanted to know what lay inside. Did God write those tablets, or did Moses? Either way, seeing them . . .

"Oh, my God!" Rhonda gasped as Brandon toppled.

For a moment, Stark thought Brandon, the mocking secular man, would bounce up and laugh at the yokels who'd believed something had happened to him. That was his style. But then the minister realized the laugh was on Brandon. He lay too still, too limp. . . .

"Oh, my God," Lester said, more softly than his wife had.

He watched them try to revive Brandon till the camera, fearing to show real death on American television, cut away. He watched the report from the hospital announcing that Brandon hadn't made it.

In the moment of Brandon's greatest triumph, the last moment of his life, Stark had thought of him as a pro's pro. That only proved he didn't always know what he was talking about. And it proved one other thing: when you talked about pros' pros, Shlomo Kupferman went at the top of the list.

"What happens now?" Rhonda asked.

Stark always had been an honest man. "Sweetheart," he answered, "I have no idea."

"I am going to approach the Ark. I wish Gabriela could be up here to do this," Brandon Nesbitt said.

Jamal Ashrawi watched an Al Jazeera feed, with an Arabic translation of the American reporter's words at the bottom of the screen. The Grand Mufti spoke some English, but was glad to have the crawl.

Unlike the late Haji Ibrahim, he'd made it down to Hebron. If the Israelis wanted him, they'd have to start a war to get him. Both Hamas and Fatah had promised. Truly God was great! Getting the militias to agree on anything these days was harder than getting either to agree with the Zionists. The fighters with whom Haji Jamal watched were Hamas men, with green armbands and head scarves.

They hooted when Brandon fell over. So did he. How could you help it? That was an obvious trick, to make the Jews' religion look true. Brandon was no Jew, but so what? Christians were full of error, too.

Some fighters went on jeering as a couple of people ran out to work on the newsman. But one said, "God smite me if they *aren't* giving him CPR. I've done it. You have to push hard enough to break ribs, and they are. You can tell."

"What?" Ashrawi said. "Do you think God struck him dead for his presumption?"

"I don't know," the fighter answered. Since he had an AK on his lap, the Grand Mufti didn't push.

Paramedics rushed in. They worked on Brandon, too. As they put him on a stretcher and carried him out, another guard muttered, "Truly there is no God but God."

"And God is great," still another whispered.

"Yes, there is no God but God, and He is Great, and He is the God of Islam," Jamal Ashrawi said. "God does not heed the Jews— they rejected His Prophet, peace be upon him."

"Can you say God didn't strike down that Christian?" asked the guard with the rifle on his lap.

"We don't *know* he's dead," Ashrawi said. "This could be a trick to make us doubt. Do you want to fall into the trap the Jews set for you?"

Two guards shook their heads. Most kept watching the TV. Before long, a woman standing in front of a hospital with her hair uncovered announced that Brandon Nesbitt had died. The guards looked reproachfully at Jamal Ashrawi.

He didn't know what to say. Brandon was prominent in the West. Taking him off the air wouldn't be easy, not when he'd been a fixture for years. *Was* he dead? Had he touched the Jews' Ark and died, the way the rabbi warned he might? If not, what *did* happen? Jamal Ashrawi had answers to none of those questions. That worried him.

* * *

Eric bounced from the Israeli channel to CNN to MSNBC to Fox to ABC and CBS and NBC. Talking heads pontificated—a hell of a word, under the circumstances—about what had happened to Brandon and what it meant. The short answer was, nobody knew. The long answer was . . . on all the networks.

Orly grabbed the remote. The TV went dark. "Why'd you do that?" Eric yelped.

"Because they aren't saying what's got to be true," she answered.

"Which is?"

"It was what it looked like. God killed him."

"But that's—" Eric stopped. He could believe God had punched Brandon's ticket. Or he could believe Brandon had had a heart attack or a stroke, just by coincidence, when his manicured paw came down on the Ark with secular intent. This when Brandon seemed in excellent shape and hadn't come close to hitting forty yet.

Which was more unlikely? Eric wasn't sure—or, if he was, he didn't want to face it.

Which was scarier? He knew damn well.

"I don't want to be *frum*," he remarked to nobody in particular.

"Tell me about it!" Orly exclaimed. "Who in her right mind would?"

Eric went into the kitchen. He came back with a bottle of nasty local brandy and two glasses. He poured one for himself, then raised an eyebrow. Orly nodded. He gave her a slug and raised his glass. *"L'chaim,"* he said, much less ironically than he'd intended.

"L'chaim," she echoed. They both drank. After what they'd watched, *to life* seemed the only possible toast.

The brandy exploded in Eric's stomach. He couldn't remember the last time he'd knocked one back before sunup—which was bound to be just as well. The room swayed when he stood again. He eyed the bottle as if eyeing a rattler.

Orly was doing the same thing. She'd drained her glass in a hurry, too. "Want another one?" she asked.

Another one would lead to *another* one would lead to . . . *Retro me, Satanas,* Eric thought. He shook his head. "Better not," he said. But the brandy gave him a shield against the slings and arrows of outrageous coincidence. Against the wrath of God, on worldwide TV? He could hope. "Let's get breakfast. I want something greasy in there to take the edge off the paint thinner."

"You're supposed to do that *before* you start drinking," Orly said. But she shed the T-shirt and sweats she'd slept in and put on a bra and a different T-shirt and some jeans. Eric dressed, too. He brushed his teeth—cheap brandy and Colgate didn't mix—and ran a comb through the hair he had left.

They got a big bowl of hummus at the falafel place around the corner. It was fancied up with olive oil and *fuul* beans, and came with pitas. It wasn't an American-style breakfast but, with more strong coffee, it was good.

Maybe it was the brandy, maybe it was the fresh coffee, maybe even the hummus, but Eric was starting to feel human—in a rattled way—when somebody said, "Hello," in English.

He looked up. Damned if Barbara Taylor wasn't standing there like a lost puppy. "Hi, Barb," he said, more cheerfully than he felt. "Grab a chair and join us?"

"Thanks. Don't mind if I do." Barb must have lived clean—well, of course she did—because somebody at the next table got up. She snagged his chair. Orly made a mutinous noise deep in her throat. She wasn't fond of Barb's relentless naïveté.

But what could you do? Eric did what he could—he waved for more breakfast fixings. "What kind of coffee you want?" he asked Barb.

"Nes is fine," she answered. Nes was instant. In a country where there was so much good coffee around, drinking that shit seemed like sacrilege to Eric. They weren't his taste buds, so he got what

Barb wanted. Orly made a soft noise. It wasn't quite *yuck*!, but it came close.

"So how are you?" Eric asked Barb.

"I'll tell you—I'm kind of upset," she said. "Did you folks watch the show about the Ark?"

"'Fraid so," Eric said. Orly nodded. She might have liked to deny it, but she couldn't.

"Me, too." Barb paused; a waiter plopped more hummus and a cup of Nes in front of her. Israeli waiters were long on attitude and short on style points, especially in a joint like this. She sipped the coffee, nodded, and started to eat. "That poor man," she said.

"Brandon?" Eric had all he could do not to choke on a chunk of pita. He'd called Brandon a lot of things himself, most of them unprintable. None was so polite as *That poor man*. Barb *was* too nice for her own good.

"He got what was coming to him," Orly said.

Barb shook her head. "Terrible to die for being curious."

"For being nosy," Orly said.

There, Eric agreed. "For being nosy and going after ratings," he said. "If the Ark wouldn't draw a bunch of"—he swallowed *fundies* at the last moment, because Barb was one—"uh, people, he wouldn't have cared about it." Was Barb a good influence? There was a scary thought.

She stopped eating to say, "Heavens to Betsy, I know that." Eric realized he would have done better to order her something more familiar. But she was damaging the bowl of smashed-up garbanzos. She went on, "Going after ratings is his job."

"*Was*," Orly said.

"That's about it," Eric agreed. "The Big Producer in the Sky called him to take his last meeting." If he stayed flip about it, he wouldn't have to admit how much it terrified him.

"If God did slay him, isn't it a sign the Last Days are coming?" Barb made what should have been an inflammatory question sound reasonable. Or maybe what seemed to be reason sprang from watching a healthy man keel over for no visible reason.

"*Whose* Last Days?" Orly snarled. The Christian, Jewish, and Muslim versions looked, as computer geeks said, incompatible.

Barb only smiled. "I don't know," she answered. "Exciting to live in times like these, isn't it? Maybe we'll find out."

"Oh, boy," Eric said. Barb seemed to think getting caught up in any of the versions out there would be good and exciting. Eric was sure it would be exciting. Good? Not so much. "I'd sooner stick to business as usual."

"Oh, gosh, so would I," she answered. "But it's not what we want, is it? It's what God wants."

"How do you know what God wants?" Orly kept throwing darts.

"I read the Scriptures and pray a lot," Barb said. If the darts stung, she gave no sign.

"How about thinking?" Eric asked.

"That, too," Barb agreed. "We've got a lot to think about, don't we? The red heifer and the bomb and the Ark and poor Brandon Nesbitt and the new Temple and—"

"Enough, already!" Eric said.

"Maybe it doesn't mean anything." Orly sounded as if she hoped like hell it didn't. Eric clung to the same hope just as hard.

Barb Taylor only smiled. "Well, sure, maybe it doesn't," she said. "But wouldn't it be neat if it did?"

"No!" Orly and Eric said together.

Barb wasn't listening to them. Her voice went soft and dreamy: "To see the Lord face-to-face . . ."

"Brandon did," Eric said. "Look what it got him."

"This would be different." You couldn't faze Barb. She saw the world through rose-colored glasses whether the world deserved it or not. "Jesus is supposed to be a lot more merciful than His Father." Then she added, "Heaven knows we need mercy."

Orly said something in Arabic and Hebrew that should have torched the table. Barb went on smiling; she didn't understand the words and ignored the tone. Orly started to say it in English so Barb couldn't not get it.

Eric kicked her under the table. She gave him a look intended to uncurl his beard. But he wouldn't let Barb's words pass unchallenged. Growing up in the States, he knew almost as much about her religion as his own. Israeli Jews never had to worry about learning the words to Christmas carols.

"What about Jesus driving the money changers from the Temple?" he asked. "What about 'I come not to send peace, but a sword'?"

"Well, anyone will do what has to be done," Barb answered. "Look at Israel. People here want to live at peace with their neighbors, but they can't always."

In a way, that was true. In another, it was a breathtaking oversimplification. A minute's conversation with a Palestinian or an Israeli would have made that plain. Barb saw the truth and didn't worry about the oversimplification. That was her style.

"Are you finished?" Orly asked Eric. Her tone said, *You'd better be.*

Unlike Barb, he took such hints. Botching this one would have meant a row. He had too many other things to worry about. "I sure am," he said, and jumped to his feet. "See you, Barb."

"So long." She was still plowing through the hummus and the *fuul* beans.

"Her heart's in the right place," Eric said.

"Maybe," Orly answered. "But her head's up her ass." And they headed back to their apartment.

The phone on the nightstand next to Gabriela's bed rang. It rang and rang and rang. She had the vague feeling it had been ringing for a long time, longer than she could actually remember. She had the even vaguer feeling it had rung before, rung and rung and finally stopped.

Weren't you supposed to do something about a ringing telephone? The proper response finally floated up into her consciousness like a walrus breaking the surface of the Arctic Ocean. When the telephone rang, you were supposed to . . . supposed to . . . answer the damn thing! Then it would shut up.

She rolled toward the phone. That made her eyes come open. For the first few seconds after they did, she saw double. Each eyeball was working on its own, and her brain wasn't up to putting two competing images together. Then it was. As the world came into better focus, the clock next to the persistently ringing phone told her it was 7:22.

That wasn't right. She wasn't supposed to be in bed at 7:22. For the life of her, she couldn't have said why she wasn't, but she knew she wasn't. She should have been . . . She didn't know where, but not here, wherever here was. She realized she was wearing a dress and panty hose and even shoes. Zoned as she was, she knew you didn't go to bed like that. So why had she?

Maybe she could find out from whoever was calling her. The first time she reached for the phone, she missed. Stubborn as a . . . as a . . . as some kind of stubborn thing, she tried again. This time, she caught it. She almost dropped the handset bringing it to her face, but she didn't quite.

"Hello?" she said. Even she could hear that she sounded like a lush on a six-day bender.

"Gabriela? My God, is that you? Are you okay?" Saul Buchbinder, by contrast, sounded as if he'd been speeding for as long as she'd been shitfaced.

Why am I shitfaced? she wondered. *All I drank last night was a glass of wine and water, lots of water.* She realized she desperately needed to pee. But that would wait—for a little while, anyway.

"It's me, Saul," she said. Remembering it was her made her remember where she was—and where she should have been. She gasped in horror. "The Ark!"

"Yeah. The Ark." Saul Buchbinder was a professionally genial man, a check-grabbing gladhander in an expensive Italian suit. Gabriela couldn't remember the last time she'd heard him sound so grim. Come to that, she couldn't ever remember him sounding grim. Something weird seemed to have happened to her memory, but even so. . . . After a few seconds, the producer went on, "Brandon did the show for you. Said you were sick after dinner—something about hot food. Couldn't get you on the phone, so I believed him. Somebody had to be there, and there he was."

"*Brandon* did the show?" Rage burned away—vaporized—much of the muzziness inside Gabriela's head. "He doped me, Saul, the motherfucker must have doped me. The food *was* hot, but I ate it okay. He was trying to screw me, and he did."

She felt at herself in sudden terror. But no, her panties were where they belonged, under her panty hose. She'd known plenty of men good at getting women's underwear off, but never one who could put it back on right. No telltale wet spot at the crotch, either. So *that* hadn't happened, anyway.

Even so . . . "I'll kill him! I swear to God I will! The biggest story of my life, and he stole it from me? He's dead fucking meat, you hear? No jury in the world will convict me." At that moment, she meant every word of it.

But all Saul said was, "Gabriela, sweetheart, I think he went and did you a favor." Despite the endearment, he sounded grimmer than ever. Gabriela hadn't dreamt he could.

"What are you talking about? That should have been me up there opening the Ark, not that shitheaded asshole. *Me,* Saul, you hear?"

"Listen to me, will you?"

"Then talk sense."

"I'm trying to. He did the back-and-forth with Kupferman. He had it down pat—I believe now he must've planned everything out way ahead of time. But it doesn't matter, not now it doesn't."

"I told you before to talk sense." Gabriela hoped she scared Saul. She sounded more than dangerous enough to scare herself.

"I'm trying to. I'm not sure I can," the producer said. "He walked up to take the lid off the Ark, right? He reached out, he touched it—and he fell over dead."

"There *is* a God!" Gabriela exclaimed. She wasn't thinking any too clearly yet, though she realized that only later.

"Yeah. I'm beginning to think maybe there is." Saul didn't sound grim any more. He'd gone past that. He sounded like someone maybe a millimeter away from crapping himself in terror. "All that stuff Kupferman talked about with you and Brandon, that wasn't bullshit. That was the straight goods. Brandon touched the Ark, and God, like, struck him dead. What else could it be?"

"He had it coming! Served him right!" Gabriela said savagely.

"I won't even try and tell you you're wrong," Buchbinder said. "The docs at the hospital are gonna do a post on him. Maybe he had a coronary or a stroke at just the wrong time. I don't believe that for a second, but maybe. Suppose he didn't, though, Gabriela. Just suppose. Suppose he wasn't a piece of shit, too, and he didn't slip you something at dinner. That would've been you going up to the Ark. That would've been you trying to take off the lid. What d'you think would've happened when you did?"

"Uh—" Gabriela slammed into that one like a power-saw disk slamming into a spike. She wasn't much of a believer. Who was, these days, except born-agains, suicide bombers, and Orthodox Jews? But what if something turned out to be true whether you believed in it or not?

Yeah. What if?

"'Uh' is right," Saul said. "If Brandon hadn't stolen your chance, way it looks to me is, that would have been you plotzing there the second you touched the Ark."

It looked that way to Gabriela, too. If Brandon hadn't died of his own nastiness or something, if God *had* reached out and touched him when he reached out and touched the Ark, wouldn't the same thing have happened to her? She wasn't in Brandon's league when it came to son-of-a-bitchery, but she knew only too well she wasn't one of the properly pious people Rabbi Kupferman talked about, either.

"What are we going to do?" she asked, as much to herself as to Saul Buchbinder.

"I dunno," he answered. "I'll tell you this, though—whatever it is, it'll send ratings straight through the roof. People will tune in to see how we can top having a guy drop dead in front of the whole wide world."

He was right. He couldn't very well be wrong. Gabriela's head whirled anyway, from Brandon's sleeping pill and from what had just happened, both. He'd acted like the worst villain in a slimy melodrama to steal her moment in the sun. And she was alive and he was dead because he had. How did any of that make sense?

God only knew. Gabriela shivered and stared up through the ceiling at what she all at once thought of as heaven, because the odds looked better and better that that was literally true.

Yitzhak Avigad walked the familiar grounds of Kibbutz Nair Tamid with an unfamiliar companion: a decontamination expert from the IDF. "So we're good to come back?" Yitzhak asked.

Ari Eitan nodded. "No problem for people. We've decontaminated the buildings, same as we did at the airport."

"And the animals? The crops?" Yitzhak persisted.

Dr. Eitan hesitated. "You can't treat fields and orchards the way you treat buildings. The background level is up a little. It will be, for a while. There are places that are more radioactive naturally than this one is now."

"Those bastards." Yitzhak looked toward Tel Aviv. "Those *stinking* bastards." He walked on, his Nikes scuffing up—radioactive?—dust. "Give me the bottom line."

"I thought I just did," Eitan answered.

"No. The bottom line is, would *you* live here? Would you eat what grows here? Would you eat meat from animals that graze here?"

"Living here is not a problem. I already told you that." Ari Eitan paused. "The Ministry of Agriculture will let you sell your produce and meat. You're within acceptable limits. I said that, too. If you ate nothing but your own stuff, you might see a small increase in . . . trouble years from now."

"Trouble." Yitzhak hated bullshit. "You mean cancer."

"Well . . . yeah." The decontamination expert nodded. "I'm not sure how much it will matter, though."

"What's *that* supposed to mean?"

"Did you see how that American dropped dead when he touched the Ark? God's paying attention to us, and we'd better start paying attention to Him. Who knows if we have to worry about cancer after the Messiah comes?"

"I hadn't thought of it like that." And Yitzhak hadn't. How would life change after the Messiah came? He'd put all his energy into working for that. What happened afterwards . . . lay in the Messiah's hands, not his.

"It's the same in Tel Aviv. The concrete, the bricks—we can clean those pretty well," Eitan said. "The parks, the grass, the trees are harder. But if you come back here, your odds are good."

Was pretty good good enough? It wasn't up to Yitzhak, anyhow. He'd take Dr. Eitan's word to Kibbutz Ha-Minsarah. The adults from this kibbutz could hash it out there. He looked toward Tel

Aviv again. No matter what the decontamination expert said, he wouldn't care to live in the city for a while.

He got into his car. Instead of heading back to the kibbutz near Beersheba, he drove into Jerusalem. A phone call told him Kupferman was at the Religious Affairs Ministry and would see him. Even in West Jerusalem, finding a place to park was an adventure.

Several people in Kupferman's outer office sent him dirty looks as he breezed past. Had he been waiting there, he would have done the same. Since he wasn't . . . he went into the rabbi's sanctum.

"Good to see you," Shlomo Kupferman said. "How is Shoshanah? How are your nephew and the other pure boys?"

"They're well," Yitzhak answered. He would have been angry that Kupferman asked about the heifer before the children . . . if the kibbutzniks hadn't moved Rosie before they got the boys out. He asked his own questions: "How soon will we sacrifice the cow? When does the Temple start going up?"

"We have some unbuilding to do before the building can begin," Kupferman reminded him. Yitzhak nodded impatiently. Then the rabbi said, "The unbuilding starts next week. Don't leak that. We won't announce it. We'll just do it."

"Next week?" Yitzhak whistled softly. That was sooner than he'd expected. The Muslim world would pitch a fit when word got out. The Dome of the Rock and the Al-Aqsa Mosque had been there a long time. But the Temple Mount was Jewish first. Didn't it deserve to be Jewish again? "About time!" he said.

"Yes." Kupferman nodded. "We could start the Temple sooner if we wrecked the trash cluttering it now, but the Prime Minister won't see reason." He sighed. "As if the Muslims will love us for preserving their buildings! But when we start erecting the Temple . . . That will be time to take Shoshanah up on the Mount of Olives."

"I know," Yitzhak said. "Chaim won't be happy. He's made that cow a pet."

"We need ritually pure priests," Rabbi Kupferman said. "Her

ashes can give them to us. Will your nephew go against the word of God in the Holy Scriptures?"

"No. He'll be unhappy, though." Yitzhak chuckled sourly. "When is a boy that age not unhappy?"

"When he isn't that age any more," the rabbi replied.

"Too true," Yitzhak said. "Next week? That's wonderful! My friends will be thrilled when I—" He laughed again, this time in embarrassment. "But I can't tell, can I?"

"Better if you don't. They would tell *their* friends, and one friend would know a reporter or be a reporter or get excited and tweet, and . . ."

"Yes. And." Yitzhak knew how Israelis loved to gab—he was one. "Something else, *Reb* Shlomo?"

"Ask," Kupferman said. "I think I know what it is, but ask."

Yitzhak did: "Do you really believe God killed Brandon Nesbitt for touching the Ark?"

"Of course." Rabbi Kupferman said. "Either you believe God does things, or you believe things happen on their own." He didn't say, *Either you're a Jew or not,* but he might as well have.

"That's not what I meant," Yitzhak said. "But God could have done so much for us if He'd chosen to. Why is He showing His power now?" *Why not during the Holocaust?* was the question behind that question—behind most questions about God these days.

"Why?" the rabbi answered. "Because the Temple *will* be rebuilt. Because the Messiah *will* come—soon, Yitzhak."

E ric and Orly went onto the Temple Mount by way of the Bab al-Silsila—the Chain Gate—north of the Western Wall. Though the Israelis had taken over the Mount, they followed old custom by letting non-Muslims get to the top only by the Chain Gate or the Bab al-Maghariba—the Moor's Gate—on the south side of the Western Wall Plaza. They could leave by any of the ten gates connecting the Temple Mount to the rest of Jerusalem.

"I don't know how you talked me into doing this," Orly grumbled, not for the first time.

"Some things you ought to see *in situ*," Eric said—an archaeologist talking. "We should take a good look at this stuff before it goes."

Her mouth twisted. "It's not our religion. If they packed up the Church of the Holy Sepulcher and moved it somewhere else, would you go gawk at that, too?"

"I hope so," he answered. Orly rolled her eyes. He pointed

toward the Dome of the Rock. "C'mon, babe. That's a lot nicer building than the Holy Sepulcher."

"If you say so. I've never been to the Church of the Holy Sepulcher," Orly said. "It's for tourists—Christian tourists."

"I saw it when I got here," Eric said defensively.

He needed to be defensive, too, because Orly pounced like a missile-toting helicopter. "Yeah, a lot of American Jews do. They feel being Christian is normal and being Jewish is weird. We don't grow up with that."

She wasn't wrong. Eric said, "I didn't go see it because it was Christian. I saw it because it was old. In L.A., there's a McDonald's from the 1950s that's a historical monument. This is different."

"Sure it is. You can't get fries or a burger at the church," Orly said. McDonald's did great in Israel. They sold cheeseburgers, too, even if nothing this side of a pork chop was less kosher.

Eric walked toward the Dome of the Rock. If he didn't notice her sarcasm, he didn't have to snap back. He didn't feel like getting into a slanging match here. This wasn't the right place, and the Israeli soldiers and their rifles had little to do with that.

Observant Jews didn't come up onto the Temple Mount for fear of setting foot inside the Holy of Holies. Only the High Priest could go there, and he only on Yom Kippur. He would offer two handfuls of incense before the Ark, then sprinkle it with blood from a bull sacrificed earlier in the day. After the offerings, he would back out in humility and fear.

Kupferman offered dispensations to people who wanted them. He said he knew where the Ark had rested: on the sacred stone inside the Dome of the Rock, the stone on which Abraham was said to have offered to sacrifice Isaac (or, if you were a Muslim, Ishmael) and from which Muhammad was said to have ascended to heaven.

To give Kupferman his due, that wasn't just expediency. His

archaeological alter ego, Sh. Nechshat, had said the same thing for years. He followed the conclusions of Leen Ritmeyer, a Dutchman who was this generation's leading Temple Mount scholar. Eric thought Ritmeyer'd got it right, too; the man had a knack for spotting things other people missed, and for seeing what they meant.

A guy in sunglasses, a cricket cap—almost a baseball cap, but not quite—and a sky-blue Manchester City T-shirt waved toward Eric and Orly. He wasn't a Brit, though, even if Eric needed a few seconds to recognize Munir al-Nuwayhi behind the shades. He waved back. Orly gave a tight little nod.

"How's it going?" Eric called.

Munir ambled over. He looked gloomy, the way he had most of the time since the Ark was rediscovered. He'd probably looked gloomy a lot before that, too. Being an Arab in Israel wasn't anyone's idea of fun.

"If I can't see history made, I may as well see it unmade, eh?" he said now, and pointed at the Dome of the Rock.

Israeli archaeologists and technicians swarmed over the building like ants over cake forgotten after a picnic. Like ants, they'd take the Dome away one chunk at a time. Unlike the picnic pests, they'd put it back together.

Yoram Louvish knew more about the disassembly project. Eric hadn't asked him much. He didn't feel good about what the Israelis were doing or about his own deliberate lack of curiosity. Hadn't otherwise decent German officers not wanted to know what was happening to Jews during the Second World War?

Nobody's getting killed here. He'd told himself the same thing again and again, trying to salve his conscience. Some days, it worked better than others. He didn't even know it was true. It might not be. When these buildings came down, who could guess what the Muslims would do?

Eric feared he could. To Munir, he said, "I wish it would have turned out some other way." Orly nodded again, this time with less constraint. She wasn't wild for the Third Temple, either; nowhere near.

Munir said something harsh in Arabic before returning to English: "It's all madness. The whole world is madness, with no way out."

"You aren't saying anything I haven't been thinking," Eric told him.

As if he hadn't spoken, the Israeli Arab went on, "It's like a bad dream, only no one can wake up from it. The monsters will get us if we don't watch out—and we can't watch out." He paused to grind out a dead Marlboro under the sole of his sandal, then light a new one. After a drag and a cough, he continued, "I've given Louvish my resignation from the team."

"You don't want to do that!" Orly exclaimed before Eric could. "Think of your career!"

"It doesn't matter now. I'm better off away from it all," Munir said. "This isn't archaeology any more. This is religion and politics. I spent my whole life trying to steer clear from both of those, and look what it's got me."

As if to underline his words, a guy in a crane swung toward the Dome of the Rock's actual dome. He taped a sheet of paper to each gold-plated panel, so the Israelis could put it back together right. Eric imagined a Palestinian saboteur sneaking among the panels and scrambling the sheets. When the building went up again, it would go up wrong. And how loud would Muslim countries yell if that happened? Loud enough so you could hear them on the moon.

"Bite your tongue!" Orly exclaimed when Eric suggested that. Munir, on the other hand, laughed harder than Eric thought the joke deserved.

"It's okay," the American said. "Nobody here but us chickens."

"You don't need to worry about me," Munir added, proving he knew too well that Orly was. "I do not care for destruction of any kind, even funny destruction. Peace be unto you both. Peace be unto all of us." He touched the brim of his cap with an oddly courtly gesture, dipped his head, and walked away.

"I want to believe him, but you never can tell," Orly said when he'd got far enough away not to be able to hear. Eric wanted to tell her she could count on Munir, but if this crazy summer had taught Eric anything, it was that you never *could* tell.

With Orly unhappily trailing, he went on to the Dome. A twentieth-century scholar said it had an elegance of proportion that outdid any other building. Eric wouldn't have argued that, either. The doors, in every other side of the octagon, faced the four cardinal directions. They were open; he supposed they would get taken down and carted away soon.

"You are?" an Israeli corporal barked when he saw they wanted to come in.

They gave their names. "We work with Professor Louvish," Eric added.

The noncom grunted. "You, too, eh? Okay, you're allowed." He stood aside.

Eric and Orly looked at each other. "'You, too'?" Eric said. Orly shrugged. Neither of them had seen any other archaeologists from under the Temple Mount but Munir al-Nuwayhi, and he hadn't come this way.

Inside the Dome of the Rock, the Byzantine architects and artisans who'd built it for Caliph Abd al-Malik let their color sense run riot. The stone paneling and columns were of marble. The columns had gilded acanthus capitals that reminded Eric of the ones in Hagia Sophia in Istanbul (or, in those days, Constantinople). The mosaics were green and blue and mother-of-pearl, with gilt accents. On the wooden interior of the dome were more splendid golden designs and inscriptions.

A fence separated the faithful from al-Sakhra—the Rock. That was just as well. When the Crusaders held Jerusalem, they'd cut chunks from the Rock as relics and sold them for their weight in gold. Not far from the Crusader quarrying was another, smaller, rectangular depression in the Rock. If Ritmeyer had things straight, that was where the Ark had rested.

Eric eyed the depression. He had an advantage Ritmeyer'd lacked: he'd seen the Ark. Damned if it wasn't the right size.

Other marks on the Rock showed the Archangel Gabriel's fingers—if you were a believing Muslim, anyway. Yet another was said to be Muhammad's footprint. Normally, those would have interested Eric. Now he had eyes only for that depression. Yes, the Ark could have fit there. And yes, it was liable to fit there—again?

"Fancy meeting you here."

Those ordinary English words, spoken in an equally ordinary American accent, almost made him jump out of his skin. He had to make a quick grab to keep his glasses from flying off his nose.

That done, he recovered such dignity as he could, like a cat that had fallen off a sofa. His voice was nearly normal when he answered, "Hello, Barb. What are you doing here?"

She beamed. "I took Yoram's name in vain to get the soldiers to let me come onto the Temple Mount. Actually, it turned out he'd left my name with the guards, said it was okay for me to come." That explained the corporal's *You, too?* Barb went on, "I wanted to see things while they're still here. There's a last time for everything—everything in the whole world."

In a different context, the remark would have been a commonplace. A lot of what Barb Taylor said was a commonplace. In the Dome of the Rock, when it was about to come down and the Third Temple about to rise in its place, things took on new meaning. Maybe Barb meant them to. Or maybe Eric's imagination was running away with him—again?

"I wish she'd shut up and get lost," Orly said in Hebrew.

"Armageddon tired of this myself," Eric answered in English, which proved that, regardless of the marbles in the Dome of the Rock, he'd lost his.

Orly looked appalled. He felt appalled. If Barb got it, she didn't let on. "Tired of what, Eric?" she asked.

"Tired of everything that's happened lately," he replied. That wasn't what he'd meant, but he wasn't lying. He would have given anything for the world to get back to normal again.

"You shouldn't be." Barb always sounded so sincere, you wanted to make her shut up. "They're signs."

"So were the ones for Burma-Shave, and look what happened to them," Eric said. Orly had no idea what he was talking about. Barb did, though he didn't think she was old enough to have seen them for herself. *He* wasn't. *They'd have to say* Myanmar-Shave *if they brought 'em back now,* he thought.

"Talk about signs . . ." Orly sounded sincere, too, enough to raise Eric's hackles. She asked Barb, "You think it will be a sign if they build the Third Temple, don't you?"

"Sure. Who wouldn't?" Barb said. "If it comes back after so long, it can't be anything else."

One of Eric's firmest convictions was that anything could *always* be something else. That conviction had taken a drubbing lately, but he clung to it. Maybe he had the courage of his convictions, or maybe he was just a jerk. How could you tell?

That wasn't the direction Orly was going in. She said, "If the Temple goes up, won't it be a sign Jesus didn't know what He was talking about? Didn't He say it would get destroyed and never rise again?"

Barb took a New Testament out of her purse. "That's in Matthew . . . 24:2: 'And Jesus said unto them, See ye not all these things? verily I say unto you, There shall not be left here one stone upon another, that shall not be thrown down.' So He did prophesy that the Second Temple would fall, but I don't think He said anything about the Third Temple rising." She flipped pages. "Almost the same text in Mark 13:2 . . . and in Luke 21:6."

Orly muttered. Eric said, "That's not how Christians in the fourth century looked at things, Barb. When Julian and the Jews tried to rebuild the Temple then, bishops quoted Matthew after they failed."

"Isn't that interesting?" Barb said. "Only goes to show there are different ways to look at things."

Orly muttered again. Eric decided arguing with Barb had no future. She was too reasonable for her own good, *much* too reasonable to belong in the Middle East.

She looked around the interior of the Dome of the Rock in wonder. "This is such a wonderful building. It's a shame they can't have it and the Third Temple here at the same time."

"American," Orly said. Eric knew what she meant. In the USA, the Dome of the Rock and the Third Temple and the Church of the Holy Sepulcher would have stood next to one another, and people would hit them all—and their gift shops—in an afternoon. Sacredland, they could call it, and build a Museum of Tolerance—and a Hindu stupa and a Buddhist shrine—close by.

He laughed. The United States *had* done that, or something close. People there didn't get shot or blown up over what they believed . . . or fall over dead for no reason. What was so bad about that?

Nothing Eric could see. Then he remembered Brandon falling dead. He remembered the Ark floating three inches off the ground in the Shrine of the Book. However neat the American arrangement might be, he feared it wasn't what God had in mind.

And wasn't that a shame?

Chaim Avigad was so glad to come back home, he didn't care whether Kibbutz Nair Tamid was slightly radioactive. Almost everybody who'd camped at Kibbutz Ha-Minsarah felt the same way. A few people stayed there. Everybody else rushed back.

Rosie came home, too. She stood in her stall chewing her cud. How much did it matter if her grass made Geiger counters tick a little? Not much, when she didn't have long to live.

Every time Chaim bumped against that, it made him unhappy. Why did God want a red heifer's ashes to purify things and make them ritually clean? It made no sense to Chaim.

Then again, God had killed Brandon for not paying proper respect to the Ark. He hadn't scared Brandon, or hurt him, or crippled him—He'd *killed* him. Along with millions of others, Chaim watched it happen. How much sense did a God Who could do something like that need to make?

Not much. If you were strong, you just needed to use your strength. God had no trouble with that.

Everything else was going as it should. Israel had chased the Arabs off the Temple Mount. The buildings the Arabs ran up there while they held the holy site wouldn't last long. Chaim thought of them that way—like shacks squatters built on land that wasn't theirs. If the Dome of the Rock was a world-famous treasure . . . so what? They had no business putting it there.

Once the Dome and the mosque got knocked down, what *did* belong on the Temple Mount could rise once more. The Temple hadn't been there for over nineteen hundred years? There'd been no Jewish state in the Middle East for that long . . . till there was again.

The Temple would rise. The Ark would return to the Holy of Holies. Priests would sacrifice by the rules the Bible spelled out. And, the way prepared for him, the Messiah would come. *Everything* would change then.

Jews had been waiting and praying for this since before the Second Temple fell. A few Jews had thought Jesus was the Messiah. A few Jews still did—a few, along with all those Christians. Chaim wasn't one of them. He never would be. He wanted the real Messiah, not a long-ago phony. And the real Messiah was on the way. How could anybody doubt it? Chaim didn't. He believed.

So why aren't I happier? he wondered.

Yes, part of it was that they were going to sacrifice Rosie. It was such a big part, it had hidden from him that it wasn't the only thing bothering him. Everybody else at Kibbutz Nair Tamid seemed excited at how things were going. Chaim didn't feel that way. He didn't wish things weren't going this way. He was as pious as he'd been raised to be. But he saw questions where others saw answers.

Why kill a red heifer to make everything ritually pure? That still topped the list. But more crowded behind it. Why did it take a dirty bomb in Tel Aviv to get people moving toward rebuilding the Temple? Why did people there have to die? Why did they deserve it?

To Chaim, they were like Job's children. They died to make God's point to other people. How fair was that? Not very, not as far as he could see. God was God. He didn't *need* to do things like that to people. He could get what He wanted without the . . . the collateral damage, that was it.

But God didn't bother. He went ahead and did stuff; tough luck for people who got in His way when He did. He was God Almighty. Chaim had no doubts about that. Things would come out as He wanted them to, whatever that was. But His work reminded Chaim of the first draft of a paper. It had everything it needed, but God could have done a better job fitting the pieces together.

You could say that about how Brandon died. Yeah, Kupferman had warned him. The Bible said bad things happened if you messed with the Ark. Brandon should have known better. If he'd believed, he would have.

Ever since the days of the Bible, God had lain low and kept quiet. He blamed Brandon for not paying attention to Him anyway. Was *that* fair? Brandon had done worse than trying to take the lid off the Ark. Were there any commandments Brandon *hadn't* broken? Maybe *Thou shalt not kill.* Any others? Chaim doubted it. And Brandon got away with everything—till then. After that, it was all over. So was he.

Was *that* fair?

Chaim looked up at the ceiling. *Where were You when the Nazis slaughtered us, when we really needed You? Why didn't You do something about that instead of killing a windbag reporter?*

He got no answer. He hadn't expected one. God had better things to do than answer kids with annoying questions. So did most grown-ups. Chaim had seen that when he asked Uncle Yitzhak about Job.

What if you didn't like any answers you came up with? What could you do about it?

Try talking to God again, maybe. Right now, in spite of the silence he'd just met, that seemed less hopeless than it would have through much of Jewish history. You *might* get an answer. But would you want it?

In Hebron, Jamal Ashrawi felt as safe as a man could when the Zionists were after him. They would cause an incident if they snatched him from the heart of Palestinian power or killed him here. That might not stop them, but the Grand Mufti hoped it would slow them down.

He felt confident enough to risk a phone call. He had a message they needed to hear. It wasn't his alone; it came from the whole Muslim world.

Navigating the Zionist entity's bureaucracy was an adventure. The first person on the other end of the call was a bored flunky, as rude as Israelis often were. "Religious Affairs," she said. *Quit bothering me,* her tone added.

"This is Ashrawi," the Grand Mufti said in Arabic.

"Who?" She didn't know or care.

"Ashrawi," he snapped. "Put me through to someone who knows something, or else watch your miserable country get what it deserves. I would laugh."

"*Cus ummak!*" she told him. An Arab woman would never say that to a man. She went on, "*Who* are you?"

"I am Ashrawi. I am the Mossad's nightmare. I am Grand Mufti of Jerusalem, misbeliever, so put me through to the minister or you and Israel pay the price."

"Who are you really?" the woman said. God made plenty of stupid Jews. Then she said, "You have to hold," and music filled his ears.

He went through more bureaucracy before he got to Shlomo Kupferman. He addressed him in English: he wouldn't admit to speaking Hebrew, and had heard Kupferman was as stubborn about Arabic. "I have warning for you," he said.

"You are in a poor position to give one," the Jew replied, also in English. What Ashrawi had heard was true, then.

"I not speak just for myself," the Grand Mufti said.

"You have a tapeworm? We'll send you medicine."

"Funny man. Listen to me, funny man, or you be sorry."

"Go ahead. Talk is cheap. No wonder Arabs like it so much."

Ashrawi reminded himself that other people depended on him. "You harm one stone from Dome of the Rock or Al-Aqsa, Muslims all over the world take it as an act of war. They avenge in God's holy name."

"They can try," Kupferman said.

"No. You not understand. They can do," Ashrawi insisted. "From thousands of kilometers off, they can. You must understand before you drown in stupidity. They have all tools they need to strike from far away, and have will to do it."

"Do you think any man's power can stand against God?"

"God is with *us!*" Ashrawi said.

"You watched that fool die when he touched the holy Ark, and you are still mad enough to say such a thing?"

"He was only a Christian." The Grand Mufti disliked Christians and Jews for different reasons. Jews were worse politically, but Christians' theology was more distorted.

"You both added to the Scriptures, which need no addition," Kupferman said. "Do your worst. God will protect us. But who's looking out for you now, Mufti?"

Ashrawi stared in all directions. Was an assassin with a scope-sighted rifle aiming at him? Would a missile-carrying helicopter swoop over the horizon? Did a drone cruise above Hebron waiting to lock on to him?

Nothing happened. The Grand Mufti hung up. If Kupferman wouldn't listen, too bad. *I tried to warn him,* Ashrawi thought. *I did my best.*

"In other news," the Israeli broadcaster said, "the Foreign Minister of Iran warned again of severe consequences if Israel rebuilds the Temple. The Israeli Foreign Minister replied that the Iranian should examine his own regime's treatment of religious minorities before scorning its neighbors."

"Oy!" Eric said. That could make you lose your appetite—though he kept eating *shawarma*. Only Israelis, who'd lived with crises since 1948, could make one sound so bland. And only an Israeli could tell the truth and miss the point like the Foreign Minister.

Orly didn't miss a bite. Nobody else in the café seemed ready to run for a bomb shelter. Eric wondered why not. Iran might be bluffing. But if the Israelis were determined to do what they were doing, the ayatollahs were as determined to stop them.

But when he said so, Orly shook her head. "It's politics," she declared. "Iran spent sixty years not caring about the Temple Mount. Why should she get excited now?"

"Muslims ran things there for sixty years," Eric pointed out. "They were Sunnis, which makes them almost as bad as Jews to the Shiites—"

"But only almost," Orly said. "Or sometimes worse, depending which way the wind is blowing and on who you need to hate on any particular day. Politics, yeah."

The TV cut to missiles on launch rails and radar dishes going around. "The alert level for Israeli Patriot batteries has been increased," the newsman said. "The Ministry of Defense has passed a warning to Iran and all other parties who feel interested in Israeli internal affairs: the country will respond to all aggressive acts. And Israel will respond drastically to any NBC attack."

"Israel doesn't like the Peacock?" Eric said.

That confused Orly, and she'd been in the States. She thought he was talking about the Peacock Throne, the name for Iran's royal seat in the Shah's day. But she knew what the acronym meant: "Nuclear, biological, or chemical attack."

"Oh," Eric said, and it wasn't amusing any more. Somebody must have used the term often enough to coin the acronym for it. Once the flunky here—or at the Pentagon, or in London, or wherever—did, other people in uniform had to decide it was useful, and to keep on saying it. And if that wasn't scary . . .

He'd had too many scary thoughts lately. Perhaps the scariest was that maybe a nuclear war wasn't the worst thing that could happen. *There's* an essay topic, students! Compare and contrast the effects of an all-out nuclear exchange with those of Armageddon and the Apocalypse. Write in blue books, ink only; be sure to organize and present your thoughts clearly. You have three hours. Begin!

The *shawarma* was good, but Eric lost his appetite. That might not be an either-or question. The world might end up with atomic annihilation *and* the End of Days, costarring or in sequence. Like Frost's ice and fire, either could do the job fine.

"We are *so* screwed," he muttered.

"What?" Orly said. Reluctantly, Eric set out his latest gloomy train of thought. She shrugged. "And so? If some maniac in Iran presses the wrong button, or if God decides He'll do what He'll do, how can we stop it?"

"We can't," Eric said. "That's what bothers me."

"So don't let it bother you," Orly said: advice on the order of, *Don't think about a green bird.* She went on, "Why lose sleep over this? I mean, seriously? If you can't change it, you may as well go on, because worrying won't matter anyway."

He thought about that. Then he touched her hand. In the States, he might have kissed her. People here got more uptight about shows of affection. "Either you're the sanest person I ever met or you're out of your mind, one," he told her.

She grinned. "You say the sweetest things."

Connections. They mattered less in Israel than in her neighbors. In Lebanon or Jordan or Egypt, what you knew hardly mattered. Without a friend who could get the ear of someone who mattered, you'd never get the chance to show it off. But Yitzhak Avigad *did* know Rabbi Kupferman, so he was on the Temple Mount when deconstruction began.

A crane swung a hard-hatted technician toward the Dome of the Rock's dome. Another crane swung a cameraman toward him for a close-up of the removal of the first gilded panels from the dome. Yitzhak wondered whether broadcasting this was the smartest thing Israeli TV could do. But what difference did it make? Nobody could keep disassembling the Dome of the Rock a secret.

Up there, the technician detached the panel from the dome. He pulled it free and stuck it in the bucket of the crane behind him. On the ground, Israeli soldiers and civilians, Yitzhak among them, cheered.

"It's quite a moment, isn't it?" someone beside him said.

There stood Shlomo Kupferman. "It is," Yitzhak agreed. "We've only waited two thousand years."

"That building has cluttered up the Temple Mount too long." Kupferman pointed to the Dome of the Rock.

"I should say so," Yitzhak replied.

Directed by the technician's hand signals, the crane swung him to another panel. The man loosened and stowed it. More cheers on the ground, but fewer and quieter. Soon it would all seem routine. The cameraman would go away, and everybody would forget it was happening.

In Israel. In the West. The Muslims wouldn't.

Kupferman said, "We have a perimeter around the Temple Mount. But if they want to bring in a mortar team or shoot rockets at us, they can. No way to cover everything inside several square kilometers."

"No, I suppose not." Yitzhak had done his time in the IDF. He knew you couldn't neutralize such a big area. If the Arabs wanted to make that kind of trouble, they could. Still . . . "This site is holy for them, too. Would they shoot at the Dome of the Rock?"

"After Tel Aviv, who knows what those *mamzrim* will do?" Kupferman said. "Maybe they won't try anything. Maybe they'll wait till we start on the Temple. Who knows? Be ready if the alarms go off."

Be ready for what? Yitzhak wondered. To hit the dirt? What else could you do if mortar rounds landed up here? Not much dirt to hit—mostly the hard walkways atop the Mount. Bursts would kick up nasty fragments.

Another panel came off the Dome of the Rock. The tech stowed it. As he reached for the next one, Kupferman's phone rang. "I'm here," he said, and then, "Oh, they do? . . . Tell them we're going ahead anyway. If they want to try something, they'll be sorry." He stuck the phone back on his belt.

"What's up?" Yitzhak asked.

"The Iranians." The way Kupferman said it, he might have been talking about the Hottentots. "They say that if we don't repair the Dome of the Rock, they'll consider it an act of war against Islam. If the Foreign Minister and the Prime Minister say yes but the Iranians say no, I'll go with our people."

"I guess so." But Yitzhak asked, "What can the Iranians do if they do something?"

"Not my worry. Whatever it is, the Defense Minister thinks we can handle it."

"He'd better be right," Yitzhak said. The Iranians had been enriching uranium for years. They insisted it was for peaceful purposes. Hitler had insisted the Sudetenland was his last claim in Europe. People'd believed him, and regretted it. Nobody particularly believed the Iranians, but nobody seemed eager to stop them, either.

Yitzhak peered east. In the 1980s, Iranian missiles had struck Baghdad. With North Korean help, they had better ones now. If they put bombs in them . . .

Seldom had he had a thought answered so fast—never one he less wanted answered. Alarms wailed, not just on the Temple Mount but throughout Jerusalem—throughout Israel, unless he was wrong. Kupferman's phone rang again. "I'm here," he said. "They did? *Oy!*"

"Who did what?" Yitzhak hoped against hope.

"Those idiots in Teheran. They've launched at us."

"Now what do we do?"

"We see how good the Patriots are. We should know in five or ten minutes."

13

"I have three birds on the screen." Tension filled the Israeli colonel's voice. The Iranians weren't making things easy for the Patriot batteries. Launching three at once, they wanted to overload the antimissiles' response capability.

They were liable to get what they wanted. The Patriots' performance in the first Gulf War was grossly overrated. The hardware was better now, the software *much* better. Still, the new algorithms hadn't been tested in combat. They would be.

Stakes were higher here, too. Saddam's Scuds hadn't carried chemical weapons, let alone nukes. They were just V-2s with different sheet metal. The colonel assumed the Iranians had nuclear weapons and were using them.

He also assumed his head would roll if he didn't kill all three birds—or go up in radioactive gas. *And you* wanted *to be a professional soldier?* he thought. *Why didn't you study the Talmud the way your grandmother wanted?*

"That bird from the northeast will get here a little before the other two," said a captain at one radar screen. The ayatollahs had launched from the northwestern corner of Iran, to shorten the flight time—that area was closest to Israel. Maybe they should have made it land with the other two. The colonel supposed they figured simultaneous launches from different directions would cause more confusion.

Maybe they were right, too.

Nobody here had time to react. Flight time from Iran to Israel was under ten minutes. If a missile dropped nuclear fire on Jerusalem or Tel Aviv, flight time from Israel to Iran was just as short . . . and the Israelis wouldn't use only three launches. Israel didn't turn the other cheek. If it got slapped, it knocked the other guy's head off.

"Bye-bye, ayatollahs," he muttered. "Bye-bye, Teheran." More people in Teheran than in Israel. If the Islamic Republic hadn't cared about that, too bad.

"Launch parameters are go for the first one," the captain said. "Optimum is thirty seconds from . . . *now.*"

"Count it down," the colonel said. This would work, or it wouldn't. Hero or goat. Nothing in between.

He thought so, anyway. Then the radar screens *flashed.* The officers and noncoms in front of them swore in Arabic, Russian, English. The screens weren't supposed to do that.

"Fix the fucking glitch!" the colonel shouted. No, the software *wasn't* combat-tested. But if it had to pick one moment to go south, why did it have to pick this one?

"Can we launch?" a sergeant asked. That was *the* question.

"At what?" the captain said. "The birds are . . . gone."

"What do you mean?" the colonel demanded. "How can they be?"

"They're not on the screens," the captain replied. "I'm picking up aircraft, but the missiles are gone."

"Did the Iranians jam us? If that was jamming . . ."

"If it was, it would've taken the aircraft off the sets, too," the captain said. The colonel nodded. That stood to reason. But if reason was wrong, his country would catch a triple whammy.

"What do we do, sir?" the sergeant said.

"We . . . wait." The colonel checked his watch again and again, as if distrusting the clocks in the Patriots' ground-control systems. He *did* distrust them. After the impossible flash, he distrusted everything about the systems.

At last, he said, "If they were going to hit, they would have by now." He breathed for the first time in what felt like weeks.

"What happened, sir?" the captain asked.

"Beats me." The colonel spread his hands. "Ask God. Maybe He knows."

The captain gave him—and the radar sets—an odd look. "Yes, sir. Maybe He does."

Bend over and kiss your ass goodbye. That was an old American joke about what to do if the missiles flew. Yitzhak Avigad didn't remember where he'd heard it. Like most good jokes, it made too much sense. What else could you do if that happened?

So he stood on the Temple Mount, waiting to see if he would live. He also waited for the roar of Patriots. At least two batteries were close to Jerusalem. He knew he was standing on the Iranians' likeliest target. If they were lousy shots and didn't use nukes, that was the best place to be.

Too many ifs, he decided, and shivered under the sun.

Kupferman was looking at his phone. He started to frown, as if a boy studying for his bar mitzvah were late. "*Something* should have happened," he said. "Either the antimissiles should have launched, or the missiles should have hit, or . . . something."

"I'm fine with nothing," Yitzhak said.

"I want to know what's going on." Kupferman peered at the phone again as he poked in a number. "Put me through to the Defense Minister," he said, and then, angrily, "Who do you think? It's Kupferman. . . . What? Somebody's knocked me out and stolen my phone, and now he's using it for this instead of calling his uncle in Bangladesh? Are you crazy? No thief is that dumb."

The rabbi's sarcasm was fun to listen to—if it wasn't aimed at you.

"Natan? It's Shlomo," Kupferman said. "Did the ayatollahs launch on us? . . . They *did*. . . . What happened? . . . It *did*?" Bushy eyebrows leaped. "Are you sure? . . . Are you as sure as you can be, then? . . . Call me back when you know more. *Shalom*."

"Well?" Yitzhak was ready to tear answers out of him if he had to.

But Kupferman didn't seem ready to give them yet. He looked up at the sky and said, " 'Hear, O Israel, the Lord our God, the Lord is One.' "

"*Well?*" Yitzhak said again, his voice harsher this time.

"Very well, thank you." Kupferman went on, "It was a real launch. Three missiles, two from the east, one from the northeast. The Patriots were about to go, and then . . . the missiles disappeared."

"Disappeared? What does that mean?" Yitzhak asked.

"What it says," Kupferman answered. "One second they were there, the next . . . gone. Off the radar. Not stealth or jamming or anything. Gone. I mean *gone*, or they would have hit by now."

"That's insane," Yitzhak said. "What could do such a thing?"

"Not what," Kupferman said. "Who"—and Yitzhak understood why he'd recited the *Shma*. Could God do *that*? If it wasn't God, what was it? Yitzhak had asked the same question after Brandon dropped dead. You could say that was a coronary or a coincidence . . . if you wanted to. Were three missiles plucked from the sky another coincidence?

Another Americanism sprang to mind. *Yeah, right*.

Rabbi Kupferman's phone rang. He held it to his ear. "Natan? . . .

Oh. *Shalom*, Binyamin." Yitzhak wondered if he should back off. Kupferman was on the horn with the Prime Minister. But, nosy as any other Israeli, he decided to stick around. "What?" the rabbi said, and then, "*What?* . . . They're crazy. We couldn't do that. . . . Yes, of course you know." He was muttering as he put away the phone.

"*Now* what?" Yitzhak said. Too much was happening too fast.

And he thought that before Kupferman said, "The President of the Islamic Republic of Iran is dead. They found him in his office. The Defense Minister of Iran is dead. He died in the middle of a phone call. The Grand Ayatollah is dead. He fell over in a mosque in Qom, in the middle of a sermon about how they would slaughter the infidel. These all happened at the same time as the missiles disappeared. There may be more we don't know about yet."

"My God," Yitzhak said, and then, in a different tone of voice, "My God."

"I think so, too," Kupferman replied.

Al Jazeera laid an Arabic voiceover atop the Farsi feed from Iranian TV. The Israeli channel put a Hebrew voiceover over that. Even at two removes, the Iranian broadcaster sounded frantic. "The murderous Zionist dogs left their handiwork in the President's office!" he shouted, pounding the desktop in front of him. "God will punish their effrontery!"

"How could we?" Orly asked Eric. "Why would we?"

They sat on their bed. They'd been watching the deconstruction of the Dome of the Rock. That turned into a missile attack, which turned into—something else—when the missiles didn't show up. And the something else turned into . . . this.

"See what they did!" the broadcaster on the TV cried, in Farsi via Arabic via Hebrew.

The picture went to the President's office. He still flopped, dead, on his desk. The camera lingered on his expressionless face, then panned to the left, to the wall near a big portrait of Ayatollah Khomeini. The ayatollah's fierce stare seemed aimed at the characters scrawled there.

"See what they did, the dirty Mossad dogs!" the broadcaster said. "They murdered the President of the Islamic Republic of Iran, but mocked him with Hebrew words from their lying scripture. It is from their Book of Daniel—what they call the writing on the wall. *Mene, mene, tekel upharsin*. They want to say that the President of the Islamic Republic of Iran has been weighed in the balance and found wanting—by God, they want the world to believe it!" He pounded his fist again. "They lie!"

"*Gevalt*," Eric muttered. Orly looked down her nose at Yiddish, but he didn't care. Nothing else fit. The Iranians had good scholars on the job—good, but not good enough.

Mene, mene, tekel upharsin wasn't Hebrew. It was Aramaic, the *lingua franca* of the Middle East in the sixth century BC. Nebuchadnezzar of Babylon wouldn't have understood Hebrew. Well, he didn't understand Aramaic, either (or, more likely, didn't read it— he probably clung to cuneiform)—he needed Daniel to interpret for him.

And the message was written in an Aramaic script obsolete for 2,000 years, though the modern Hebrew alphabet sprang from it, not from the one the Hebrews originally used. If a Mossad hit man killed the President of Iran, would he have added that message? Would he have known enough to add it in that script?

This on top of how could an Israeli hit man take out the President of Iran at the instant the Iranians were launching missiles at Israel? Were his guards asleep? At *that* moment?

What about the Defense Minister's guards?

What about the Grand Ayatollah, who dropped dead in front of thousands of people? Didn't *he* have guards, too? He had to have more than the President of Iran did.

"The Mossad's good, but not *that* good," Orly said. "Nobody's *that* good."

"Well, if they didn't nail the Iranians, who did?" Eric asked.

"*I* don't know." Orly sounded impatient. "The same person who grabbed three missiles out of the air."

"Nobody could do that, either." Rationally, Eric knew he was right. But the rational and what happened kept getting disconnected from each other.

Orly shook her head. "*Somebody* could. *Somebody* did," she said. Ice walked up Eric's spine, because he knew Whom she meant.

Jamal Ashrawi *believed*. You didn't get to be Grand Mufti because you knew the right people, though that helped. But you needed fire in your belly, too. Ashrawi had it, and it had sustained him through thick and thin—through years of thin.

The Iranians also believed. They might believe wrongly, but they weren't as bad as the Jews. And they believed fiercely. That often counted more in the *jihad* against Zionism.

Now, Jamal Ashrawi didn't know *what* to believe.

Iran *had* launched missiles at Israel. (What would have happened to Hebron if a missile came down on it instead of Jerusalem a few kilometers away never crossed his mind.) The Israelis *hadn't* launched antimissiles. They couldn't have kept it secret. Ashrawi couldn't think of anything more public than a missile launch.

But the Iranian rockets hadn't come down anywhere. If the Israelis knew why not, they weren't saying. If the Iranians knew, they weren't, either.

They *were* saying the Israelis had decapitated their country. They weren't saying how; either they didn't know or were too embarrassed to admit they did. The nonsense from Daniel . . . Ashrawi had to borrow a Bible from a Christian Arab to understand that.

When he did, a shiver ran through him. Jews and Christians

distorted their holy books. But not *everything* in the Bible was a lie. The holy Qur'an made that plain. Figuring out what was true, what twisted, and what false . . . God knew, and the Prophet, but it was harder for an ordinary mortal.

Daniel had prophesied that Nebuchadnezzar would fall, and Nebuchadnezzar fell. So Daniel was a true prophet. Then the Persians took over the Near East, which to Ashrawi only proved God had lapses in taste.

And now the Israelis were mocking those Persians (well, their descendants, but memories ran deep in this part of the world) with the prophecy that brought down the King of Babylon! It had to be the Israelis. Though how they'd bagged the Grand Ayatollah in the mosque in Qom . . . If they could do that, Ashrawi knew he wasn't safe himself.

Al Jazeera cut away from the Iranians. An announcer said, "American sources confirm the Islamic Republic of Iran launched three missiles at Israel. Halfway to their destination, they disappeared from radar for no known reason."

Halfway between Iran and the Zionist entity was over western Iraq. Suspicion flared in the Grand Mufti. Maybe the Americans had something to do with it. Who could guess what secrets were hidden in the desert?

The newsman went on, "These sources deny the United States shot down the missiles. The Americans are as baffled as the Israelis, who were about to launch Patriots against the rockets from the east."

Someone handed him a sheet of paper. "This just in," he said. "Russian sources confirm the missiles vanished from their radar installations in Syria. 'We don't know who did it, or how,' one Russian said. 'We wish we did.' "

If the Russians doubted the Americans knocked down the missiles, they probably didn't. Did the Zionists? Ashrawi couldn't believe it. If they did, they would have bragged about it.

"The Americans didn't do it," a Hamas man said. "The Jews didn't." He must have been thinking with Ashrawi. "Who did?"

"Maybe the missiles were flawed," another man said. "Maybe the same thing made all three blow up. I wouldn't drive a car an Iranian made." Several people nodded.

"But they didn't blow up," the Grand Mufti said. "They just disappeared. That's why the scientists are going crazy." All Arabs knew Iranians were arrogant and incompetent. But they also knew Western scientists *weren't* incompetent, no matter how arrogant they were.

"I don't see how the Zionists could have done all that," the Christian Arab said. "The timing is too good."

"Who did?" Ashrawi said. "The Americans?" Everybody laughed. The Americans might have knocked down the missiles. But those assassinations? Not a chance. Saddam Hussein in his glory days couldn't have brought off three simultaneous, widely separated hits in Iran. The FSB couldn't, either. And the Americans had always been inept at such things.

The Christian Arab took back his Bible. "God knows who did it," he said.

"God wills it!" Lester Stark's fist crashed down on the pulpit. The gesture wasn't scripted. You had to leave room for spontaneity, or your preaching would feel canned. "God wills it!" he repeated. "Can there be any doubt?"

There could always be doubt. Still, he hoped some of his listeners would remember that *God wills it!* was the Crusaders' battle cry. Then he remembered the hysterical Iranian broadcaster slamming his fist down on the desktop. He wished he hadn't done it himself.

He couldn't take it back. "In destroying the missiles aimed at holy Jerusalem, and in destroying the men who sought to harm it and prevent the Third Temple, God has shown His power over our world."

"That's right, Reverend!" somebody yelled.

"Tell it!" someone else added.

"God wants the Temple to rise again *now*," Stark said. "Do you know what that means?"

"Tell it!" The shout rose again.

"It means the Last Days may be upon us," the preacher said. His televised colleagues said more than that. They left their listeners no room for doubt. For them, the Second Coming would happen week after next. If it didn't . . . They'd find some way to get around that, too. They always did.

He worried again about being lukewarm. He also worried about his colleagues' sincerity. Of his own he was sure. He hoped his listeners would notice. He *really* hoped God would. If God saw the falling sparrow, He might glance toward Lester Stark.

He stretched his hands toward the congregation. "I'm going to talk about the elephant in the room," he said. "The elephant in the room is God. I've talked about God for a long time. But when I talk to you about God, I'm preaching to the choir."

The camera cut away from him to show the choir in their blue satin robes. Some smiled self-consciously. Others nodded. Still others looked straight ahead.

"When I talk now, I'm talking about people in power," Stark went on. His image returned to the monitors. "They pretend the elephant in the room isn't there. They want to pretend *He* isn't there. Then they can keep doing things the way they always have.

"But it won't work any more, will it? Because the elephant *is* in the room. They can pretend all they want, but pretending won't make it go away. Pretending won't make *Him* go away.

"In a news conference, the Secretary of Defense said he didn't know why the Iranian missiles disappeared. As far as he knew, it was impossible. But it happened anyway. When something is impossible but happens anyway, what do we call it?"

"A miracle!" The congregation didn't let him down.

He nodded. "That's right. It *is*. When the three men responsible for launching those wicked missiles die at the same time as the rockets disappear, what's *that*?"

"A miracle!"

"Right again," Stark said. "Our friends in Israel say they didn't do it. I have assurances from my friend, Rabbi Shlomo Kupferman, the Israeli Religious Affairs Minister, that they didn't. I believe him. He was on the Temple Mount when the missiles flew. He would have been at ground zero, but he lived, praise the Lord."

"Praise the Lord!" the congregation echoed.

"The Iranians admit their best doctors can't say why their leaders died. They just did—the way Brandon Nesbitt died when he transgressed God's will." Stark paused. "What more do world leaders want? What more do our leaders want? Can't they see? *The times have changed.* How loud must the elephant trumpet before they hear? When the Tribulation comes, which side will they be on?"

He paused again. "I want to make sure they're on the Lord's side. I want you to help me. Contact your Representative or Senator. If you don't know how, go to my Web site."

The monitors ran the URL superimposed on his picture. Some people in the congregation wrote it down. Most already had it bookmarked, though. Fewer in TV land would. If they didn't need to Google it, they were more likely to use it.

"My site has mailing, e-mail, and Twitter addresses for every Representative and Senator. If you don't know whose district you're in, enter your Zip code and find out. And it has the President's mailing address and e-mail address and Twitter handle, too. These people will only know what you think if you tell them. So tell them!"

Other ministers pushed more political buttons than he did. He hoped that meant Congress would take more notice when his audience sent messages. He hoped to make Congress pay attention. Lots of Congressfolk were secular. If God walked into their office, they might not believe He was there.

But if enough voters believed . . . their elected representatives would act as if they did. It might not save their souls. With luck, it would save the country.

As Stark stepped away from the pulpit, he nodded. He couldn't make politicans come to him or Jesus. That lay between them and God. If he could make them act responsibly, he'd be satisfied.

"What happens after the Temple goes up again, Reverend?" a plump woman asked.

"I'd expect the Antichrist to follow," Stark answered. "In what form and when? I don't know. That's in God's hands."

She nodded. "Isn't it exciting?"

"It is," Lester Stark agreed. "But frightening, too, because it's so easy to be led astray. We think it can't happen to us, and that's the Antichrist's greatest weapon."

"*You* don't need to worry, Reverend," the plump woman said, which proved she wasn't listening.

But, because she wasn't, she wouldn't understand if he explained—she had preconceptions filling the slot where the explanation fit. So many people were like that. "I pray, that's all," Stark said, and left it there.

Why this is hell, nor am I out of it. Gabriela Sandoval first ran into that line of Marlowe's in a sophomore English Lit class. It had stuck with her ever since. When things went wrong, it seemed to describe life in ten words. When César dumped her, when the judge said he could keep Heather all the time, when she did her damnedest to scuttle her own career . . . Yeah, the world looked inescapably hellish at times like that.

As it did now. People didn't know why she hadn't shown up at the Shrine of the Book. She and Saul both knew they had to keep that quiet. *Gabriela and Brandon* would have been a bad reality show, not something real, if word ever got out that Brandon doped Gabriela. And that would have been a total catastrophe just when the show was starting to win its cohosts some fresh credibility.

Just to make things more fun, she and Brandon had partnered with Saul on the business side of the venture. Saul had a will. Gabriela had a will. Brandon, it turned out, had shuffled off this mortal coil without one. All of his relatives, by blood or by former marriage, thought they were entitled to all of his assets. All of them lawyered up as fast as they could. Dorsal fins started circling in the blood-stained legal waters.

Gabriela and Saul had lawyers of their own, of course. So did *Gabriela and Brandon*. It got complicated and expensive, because not all the attorneys pulled in the same direction. Gabriela—and *Gabriela and Brandon*—could afford that for a while. But the entity that had been *Gabriela and Brandon* was in deep financial kimchi if this trip to Israel went down the toilet without yielding a lot more than it had so far.

"Lemme lay it out for you," Saul said to Gabriela when she was fully functional and when the excitement about Brandon's untimely demise had died down a bit—though it still wasn't as dead as he was. "We had a blockbuster here. The way Brandon bought it proves we did. We should ride that as hard and as far as we can."

"I know." She sat on the edge of her bed, head down, the heels of her hands pressing against her eyes. "But it makes me sick. Everybody goes on about how bravely he died—"

"Not everybody," Buchbinder broke in. "There are all the *He-messed-with-God-so-he-deserved-what-he-got* folks, too."

"He deserved what he got, but not on account of that." Gabriela still didn't want to think God could reach out and strike someone dead. She *really* didn't want to think she would have been that someone if Brandon hadn't drugged her. No matter what Rabbi Kupferman said, she hadn't believed touching the Ark could kill. Who in his or her right mind took that Old Testament shit seriously?

Evidently God did. There sure wasn't any other explanation for Brandon Nesbitt's death.

"This is what we've got right now." Saul plainly didn't like contemplating a large, muscular, divine thumb coming down on the earthly scales, either. "We have all the stuff from Tel Aviv after the dirty bomb went off. We have the footage of the Ark coming out and going across Jerusalem. We have the interviews you and Brandon did. We still need to film at the kibbutz with the red heifer."

"If we add all that in with what we'll get from the Dome of the Rock coming down and the Third Temple going up, we can put together a pretty fair Last Days package. That should pay some bills," Gabriela said.

"Some, yeah." Saul paused. Gabriela knew that meant things were going to get difficult. The producer didn't like quarrels. He got into them, but he had to nerve himself for them first. "But this is a religious mess, and you aren't the most religious person who ever came down the pike. Brandon wasn't, either. That'll hurt marketing."

"What have you got in mind?" Gabriela asked carefully.

"It's not my idea, actually. One of my lawyers suggested it to me." No, Saul wasn't going to take any heat he didn't have to. After the disclaimer, he went on, "He said maybe you should get an evangelical trained seal to narrate some of this stuff—put a pious spin on it, like. That'll help pull in the born-agains, the folks who look for a preacher-man to talk to them about religion." *Trained seal* was lawyerspeak for an expert who'd trot out what he knew for cash.

Preacher-man grated. Gabriela got that one of the reasons people didn't take her as seriously as they should have was that she peed sitting down. But, while she hated that, she knew it was there. And she knew she wasn't religious enough to satisfy all the target demographic. Cautiously, she asked, "Who does your lawyer have in mind?"

"He started down from the top," Saul said. "First name he picked was Robertson, but Pat's pissed off the Israelis, so that won't fly."

"He's old as the hills, too," Gabriela said.

"Older," the producer agreed. "He also mentioned Falwell's kid, but we would like to sell this in blue states, too, right?"

"Might be nice," Gabriela said. *Don't throw away audience ahead of time* was good advice any time. "Who, then?"

"The next name Moishe came up with was Lester Stark. He's into this stuff," Saul said.

"Is he?" Gabriela knew Stark's name—who didn't?—but little about the preacher's interests.

"Yeah, he is. I did my homework after Moishe mentioned him. The guy is pretty sane. I think you can work with him. He's not poor—don't get me wrong—but the place he lives in wouldn't make Trump jealous or anything. And he's still married to the gal he started dating in high school. No sexy secretaries, no choirboys, none of that crap. I even read some of his sermons online."

"*Did* you?" Gabriela made sure she sounded impressed. By the way Buchbinder said it, he wanted a medal for courage above and beyond the call of duty. He might deserve one, too.

"Sure did." Yeah, Saul was proud of himself. "And you know what? They aren't too bad. The guy can write English, which not everybody can these days. He talks about stuff that worries people.

When he quotes the Bible, he doesn't sound like he's twisting its arm to get it to say what he wants it to, either."

"All right, you've convinced me," Gabriela said. "I'll call him. If he says no, we take another step down, that's all. Thanks."

"All part of the service," the producer answered.

As soon as he left, Gabriela phoned Birmingham, Alabama. She didn't think she'd ever done that before. She needed a few minutes to wade through flunkies and get to Stark's administrative assistant, and a few more to convince the man she was who she said she was.

"Hold, please, Ms. Sandoval," the administrative assistant said. "Reverend Stark should decide whether he wants to hear more about this."

Music played in Gabriela's ear. It didn't sound sappy, the way she'd figured a televangelist's hold music would. It was just . . . there. Then it wasn't. "Lester Stark here, Ms. Sandoval. Jeremy says you have something on your mind that might interest me."

Wow! That's a hell of a voice. The thought was more reverent than not. A TV preacher had to have good pipes. But Stark's warm baritone was better than good. He would have pulled people in reading the phone book, never mind Revelation.

His voice was so good, Gabriela needed a beat before answering, "That's right, Reverend." She'd dealt with a good many clerics, even if most of them came from Stark's left. "I was wondering if you'd like to help continue and complete the work Brandon Nesbitt and I began before his untimely demise." *The filthy turdface,* she added, but only to herself. Yes, you had to sit on some stories.

"I must tell you, I don't care for much of the coverage you folks gave from Israel," Stark said. "Mr. Nesbitt struck me as being out for his own glory first, for anything sensational after that, and for faith, which lies at the heart of everything, only as an afterthought. He might still be living had he taken faith more seriously."

Yeah, and I might be dead instead, Gabriela thought. *But you're right the first time, and the second, and the third*. She said, "Brandon was who he was. If you join me, you can help give future work the balance you feel it should have."

"You don't balance mistaken views, Ms. Sandoval. You correct them." Lester Stark had his own opinions, all right.

So did Gabriela, but she was convinced reasonable people could reach reasonable compromises . . . most of the time, anyway. If she and Stark couldn't here, she *would* try somebody else. She said, "I think we're saying the same thing in different words, so let's not get anti-semantic, okay?"

She also needed to know if the horrid pun would be too pungent for him. After some silence, he said, "Go on."

"Nobody knows how this will turn out. Well, God does, but He's not telling us ahead of time," Gabriela said. "Brandon knew what he thought—"

"And he touched the Ark after repeated warnings not to, and paid for his transgression with his life," Stark said.

And I would have done the same thing if the motherfucker hadn't doped me, Gabriela thought. *There but for the grace of God went I—the grace of God or a bad-odds roll in the crapshoot of life.*

She wouldn't tell Stark any of that. It still freaked her out, and likely would for years. "What you say is true. Brandon was a long way from perfect," she said. *You have no idea how far, either*. More things she wouldn't say. She did go on, "But he was right a lot of the time, and he was brave most of the time. Yes, he had an eye for the main chance. We wouldn't have been in Israel or been able to get those great reports after the Arabs dirty-bombed Tel Aviv otherwise. He deserves credit." *And I deserve an Emmy for Best Bullshit in a Starring Role, and* Gabriela and Brandon *deserves a helping hand. Needs one, anyway.*

"You're right when you say no man is of a piece," Stark replied. "I wish Mr. Nesbitt hadn't put his talent to some of the uses he did. . . . What do you want me to do, and what arrangements do you propose?"

For Gabriela, explaining what she had in mind was easy. How much to offer . . . With most people, she would have lowballed the first time. With Stark, she made her best offer right away. Sometimes you had to know when not to bullshit.

"Well," Stark said—the number must have been bigger than he expected. While he might not crap in a solid-gold toilet like some TV preachers, he wasn't allergic to cash. Who was? He continued, "That . . . does appear satisfactory. If our legal and financial people can firm up everything along those lines, discussions will definitely go forward."

Once I'm sure you can pay what you say you'll pay, Gabriela translated without malice. "Wonderful!" she said. "Thank you!"

"And in case of Rapture, all debts are paid," Stark added, which wasn't a bad comeback for *anti-semantic.* He added, "I was thinking about going to the Holy Land soon. I take this as a sign I should."

"Wonderful!" Gabriela said again. She felt redeemed. Brandon was gone—to hell, with any luck—but *Gabriela and Brandon* would have more product.

14

"Come on, Shoshanah! Come on, Rosie!" a man coaxed.

Chaim Avigad watched helplessly from his apartment window as the red heifer got into her trailer. A couple of carrots were more persuasive than her Hebrew or her English name.

"She's going to Jerusalem!" Despair filled Chaim's voice.

"Of course she is," his mother answered. She'd never understood what was bothering him.

"They're going to kill her!" Chaim cried.

"They have to, sweetie." Rivka Avigad did her best to sound consoling, but her heart wasn't in it. Chaim could tell. She went on, "The Temple's about to go up. We'll be able to celebrate our religion the way God always meant us to. They need to sanctify the ground, and the workers, too. And they have to sacrifice a red heifer to do that. I know you're fond of Shoshanah, but—"

Chaim spun away. "God is stupid!" he yelled. "If you have to kill something to make something else holy, what's the use?"

"I don't know what you want me to say," his mother replied. "It's in the Scriptures. It wouldn't be if God didn't want it. If it's something He needs, who are we to question Him?"

"Somebody ought to," Chaim said. "It's silly."

"Is it any sillier than raising children in buildings on stilts?" his mother replied. "I thought that was worthwhile, and so did your father. We never argued about that." Her mouth twisted. They'd argued about plenty of other things; Chaim remembered the fights from when he was little. She'd raised him by herself since, and she got on a lot better with Uncle Yitzhak than she ever had with Chaim's dad. He couldn't remember the last time Tzvi Avigad came around. He had his own, much less pious, life now.

"Nobody ever asked me what I thought about that," Chaim said.

Rivka Avigad sighed. "No, nobody did. So what? All of us who agreed to bring up our boys like this, we were doing God's will. See how things are coming together? The red heifer, and the Ark, and rebuilding the Temple at last, and the miracle He worked when He stopped the rockets and killed the wicked leaders who launched them . . ."

"Why didn't He keep the terrorists from setting off the dirty bomb in Tel Aviv, then, if He's working miracles?" Chaim asked.

Down below, they were closing the trailer and hitching it up to a muscular American pickup. Armored personnel carriers belched diesel fumes into the air. They would protect Rosie all the way. *Oh, boy,* Chaim thought. *They don't want anybody killing her till they can do it themselves. Big deal!*

He missed some of his mother's answer. When he started paying attention again, she was saying, "—think we needed that bomb in Tel Aviv. It woke people up. It made sure Israel has the government to want to restore the Temple."

"So God blew up a thousand people and made lots more radioactive, so He could get His temple back?" Chaim said. "Wasn't there an easier way?"

"God doesn't worry about easy. He does what suits Him, not what suits us."

Brandon could have argued with her. He was weird, but Chaim didn't think he'd been *bad*. God evidently had a different opinion. And He'd massacred Job's family—or let Satan do it, which was the same thing—without blinking. Chaim had already gone 'round and 'round on that with his mother and his uncle. You couldn't win, not against them or against God.

"You'll be one of the boys who carry water from the Pool of Siloam for the sacrifice," his mother said. "You'll remember it the rest of your life. There can't be a bigger honor."

"Mom—" What could he say? "How is it an honor when I have to help them kill my friend?"

"Abraham was ready to give God his son where the Holy of Holies will be again," Rivka Avigad said. "If Abraham would do that, can't you can spare God a cow?"

"But God didn't take Isaac," Chaim said.

"No. He took a ram. How is a ram different from a cow?"

Chaim knew the answer. The ram was just there. Abraham hadn't got to know it beforehand. No wonder he didn't feel bad sacrificing it. Whoever sacrificed Rosie wouldn't know her the way Chaim did, either. Maybe it wouldn't bother him. It would bother Chaim.

"It's not right!" he said. "We haven't sacrificed anything for all these years. Why do we need to start over now?"

"Because God wants us to. Because He knows we're supposed to now," his mother answered. "Why are we here, if not to fulfill His plan?"

For ourselves, Chaim thought. Brandon would have said something like that. Chaim didn't believe it—except now he wanted to. But he believed what he'd been taught since he was old enough to understand it. How could he help believing it?

"It's not fair to Rosie," he muttered. "She didn't ask to be born to get her throat cut."

"You're looking at it backwards," his mother said. "God made a perfect red heifer be born now, when we need it most. Wouldn't it be a sin to waste what He's given us? Everything would stay impure forever if we did."

"I guess." But defiance died hard in Chaim. "He still should have found some other way to take care of it."

"I can't do anything about that, and neither can you," Rivka Avigad replied. "It's in the Scriptures, so that's how God wants it. Even the sages in days gone by didn't understand why He wants it like that, but He does. We make the sacrifice *because* He wants it. We don't have to know anything else."

"I guess," Chaim said again. His gaze slid toward Jerusalem. *You can't do anything about it, Mom, but maybe I can.*

How long had it been since the stone where Abraham almost sacrificed Isaac (or Ishmael), on which the Ark probably rested (or above which it possibly floated), from which Muhammad ascended to heaven, the stone that carried more myth, legend, *baggage* than any other chunk of rock in the whole world, last saw the light of day?

Over 1,300 years: Eric had made the calculation before. How long had the baggage been piling up? Close to 4,000 years. By that reckoning, Muhammad was a recent visitor, and the time where the stone stayed under the Dome of the Rock not so long.

When he said so to Orly, she nodded. "Some people will tell you this is where God made Adam, too," she said. "That stretches things back even further."

"It does," Eric agreed. He lived in a Darwinian world, where apelike things evolved into more manlike things, where life stretched back billions of years. Next to that, the 5,700-odd years the Jewish calendar reckoned since the creation of the world weren't much. When you looked at them by themselves, though, they made a fair chunk of change.

But hadn't God—if not the guy in the Old Testament, a mighty reasonable facsimile—struck a man dead for touching the Ark? That said nothing about more recent developments, about which your views could differ according to your religious and political prejudices. Nobody could deny that some powerfully weird shit was going down.

"Duh!" Orly said when Eric came out with that. "I'd rather believe in Mossad men who learned Aramaic to spook the Iranians, but I can't. Where did the missiles go?"

"Into the place between the stars?" Eric suggested. Orly gave him a quizzical look. He went on, "That's what a lot of believers are saying."

"Those people are crazy." Orly spoke with her usual self-assurance. It didn't last this time. "They may be crazy, but that doesn't mean they're wrong."

"I know," Eric said. "That's what I just figured out, and that's what I'm worried about."

At the southern end of the Temple Mount, saws like the one that had cut through the wall in front of the Ark were biting into Al-Aqsa Mosque. The din wasn't the only thing that raised Eric's hackles. Muslims from Rabat to Jakarta were screaming their heads off. But after what had happened to the Iranian rockets—and to the men who'd launched them—no one was doing anything but screaming.

The mosque's silver dome—it suffered by comparison to the Dome of the Rock—had already come down. The handwritten Qur'ans and other exhibits in the museum next door had already been moved . . . by Israeli Arabs. Cooperating with the government to handle that took either courage or collaboration. Eric was damned if he knew which. He also wondered whether Munir al-Nuwayhi had been involved in any of that. He hadn't run into the Muslim archaeologist since the last time he was up on the Temple Mount.

Yellow tape marked off a square around the sacred stone. It showed the dimensions of the Holy of Holies in the First Temple—and, presumably, those of the Holy of Holies in the Third Temple.

Eric and Orly had both stepped way inside that perimeter when they looked around in the Dome of the Rock. "How does it feel to violate religious law?" he asked.

She gave back an impish grin. "Which one?"

His answering smile was forced. She'd been shocked to find he ate pork. Lots of American Jews did. Hardly any Israelis matched them, even Jews who called themselves secular. Only the tiny Christian minority here had anything to do with pork. Jews and Muslims who agreed on nothing else joined in despising it.

Depends on what you're used to, he thought, and laughed at himself. Talk about unoriginal! The ancient Greeks put it into a handful of words: *custom is king of all.* Wasn't that the truth? And couldn't so much *tsuris* have been avoided if it weren't?

"Do they know where they'll rebuild the Dome and Al-Aqsa?" he asked.

"Nobody's told me," Orly answered. "Maybe Yoram's heard."

"Maybe," Eric said. "Hard to see him these days, or even talk to him."

"Tell me about it," she said.

He tried to be sympathetic: "If you've just made the biggest archaeological find ever, what do you do for an encore? What *can* you do? Maybe he needs time to figure that out."

"Or maybe he's fixing things so he and Kupferman get to publish and nobody else does," Orly said.

"I don't like to think he'd pull anything like that," Eric said slowly. Not liking it didn't mean it couldn't happen. Archaeology was as political as other academic disciplines. Who got credit and who lost it made and broke careers—and friendships. "He's good olive oil." The Israeli phrase meant somebody you could count on.

"*Alevai,*" Orly said. But she rubbed her first and second fingers against her thumb. "I just hope he isn't slippery like oil. And Kupferman . . ." She didn't go on.

She didn't need to. Eric would have trusted Shlomo Kupferman to do all he could to give the Arabs one in the nuts and rebuild the Temple. If that involved screwing people he worked with, he would. Eric was convinced of it.

Before his gloomy reflections could go any further, Orly made a different discontented noise. "What now?" Eric asked.

"Little Miss Sunshine," Orly answered.

Here came Barb Taylor, glistening with sunscreen but pink anyway. Her floppy hat kept her from burning worse, but only at the price of making her look even frumpier than she would have otherwise. *She's on Yoram's list,* Eric reminded himself. *I wonder why.* She waved to Eric and Orly.

"Isn't it exciting?" she said. "He's coming!"

"I thought you said He came a long time ago," Orly said snarkily. Jews in the States didn't mock Christians like that. It had to have something to do with growing up as a majority, not two percent of the population.

But it didn't faze Barb. Hardly anything did. "Oh, I didn't mean Him," she said. "I meant Lester Stark. If he's coming to Israel, he must think the Last Days *are* close."

"Oh, joy," Orly said. "Another know-nothing preacher. Just what we need."

"He is not!" Barb sounded as close to indignant as Eric had heard her. He didn't blame her, or not too much. As televangelists went, Stark seemed fairly sane. The competition got stiffer on what looked to him like the other end of the woo-woo scale.

"He'll probably come down with Jerusalem Syndrome," Orly said.

Maybe the background snarl of saws ripping into Al-Aqsa Mosque kept Barb from hearing that. Or maybe she didn't know what Jerusalem Syndrome meant. Eric did. Every year, tourists flipped out and decided they were Biblical characters—David or Samson if they were Jews, Jesus or Mary if Christians. That sort of craziness had been going on since before Israel gained independence. Usually, getting the sufferers out of town was part of the cure.

"I like the way he looks at the Bible," Barb said.

"The Bible he looks at is too fat," Orly retorted.

"I don't think so," Barb said tranquilly. "It's all God talking. I suppose He was talking to the Muslims, too, even if they don't hear Him the way we do."

Where *did* she buy her theology? Next thing you knew, she'd be saying kind things about Hindus or Buddhists. That wasn't the usual born-again style.

Orly didn't want to let Barb off the hook. "You don't hear Him the way *we* do." She held Eric's hand to show who *we* was. Nothing like a Christian to make a secular Jew sound Orthodox.

Barb only shrugged. "I know you don't believe Jesus was the Messiah. That's okay. When the Last Days come and it gets sorted out, you'll see. God's working this through you, after all."

"Let it alone," Eric said in Hebrew to Orly, who looked ready to spit rivets. "You won't change her mind and you won't make her mad, at least not where it shows."

Deliberately using a language Barb didn't speak was patronizing if not insulting. Since Orly was being more insulting in a language Barb *did* speak, Eric felt only a small twinge of guilt.

The plain, middle-aged American woman kept smiling. She touched the brim of her hat and said, "I'm off to watch them take down the mosque. That's not something you see every day." Away she went. She pulled a disposable Kodak from her purse and started snapping pictures. She *would* be somebody who clung to film after the rest of the world used ones and zeros.

"The nerve!" If Orly couldn't take it out on Barb, she would on Eric. "If she thinks her crappy God is doing this—"

"Whose God do you want?" Eric broke in. "Rabbi Kupferman's? The Grand Ayatollah's?"

Orly's suggestion about what Kupferman and the late Grand Ayatollah could do violated Leviticus 18:22. She added, "Or with a sheep," which took care of the next verse. That seemed to soften her temper; she went on, "What I *want* is for things to go back the way they were before this started."

"Sure. Me, too," Eric said. "But what are the odds?"

A crane took hold of a wall section that had just been separated from what remained of Al-Aqsa Mosque. Diesel engine belching, the crane swung the panel onto a truck that took it down a ramp laid over the steps of the Bab al-Maghariba. Eric didn't like seeing the Temple Mount turned into a dusty, smelly construction site, but he couldn't do thing one about it.

Was this what God had in mind? Barb Taylor seemed to think so. If it wasn't God's idea, who was in charge? Anybody?

Satellite dishes sprouted all over the West Bank, occupied though it was. Jamal Ashrawi wondered whether there was any place these days where they didn't sprout. He could watch Al Jazeera. He could watch the Hezbollah station, which made Al Jazeera seem reactionary. He could look at the Zionists' lies. And he could watch as much American television as he could stand.

The Grand Mufti of Jerusalem stayed away from CNN and Fox. To him, they were as bad as the Israeli stations. He found himself watching preachers who sold their lying religion over the air.

"Will you convert to Christianity?" a guard asked him with a mocking grin on his face.

"By God, no!" Haji Jamal answered. "The Prophet, peace be unto Him, rightly ordered death for those who abandon Islam."

"Then why poison your eyes with these talking turds?" the younger man said. "Whenever they open their mouths, filth comes out."

"What they say is filth," Ashrawi agreed. "How they say it, though . . . is very clever. They persuade those who believe as they do to do as they say and send them money: millions of dollars."

"And so?" the guard sneered. "What does that show except that American Christians are fools, sheep who deserve the fleecing their holy men give them? This we knew."

"One other thing," the Grand Mufti said. Despite the fighter's skeptical grunt, he went on, "It shows how to inspire people. The American Christians do it for wicked purposes, but the things they do we can use to promote God's truth. They know how to work their people up. We could use that now."

He got another grunt from the guard. Morale on the West Bank was low. Ashrawi knew he wasn't the first Muslim to use the Christians' notions against the Jews. In the 1990s, an Egyptian had written a book called *The False Messiah* that drew on one distorted faith's beliefs to discredit another. The book had had imitators, too. But now the hour was at hand.

The Grand Mufti preached in the main mosque in Hebron after noon prayers on Friday. Somebody was bound to inform on him, so he was ready for a quick getaway. He and the men outside the mosque with assault rifles were also ready for a fight.

"You think times are hard," he told the faithful. Men with phones filmed his sermon. Soon TV and the Internet would take his words around the world.

"You think times are hard," Haji Jamal repeated, "and, by God, you are right. The Jews gloat that their foolish Temple will rise, replacing the holy Dome of the Rock and Al-Aqsa Mosque. They think their Messiah is at hand. The Christians, who lie when they say the prophet Jesus, peace be upon Him, is the Son of God, believe the rebuilding of the Temple foretells the rise of the Antichrist and the Second Coming of Jesus."

He made a slashing motion with his hand. "The Jews and Christians are right—and wrong. They are right when they say the Hour is nearly come. God will do what He wants in this world when He wants to—and the time is near.

"But it will not be what the misbelievers think. Take heart, believers! Let the Jews and Christians fool themselves by believing God will be good to them at the Hour. He whom the Jews proclaim the Messiah will be the False One instead.

"Let him seem to conquer. Let him seem to grind us underfoot. But Jesus will return—not as the Christians say, but with the holy Mahdi at His side. Together, they will smash the Jews and their lies. In the last battle, trees and stones will shout out that they have Jews hiding behind them, and Muslims will go forth and kill them. Believe this, for God ordains it."

He could see they wanted to believe. They called the war that created the Zionist entity *al-naqbah*: the catastrophe. They'd seen another catastrophe in the Setback—what the West called the Six-Day War. Ashrawi had been just too young to fight then. Now the Israelis were grinding their faces in the dirt again. How could they bear it and remain men? No one with red blood could.

"Once the False One is defeated, Christians will go down, too. Their crosses will break. The whole world will become Muslim. At the valley of Jehosaphat outside Jerusalem, God will judge everyone who ever lived. Sinners and misbelievers will get what they deserve, and good Muslims will know Paradise for eternity. You have only to believe, and you can make it happen.

"When the Jews lay impious hands on Al-Aqsa Mosque, do they not follow what is foretold in the Qur'an? For does not the blessed Prophet say in the sura called The Night Journey that the Jews would be twice corrupted, and that God would send an army to enter the mosque and punish them for it? You know the verses— see here the interpretation. So I say again, take heart! Yes, they ravish the mosque, but they will pay!"

When he looked out at the sea of men listening to him, he saw they were *hearing* him, too. If you saw things the right way, the way God wanted you to, you saw they weren't disasters after all, but part of His plan.

"Let the Jews gloat and strut. Let the Christians broadcast their nonsense. We will see who rejoices and who laments when the Hour comes—and I do not think we have long to wait."

Cheers buoyed him, sweet and strong as wine in Paradise. *Let the Zionists howl,* he thought. *It will be too late, for the truth will run ahead of them, the way truth always does.*

The Holy Land! Not even a long flight and the indignities of customs could remove the exclamation point from Lester Stark's mind. Rhonda was even more excited; she came here less often than he did.

The Israelis did their best to show him their land was mundane as well as holy. They closely examined his luggage. An inspector said, "You're a Christian minister?"

"That's right," Stark answered.

"Purpose of your visit to *Eretz Yisrael*?"

"Journalism, mostly. I want to see the Temple rise."

If that wasn't a skeptical snort, Stark had never heard one. "You aren't going to try to convert any Jews, right?" the customs man said. *You'd better not,* his tone warned.

"No, I'm not here for that." Stark could have added commentary on what would happen when the Last Days came, but he doubted the Israeli official would have appreciated it.

"You're sure?" the man said. He had bad breath.

"Yes, I'm sure. If you doubt it, call Rabbi Kupferman. He'll vouch for me." Stark's patience frayed.

But he'd found a name to conjure with. "You . . . know the Religious Affairs Minister?" the customs man said.

Stark took out his phone. "Look—here's his number. Shall *I* call him?"

The customs official weighed the risks. "No, never mind," he said. The inspection didn't last much longer. Stark's luggage passed. He hadn't expected anything else.

Gabriela Sandoval waited beyond the customs area. She looked casual, but professional. She wore jeans, but plainly designer jeans, and her makeup was almost camera-ready. "So good to meet you, Reverend," she said. "And you, Mrs. Stark. Rhonda, isn't it? May I?"

"Of course, Gabriela." Rhonda Stark smiled. So did Lester; he thought better of the TV personality for including his wife so naturally.

Gabriela had a limo waiting for the trip to Jerusalem. "We can afford it," she told Lester. "And the other choice is a *sherut*— a shared taxi. You'd never fit all your bags in, and the people we'd share it with wouldn't like it if you tried."

"I've ridden in limousines before," Stark said dryly. "I don't mind." He knew the verse about the camel and the eye of the needle. You couldn't be a minister without knowing it. But, while he enjoyed wealth, he didn't flaunt it the way some of his colleagues did.

The limo took them to the Sheraton Plaza. "We stayed at the Holyland the last time we were here," Rhonda said.

"My producer and I looked at it before we came over," Gabriela replied. "This is newer and nicer and has a better location."

"I'm a little surprised you didn't move somewhere else after Mr. Nesbitt, ah, passed away," Lester Stark remarked.

Gabriela's face clouded, but quickly cleared. "To take the bad luck off, you mean?" she said.

He nodded. "That's right. Superstition, I know, but people still knock wood after two thousand years of Christianity. I do it myself."

"We thought about it," Gabriela said, "but the location *is* good, and in a Sheraton you always know what you're getting." Her eyes, which he'd thought quite expressive, suddenly went wary, opaque. Or maybe he was just jet-lagged and worn out and imagining things.

Getting settled at the Sheraton went as smoothly as it would have in the States. Afterwards, the Starks and Gabriela had an early dinner. The Reverend ordered Sichuan noodles with lamb. "Yes, sir," said the waiter, who was certainly no Israeli. "How spicy would you like that?"

"Don't tell them to go all out," Gabriela said quickly. "They'll take the top of your head right off."

"I wasn't going to. Medium will be fine," Stark replied.

"Yes, sir." Did the waiter tip Gabriela a wink? Stark thought so, but, again, he couldn't be sure.

Over the food—even medium-spicy seemed plenty hot to Stark—the minister said, "I'll want to see the Ark. I'll want to get up on the Temple Mount. And I'll want to talk to the Israelis from the Patriot batteries that were about to launch on the Iranian missiles till they went off the radar."

"Talk to Rabbi Kupferman for the first two. If he gives you trouble, I'll have our producer do what he can. Saul's known him for years," Gabriela said.

"Thank you," Stark said. He'd known Kupferman for years, too, but he wasn't a member of the tribe. Saul Buchbinder was.

Briskly, Gabriela went on, "Saul and I both have some contacts in the Defense Ministry, so we'll see what we can do about the last one. No guarantees there, though. The military doesn't like showing its cards."

"Do what you can, and I'll do what I can—I know a few people there, too—and we'll see what happens," Stark said.

She smiled. "Sounds like a plan. I think I'm going to enjoy working with you."

"And back at you." Stark didn't think polite lies were sinful—who was more obnoxious than people who prided themselves for being brutally frank?—but, rather to his surprise, he found he was telling the truth.

Eric tracked Yoram Louvish to his lair: a cramped office on the Hebrew University campus at the west end of Jerusalem, with steel bookcases full of books in half a dozen languages and boxes stuffed with old journals. Yoram was swearing at his computer when Eric knocked. What the Israeli archaeologist said about Windows wasn't anything a lot of people hadn't said before him.

He looked up and saw Eric. "Oh. It's you." He sounded as glad to see the American as he was about whatever horror Bill Gates had wrought.

"Yeah. Can I come in?" Eric said.

"I won't shoot you if you try." From an American professor, that would have been a joke. From Yoram, it sounded more like a statement of fact.

Eric edged into the office. He took a box off a steel-framed chair and sat. He said, "Who do I have to kill to get a look at the Ark in the Shrine of the Book?"

"Me," Louvish said. "And if that doesn't do it, Professor Sh. Nechshat."

"Let's start with you." Eric didn't want to beard Shlomo Kupferman in his den. Kupferman already had a fine beard.

"Okay." Yoram grabbed a piece of paper and wrote rapidly. He handed the sheet to Eric. "Here. Happy now?"

Admit Professor Eric Katz and Professor Orly Binur to the Shrine of the Book to view the Ark of the Covenant. I vouch for them. If you have any doubts, call me. Yoram Louvish. Hebrew script was as different from the printed version as Roman-alphabet cursive was from printed caps. Eric needed to work his way through it before he finally nodded.

"Thanks," he said. "And thanks for putting Orly there, too."

"*She* would have killed me if I didn't. You talk about it—she would have done it."

"I guess." Eric folded the note—the paper was Hebrew University stationery—and stuck it in his pocket. "You okay, Yoram? You've pulled a disappearing act."

"They don't need me now, so I'll work up some publications," Louvish said. "Hardly ever time to do that right. Just making the bibliography work . . . You know about that."

"Just a little," Eric said. Yoram grinned tightly. Eric was like a lot of archaeologists—his career would have been further along if he'd published more. But he dug digging, not pawing through journals to compare what he'd found to what others unearthed twenty or fifty or ninety years earlier. You needed to do that. It was part of the game and of the record. But it wasn't nearly so much fun as getting your hands dirty.

Yoram felt the same way. Seeing him stuck in this airless office was jarring. "Everything okay?" Eric asked.

"Why wouldn't it be?" Yoram didn't usually answer a question with a question. If he had something on his mind, he said it.

"I don't know," Eric said uncomfortably. "You've got . . . shunted to the sidelines since the Ark came out from under the Temple Mount. It doesn't seem right."

The Israeli archaeologist looked at him—looked through him,

really. "You've always been secular, pretty much," he said, as if that explained everything.

"Well, yeah." Eric nodded, more uncomfortably still. "And you're not. But you never held it against me before."

"What do you think of everything since we found the Ark?"

"I don't know what to think. It's weird." Eric asked the question Yoram had to be waiting for: "What do *you* think of it?"

"It scares me." Yoram muttered something, then nodded. "Yeah, it does. When Brandon touched the Ark and dropped dead . . . I've never been so frightened, not under mortar fire, not ever."

"I think maybe Munir feels the same way," Eric said. "He bailed out even before you did."

"It could be," Louvish said. "He's more like you, though. He thinks politics before he thinks religion. And that doesn't work any more."

"But . . ." Eric knew he was floundering. "Why aren't you happier, dammit? If what's happening goes with what you already believed—" He thought about Rabbi Kupferman, who seemed sure Brandon had got what was coming to him.

Yoram cut him off. "It doesn't. That's what I'm telling you."

"Okay." Eric blinked. "You've lost me."

"I'm a Jew like you, only more observant. I'm a post-destruction-of-the-Temple Jew. You do what God says, and He treats you fair. Now I've seen the real thing, and He's as mighty and arbitrary as He was in the days of the Bible. He'll do what He wants. It scares the crap out of me."

"Oh." Eric had to shift gears. Recent events had sent most believers into ecstasy. Eric said, "I don't think your reaction is too different from mine."

"You didn't want to believe to start with, any more than Munir does. Of course a God Who shows Himself scares people like you. Me . . . A God Who would do some of the things we've seen . . ." Yoram looked drawn and old. "A God like that, you begin to see how the *Shoah* could happen after all."

Little fingers of ice walked up Eric's back. An arbitrary God Who did as He pleased with the world *might* throw six million people into the fire of the Holocaust if that furthered His purposes. "What can we do?" Eric whispered.

"Nothing," Yoram said flatly. "You don't fight God."

"Oh, yeah? What about Jacob?—I mean, Israel. This country got a name because he wrestled with God and prevailed."

"God let him. If that happens, fine. If it doesn't, you end up like Sodom and Gomorrah—or like Brandon," Yoram said. "And this thing is just starting to play out. We think we know how it goes. So do the Christians and the Muslims. Somebody's wrong. Lots of somebodies. That scares me worse than anything."

15

Yitzhak Avigad watched the Third Temple rise. He'd always prayed for such a thing, but he'd never really believed it would happen. Here it was, though. Christian evangelists were screaming their heads off. So were the Muslims, Sunnis and Shiites alike. But not even the Iranians thought launching more missiles was a good idea.

Trucks rumbled, on top of the Temple Mount. The Reconstruction Alliance had delivered two six-tonne cornerstones. They'd had them ready for years. The police always turned them back before. No more.

Cement mixers churned and growled. Yitzhak wished for earplugs, as he would have at a raucous concert—except he didn't go to raucous concerts. He'd wondered whether the religious authorities would insist that the Third Temple rise by hand, as the First and Second had. But they were limiting that to the Holy of Holies. For everything else, their motto seemed to be, *Get the Temple up and running as fast as we can.*

The Temple would be bigger than the Dome of the Rock (which wasn't getting reassembled nearly so fast). Even Yitzhak had to admit that it wouldn't be so beautiful. The Dome of the Rock had delicacy, subtlety. None of that in the plan for the Temple. Its court and buildings were big rectangles. Most of it would be reinforced concrete, with thin stone veneers on the outside for decoration. That only added to the brutalist massiveness.

Computer re-creations of what the Temple would look like showed it shining with gold leaf. On a monitor, that looked fine. Yitzhak was less sure about the real building. Gold leaf slapped onto those big square spaces? They made him think the architect knew Donald Trump.

Nobody'd asked his opinion. He wasn't an architect himself. And what difference did looks make? The Second Temple lasted 500 years before Herod redid it in style. Nobody'd had the money or anything else to fix it up till then. God hadn't seemed to mind. Chances were He wouldn't this time, either.

Just watching this happen, watching Judaism reclaim something most people had thought lost forever, made his heart beat faster. To him, this was Judaism as it was meant to be. After the Romans sacked the Second Temple, Jews had had to figure out how to go on without it. They'd done a good job, but it was an adaptation. He imagined Islam trying to get along without Mecca. How would the Muslims do it? He had no idea. But now the real faith, the Biblical faith, would return after a hiatus of more than 1,900 years. If that wasn't a miracle, what was?

He looked around. Jews in hard hats were yelling at other Jews in hard hats to go faster. It might have been a battlefield, except the stench was different. Diesel exhaust was a constant; so was hot metal. But he didn't smell shit or burnt meat or fear. Without fear, you didn't have a battlefield.

Here came a camera crew, with a soft bald guy telling the camera where to go and how to set up. An American: he was talking English, his accent half New York, half L.A. He looked like the kind of American Jew who would boss a camera crew.

The people with him who'd be on-camera were fish from a different pool. The man was tanned and elegant, with capped teeth, an expensive haircut, and a more expensive suit. He deferred to the stylish woman in the brown pants suit, but did more of the talking. Though the day was warm, he didn't glow or glisten. Maybe he'd had his sweat glands removed.

When he spoke, his voice penetrated the racket around him. That, and the Southern accent Yitzhak followed because of his dealings over the red heifer, shouted *preacher* to the Israeli. The woman had an equally strong voice but spoke as general American as anyone could.

In the States, Jews and Christians teamed up all the time. Yitzhak had spent enough time in America to know that. It wouldn't happen here. Here, each Christian sect clung fiercely to what had been its for generations. The Jews wished they'd all go away, but they wouldn't.

"They'll build a causeway across to the Mount of Olives," the preacher said, pointing east from the Temple Mount. "That's where they'll sacrifice the red heifer, to help them sanctify the Temple and the people and holy implements that will serve here."

Plenty of *goyim* hadn't the faintest idea what they were talking about when they did deal with Jewish affairs, but he wasn't like that. The trim woman said, "That's fascinating, Reverend Stark, Tell me—"

"Cut!" the bald guy yelled. "We gotta do it again. Background noise is just too loud."

Then Yitzhak recognized the woman. An American would have been quicker on the uptake, but even he'd heard stories about how a too-spicy dinner had kept her from trying to take the lid off the Ark of the Covenant—and, almost surely, kept her in this world.

He walked over to her. "You're Gabriela Sandoval, right?" An American would have said *Excuse me* first, but he wasn't.

"Yes, I am." She nodded. "You're one up on me, I'm afraid."

"Yitzhak Avigad. You and Brandon were going to do a show about the red heifer before Tel Aviv."

"Oh, of course! Good to meet you in person." She held out her hand.

Yitzhak shook it. Her grip was smooth and practiced, but it wasn't like shaking a man's hand. "Who's the fellow with you now?" he asked. Brandon Nesbitt would never be part of *Gabriela and Brandon* again.

"The Reverend Lester Stark. He's an important minister in the States," Gabriela answered.

"What's he doing here? How come you're working with him?" No, Yitzhak didn't cotton to ministers, important or not.

"He'll do some narrations and commentary about all this," Gabriela said. "We'll add those together with what Brandon did before he, uh, died, and we'll have programming and streaming video and DVDs lots of people will want to see."

And so? But Yitzhak didn't ask that. He could see the answer. *And so we'll make lots of lovely money.* Living on a kibbutz largely insulated him from the urge to pile up cash. Some who got rich bailed out of kibbutz life. Others plowed the money back into the general fund. Yitzhak didn't know what he'd do. Since he wasn't likely to get rich, he'd never worried about it.

Stark coughed when dust blew in his face. So did Yitzhak. Gabriela didn't. Waving to the preacher, she said, "Reverend, I've got someone here I'd like you to meet. This is Yitzhak Avigad, from Kibbutz Nair Tamid." Yitzhak was impressed she remembered that.

He was more impressed when Stark knew what it meant, literally and metaphorically. "Eternal Light Kibbutz! The people with the red heifer! Pleased to meet you, Mr. Avigad." That baritone was made for preaching or TV, all right. It was made for preaching *on* TV, too.

"Nice to meet you." Yitzhak also shook hands with him. "What do you think of all this?"

"It's wonderful. Prophecy is being fulfilled," Lester Stark answered. "The Last Days really do seem to be upon us." He was more cautious than some Christian preachers. If you listened to them, Jesus would be buying *shawarma* and coffee in the Jewish quarter of the Old City day after tomorrow.

Which reminded Yitzhak . . . "And what happens when the Last Days do come?"

Stark's cough this time had nothing to do with the dust. "As I'm sure you know, Mr. Avigad, Christians believe Jesus Christ will return to judge the quick and the dead."

"And the Jews will get left behind again, same as they did the last time?" Yitzhak didn't know why he pressed it. Probably for the same reason Christians pressed Jews where they had the numbers. Because he could.

Lester Stark wasn't easy to press. "You said it. I didn't."

"You've got—what do they say in English?—the courage of your convictions." But Yitzhak wouldn't let him off the hook so easily. "The Grand Mufti of Jerusalem has his, too." He wished something permanent would happen to the Grand Mufti.

"I don't think his convictions are accurate," Stark said.

"You don't think mine are, either," Yitzhak pointed out.

"Yours come from the Old Testament, which is divinely inspired," Stark said. "I don't think the same is true of the Qur'an."

"I don't think the same is true of the New Testament." To Yitzhak, Christians and Muslims stole the parts of Judaism they liked, then made up other stuff to go with them.

"You're frank." Stark smiled when he said it, anyhow.

"Why not? This is my country." *It doesn't belong to Christians. Jews were here first. That goes double for Muslims.*

"Well, so it is." Stark was smooth and slick. Was he good olive oil? Yitzhak had trouble deciding. The preacher went on, "Tell you what, Mr. Avigad. We'll see what happens. Then we'll have a better idea of who was right and who was wrong and what it all means."

This time, Yitzhak stuck out *his* hand. "That's a deal."

Eric and Orly got fewer hassles from the guards around the Shrine of the Book than he'd expected. "I remember you guys," a trooper said. "You were part of the mob that came behind the Ark."

By the way he looked at Orly, he remembered her better than Eric. If you were male, straight, and alive, that wasn't a hot headline. "Can we go in, then?" Eric asked.

Fewer hassles didn't mean none. The guard pulled a phone from his pocket. "Let me call Professor Louvish, make sure he wrote this," he said. For a wonder, he got Yoram. They talked for a minute. Then the guard nodded. "Yeah, he wrote it, and you're you. Go on in."

Eric left his hat on. He didn't have the urge to uncover here that he might have had in the States or England. When he went to Salisbury Cathedral after visiting Stonehenge, a matron had snarled at him because he left his hat on. But he wasn't an uncouth American—he hoped not, anyhow. He was just somebody unused to baring his head in a house of worship.

"I should have come here a long time ago," he said to Orly as they walked into air-conditioning. "Not for the Ark—for the Dead Sea Scrolls. Not seeing them is like going to Dublin and missing the Book of Kells."

"Oh, more than that," Orly said. She had a point: the Dead Sea Scrolls were twice as old as the Book of Kells. But they were straightforward manuscripts, while there would never be a more splendidly illuminated Gospel than the one at Trinity College.

Which counted for more, history or beauty? Eric supposed it depended on what you wanted.

More armed guards stood inside the Heikhal Ha-Sefer. How much firepower could the Israelis bring to bear to protect the Ark? In a way, having lots made sense. Lots of people were unhappy it was here. In another way . . . Hadn't the Ark shown it could take care of itself?

The guards stood close to the Ark, but not *too* close. You didn't want to trip and fetch up against it. Not after what happened to Brandon, you didn't. That was for sure.

Orly stared at the Ark. So did Eric. It drew the eye with irresistible power. The model at the Reconstruction Alliance's museum was impressive. The real thing went way beyond that.

Or is it my imagination? Eric wondered. If you didn't know which was the real Ark and which the model, could you tell them apart? Sure you could—the real one laughed at gravity. Assume it didn't. Could you tell then?

He thought you could. And that was an archaeologist's professional opinion. He hoped so, anyway. The model was a good reconstruction. The real McCoy was more like a punch in the teeth. Whoever'd made these cherubim was on a wavelength no modern Western man could receive.

Orly eyed them, too. "I swear they change expression," she said.

Eric almost kissed her, right there in front of the guards and God. The guards didn't intimidate him. God did. "Oh, good!" he said. "I wondered if I was the only one who thought so."

She shook her head. "Unh-unh. Now they look . . . statue-y, you know? But they were licking their chops when Brandon reached for the Ark."

Eric wouldn't have put it so strongly, which didn't mean he was sure she was wrong. Remembering Brandon's last TV spectacular, he thought the cherubim seemed more attentive then than they had when the Ark came out of its hiding place—or now. Maybe it was all in his head.

Maybe it wasn't.

The doors opened again. In came several people speaking English. You heard it a lot in Jerusalem. Eric was used to it. Such authoritative, perfectly punctuated English? No.

Then he recognized two of the people. One was Gabriela Sandoval, the broadcaster who'd come down with what had to be the luckiest bad stomach in the history of the world. The other was Lester Stark. He wondered if Barb Taylor knew that Stark was already in town. He also wondered why Stark was buddy-buddy with someone so much more secular than he was. They weren't quite Felix and Oscar from *The Odd Couple*, but they came close.

What they were doing together soon became obvious. The people with them were a TV crew: camerapeople, lighting techs, and so on. They were going to film the Ark. With luck, they'd be more careful than Brandon Nesbitt had.

Gabriela walked over to Eric and Orly. "You two are part of the team that found the Ark," she said. "Eric Katz and Orly Binur."

"You remember!" Orly sounded as impressed as Eric felt.

Something in Gabriela's smile made it clear why the cameras loved her. "Being good with names is part of what I do," she said. "We're here to get some shots that . . . didn't quite happen the last time we filmed the Ark." The smile slipped.

"Is Reverend Stark, ah, filling in for Mr. Nesbitt?" Eric asked.

"To some degree. We've found we do point-counterpoint pretty well together." Gabriela Sandoval's smile came back, though a few watts dimmer than it had been. "Would you like to meet him?"

"Um, okay." Eric couldn't find a polite way to say no. Orly looked as if she was on the edge of an impolite one.

But the preacher proved professionally charming, or a bit more than professionally. He kept Orly from spitting in his eye. Given what she thought of preachers in general and televangelists in particular, that put him way ahead of most of his kind.

"I understand you were the second person to see the Ark, after Professor Louvish. Is that right, Dr. Katz?" Stark asked.

"Well—yeah." Eric felt reluctant to admit it.

"And what did you think when he called you to the opening?"

"Wanna know? I wondered if he was playing a joke on me. Archaeologists do that. I was waiting for him to give me the horse laugh. But it turned out to be real."

"Yes. It did." Stark's gaze swung toward the Ark. If you were anywhere near it, you looked at it. You couldn't help yourself.

"Would you like to go on the air and talk about the discovery, Dr. Katz?" Gabriela asked.

Reluctance again. Eric wondered if it was just that he wanted nothing to do with televangelists. That wasn't PC. Weren't you supposed to tolerate everybody's beliefs? But Stark was bound to haul in the Apocalypse. Eric didn't want his name associated with that. It wasn't what *he* believed, and he didn't want anyone imagining it was.

"I'll pass," he said. "Archaeologists don't need much publicity."

"Are you sure you won't change your mind?" That wasn't Gabriela; it was Stark. "You have a unique perspective, and your contribution would be valuable."

"We'd make it worth your while, too," Gabriela Sandoval added.

Retro me, Satanas went through Eric's mind again. "I don't think so," he said. "Thanks, though. I appreciate it." He didn't say he'd lose his colleagues' respect if he went on a show with Stark and Gabriela, which was also true. But it wasn't the main reason he didn't want to perform.

"Too bad." Gabriela recognized no when she heard it. But she didn't quit. She turned to Orly. "How about you, Professor Binur?"

"I'm not a professor. I'm only a grad student." Orly might have said, *I'm not a master. I'm only a slave.* In Academese, she had.

By the way Gabriela chuckled, she understood that. "All the same," she said. "You're a researcher on the project."

Orly shook her head. "I don't want to do it."

"Are you sure?" Reverend Stark asked, which proved he didn't know her.

"I'm sure," Orly said. This was her country and her religion. If he didn't like it, too bad. By her look, too bad anyway.

Stark also saw as much. "However you please," he said easily. "I hope you'll excuse us, because we're going ahead." Orly didn't seem thrilled about that, either. But she couldn't do anything about it, not when Stark and Gabriela and their crew obviously had permission to be here.

"We're ready," a cameraman called. With a small shock, Eric recognized the guy. He was the one who'd tried to revive Brandon after he touched the Ark. As many people had seen him as any cameraman ever born.

"Thanks, Danny," said an older man who looked like a producer or director. He raised his voice: "Places! Quiet on the set!"

Orly bristled anew. So did Eric. Calling the Shrine of the Book, with the Ark as its new centerpiece, a *set* . . . Why did the God Who killed for setting a fingertip on the Ark let that go unpunished?

Gabriela said, "You're welcome to watch if you stay quiet."

Gee, thanks went through Eric's mind. Being American rather than Israeli, he swallowed the sarcasm. "What do you think?" he asked Orly.

"I've seen plenty," she said. If that wasn't enough to damn Gabriela and Lester Stark and all their works . . . Eric was also glad to escape the Heikhal Ha-Sefer.

Tanks squatted by the churches on the Mount of Olives. Chaim Avigad knew he wasn't seeing them all. Walls and trees hid some, and camouflage paint and branches made them harder to spot. But he could hear engines rumbling: a deep bass background note that never went away.

In the foreground was ordinary construction noise. They needed a causeway from the Temple Mount to the Mount of Olives. The firepower was there to make sure nobody started lobbing mortar bombs at the causeway or the workers.

You had to sacrifice the red heifer on the Mount of Olives. That was in the rules, like everything coloring Chaim's life these days. When you said it like that, it didn't sound so bad. Sacrifice the red heifer . . .

They were going to kill Rosie!

He watched from a platform near the Pool of Siloam that people from Kibbutz Nair Tamid had set up so he and the other ritually pure boys could go where the action was without polluting themselves. The pool lay 400 meters south of the southwestern corner of the Temple Mount. He could see everything, and he couldn't do anything about it. That drove him crazy.

When they built the causeway, he and the other boys would bring water from the Pool of Siloam over to the Mount of Olives for the sacrificial ceremony. They still wouldn't touch the ground. They would ride on boards atop oxen. If not for why they'd be doing it, that sounded like fun.

The pots they would use to carry the water were special, too. In ancient days, the village of Modin, halfway between Tel Aviv and Jerusalem, had been a stopping point for pilgrims to the holy city. (It was also where the Maccabees came from, but that had nothing to do with the pots.) Since most people who'd lived there were of the priestly class, the ruling was that all pots from Modin were ritually pure.

Nowadays, though, nobody lived at Modin. Nobody had for years. But the Reconstruction Alliance had set up a clay works and a pottery studio there, to make new ritually pure pots. Kupferman had ruled that those pots met the ancient standards. No one cared to argue with him. If you quarreled with a ruling like that, you'd end up with no ritually pure pots.

Again, that was nice when you thought about it the right way—or, to Chaim, the wrong way. He would have been happier about everything if it hadn't pointed toward sacrificing the red heifer: toward killing his friend.

He couldn't get anybody to take him seriously. That was the curse of boys his age, but he thought it was his problem alone. (That was also part of the curse of boys his age.) His mother wouldn't listen. Neither would his uncle. The other ritually pure boys seemed excited at ushering in the new Temple by sacrificing the red heifer.

Rosie was just a cow to them. They ate beef. So did he. But he wouldn't have wanted to eat beef from a cow he knew personally. Anyone who'd grown up working on a farm would have laughed. Kibbutz Nair Tamid *was* a farm, but the ritually pure boys hadn't worked on it. How could they without polluting themselves?

No matter what everybody else thought, Rosie wasn't just a cow to Chaim. His hands curled into fists as he watched the causeway stretch from one mountain to the other. Slowly, but with more determination than he'd ever known before, he nodded to himself. He *would* stop the sacrifice if he could.

From such selfish willfulness sprang martyrs, heroes, madmen, and . . .

Targeted killings. The Zionists denied that they assassinated anybody. They called it something else and thought that made it different. Jamal Ashrawi thought they would kill him if they got the chance.

So the Grand Mufti went around Hebron with his squad of guards. Some carried assault rifles, some RPGs. Ashrawi wished his people could get a Stinger—or even a Russian antiaircraft missile.

None of his friends in high places had coughed up a missile. He resented that. He also resented being unable to get an Arab-made missile. The Americans manufactured them, and the Zionists, and the Russians. Godless, one and all.

Muslims? The community of believers? Those who submitted to God? They lacked the know-how. Oh, the Iranians made missiles, but big, hulking things, descendants of Russian Scuds that were descendants of German V-2s. The ayatollahs bought the small ones from unbelievers, too. Why did God permit the embarrassment? He had His reasons, but they weren't apparent to Jamal Ashrawi.

If he looked north, he could almost watch the Jews profaning the Haram al-Sharif. The Dome of the Rock, the monument that marked Muhammad's ascension to heaven, taken apart like a child's toy made of blocks? Al-Aqsa Mosque, too? For what? So a lying Temple could go up where no Temple ever stood before! How did God tolerate such abominations?

Ashrawi thought he knew. God would let the Jews triumph for a while to set up their downfall, and the Christians' with them. In the end, Islam would prevail. But the waiting was hard! Humiliation, subjection—how could a proud folk find that easy, especially when it went on so long?

Something mundane happened then: his phone rang. He took it off his belt. "Yes?" He didn't give his name.

"How is it with you, Haji?" An educated man speaking excellent classical Arabic with a slight mushy accent: an Iranian.

Haji was safe enough—millions had made the pilgrimage. "I am well, God be thanked," Ashrawi answered. "How is it with you and your martyred country?" Normally, Haji Jamal had little use for Iranians. But they'd *tried* to strike the Zionist entity—more than any Arab country had.

"We still suffer . . . some confusion," the other man answered.

Ashrawi believed that. You couldn't lose your president, your top mullah, and your top general without going into a tailspin. After a moment, the Iranian went on, "But we have not abandoned the fight. If Israeli raiders lurk inside our land, we shall root them out without mercy."

"That is good to hear." But Jamal Ashrawi could not help murmuring, *"Mene, mene, tekel upharsin."*

"The Zionist dogs did that!" the Iranian exclaimed. "They try to shake our faith in God. But they fail."

"Good."

"We will bring you what you need for a distraction, and what you need for something more important," the Iranian said. "You know of men with fire in the belly?"

"Such men can be found, *inshallah,*" the Grand Mufti said. *God willing* gave a handy excuse if something went wrong.

The Iranian knew that, too. "Some people need to remember that God works through men. What greater blasphemy than if men fail and then blame God?"

"Send what you can," Ashrawi said, wondering how foolhardy the plan would be. Martyrdom was martyrdom, but most people liked to think they gave up their lives in hope of striking God's enemies.

"Expect it soon," the Iranian said, and the line went dead.

Jamal Ashrawi muttered. Yes, the Iranians were still willing to fight the Zionists. But it sounded as if they were willing to fight to the last Palestinian.

Well, the Grand Mufti thought, *their own efforts failed. Maybe ours will do better. They couldn't do much worse.*

Yitzhak Avigad looked from the Temple Mount to the Mount of Olives. He wasn't paying attention to the golden domes of the Russian Orthodox church on the mountainside, or to the Jewish cemetery nearby. You could still be buried there, but it cost a not-so-small fortune.

Tradition said that when the Messiah came to Jerusalem, he would round up the dead on the Mount of Olives and lead them into the city through the Gate of Mercy, also called the Golden Gate, on the east side of the Temple Mount. But the Golden Gate had been closed up for centuries.

How God would get around the difficulty, Yitzhak had no idea. That God would . . . he grew more confident as the causeway stretched toward the Mount of Olives. They would sacrifice the red heifer. They would purify the Temple Mount, the Temple, and the men and implements who would serve there. And after that it would be up to God.

"Mr. Avigad?"

The question, in American English, made Yitzhak turn around. "Yes?" He needed a moment to recognize the pale, dumpy woman in the broad-brimmed hat. He hadn't seen her since Kibbutz Ha-Minsarah, and a lot had happened since. "How are you, Miss—?"

"Taylor. Barb Taylor. I didn't expect you to remember—don't worry." Barb Taylor seemed resigned to being forgotten.

Seeing as much made Yitzhak feel worse. "Sorry," he said. That was a rare admission from an Israeli, so rare that people joked about it. "How are you?" He could make small talk—you had to when you dealt with people from the States—but he rarely wasted time on it here at home.

"I'm well, thank you," the American woman answered. "And so are you people." Her wave took in the construction on the Temple Mount and the causeway. "It's so exciting."

The trouble was, he knew what she meant. The Jews would rebuild the Temple, and then Jesus would come down and leave them out in the cold. Again. He thought she was full of crap.

But she was full of crap in a sweet, polite way, so he didn't tell her to piss up a rope. He just said, "I think so, too." She could take that any way she wanted.

And she did. Which only went to show that no good deed went unpunished. "You're not the only one," Barb Taylor said. "Lester Stark is here." She didn't sigh over the preacher's name with the same reverence a kid would give the latest singing idol, but she came close.

"I know," Yitzhak said. "I've talked to him."

"I'm jealous. That must have been so interesting," Barb said. Yitzhak managed a jerky nod. She continued, "It's especially exciting because a lot of ministers are more . . . more pumped up, about everything that's been going on than Reverend Stark is."

"Are they?" Yitzhak Avigad cared about the theological opinions of Christian preachers as much as he cared about the performance ratings of NFL quarterbacks. Zero equaled zero.

Barb Taylor nodded anyway. "They sure are. So if Reverend Stark decided to come to the Holy Land, he must think the Last Days are close." She looked up into the bright, brassy sky, as if expecting angels right now. When she didn't get any, her shoulders sagged a little. She perked up in a hurry. "And if he thinks so, he's likely right."

Yitzhak nodded again. He thought the Last Days were close, too. Whether his version matched Stark's or Barb Taylor's was a different story. "He's also here with Brandon Nesbitt's cohost, to finish the video work Brandon started before he . . . died," Yitzhak said with malice aforethought.

He didn't faze Barb. "It's Christian charity, helping poor Mr. Nesbitt finish his work after he's gone."

Anyone who called Brandon *poor Mr. Nesbitt* had never dealt with him. He'd been a self-loving bastard his whole short life. Pointing out an obvious truth seemed safer: "Christian charity? Reverend Stark isn't doing it from the goodness of his heart, you know."

"Well, sure." Barb Taylor didn't even blink. "Ministers can make a living like anybody else, can't they? I mean, I don't suppose Rabbi Kupferman is exactly poor, either."

Yitzhak didn't think Kupferman was in the same league as Lester Stark when it came to cash. In other ways, he didn't think Stark was in the same league as Kupferman. Still, no denying the plump American had a point of sorts. The Religious Affairs Minister *wasn't* poor.

Before Yitzhak could put that into words, he heard a whistle in the air, and then a sharp, harsh *crump!* down in the Kidron Valley between the Temple Mount and the Mount of Olives. A few seconds later, he heard the same thing again, this time closer. Dust and smoke sprang up where none had been before.

"Those are funny noises," Barb said. "Is one of the bulldozers down there having trouble? Sounds like it's backfiring."

"Those are"—*crump!*—"mortar rounds."

"Somebody's *shooting*?" Barb sounded incredulous, as if wondering how God could allow such a thing. Yitzhak was wondering, too. If Iranian missiles got swatted like flies, shouldn't mortar rounds walking up to the Temple Mount?

Of course they should. Only they weren't. *Crump!* Those were *big* mortar rounds, too—they sounded like Russian 160mm jobs. Portable heavy artillery. Yitzhak looked around in raw fear. Up here on the Temple Mount, especially with the Muslim structures gone, you were alone with God under the sky. That was the stuff of exaltation . . . till somebody tried to blow you up.

Crump! Yitzhak knocked Barb Taylor down. She squawked. He flattened out himself. *Crump!* A mortar bomb slammed the Temple Mount.

16

E ric was fixing a sandwich when explosions rattled his windows. "What the hell?" he said. Explosions in the States were likely to be accidents. Here . . .

"Mortars," Orly said. "Big ones, too. Terrorists' favorite toys." Eric couldn't have told a big mortar from a little one if his life depended on it (and, here, it might). Having a girlfriend who was a vet got strange sometimes.

He looked at the bread and turkey loaf. His appetite wilted like the lettuce he'd been about to add. "We'd better find out what happened."

More *crump!*s punctuated Orly's nod. "See what the Arabs did now." She took terrorism for granted. She'd grown up in a country where it happened all the time.

He wondered if she would head for the Temple Mount. The west Jerusalem apartment building was only a mile away. Nothing in Jerusalem was far from anything else—except Jews, Muslims, and Christians.

But Orly flipped on the TV. She assumed anything horrible at the Temple Mount would cross the country in nothing flat. *If it bleeds, it leads* was as much a rule here as in L.A. or New York.

She was right. Of course Israeli TV had crews all over the Temple Mount. The last time there was news as big as building the Third Temple was the sack of the Second Temple in 70 AD/CE. Eric didn't suppose the attempted rebuilding during the brief reign of Julian the Apostate counted. If that partly restored Temple hadn't burned down, though . . .

Judaism wouldn't look the same today. Eric wasn't sure how it would have synthesized the sacrifice-based cult and the synagogue-based religion that grew after the Second Temple fell. An interesting question, but one that would never have an answer.

Smoke and flames rising from a bulldozer in the valley between the Temple Mount and the Mount of Olives made ancient might-have-beens less urgent. "One man dead and two wounded by this 160mm mortar bomb," a newsman gabbled. His voice was shrill and scared, the voice of somebody who'd just got shot at.

Orly didn't look smug. She knew what she knew—so well, she took it for granted.

"Other bombs fell here in the valley and at the edge of the Temple Mount," the Israeli newscaster said. "There are more casualties, and it is—" A helicopter thuttered by, loud enough to drown him out. Still sounding shaky, he tried again: "It's worth noting that the Muslims didn't hesitate to shell their third-holiest site."

This editorial brought to you by . . . Eric thought. But Israeli news was more objective than anything from other Middle Eastern countries. He couldn't be too scornful. News in the USA also split right and left, leaving a chasm where the center used to be.

"Fortunately, no rounds struck the causeway from the Temple Mount to the Mount of Olives," the newsman said. "At least one did descend on the retaining wall that upholds the Temple Mount.

Shell fragments and bits of flying stone wounded several people on the Mount."

The camera in the valley panned the eastern side of the supporting wall. The gap in the masonry looked bigger than one mortar round should have managed. Then Eric realized what had happened.

"Talk about lucky shots," he said. "They knocked down the masonry that's closed the Golden Gate for so long."

Orly looked at him. Her expression seemed as ancient and unreadable as the ones on the cherubim that topped the Ark. "What makes you think it's luck?" she asked.

"Huh?" Eric said.

"What makes you think it's luck?" she repeated. "The Messiah enters Jerusalem through that gate. How can He if it stays closed?"

"Wait," Eric said. "You don't think ISIS or Hezbollah or whoever is trying to help the Messiah, do you?"

"I don't care what they're trying to do. I don't think God cares, either." Orly sounded weird, spooked. She was starting to believe in everything that was going on.

Eric shook his head. That wasn't the right way to say it. How could you not believe in what was happening? There it was. Believing in the hand of God . . .

She might have picked that from his mind. "You still think this is coincidence, don't you?"

"I'm trying to," he answered.

"Why?" she said. "When it gets this obvious, isn't it easier to believe what you see and what's behind it?"

"Maybe for you. You take this place for granted. You can say plenty of things about the San Fernando Valley and the Westside, but the Holy Land they ain't. I'm not used to God looking over my shoulder. I like to think I'm a free agent." *Even if I'll never sign for millions.* Eric didn't say it. It wouldn't have meant anything to Orly.

"He's looking any which way," Orly said. "That's what you need to get used to."

He knows when you've been sleeping. He knows when you're awake. He knows when you've been bad or good. . . . Eric needed an effort to cut off the song inside his head. It was cute when you talked about Santa Claus—till you heard it selling everything from condoms to BMWs. When you talked about God and meant it literally, the overtones were different.

Waaay different.

Eric felt more like *Big Brother is watching you* than *Santa Claus is coming to town.* Except God didn't need hidden cameras and secret police. You couldn't hide from Him by gabbling the right phrases while you thought your thoughts in the privacy of your mind. You had no privacy from God.

Thou shalt love the Lord thy God with all thy heart and with all thy soul and with all thy might. Not *Thou hadst better.* No compromise. No bargains. This was how it would be.

The camera cut to the reopened Golden Gate. It wasn't elegant, but Orly was right: it would do. "I'm so scared," Eric said.

She nodded. "Welcome to the club."

Lester Stark had no congregation before him. He didn't like preaching without one, but you could do things in Birmingham you couldn't in Jerusalem. The Israelis probably weren't happy to have him preaching at all. They would put up with it, since this wasn't aimed at them.

"I take as my text today Romans 8:28," he said into the camera. "We have seen it in action here lately. For those who don't have the Bible open before them, I'll quote it: 'And we know that all things work together for good to them that love God, to them who are called according to his purpose.'

"Look at the faith and confidence. 'And we know!' it says. Not 'we hope.' Paul was right when he wrote that to the Romans. The Roman Empire tormented and killed our Lord and Savior, Jesus Christ. They thought they settled Him forever. But the Roman Empire is gone, while Christianity thrives today."

He wouldn't say the Jews had anything to do with crucifying Jesus. He didn't believe it, and it would infuriate his hosts. He didn't fear taking on the Israelis, but he wanted reasonable cause first.

"Terrorists trying to delay the rebuilding of the Temple launched a cowardly attack against the Temple Mount. They killed and wounded several people who never harmed them. Maybe they think they accomplished something—besides making decent folk all over hate them, I mean.

"But they did more. They opened the gate in the eastern wall of the Temple Mount, which has been closed for centuries, through which the Messiah will enter Jerusalem: the Golden Gate, also called the Gate of Mercy.

"Could they have done that by themselves or by chance? Maybe. Coincidence has a long arm. But, after the other remarkable things lately, which is more likely? Coincidence or God's plan?

"Believe whatever you choose—now. You'll learn the answer, and I don't think you'll have long to wait."

The red light went out. He was off camera. He sighed in relief. Preaching to a real congregation was a joy. This felt like hard work.

"Nice job, Reverend." Gabriela Sandoval made silent clapping motions: emoji brought to life.

Lester smiled. "Thanks. Is it good enough to persuade you?"

"That you know more about how religion and history fit together than I ever will? You bet it is," Gabriela said. "I figured you would when I asked you to join me, and boy, was I ever right."

"Not quite what I meant, though I'm grateful," Stark said. "What I meant was, is it enough to persuade you the Second Coming of the Messiah—of our Lord and Savior, Jesus Christ—can't be far away?"

Gabriela coughed in faint embarrassment. "I've always worried more about this old world than the next one. I think I still do. It's a hard habit to break, if you know what I mean."

"I suspect I do. I have many other friends who feel the same way," Stark said. "But can you go on doing that when you see more plainly by the day how your eternal soul's fate depends on your relationship with God?"

"I've never spent much time worrying about what happens to my soul when I'm gone," Gabriela said slowly. "When I'm dead, it will do . . . whatever it does. Are you sure your ideas are any better than Rabbi Kupferman's, say? If they locked the two of you in a room, who'd come out on top?"

That made Stark chuckle. He was between ten and twenty years younger than Kupferman. But would that matter in a brawl, or in a theological disputation? *How do I know I'm right and the Jews are wrong?* Stark asked himself.

Because the New Testament tells me so. The argument carried weight for him. It wouldn't for a Jew, though. A Jew would deny the New Testament was the word of God.

You couldn't even say it came down to faith. Jews had plenty of that. Their religion never would have survived without it. Muslims had it, too. Without faith, you wouldn't blow up a truck full of explosives and radioactives when you were sitting in the driver's seat. *Which leaves me where?* Stark wondered. Either you believed what you believed for reasons you found good, or you believed in nothing and found that good.

Depressing numbers of intelligent, caring people—people like Gabriela, for instance—had turned their backs on faith. Maybe what was going on in the Holy Land now would bring them back to it. Something needed to, or hell would overflow. And wouldn't that return almost be miracle enough in itself?

"I won't bother you with the question any more," Stark said. "I'll tell you what I told Yitzhak Avigad. You'll do what you'll do, I'll do what I'll do, God will do what He'll do, and when it's over we'll see what it means."

"Hard to be fairer than that, Reverend," Gabriela said.

But Lester Stark still thought he was right about what the passage in Romans meant.

Some who'd fired at the causeway leaping east from the Haram al-Sharif and at the Haram itself were no longer around to be questioned. The Zionist entity's helicopters and tanks started hunting before the last mortar bombs landed. In spite of everything the Jews could do, several gunners got away.

Habib al-Bedwani was a lean, scarred man with one finger missing from his left hand. "Did you aim at the Golden Gate?" Jamal Ashrawi asked. "Why would you try that?"

"We aimed where we should have aimed," al-Bedwani said stolidly. "The bombs came down where God willed they come down."

That was the last thing Haji Jamal wanted to hear. "Do you think God wanted you to open the Golden Gate? More likely Satan did, Satan or the djinni!"

The fighter shrugged. "Well, what can a mere man do against God and Satan and the djinni?" he asked.

"You were supposed to hurt the Jews! Instead, you made it easier for their Antichrist to do his work."

"We blew up a bulldozer, I hear," al-Bedwani said. "We killed Jews and wounded more. How can you complain?"

"You opened the Golden Gate! The Zionists might have, but you did. Do you think they won't thank you for it?"

"Be careful how you talk, old man, or you won't get much older." Habib al-Bedwani turned his back and walked away.

"Wait!" Haji Jamal sputtered. That a nobody should talk to the

Grand Mufti this way . . . ! What the other man did have was skill with weapons. He thought he could use it to make Ashrawi afraid—and he was right.

A bodyguard must have understood the way his mind worked. "Shall we teach that son of a poxed she-camel to regret his bad manners, Haji Jamal?" The man hefted his Kalashnikov.

Any lesson he taught would have a funeral at the end. The Grand Mufti shook his head. "No, let it go," he said. "We need to fight the Zionist entity, not our brethren." Arabs had too much trouble remembering that obvious truth. The Jews didn't fight among themselves about anything that mattered.

"Anyone who insults you is no brother of mine," the bodyguard said, which proved he couldn't see the obvious, either.

But Ashrawi repeated, "Let it go. He is angry at me because he didn't hurt the Zionists more."

"Let him be angry at them, then," the man replied. "A one-eyed donkey could have aimed better."

"It is as God wills," Jamal Ashrawi said.

Inshallah was usually a commonplace. Here, though, he wondered if it wasn't true. Had God willed that that heavy mortar round should fall on the long-closed Golden Gate? Hard to imagine such bad shooting from an experienced mortar crew unless some power stronger than mortal was involved.

The Zionists and their Christian stooges believed God had a hand in opening the Golden Gate. To hear them talk, the Messiah or Jesus would lead souls into Jerusalem through the gate any minute now.

Ashrawi's first instinct was to deny they could be right. But what if they were? A slow smile spread across his face. They thought God was paving the way for the Messiah? They'd let the Antichrist seduce them even before he appeared.

They would be judged. But God would not dispose of them the

way they expected Him to. "Truly there is no God but God, and Muhammad is the Prophet of God," Ashrawi murmured.

"Well, of course," his bodyguard said.

Despite everyone's best efforts, working with a sincere believer proved more complicated than Gabriela had looked for. She was getting good TV out of it, but her stomach lining paid the price. She watched the Israelis grind their teeth at some of the things Lester Stark said, which also made life harder for her. This even though they *liked* Stark, at least compared to most televangelists.

When she grumbled, the preacher only smiled. "I didn't come here to censor myself. You wouldn't want me to censor myself, would you, Ms. Sandoval?"

"No-o," Gabriela said, and clenched her own teeth. Stark knew how to push buttons, all right. Censorship was a dirty word to her. But when she thought about it, she meant dirty words, tits and ass too early in the evening, or maybe too much violence. She hadn't worried about suppressing religious opinions that still struck her as medieval . . . till now.

Weird thing was, even medieval religious opinions might be too modern. God's comeback was looking more impressive and unlikely than George Foreman's. As Brandon had found out the hard way, God still packed a punch—and He probably hadn't got fat sitting on the sidelines the past 3,000 years.

Whenever Stark talked about the Last Days, he talked about the Second Coming of Jesus. That made the Israelis jerk and twitch. They didn't just not believe it. Hearing anyone suggest it *might* happen pissed them off.

Gabriela got a text from Shlomo Kupferman after the minister preached on Romans 8:28. She called back with more than a little apprehension. The Religious Affairs Minister could pitch her and Stark out of Israel, and they hadn't done everything she wanted yet.

She figured she'd reach a secretary or voicemail. But a gruff voice barked in her ear: "This is Kupferman."

"Oh, hello, Rabbi. Gabriela Sandoval."

"I know who you are," Kupferman growled. "What I don't know is how you put up with Lester's bullshit. He's my friend, but he knows about God the way my cat knows about hang gliding . . . and I don't have a cat."

"Heh," Gabriela said, but then, her spine stiffening, she added, "That hasn't kept you from working with him before."

"What did the English say about American soldiers during the war? 'They're overpaid, oversexed, and *over here.*' Lester's over here now."

Gabriela couldn't say it wasn't her fault Stark was in the Holy Land. It damn well was. *Smooth,* she told herself, and tried to turn the subject: "He's not trying to convert any Jews."

"He knows better. But I'm so sick of the more-in-sorrow-than-in-anger *dreck* from *goyim,*" Kupferman said. "You think the Last Days are all about Jesus and the poor stupid Jews'll get it in the neck again for not believing in Him. And you know what? When Jesus doesn't show, you're going to look mighty damn dumb."

Gabriela had to hide her surprise at hearing the rabbi so profane. "Include me out of that, please," she said. "I don't have any idea what will happen."

"That's right, you're one who doesn't believe in anything. You signed the release that proved it. So did your associate. How did that work out for him?"

"Not too well," Gabriela said tightly. If Brandon hadn't been such a thoroughgoing asshole, Kupferman would be having this conversation with him right now, because she'd be dead. Some of what she felt for him was honest hate, which he'd earned. But a little was survivor guilt. She couldn't help it, no matter how much she wanted to.

"No, not too well." The Religious Affairs Minister bore down on the words. "And Lester sounds like such a jerk." Kupferman muttered something that wasn't English or, by the sound of it, polite. "Still, what the Muslims spew about the Last Days is *really* poisonous. Breaking all the crosses? Or killing all the Jews? That's not going to happen again, no matter what the Grand Mufti preaches. He should have an accident—with a rocket or a bullet, *alevai omayn*."

"Do they take that kind of vicious propaganda seriously?" Gabriela said. "Or do they just cook it up to keep their people happy?"

"They believe it," Kupferman said. "That makes it worse, not better, because it won't end up the way that dumb-ass camel driver told them it would, and they'll go nuts when they find out they've got it wrong, too."

Dumb-ass camel driver? Gabriela almost swallowed her teeth. In the USA, most Jews were good, tolerant liberals—Saul Buchbinder jumped to mind. Everybody'd dumped on them so much, they didn't want to take shots at anybody else. Things here were different. Here, Jews were top dogs, and looked down their noses at their neighbors. It felt bizarre.

"If the Grand Mufti is the one who's getting on your nerves, why worry about Lester Stark?" she said. "His heart's in the right place."

"Yes, but his head's up his—" Kupferman broke off. "I've got enough *tsuris* I don't need without him."

Gabriela had heard that word often enough from Saul to know what it meant. "No trouble from me," she said soothingly. "And none from Reverend Stark, either, not really. He's talking to his home crowd, with language they understand."

The Religious Affairs Minister made a discontented noise. "I'd be happier if things were different."

"If things were different, Rabbi, we wouldn't be worrying about any of this, would we?"

Kupferman hung up on her. For a moment, she was offended.

Who did he think he was? What did the sudden case of dial tone mean? Slowly, she began to smile. What was it likely to mean, except that she'd convinced Kupferman but the rabbi didn't care to admit it?

"What's going on now?" Eric eyed the fancy tent going up where the Dome of the Rock had stood, inside the rising Third Temple.

Orly shrugged. "Beats me." She called out to one of the workmen and asked him. Eric grinned wryly. That never would've occurred to him. Orly was way more outgoing than he was.

Even if he'd asked, the workman might have told him to stick it. When the guy looked at Orly, he was all smiles. "We're making the —," he answered; Eric didn't know the key word.

"They're making the what?" he asked Orly.

She repeated it in Hebrew, which did him no good. Then she translated it: "The Tabernacle, I think you would say."

Eric didn't think he would say that. Then he got it. "The tent where the Ark lived before the Hebrews took Jerusalem and built the First Temple?"

Orly nodded. "That's right."

"So are they going to move the Ark here?" If they were, nobody'd told Eric anything about it.

"Beats me," Orly said again. She asked the workman another question. It was so simple! Eric wondered again why he didn't think to do things like that.

"That's the plan," the guy said. "If the Ark shows it doesn't want to get moved, we back off and try something else."

If the Ark didn't like something, somebody might end up dead. Eric changed the subject: "How do you know what the Tabernacle is supposed to look like?"

The workman gave him a look he'd seen before in Israel, more often than he would have liked to. It was the look the Orthodox gave their secular cousins, and it said, *Call yourself a Jew? Some nerve!* This guy, at least, answered: "It's in Exodus." He started quoting chapter and verse in Biblical Hebrew, which bore the same relation to Amos Oz as Chaucer did to Martin Amos.

Eric let the archaic language roll over him. Then he said, "All right. I'm convinced," and walked away.

No doubt the workman would feel smug—he was a hell of a Biblical scholar. Eric didn't care. He didn't mean the hard hat's arguments had convinced him they were right. He just meant they'd convinced him the Bible laid out marching orders for assembling the Tabernacle.

Walking up onto the Temple Mount was a man who looked familiar. When he crushed one cigarette underfoot and lit another at the same time, Eric recognized Munir al-Nuwayhi. He waved to the Israeli Arab before he thought about what he was doing. Al-Nuwayhi ambled over, shook hands with him, and nodded to Orly. Orly nodded back, polite but cool.

"How's it going?" Eric asked. He knew what Israeli Jews and Arabs too often felt about each other, but told himself he was above all that. Making himself believe it was harder these days. "Haven't seen you in too long."

"You know how it is," Munir said with an expressive shrug. "I'm not exactly welcome up here. I'm permitted—I give Yoram credit for that—but I'm not welcome."

"So what are you doing here, then?" Orly asked bluntly. She didn't add *Spying?* Not out loud she didn't, anyway.

Munir shrugged that shrug again. "I came back to visit . . ." His voice trailed off, as if he also didn't want to say all of what he was thinking. But then he came out with it: "To visit the scene of the crime."

Orly bristled. Eric didn't want a fight. There'd already been too many bigger fights over the Temple Mount, what was on it, and what should be on it. Quickly, he said, "They're doing the best they can, I think."

"You would say so," Munir replied. "It doesn't look that way to me. But what you think, and what I think, and what Ms. Binur thinks, that doesn't matter so much these days, does it?"

"How do you mean?" Eric asked, though he feared he knew.

Sure enough, the Israeli Arab answered, "What God thinks is what matters. I prayed in a mosque the other day, for the first time in a couple of years. It felt odd, but I still know what to do."

"Did it help?" Now Orly sounded genuinely curious. She'd been talking about how everything was in God's hands, too. Eric kept trying to resist the idea. He had less and less luck with each passing day.

"I don't know," Munir said with one more shrug. "I am a sinner, a backslider. I know it. God knows it. Maybe He will forgive me. Maybe He won't. *Inshallah*, as they say. Peace be unto both of you." Away he went, pausing only to fumble for a fresh Marlboro.

"He has the willies as bad as you do," Eric said to Orly. Then he had to explain what the willies were.

When she got it, she nodded. "You're right. And we're secular, remember, he and I. Some Orthodox Jews still won't come up here," she answered. "No matter what Kupferman says, they worry about trespassing on the old Holy of Holies."

In a way, with the real Ark in the Shrine of the Book, that was funny. In another way, it was admirable: some people stuck to tradition come what might. In yet another way, it added more complications to what was already complicated. "Are they more Orthodox or less than the guys who *are* up here?" Eric asked.

"I don't know." Orly looked startled. "I don't think it's a question of more or less. They're just different."

"I guess." Eric snapped his fingers. "I know what we should have asked Lester Stark when we ran into him."

"What he's doing here?" His lady love liked Christian ministers even less than secular Muslims.

"Well, that, too," Eric said. "But I wondered if he was a pre-, a mid-, or a post-Tribulationalist."

"A what?" Orly didn't speak this lingo.

"Whether he thinks the Rapture is coming before, during, or after the Tribulation."

"Rapture?" Her blank look proved she didn't grow up in the States. Whether you believed in it or not, you couldn't not hear about it there.

"Where all the believing Christians get snatched up bodily into heaven to be with Jesus in the Last Days," Eric explained.

"They really believe that?" Orly sounded as if she didn't trust her own ears.

"They do." Eric held up his right hand. "So help me, they do." He hesitated. "You know what else? After so many freaky things already, ruling *anything* out is harder than it used to be."

"No, it isn't. I know bullshit when I hear it." Orly came straight to the point.

"Did you think we'd find the Ark? Did you think somebody would die if he touched it? Did you think it would knock rockets out of the sky and treat the President of Iran like King Nebuchadnezzar?" Now Eric sounded like the believer.

"The President of Iran had it coming," Orly said, which wasn't the point. "Besides, the Ark comes out of the Old Testament, not the New Testament."

That *was* to the point. *The stories I grew up believing in are true,* she was saying. *The stories those other people grew up believing in are nonsense.* Everybody was saying that, even if everybody couldn't be right. There were at least three competing stories. Some people would end up disappointed. Some people were liable to end up a lot worse off than disappointed: dead, maybe toasting in hell forever.

One of Orly's eyebrows quirked as she tried to make a joke: "Some people ought to disappear. Nobody would care if they didn't come back, either."

"Yeah." Eric grinned, but his heart wasn't in it. He looked back to the Tabernacle that would house the Ark till the Third Temple grew over it. A year earlier, he would have figured the Ark was lost for good and the Dome of the Rock was a permanent feature of the Temple Mount.

Permanent? The word made him want to laugh—or shake. What was permanent? God only knew. Then he *did* shake, because chances were that was true.

Yitzhak Avigad hadn't pulled strings to help carry the Ark back through Jerusalem to the Temple Mount. There were no strings *to* pull, as far as he knew. But when Rabbi Kupferman called to ask if he wanted to do it, he didn't turn him down.

Kupferman waited outside the Shrine of the Book to get him through security. "Are you ready?" the rabbi asked gruffly.

"What? You think I'll tell you no now?" Yitzhak said.

Kupferman's mouth twitched. "Mm—maybe not. Come on."

Yitzhak thought he'd been early, but most of the other men who would bear the Ark waited inside the Shrine of the Book. They were praying before it. He joined them. You had to be careful not to pray to the Ark itself, but to God through it. Otherwise, how was it any different from praying to the Golden Calf?

After Kupferman brought in the other bearers, he too paused for a moment to pray. Then he said, "Let's go," as if they were furniture movers. And they were, though the furniture belonged to God, not man.

As Yitzhak bent to take up a gold-plated *shittim*-wood pole, fear ran through him. If this wasn't what God wanted, he would be dead the next instant. Well, he probably wouldn't know what hit him. Brandon hadn't seemed to. Worse ways to go: his stretch in the IDF taught him that.

His hand came down on the gold. It felt cool. That he knew it felt cool meant he still lived, meant God approved of what he was doing. "Lift!" Kupferman said.

Some bearers grunted with effort. Yitzhak started to, but caught himself. The massy Ark should have been far beyond their power to lift, but it wasn't. Yitzhak felt he might have been lifting ten or fifteen kilos, no more.

How was that possible? Only one answer occurred to him: the same way it was possible for a man to drop dead after he touched a box made of gold and gold-covered wood. It was a miracle.

Out of the Shrine of the Book they went, out and east. They reversed the journey the Ark made when it left its long seclusion under the Temple Mount. Security was as tight as before. Crowds were, if anything, larger and crazier.

Red-gold light from the rising sun shone into Yitzhak's face whenever buildings didn't block it. It seemed to strike fire from the Ark. Yitzhak let awe wash over him. King David's men brought the Ark into Jerusalem like this after the children of Israel took the city from the Jebusites. After that? No one had had such a moment since, not for the past 3,000 years.

As David had then, Shlomo Kupferman danced ahead of the Ark. Yitzhak had watched him do it when the Ark came forth from the Temple Mount. He wasn't a young man, but danced as if he were. And if his heart gave out and he keeled over—well, again, what better way to go?

By all the signs, he might have been ready to run the 10,000 meters at the next Olympics. A couple of bearers were paunchy and starting to sweat just from the walk. They never would have lasted kicking up their heels the way Kupferman did.

Into the Old City. It wasn't as old as the Ark. Nothing from those days survived except a little stonework on the Temple Mount.

Yitzhak set his jaw as they went through the Jewish Quarter. Back when the Jordanians held it, they'd used grave markers from the Jewish cemetery for paving stones and in latrines. The God of the Old Testament was jealous and vengeful. Maybe He was laughing, as His Ark went through these streets held by Jews once more.

How the soldiers held back the crowds by the Western Wall, Yitzhak never knew. For so many years, the Wall had been the Jews' closest approach to the fallen Temple. As Israel had revived, so would the Temple.

Up the steps of the Bab al-Silsila to the top of the Temple Mount. The Tabernacle did duty for the Temple, as it had till Solomon got busy. The cloth fluttered and flapped as helicopters skimmed low. Were more Arab mortars zeroing in here? Would it do them any good if they were?

Those cloth walls turned sunlight to gloom as Yitzhak and the other bearers entered the Tabernacle. Two curtains separated the Holy of Holies from the rest of the tent. "You have leave to enter," Kupferman said, holding them apart with his hands. "After this, it is forbidden to all but the High Priest on Yom Kippur."

They carried the Ark of the Covenant into the Holy of Holies. Rabbi Kupferman pointed to the exposed stone of the Temple Mount, showing them exactly where to place it. Yitzhak thought it would go on floating above the stone. But it settled into place there. The Mount trembled and creaked beneath his feet, as if taking up the weight of the world . . . or more. The Ark was home.

17

Israel was the only working democracy in the Middle East. *Working* often meant like yeast in dough. You could get caught in a demonstration in Jerusalem any time except during Shabbat.

The protesters were noisy and passionate. In the States, they would have been screaming about war or abortion. Not much else got people there so worked up. Israelis had a lower boiling point. This *was* the Middle East.

And these demonstrators, shouting and waving placards and beating on drums and messing up traffic were marching because . . . the people rebuilding the Temple intended to sacrifice their red heifer. Some demonstrators were Orthodox Jews who didn't believe mere mortals should do anything to hasten the Messiah. HE WILL COME WHEN THE LORD WILLS! shouted a sign held by a bearded man whose wide black hat and long black coat would have been stylish in Vilno or Cracow in 1791.

Others were dressed like anybody in the twenty-first-century West. They were left-wing, secular, and marched for the Israeli

SPCA. ANIMAL SACRIFICE IS ANIMAL CRUELTY! their signs read, and SAVE THE HEIFER! They were even more raucous than the ultra-Orthodox.

Adding to the din were car horns from drivers stuck because people were marching down the street. Israeli drivers honked when everything went smoothly. To Eric, it was their least endearing trait—along with passing on the right whenever they felt like it. Drivers also screamed at the cops trying to shepherd the demonstrators along.

"*Cus ummak!*" the drivers bellowed, and other endearments. Demonstrators yelled back. A good time was had by all.

TV crews filmed the chaos so the rest of Israel and the world could see the good time. Eric thought he spotted one of Gabriela Sandoval's cameramen. He wondered what Reverend Stark would say about this. Nothing nice about the demonstrators, not unless Eric was way off base.

"Save the heifer!" a woman yelled. "Meat is murder!" She was skinny, with spiked, gelled hair dyed the same shade of green as her environmentally friendly T-shirt.

An Orthodox demonstrator swung his placard at a policeman. The cop clouted him with a nightstick. What had been noisy and melodramatic suddenly got more serious than Eric wanted. Protesters and police waded into each other, swearing and swinging and assaulting. He ducked into the first open door he saw.

It was a *shawarma* shop. The smell of roasting lamb reminded Eric he was hungry. "Some fun," said the skinny bald guy behind the counter.

"Fun. Right." Eric pointed to the meat. "Let me have one."

"Sure." The counterman chuckled. He saw the irony, too. He stuffed lamb into a pita pocket, then held out his hand. Eric gave him a 20-NIS bill. After pocketing his change, he filled the pita to bursting with salad fixings, then bit in.

"Good," he said. "What do you think of all this?"

"You were smart to bail out of it." As the man spoke, a tear-gas grenade, trailing smoke, flew into the crowd. Eric thought it had been loud before. The counterman ran out and slammed the door. "Keep some gas out of here, *alevai*," he said. When he went back, he pulled out a gas mask. Israelis were ready for anything.

Eric wasn't. "Do you have a back way out?" he asked. His eyes started to burn. He hoped it was his imagination. When the counterman put on the mask, he knew it wasn't.

"Follow me. Don't know how much good it'll do you," the counterman said. The mask muffled his voice.

Still clutching the *shawarma*, Eric let the fellow take him out to an alley. It was narrower than Jerusalem's streets—not wide enough to let Eric spread his arms. It stank of garbage. Other people with streaming eyes came running down it, fleeing the gas. An Orthodox man vomited, then staggered on, wiping his eyes with his black wool sleeve.

"Some fun," the *shawarma* seller said again.

It was either stand there and get trampled or go with the flow. Eric went. The gas didn't help his appetite, which was a shame—it was a good *shawarma*. He ended up throwing out half, and hoped the rest would stay down.

Then he spotted a McDonald's. He hurried in, not for the food but for the men's room. He wasn't the only one splashing his face to get the tear gas out of his eyes.

"They'll kill the cow anyway," said another man, yanking out paper towels and drying his face. He was secular: he wore a tank top that showed off his muscled, tattooed arms.

Jews who weren't secular didn't get tattoos. They thought the marks distorted the image of God . . . and they remembered the Holocaust. Eric had known a couple of survivors who'd carried Hitler's numbers to the grave with them. At a different time, the Orthodox man drying his beard might have said something sharp to his fellow demonstrator. Now he nodded mournfully. "They are," he agreed. "They think you can bring the Messiah any time, like you raise hothouse flowers. Can you push God like that?"

Eric said, "Maybe they think God is pushing them."

He won himself two glares. The guy with the tats had *really* big arms. The Orthodox man was wiry, but fifteen years younger than Eric. *Me and my big mouth,* the archaeologist thought. "If they do, they're wrong," the Orthodox man said, and proceeded to start quoting the Bible to prove his point.

Eric had had enough of that. To change the subject, he asked, "What do you think will happen if the Temple goes up?"

The man threw wadded-up paper towels in the trash bin. "Trouble," he answered. Eric couldn't quarrel with that.

After more than 1,900 years, the hour was come 'round at last. From the Pool of Siloam, Chaim Avigad and the other ritually pure boys watched through binoculars as attendants led the red heifer across the causeway to the Mount of Olives. Soon, people would be able to become ritually pure without living the life Chaim and the others were stuck with. They were excited about it.

He wasn't. There went Rosie, and he couldn't do anything to help her. He would be on the Mount of Olives, and he would watch while they cut his friend's throat. Didn't God have another way to let people become ritually clean?

Everybody said no. Everybody said this was how things worked in ancient days, so this was how they had to work now. Chaim thought that was hooey. Had tanks protected the site the last time someone killed a red heifer? Had helicopters flown about it? Had TV waited to broadcast the sacrifice?

Not likely! Things had changed since the Second Temple. Wouldn't God also have changed in all that time? Chaim thought so. No one else seemed to. Maybe he was the stupid, impious one.

But, as boys his age often will, he was sure the rest of the world was out of kilter.

"Come on, boys!" said the man in charge of this part of the ceremony. "Dip your jars in the pool, then we'll help you onto your oxen and you'll get going."

Soldiers held a perimeter around the pool, to keep anybody from sniping at the boys. If someone had a mortar or some rockets . . . In that case, it would be in God's hands. So far, He'd handled things. Chances were He could do it again.

Chaim believed that along with believing God didn't need this old-fashioned, cruel ceremony. It was like believing the earth was flat and round at once. He didn't notice.

Bubble wrap popped under his knees when he bent to fill his jug from Modin. The water chilled his fingers. The vessel, once full, was heavy. He grunted when he pulled it out of the pool. More bubbles popped when he set it on the plastic.

He stood. A man led an ox with a board across its back up to him. The board didn't have stirrups. The man lifted him up onto it. He sat crosslegged, the way they'd told him to. The man handed him the ritually pure jar of Siloam water. He held it in his lap.

"Ready?" the man asked. Numbly, Chaim nodded. The man tugged at the ox's lead rope. The stupid animal walked forward. The man nodded. "Here we go," he said over his shoulder. As far as he was concerned, everything was fine.

The Pool of Siloam lay in David's City, below the walls of the Old City. Slowly, the ox climbed toward the Dung Gate, the one closest to the Temple Mount on the south side. More soldiers stood at the gate and on the wall. They looked ready for anything. Maybe because they were, nothing happened.

It wasn't till you neared the Western Wall that you realized how massive it was. Chaim wouldn't have wanted to build anything like that without earth-moving machinery. People had carved those massive blocks by hand. No jackhammers. No dynamite. They'd moved them by muscle power—men, oxen, maybe horses and donkeys. No engines. No electricity. Only faith. People said faith could move mountains. How about building one?

A ramp led to the top of the Temple Mount. It had been a stairway. It would be again, once heavy machines no longer needed to go up there. In the meantime, it helped the oxen carrying the boys with water from the Pool of Siloam to the top of the Mount.

Chaim stared at the Tabernacle. That was something even more ancient than the Temple. Seeing the fabric flutter in the breeze reminded him the children of Israel had been the Bedouins of their day: nomads wandering the desert. They and the Arabs had the same roots. *But we're different plants,* he thought.

The thud of the ox's hooves on the paving stones was a sound old as time. David would have heard it, and Moses, and Abraham. Like the Tabernacle, here it was again. What was old was made new again. *Like Israel,* Chaim thought.

They went onto the causeway, passing over the Kidron Valley. The causeway was new, thrown up by machines: steel and cement. Nothing like it existed in ancient times. But they'd spanned the valley when they needed to sacrifice a red heifer. They'd used hand tools to build their causeways. But they'd done it.

He looked ahead. There stood Rosie, calm with bovine placidity. She didn't know what they'd do to her. She'd known nothing but good since she came to *Eretz Yizrael*—and before that. Rabbi Kupferman was feeding her some grain. She didn't know he had a knife no doubt carefully inspected to make sure the edge was nick-free.

She didn't understand the pyre of cedar and fig and pine, either. It was pyramid-shaped, and had an opening facing west toward the Temple Mount. They would lead her in, and they would turn her around so *she* faced west, and Kupferman would . . .

Don't think about that, Chaim told himself. It was like trying not to think about an elephant. Every stride from the ox brought him closer to . . . what he was not thinking about.

He tried thinking about the rabbi instead. There'd been some grumbling when Shlomo Kupferman announced he would conduct the sacrifice. *Would be here,* Chaim corrected himself frantically. In ancient days, the person who would be here was the High Priest's son and heir. By doing this himself, Kupferman announced that he intended to become the High Priest when there was a High Priest again. Nobody was in a good position to tell him he couldn't. He *was* the Religious Affairs Minister. That wasn't the same as being the High Priest's son, but you could say it was the modern equivalent. Kupferman had. And he'd got away with it.

He wasn't claiming to be High Priest yet. He wore an ordinary priest's white vestments, like the ones in the Reconstruction Alliance's museum. Chaim had never been to the museum, but he'd seen online pictures of the vestments and Temple goods there.

In olden days, the officiating priest would have stayed secluded in a room of the Temple before he . . . officiated. Every day, he would have been sprinkled with ashes from all the red heifers ever sacrificed before (careful there!), to make sure he was ritually pure.

You couldn't do that now. The chain had been broken all these years. Some rabbis said that was reason enough to let it stay broken. Not Kupferman. He insisted that if modern Jews did their best, God would accept it. If you rebuilt the Temple . . .

You had to sacrifice a red heifer.

Chaim started to puddle up. *I won't cry,* he thought fiercely.

The elders of Israel would have gone up onto the Mount of Olives to witness the sacrifice in days gone by. In a way, the elders were there now: TV would broadcast the ceremony. Kupferman used modern things when they suited him.

Chaim looked down from the causeway. It passed over the

graves of the rich who waited there for the Messiah. The causeway was double-arched, to keep pollution from rising from the ground and invalidating the ceremony.

"Welcome!" *"Shalom!"*

A man's voice, and a woman's. Chaim didn't see anybody, but he knew he'd heard them. "Did you say something?" he asked the man leading his ox.

"No." The fellow shook his head. "Nobody said anything."

"But—" Chaim looked around again. None of the other boys or the men leading their oxen had heard the voices.

Am I going nuts? he wondered. How could he help Rosie if he couldn't help himself? How could he help Rosie even if he *could* help himself?

He heard more voices. Some spoke Hebrew, some Yiddish, the way some pious Jews did with everyone except God. Some spoke Russian, some English. Some spoke languages he didn't recognize. Their rising tide meant he couldn't understand any of them. Nobody else near heard anything.

He looked to the heavens. *Why me?* he asked God, as Job might have. God didn't answer Job, and He didn't answer Chaim, either. God wasn't in the habit of answering. He usually asked questions. Answers were up to you.

How am I supposed to know what the answers are if I don't even know whether I'm in my right mind? Chaim demanded of Him.

One more thing God didn't answer.

"The Jews will not build their Temple," Jamal Ashrawi preached. "It would insult God if they succeeded. They took down the Dome of the Rock. Will they build on the spot from which the Prophet, peace be unto Him, left earth behind to go with the angel Gabriel to heaven?"

"No!" shouted the crowd in the mosque in Hebron.

Jamal Ashrawi said no more. He knew he'd already said everything that needed saying. Some who listened would have weapons.
Some would be hot to use them. Even with the mortar from Iran,
they hadn't stopped the Zionists from building the causeway. If
they could ruin the rabbis' ceremony, though . . .

Officially, Ashrawi didn't know any crews were operating. If the
Israelis caught him, he could say he'd spoken abstractly. It would
embarrass the Zionist entity. It might save him.

He stayed in Hebron and watched TV. He, who had killed a kid
after his pilgrimage, scorned the Jews for wanting to kill the red
heifer.

It *was* an impressive ceremony. The rabbi's plain white costume
reminded him of a pilgrim's robe that destroyed the difference between rich and poor. The red heifer was a handsome beast. The
pyre where it would burn was large and well made. No doubt the
pagans in Arabia before Muhammad's time had had impressive
ceremonies. But they worshiped idols. Ashrawi thought the Zionists did, too.

He watched boys ride across the causeway on boards fixed to
the backs of oxen. Something about them—or maybe about one of
them—raised his hackles. A slow smile stretched across his face.
He thought they were in for a surprise.

The Grand Mufti didn't know what kind of weapons the *mujahidin* would use. The 160mm mortar was lost. But the Palestinians
had plenty of smaller, more portable 120mm and 82mm models.
They had rockets and machine guns. Maybe an artillery piece hid
in a cave whose mouth God had turned in the right direction.
There was also the simplicity of assault rifles and explosive vests.

A rising shriek came from the TV. Jamal Ashrawi knew what
that meant. Somebody had fired a rack of *Katyushas*. Two dozen
rockets smashing down at once could tear up a square kilometer.

One burst in the Jews' cemetery, not close to the red heifer and
the rabbi who would kill it. The picture slewed crazily as the cam-

eraman ducked for cover. For a moment, only cloud-flecked blue sky showed on the screen Ashrawi was watching. Another rocket blew up, this one also, by the sound of it, not close enough to the sacrifice.

Hillside replaced sky: the cameraman found his courage. Haji Jamal saw graves blasted open and tombstones shattered and tilted. He waited for the rest of the barrage to devastate the area.

He waited . . . and waited. One more Russian rocket smashed to earth only ten or twenty meters from the red heifer—but the charge in its nose didn't go off.

"You idiot!" Was Haji Jamal screaming at the rocket or the man who'd launched it or the drunken infidel who'd botched its assembly?

Katyushas were reliable. Armies and guerrillas everywhere used them. Why were the Palestinians cursed with a defective batch?

"*Inshallah*," Haji Jamal muttered. Of course it was as God willed it. Everything was—everything had to be.

This was the second time an attack on the Jews rebuilding their Temple had failed—the third, if you counted the Iranians' fiasco. If God willed it to be so . . . But that was not an *if*. Such failures argued that God might want the Temple built—rebuilt, the Zionists claimed.

Why? Not for the reasons the Jews thought He did. If God wanted the Jews to build the Temple, then it had a role to play in the Last Days.

Well, then, let them build whatever they pleased now. Why not? It would only make their downfall sweeter. When Jesus and the Mahdi came to sweep them away, when the stones and the trees cried out that they had Jews hiding behind them so the Muslims could kill those Jews . . . How the Zionist dogs would howl then!

One of the bodyguards scowled. "Why do you smile, Haji?" the man demanded. A chill ran through Jamal Ashrawi. Just because the guards protected him from the Israelis, that didn't mean they wouldn't turn on him. "Why do you smile?" this fellow repeated. "Everything we try goes wrong."

"It is as God wills, Ishak," the Grand Mufti said. Several guards frowned and muttered. Ashrawi explained what he thought God's will meant. "Let them build," he finished. "Are they not building their own destruction?"

The guards didn't say yes right away. They put their heads together. At last, one by one, they nodded and smiled carnivorous smiles. "It could be so, Haji Jamal," Ishak said. "How they will shriek when God shows them they have built on sand."

"Why didn't you see this sooner?" another bodyguard asked.

Ashrawi spread his hands. "I am only a man, Ali. God holds everything in His mind, from the Creation to the Last Days. I have to judge by signs and portents. Usually, we oppose the Zionists with all our power. It took me longer than it should have to realize the best way to oppose the Jews now is not to. If God opposes them—"

"And He does," Ali broke in.

"Yes." The Grand Mufti nodded, too. "He does. And, since He does, the best thing is to let Him confound them. Let their hopes grow. God will deal with them, and they will not have joy of it."

The guards muttered more among themselves. Then they also nodded again. "We shall be here for the Last Days!" one said.

"It is an honor," Ashrawi agreed. "We must deserve it."

When the *Katyushas* screamed in, two boys jumped off their oxen and ran back toward the Temple Mount. So did a man leading the oxen. Chaim had a hard time blaming them. The rockets' screech was made to terrify. And there wasn't an Israeli who didn't know what they could do. *Eretz Yisrael*'s neighbors had launched them too often to leave anyone in doubt.

He wondered why he didn't run, too. He wouldn't pollute himself if he did—probably. The causeway was made to carry the red heifer and the man who would sacrifice it above the religious pollution that rose from the ground. But he stayed, even when first one rocket, then another, burst in the graveyards below.

Ahead, Rosie looked around in mild surprise. She showed no fear. *She's too brave to sacrifice,* Chaim thought. Rabbi Kupferman wouldn't have agreed. He stood by the pyre as if carved from stone. Chaim admired Rosie's courage without noticing his. That wasn't fair, but he couldn't do anything about it.

More *Katyushas* crashed down. These didn't go off. Chaim heard thumping and clattering as they struck and rolled away. "It's a miracle," said the man leading his ox. "God wants us to go ahead. Otherwise, all those . . . miserable things would have blown up, like they usually do."

Was it a miracle? Was God putting His oar in again? Did He really want Rosie dead so much? Chaim *wouldn't* believe it. But what else was he supposed to think?

He didn't have much time to make up his mind, not any more. He was almost to the sacrificial pyre. He looked down into the ritually pure jug. He hadn't spilled a drop of water from the Pool of Siloam. If that wasn't luck . . . What difference did it make? They'd kill Rosie, and soon.

Even here, Rabbi Kupferman or somebody had gone all out to avoid pollution. The rabbi and red heifer and pyre stood on a concrete platform raised on little concrete arches. Those kept pollution from rising up, like the arches on the causeway.

Off in the distance, bombs burst and machine guns chattered. Was the *Heyl Ha-Avir* paying back the people who'd launched the *Katyushas*? Chaim didn't get the chance to wonder. The man who led his ox said, "Time to get on with the show."

He didn't want to get down. But his shoes thumped on the concrete. His heart thumped, too. The rest of the boys who hadn't run descended from their oxen, too. *Maybe there won't be enough water now,* Chaim thought. *Maybe they'll call things off.*

Kupferman showed no sign of that. He stood with Rosie, waiting for everything to be ready. Everyone except Rosie looked solemn: the rabbi, the men who'd led the oxen, the other boys, even the cameraman. Everyone except Rosie and Chaim, rather. The heifer was calm, and Chaim was frantic.

Suddenly, he knew what to do. The insight was almost blinding. Was God talking to him? Did prophets feel this when He spoke through them? Chaim wouldn't have been surprised. He felt that sure, that exalted, that *right*.

He ran up to Kupferman. The old man's frown was fearsome. This wasn't in the program. "What do you want, boy?" Kupferman said gruffly. "Get back where you belong."

Chaim knew exactly what he wanted: "Take me instead!"

"*What?*" The rabbi's eyebrows came down and together in a scowl that should have petrified Chaim.

It didn't. "Don't sacrifice the red heifer," he said. "She hasn't done anything to get her throat cut for. She's . . ." He found the word. "She's innocent. Use my ashes instead."

Kupferman stared at him as if noting him for the first time. After staring, he did Chaim the courtesy of not laughing at him. "When Abraham was about to sacrifice Isaac, God gave him a ram instead. So you want to turn it around and die in place of a beast?"

Chaim nodded. "I'd know what I was dying for. Rosie has no idea. That's not right."

"The purity of the red heifer is what the ritual requires," Kupferman said. "Not even a cloth has ever lain across her back. That would be pollution, and would render her unfit."

If that was what it took . . . Chaim grabbed for the handkerchief in his trouser pocket.

Hands seized his arm. Two who'd led oxen had come up without his even noticing. He wouldn't have had much chance against one of them. Against two men, he had none. "Come on, son," one said, not unkindly. "Don't mess things up."

"But—"

That man twisted his arm, enough to show how much it might hurt if he twisted more. "*Don't* mess things up," he repeated.

"We go on." Kupferman sounded half pious, half relieved. *I scared him,* Chaim thought. That didn't do anybody any good, though: not Chaim, not Rosie.

Kupferman prayed in Hebrew that sounded more Biblical than modern, and in Aramaic, which was more like Hebrew than Arabic was, but not much more. Chaim wondered how he knew what prayers to offer when no one had conducted this ritual in close to 2,000 years. The verses were bound to be in the Mishnah. Everything was: it was Judaism's file cabinet, for those who knew where to look. And Kupferman would.

He led Rosie into the hollow space inside the pyre and turned her so she faced west. The last thing the red heifer should see was the Temple—or, here, the Tabernacle. Rosie let out a surprised grunt when Rabbi Kupferman stooped and tied her feet together, but no more. She *was* innocent; she expected no evil.

Kupferman looked toward the west. No doubt he *was* seeing the Temple in his mind's eye. He took the knife in his right hand. "No!" Chaim cried bitterly.

Swift and practiced as a *shochet,* Kupferman cut the red heifer's throat. Ritual slaughterers weren't supposed to cause much pain. Rosie's grunt, again, sounded more surprised than hurt. But blood spurted from her. There was red, and there was *red*. Her hide and her blood told of the difference.

Rabbi Kupferman, his face exalted, caught the blood in the cup of his left palm. He dipped his right forefinger in the gore seven times and sprinkled it toward the Holy of Holies. "O God, I thank Thee for letting me live in such times!" he cried.

Rosie no longer lived in them. Pampered her whole life but betrayed at the end, she crumpled. A man holding Chaim murmured, "The sacrifice is accomplished." No Jew had meant those words literally from the days of the Second Temple till now.

Kupferman lit the pyre. It caught at once—did oil soak the wood? He held up another piece of cedar. "Is this cedar?" he asked three times. He held up a small plant with long, narrow leaves and a spike of blue flowers. "Is this hyssop?" Once more, the question rose three times. He held up woolen fabric dyed almost the color of Rosie's blood. "Is this scarlet?" he asked three times.

No one tried to tell him it wasn't. He tied the piece of cedar and the hyssop plant with the scarlet fabric and cast them onto the red heifer's burning body. They were not so rare as the heifer, but they made an essential part of the sacrifice.

After the pyre burned down, the remains would be quenched with the water from the Pool of Siloam. Then they'd be beaten into ashes with sticks and stone mallets and sieved to make sure they were fine enough. In olden days, one third would have been stored on the Temple Mount, one third on the Mount of Olives, the rest shared among priests all over *Eretz Yisrael*. Till the Temple rose again, the priesthood was extinct. Would half stay here and half go to the Temple Mount?

What difference did it make? Rosie was dead. "Let go," Chaim told the men who'd grabbed him. "I won't do anything now."

They did. They weren't mean. They were just doing what they thought was right. That made no difference to Chaim.

The pyre blazed into his face. Nobody would pound Rosie's remains into ashes right away. Despair and disgust filled Chaim. He'd been kept ritually pure all his life . . . for *this*? What a stupid, pointless waste!

He jumped off the concrete platform and ran. Behind him, Kupferman and the boys who'd spent their lives in ritual purity shouted. Chaim didn't care. With one leap, he'd thrown that away. He was free now, free to be ordinary the rest of his life.

He ran downhill—that was easier. If he ran straight toward the graveyards there, so what? It didn't matter any more. He was just a regular Jew now. And if that turned out not to be good enough, the ashes of a red heifer—of his friend—could purify him again.

Tears stung as he dodged among the headstones. Those *Katyushas* had knocked down many and blasted graves open. Chaim swore. Even regular Jews had no good word for terrorists.

"*Shalom!*" "Welcome!" "Here he is at last!"

Those voices again! Chaim looked around wildly. He didn't see anybody . . . and then he did. What seemed a ghostly army gathered around him—if an army could include old men and women, children, even babies, as well as people in the prime of life.

They were there and they weren't. He could see them. But he could also see *through* them. And when he heard them, he didn't think he was hearing with his ears, or not just with his ears. Farther up the Mount of Olives, Rabbi Kupferman and the ritually pure boys and the men who'd held the oxen stared down at him. Could they see all this? When the TV camera swung his way, he decided they could.

Fear seized him then. He didn't think of the spectral shapes as ghosts, but as the risen dead. Yes, he knew what this place was and what it meant. He knew—and he wanted no part of it. He fled into the Kidron Valley . . . and the dead streamed after him.

Before long, he wasn't going down any more. He was going up toward the Temple Mount. More dead rose at every moment. Some called to him in Hebrew; some, ancient ones in strange garments, in Aramaic; some in Arabic—the Muslims had put a cemetery in front of the Golden Gate, too.

That gate had stayed closed for more than 1,200 years. It had . . . till the Palestinians' mortar bomb blasted it open again. The way was narrow, but Chaim squeezed through. And the dead streamed after him into Jerusalem.

18

Yitzhak Avigad watched the sacrifice from the Temple Mount. He had IDF binoculars. They didn't put him right there, but they let him see what was going on. That would do.

When a boy ran over to Rabbi Kupferman, Yitzhak knew it was Chaim. His nephew had gone on about how he didn't want Rosie killed. She mattered more to him than to any of the other boys; he'd been along when Yitzhak accepted her.

The binoculars didn't magnify sound. Yitzhak couldn't hear what was going on on the Mount of Olives. Whatever it was, it didn't go very far. Two guys grabbed Chaim and hung on to him. The ceremony proceeded as if nothing had happened.

As if. Yitzhak wondered why those words echoed. Things weren't finished over there, and he wasn't just thinking of the sacrifice. He didn't know how he knew, but he did. He watched, waited, and worried.

Kupferman cut the red heifer's throat. He caught the blood in his cupped hand and sprinkled it toward the Temple Mount. He lit the heifer's pyre. Then he held up the cedar, hyssop, and scarlet and cast them into the flames. Yitzhak had imagined the ceremony so often, he hardly seemed to be seeing it for the first time.

All the drama should have been over. After the pyre burned itself out, the ashes would be prepared following the ancient rules. That would take some time; you needed a lot to char a carcass. Yitzhak didn't know why he kept watching so intently.

It was like being in the Army again. Sometimes you couldn't say why you knew gunmen holed up in one house and not another, but you did. And you'd be right most of the time, too. People talked about vibes or feelings or hunches. The hair prickled up on the back of his neck. It wasn't over, there on the Mount of Olives.

He groaned when Chaim jumped down from the sacrificial platform and ran back toward Jerusalem. Ritual purity gone . . . Then Yitzhak brightened. Not necessarily, not with the red heifer's ashes to restore it.

He wasn't the only one watching from the Temple Mount. "What's that crazy kid doing?" said somebody. Yitzhak glanced over. The man wore khaki, with a brigadier general's crossed swords on his shoulder straps.

"What the—?" Startled exclamations rose from several places. Yitzhak's attention snapped back to his nephew. *Something* was going on around Chaim. Even without binoculars, Yitzhak could tell as much. It looked as if the air around him was boiling—almost like heat waves from the ground on a scorching day. This was stronger than any heat waves Yitzhak had ever seen or imagined.

When he raised the field glasses . . . For a heartbeat, he didn't believe what he saw. He thought he was in a theater watching a movie full of special effects. If those writhing, half-transparent things weren't ghosts, what were they?

What indeed?

And if they *were* ghosts . . . What then? Why would ghosts come forth? Why would they throng around Chaim as he dashed across the Kidron Valley toward the Temple Mount? Why would they follow him that way? Why, unless he was . . . ?

"No," Yitzhak whispered. But he'd known cats bigger than newborn Chaim. He'd changed the kid's diapers. It wasn't angels that came out of there, either. When you'd done that stuff, it was hard to think you might be looking at . . .

The Messiah?

"You've got to be out of your mind," Yitzhak said. The brigadier glanced toward him and sidled away a couple of steps.

But if his nephew wasn't, how was he raising the dead? What else would you call this? Yitzhak shivered. Even Chaim's name meant *life*.

"It's the Messiah. *He's* the Messiah. Who else can he be?" That was a member of the Knesset—not a man from the ruling coalition, but a Labor stalwart about as secular as any Israeli ever born. Yitzhak had no idea why he would have wanted to come here. If *he* was saying things like this . . .

Yitzhak's thoughts trailed away in confusion. Why not, when his nephew'd started working miracles before his eyes?

He wondered how Mary and Joseph felt when Jesus started doing impossible things around the house. That was absurd on several different levels, but he hadn't dreamt his nephew was the Messiah. As far as he knew, Chaim hadn't, either.

So what was he doing raising the dead?

It was a good question. He wished he had a good answer.

Chaim ran through the Golden Gate. He couldn't have done that if the Palestinians' big mortar hadn't busted it up. What were *they* thinking right now? Yitzhak started to laugh. He would have paid money to see their faces.

* * *

"It's impossible!" Haji Jamal Ashrawi howled as ghosts swirled up around the Jewish boy running through the graveyard. "It's a special effect, like the ones in the movies!"

But even a bodyguard betrayed him. "Is it, Haji?" the man asked. "Is it really? See how scared the kid looks? He didn't expect this to happen—you can tell." Several of the other armed men nodded.

"No, by God!" Ashrawi insisted. "He has to be an actor! He's the Jew who tried to get the old man not to cut the cow's throat. If this isn't a script, what is it?"

"Maybe," the guard said—not as if he agreed with the Grand Mufti, as if he was still open to argument. "How will we tell?"

That was a shrewd question. Haji Jamal answered, "Look—he's running through a Jewish cemetery now. If more ghosts come up when he gets to the Muslim cemetery closer to the Golden Gate, we'll know he's a fraud. Muslim dead would not rise for a Jew."

He thought that nailed things down tight. But the bodyguard said, "Unless he really is the Messiah."

"Don't be silly!" the Grand Mufti said. "How could a Jew be the Messiah?"

"God can do whatever He pleases." The guard *was* stubborn.

"God gave us Muhammad, the Seal of Prophets—peace be unto him—to teach us how to live," Haji Jamal said. "He doesn't need to have anything to do with Jews who wouldn't accept the Prophet when he was there before them, and who still deny Him now."

The guard grunted. "It's possible," he said at last—as much of an admission as Ashrawi was likely to get.

With ghosts boiling around him on the TV screen, the Jewish boy ran on. Ashrawi sometimes thought he could make out faces, mouths and eyes wide open. Other times, it was all swirling motion. It centered on the boy, and trailed after him.

"Here's the Muslim cemetery," Ashrawi said. "Now we'll see."

More ghosts rose. These looked like Muslims, not Jews. When

you could make out clothing, it was clothing Arabs might wear. Some was the kind they might have worn in days long gone. Whoever directed these special effects paid attention to detail. But they could only be special effects.

He said as much.

"It's possible," the bodyguard repeated. Haji Jamal almost kicked him. But he restrained himself. Jerusalem would need a new Grand Mufti if he yielded to temptation. He didn't believe that a Jew could raise the dead, and he wasn't about to gamble he might be wrong.

Yes, there were times when Gabriela wished she hadn't invited the Reverend Lester Stark to the Holy Land. Because Shlomo Kupferman was irked at Stark, she and the minister had to comment on the sacrifice of the red heifer by what they could see from studio monitors. Stark hadn't wangled an invitation to the Mount of Olives or even the Temple Mount for their camera crew. Kupferman might have said, *This is ours. It's not for* goyim *to mess with.*

So naturally, Stark started messing in the studio. Gabriela wasn't happy. A lot of this commentary might have to get tossed for the more permanent versions of the production. Stark wasn't so snarky as he might have been—he *was* a good-natured man. He was determined to get his licks in, though.

"Our Jewish brethren find this purification ceremony most important," he said. By his tone, he might have been narrating a 1950s documentary about the natives' quaint customs.

That tone pissed Gabriela off, and she wasn't Jewish or observant. Not even Brandon, shit that he was, would have sounded so condescending. But Brandon was dead of his own arrogance, and Gabriela stuck with the reverend.

"Jewish people believe the sacrifice of the red heifer is enough to render things its ashes touch ritually pure," Stark went on. "I could do worse than to quote Hebrews 9:13–14: 'If the blood of bulls and goats, and the ashes of a heifer sprinkling the defiled, sanctifieth to the purifying of the flesh: how much more shall the blood of Christ, who through the eternal Spirit offered Himself without spot to God, purify your conscience from dead works to serve the living God?'"

This isn't Sermonette, *dammit,* Gabriela thought. She could cut some in the edits if Lester piled it on too thick. But she didn't want people thinking she agreed with everything he said, so she re-marked, "Hebrews is in the New Testament, though." She knew that much, anyhow. "People who don't accept that as the word of God aren't bound by what it says."

They'd already had this argument off camera. Now they could have it on-. Again, Gabriela would just have to see if it stayed in later. But Stark, being a trained minister, could wheel out the theo-logical heavy guns and let fly with them. *You're so smart, why didn't you remember that sooner?* she thought.

Before they could start making like liberals and conservatives on a CNN panel, though, one of the kids who'd crossed the cause-way on oxback tried to interrupt the ceremony. Stark came on point like a good bird dog. "Here's something Rabbi Kupferman didn't expect!" he exclaimed. He could be a terrific analyst when he steered clear of the pulpit.

Things weren't different enough. Whatever the kid tried, it didn't work. And Kupferman had as much bend as a boulder. Once a couple of ox-handlers corraled the youngster, the rabbi cut the red heifer's throat.

Here was a deliberate killing on camera, going out to Israel and the world (though little to the USA, which was hinky about such things). Gabriela wondered how people watching it live liked it. That boy wasn't the only sign the world had got more squeamish the past two millennia. Watching the heifer's carcass burn might also turn a stomach or two—million.

When the kid who'd tried to stop things jumped off the platform, Stark gasped. "He's been ritually pure his whole life," he said. "He just threw it all away."

Gabriela found herself nodding. Sure enough, this was the kind of commentary she wanted from the minister. "When he's older, do you think he'll regret what he's done?" she asked.

"In his place, I would, given what he's always believed," Stark said.

The boy ran down the Mount of Olives. A camera followed him. He was a lot more dramatic than the pyre and the heifer. He ran through the Jewish cemetery . . . and strange things began to happen.

Lester Stark caught it fast—ahead of Gabriela. "What are we seeing?" he asked sharply. "It looks like—ghosts?—are surrounding the boy as he runs. Can that be possible?"

"Yes. Look!" Gabriela's voice rose in excitement as she responded. "You can see them rising from the ground as the boy runs past, rising and hurrying after him!"

You could see them, but for her seeing wasn't necessarily believing. Since video-editing software came along, you could do anything with images. With enough money and computing power, you could do it in real time. Did Israeli TV have enough? As Saul Buchbinder would have said, did the Pope shit in the woods?

Then the TV feed cut to the people on the Temple Mount who'd been watching the ceremony. They looked as if they'd just staggered out of a car crash. All their faces had that poleaxed expression. Their eyes were seeing what the monitor showed.

Or else they were fake, too. Gabriela shook her head. She didn't believe it. That would have taken advance planning, and would have meant the kid was scripted from the git-go. She couldn't imagine Shlomo Kupferman playing along.

"Unless I'm completely off-base, that young man is raising the dead," Lester Stark said. "I can see two explanations for that."

"You're two up on me, Reverend," Gabriela said. "When I see

something impossible, I know there's no explanation for it. What else does impossible mean?"

But raising the dead evidently wasn't among things that couldn't happen for Stark. He said, "One possibility is that this young man is the Jewish Messiah. That goes against everything I ever believed, but it could be."

Gabriela admired the admission. It took moral courage, not a quality in large supply these days. She asked, "What's the other one?"

"That we're witnessing the advent of the Antichrist, his miracles powered not by God but by Satan."

Too much! Gabriela thought. *Way too much! He's trying to get us thrown all the way out of Israel, not just exiled to this studio.* She made a chopping motion with her right hand, and sound recording stopped. "How much hot water are you trying to land us in, Reverend?" she asked. "A Jewish kid who doesn't shave yet is the Antichrist? Come on!"

The way Stark looked back chilled her. He might be wrong, but he was serious. "I didn't say he *was* the Antichrist," Stark replied. "I said he might be. And he might. Too many strange things have happened lately to leave anything in Scripture out of the mix. Or will you tell me I'm wrong?"

Gabriela thought about it. She remembered the floating Ark, Brandon dropping dead on live TV (*instead of me,* she thought with one more internal shiver), missiles disappearing in midair, and the writing on the wall of the suddenly defunct President of Iran's office. She remembered some other things, too.

Shivering again, she shook her head. "I guess not. I don't know anything about anything any more."

Lester Stark gave back the thinnest of smiles. "We're even."

* * *

Eric Katz stood on the Temple Mount, watching the Jewish kid run through the graveyard and . . . stuff happening around him. Even through the field glasses he and Orly passed back and forth, he had trouble making out what was up on the Mount of Olives.

He shook his head. The trouble lay between his ears. He could see what was going on. He could see it, but he was damned if he believed it.

"He's raising the dead," Orly said. "He is."

"But that's impossible." Eric couldn't blame it on special effects—not through binoculars—but he would have if he could.

Orly gave him a look that came not only from another planet but from another time as well. "I know." She sounded calmer than anyone had any business being. "He's doing it anyway. *Possible* and *impossible* don't matter any more, Eric. Don't you get it?"

He did. The difference between understanding and liking was wider than the sky, deeper than the sea, and real as a right to the jaw. He hadn't thought anybody, including God, could raise the dead. He'd figured that when you died, you were gone. Evidently not. Which meant . . . what?

Good question. If there *was* life after death, people would be arguing about what it meant for the next 10,000 years.

If God didn't decide to ring down the curtain sooner than that, anyhow. By the look of things, He was liable to. If this wasn't the beginning of the End of Days . . . then it was something else. As the old song put it, it was the start of *something* big.

Not far away, Yoram Louvish peered down into the valley with his own binocs. With the Israeli archaeologist was a guy Eric didn't know: early forties, black hair, a dark beard streaked with gray. Not least to escape Orly's terrifying truths, Eric walked over to them. Orly came along, so he didn't escape. All the same, he asked Yoram, "What do you think?"

"I think God is doing strange things. A Messiah without a

beard?" Yoram answered in Hebrew, which Eric had also used. *No, I didn't escape,* Eric thought. Then Yoram switched to English: "Eric, this is Keith Rosenthal. He's over from Chicago to do something perverse to the university computer system. Keith, Eric Katz. He's like me—he'd rather deal with tablets and potsherds than Windows."

"Who wouldn't?" Keith said. He stuck out a hand. "Hi, Eric."

"Hi." Eric shook. They grinned at each other: one American Jew with a Norse first name, the other with a Celtic. Carrying a handle that fit in with the dominant culture went back at least as far as Flavius Josephus, likely further.

Yoram raised the field glasses again. "He's going through the Muslim cemetery now, and the dead there are rising, too," he said, sticking to English.

"This is weird, man," Keith Rosenthal said. "I mean, I'm Jewish, but—"

"Tell me about it," Eric said. Orly let out a small sniff, as if to say she could tell him plenty. For an Israeli to hold back might have done for a miracle if Eric hadn't witnessed too many fancier ones lately.

Now he and Yoram had to lean over the wall to see what the kid was doing. *If I fall and break my neck, will my ghost rise up and follow him?* Eric didn't want to find out.

The boy had plenty of ghosts on his trail. They looked half real, half like curdled air. Some were plainly Jews, some Muslims. A couple might have been Crusaders. Some went back . . . God only knew how far. Eric shivered. One more true cliché.

If the kid trotted by a Neandertal skeleton, what would happen? How long till an anthropologist started wondering about that? Before the End of Days?

Were Neandertals enough like real humans to have the Messiah resurrect their souls? Or was that the real question? Wasn't it something more like, Did God breathe His spirit into Neandertals, too? Eric shook his head. Talk about unscientific!

Or was it? Now he had evidence he hadn't had before. If the evidence pointed this way, wasn't he supposed to go with it?

The kid squeezed through the opening blown in the long-sealed Golden Gate. The Messiah was supposed to bring the resurrected dead into Jerusalem by that route. Jesus had done things the Messiah was supposed to do. Jews who didn't accept Jesus thought that was staged. How about this? Eric had no idea.

The stairs up from the Golden Gate hadn't been climbed much the past 1,200 years. What had been the point? Archaeologists had explored the gate while Britain held Palestine, but the Waqf didn't encourage them. The Muslims didn't want anyone finding anything there, since they denied that the Haram al-Sharif ever housed Jewish Temples.

Battered or not, the stairs were climbable. The Israeli boy came out on the Temple Mount and ran across it as fast as he could.

Eric got a good look at his face. The kid looked scared to death. If he was the Messiah, it hadn't been his idea. And, considering the ghosts or spirits or whatever the hell they were that streamed after him, Eric didn't blame him.

Several people took a couple of steps toward the boy. After those couple of steps, everyone thought better of it. Eric didn't blame them, either. He'd taken his own step and a half, then stopped. He glanced at Orly, wondering if she'd flay him for acting like a gutless American. She didn't. Her feet stayed rooted to the paving stones, too.

Get out of my head! Chaim wanted to scream it. Maybe he *did* scream. He wasn't sure what was really going on and what was in his mind. He also wasn't sure there was any difference.

Ghosts . . . Spirits . . . Souls . . . They howled within him in languages he knew and ones he didn't. They wanted something from him, something he didn't know how to give them.

Now he understood why Jewish law reckoned graveyards sources of pollution. The ancient rabbis must have stumbled across cases like his. Running into ghosts could drive anybody out of his mind. Chaim feared they were driving him out of his.

He almost broke his neck scrambling up the cracked and pitted stairway up from the Golden Gate. What would have happened if he did? Would he have turned into a spirit, hovering around his body like the rest of them? How weird was that?

When he got onto the Temple Mount, he kept running. He looked toward the Tabernacle and rising Temple. If he rushed in there, maybe the Ark would solve his troubles. Or it might strike him dead—he was carrying as big a load of pollution as anybody could.

Chaim didn't want to chance it. If he ran far enough and fast enough, maybe . . . Maybe he could somehow shake the ghosts. He would have done anything just then to get free of them.

Someone pointed at him and yelled, "Look! It's the Messiah, come at last! God bless him!"

Even bedeviled by spirits, Chaim almost burst out laughing. The Messiah? Him? That was the most ridiculous thing he'd ever heard. He was nothing but an ordinary kid who wasn't even ritually pure any more.

Or was he? He hadn't had a chance to wonder. Things were happening too fast. If he wasn't the Messiah, how was he raising the dead? For that matter, if he *was,* how was he doing it? He had no idea. He only knew he was. No—he knew one other thing, too.

It scared the crap out of him.

If Rabbi Kupferman had only listened, if he hadn't stuck the knife in Rosie . . . Chaim wouldn't have jumped off the platform.

He wouldn't have run through the cemeteries or found out he could do—this.

He would have been much happier, even if he'd stayed on the platform and watched Rosie's body burn. He hadn't imagined that could be possible. Well, it was.

The roaring between his ears wouldn't go away. He feared it would keep getting louder, till his head exploded. Every time he went near a place where somebody was buried, that added one more voice to the clamor. And people had been buried all over the place. That was why everybody'd gone through such contortions to keep him ritually pure till now.

Chaim laughed wildly. He didn't have to worry about *that* any more. He'd spent his life looking forward to the day he didn't have to. Now the day was here—and he had bigger things to worry about. Not fair!

If you looked at things like the Book of Job, what did you see? You saw God wasn't fair. At least Chaim thought he did. God didn't have to be. He just had to be strong. And was He ever!

If one spirit at a time had spoken to Chaim, he might have figured out what they were trying to tell him. He'd heard the first few as individuals while he was on the causeway, though he'd had no idea what was going on then. But now they were all screaming at the same time. He couldn't understand any of them.

Once, God confused everyone's speech at the Tower of Babel. Chaim had his own Tower of Babel inside his head. He felt as if the original, which reached to the heavens, were weighing him down.

He ran down the ramp on the Bab al-Maghariba. As soon as his feet hit the plaza in front of the Western Wall, the chorus got louder again. Not many people were buried on the Temple Mount—it was both rocky and holy. Not many had been buried here, either, but enough to stoke the din.

Men praying at the Western Wall stared at him—and at his semitransparent entourage. Some ran way. Some pointed. Someone shouted, "The Messiah has come!" People trotted toward him.

That was the last thing he needed. He didn't feel messianic. He felt exhausted. He'd done a lot of running—which he hadn't been able to till then. He was sweaty. He could smell himself. He wished everybody, living, dead, and divine, would leave him alone.

"It's the Messiah! He's come!" The cry rose from a dozen throats.

"*Shut up!*" Chaim screamed. "*Stop that!*"

The Jews running toward him skidded to a halt, faces gray with fear. Some prostrated themselves before him, as priests had prostrated themselves before the Holy of Holies back in the days of the Temples.

Chaim hardly noticed. What he noticed was that, when he shrieked, the spirits roaring and bellowing and calling through the fastnesses of his mind fell silent.

Sudden hope filled him. Maybe he could deal with this after all. Maybe he wouldn't go crazy trying. Or maybe he already had.

Yitzhak Avigad wanted to run to his nephew as Chaim dashed across the Temple Mount, but his courage failed him. Shame filled him; he'd seen combat, so nothing should have fazed him. But what should have been and what were were two different beasts. Arabs with rifles and RPGs fell within his mental horizon; the Messiah didn't.

He stayed where he was, then, and let Chaim dash by. Only after Chaim was gone did Yitzhak shake himself and get moving. Even then, he was ahead of everybody else. What were you supposed to do when something miraculous went by in front of your nose?

You were supposed to praise God. Saying it was easier than doing it. It wasn't that Yitzhak didn't want to praise God. But he was too freaked out for that to be easy.

He'd thought he knew how things were supposed to work. They'd rebuild the Temple. Finding the Ark just seemed a lucky bonus. Once the Temple went up, they'd worship the way Jews had in ancient days—the right way, he was convinced. And that, *alevai*, would hasten the coming of the Messiah.

It seemed logical, as far as religious matters could. But man made his plans and God made His. When man's plans bumped against God's, man's came in second. Anyone who didn't believe it could ask Brandon Nesbitt.

Yitzhak started down the ramp after his nephew. He was halfway to the bottom—halfway down to the plaza in front of the Western Wall—when Chaim let out a shriek: *"Shut up! Stop that!"* His nephew's voice didn't just break. It shattered—baritone at the start, shrill soprano at the end.

Part of Yitzhak wanted to go faster. Part wanted to run away. He didn't freeze in place, but he didn't speed up, either. Shame washed over him again. But he was doing everything a man could do. If that wasn't enough, he would have to take a beating from his conscience.

He got to the bottom of the ramp, even if not so fast as he wanted. Orthodox Jews surrounded Chaim and the spirits of the dead he'd raised. Moses in the middle of the Red Sea with it pulled back around him might have looked like this.

"The Messiah!" The Orthodox had been shouting when Yitzhak started down from the Temple Mount. They weren't shouting now, in deference to Chaim's scream. They weren't shutting up, though.

"What are you doing?" a man asked as Yitzhak pushed past him. "Who do you think you are?"

"That kid's uncle," Yitzhak growled. He didn't wait for more argument, but went up to Chaim—and Chaim's ghostly retinue. Yitzhak heard only a distant rumble from the spirits, like voices in a far-off room. By Chaim's anguished look, he'd heard much more.

"You all right?" Yitzhak asked, as casually as he could.

"I'm better now," Chaim replied. "I was really yelling at all these people, but the dead ones listened to me, too."

"If you're . . . If you're . . ." Yitzhak needed three tries, but he brought it out: "If you're the Messiah, they would."

His nephew winced. "Don't you start, too."

"I don't want to start anything," Yitzhak said truthfully. "I just want to help if I can."

Chaim's voice was bleak: "I don't know if anyone can. I don't know if I can help myself. I don't know what to do about it." He looked even younger than he was. "I'm scared."

Remembering his own thoughts of a moment before, Yitzhak said, "You aren't the only one."

"I guess." Chaim sounded shaky. "But it's not happening to anybody else. I'm in it."

He was the heart of it. It was what it was because he was what he was. Yitzhak was convinced of it. As gently as he could, he asked, "What do you want to do now?"

"I don't know. Could I get something to eat, and maybe a soda?" Chaim was still a kid, all right. Or if he was something more, he was something more with its head on straight.

He startled a laugh out of Yitzhak. "If we can't find a place that sells falafel or *shawarma,* we aren't trying. C'mon."

His nephew came. So did the ghosts. More seemed to pop out from between the paving stones with every step Chaim took. People weren't supposed to be buried here, but Jerusalem had been around a long time. Maybe they were Jordanian soldiers killed in the Six Day War, or Turkish troops from World War I. Or maybe they were Jebusites, from the days before King David took the town. Or they could have ended up dead anywhere in the 3,000 years between.

With the souls of the dead came the curious and awestruck living. After Chaim screamed at the Orthodox who'd been praying at the Western Wall, they kept their distance. But they followed nonetheless. They'd been waiting for the Messiah since the Second Temple fell. Now they thought they had Him.

Yitzhak wasn't sure they were wrong, either. He *was* sure he could find a falafel stand. Even the Messiah got a yen for deep-fried garbanzos. Everybody else did.

An old, bald Israeli and a girl a couple of years older than Chaim—the old guy's granddaughter?—stood behind the counter. Yitzhak ordered and paid. They had a TV. The girl stared at Chaim, and not on account of the ghosts. "Oh," she breathed. "You're . . . him. I just saw you." Her eyes were enormous.

So were Chaim's, for a different reason. "Uh, hi," he managed. He'd never had anything to do with girls before. This one was, if not beautiful, definitely cute. Chaim noticed. Definitely. *Well, well,* Yitzhak thought. *Something new has been added.*

19

Sometimes too much happened at once. You needed to pay attention to six things at the same time. You couldn't pay proper attention to any. If you did, you'd lose track of the rest.

Lester Stark felt that way now. Chaim Avigad—Messiah or Antichrist? The red heifer's sacrifice measured against Jesus Christ's. The red heifer's sacrifice as a harbinger of the rebuilt Temple. The Resurrection of the dead? Was it that? Was it a warning the Last Days were near? And what would they be like when even North Korea could throw nukes?

Try as he would, Stark couldn't track all his worries at once. Whenever he got a handle on one, others slipped from his ken.

"It's enough to drive you crazy!" he complained to his wife.

"Not me." Rhonda looked up from her mystery. "God will do what He does. I can't change it, except maybe by praying. So I pray, but maybe I'm praying 'cause I'm destined to pray."

That only made Lester Stark groan. Adding free will and predestination to everything else felt like something that would bring a piling-on penalty in a football game. His own prayers had been for the strength and wisdom to keep track of everything going on in Jerusalem now. That seemed too much for one man to get.

He nodded sheepishly. "You've got better sense than I do."

"Ha!" she said, which might have meant anything.

Stark pressed ahead with his own thoughts: "I have to talk to that boy. But why would he talk to me? To him, I'm only a Christian."

Rhonda said, "Talk to Rabbi Kupferman. If anybody can fix it, he can. Of course, he'll want to talk to the boy, too."

"I told you you had good sense." Stark kissed her. He was embarrassed he hadn't thought of it. And if he couldn't talk to the boy, talking to Kupferman would be the next best thing. He hadn't wanted to call the rabbi because of the pressure Kupferman would have felt to bring off the sacrifice of the red heifer to perfection. Well, now that was over—and Kupferman, and everybody else, had something new to worry about.

When Stark called Kupferman, he got voicemail. He knew he shouldn't have been disappointed, but he was. Rabbi Kupferman had always answered for him—but not today. It wasn't as if nothing was happening. Still . . .

"This is Lester Stark," he said after the beep. "Call me back when you get a chance, Shlomo. A lot going on, isn't there?"

Ten minutes later, his phone rang. He'd hoped it would, but jumped anyway. When he answered, Kupferman's gravelly voice growled, "What do you mean, Chaim's the Antichrist? You've got some nerve."

"I didn't say he *was*," Stark answered. "I said he might be. And I said he might be the Messiah, too."

"He's raising the dead. Who else is he?" Kupferman said.

"Neither of us knows by Whose power he's doing that," Lester said. "Till we do, we'd better keep an open mind, eh?"

"Better an open mind than an open mouth," Kupferman said.

"Why did he try to keep you from sacrificing?" Stark asked.

"Because he cared more about the stupid cow than about the Temple," the rabbi answered. "Because even if he is the Messiah, he's still wet behind the ears."

Was he? Lester Stark held his tongue. To him, it looked as if the Jewish hierarchy now was doing what it had 2,000 years before. It had an authentic miracle in front of it, and what did it care about? The minutiae of running the Temple or rebuilding it. Jews couldn't see that what went on beyond their corset of laws was more important than what the corset shaped. They couldn't . . . think outside the box. Stark smiled. The modern catchphrase fit what had happened long ago.

He did say, "Maybe you should pay more attention to him and less to the Temple."

"I don't tell you how to run your religion. You wouldn't listen if I did," Kupferman said. Lester Stark flushed; the rabbi was right. "Why do you think you can mind my business?" he added.

But a question like that demanded an answer. "Because this is the most important time in the history of the world. If things go wrong now, *disaster* isn't a big enough word."

"Why worry so much? Don't you trust God?" Kupferman asked.

"Of course," Stark said. "But Satan is in this game, too."

"Christians worry about Satan a lot more than Jews do," Kupferman said. "Besides, even you believe God will win in the end. You wouldn't be a Christian if you didn't—you'd be a Manichee or a Zoroastrian. Right?"

"Well, yes," Stark said. Jousting with Kupferman was like getting grilled by an older brother. That was true on a personal level and a religious one. Judaism was Christianity's older brother. Judaism had borrowed Satan from the Zoroastrians by the time Job got written, but still recalled days before that. Satan as God's opponent was always part of Christianity. Stark took the notion for granted. Running into someone who didn't was a jolt.

Kupferman realized as much. "Okay. So relax. God *will* take care of things. Everything *will* be all right."

"It will if we help God," Stark said. "I don't want to work against Him."

Rabbi Kupferman's amusement flickered and went out. "Then shut up about the Antichrist. You'll get people killed if you don't. You're liable to get Chaim killed. Muslims believe in the Antichrist, too. But your happy ending isn't the same as theirs. The only thing that's the same is, Jews get screwed both ways."

Lester knew his own ignorance about Muslim beliefs. To him, Muhammad had plagiarized the Old and New Testaments and added his own flourishes. That Muslim beliefs could be true struck him as wildly unlikely. That Kupferman might feel that way about Christianity had never fully struck him . . . till now.

In numbers lay strength. In Alabama, Stark was always part of a large majority. Not in Israel. And, while there were a billion and a half Christians, there were also more than a billion Muslims. You couldn't ignore them.

"We all have to do what we think is right," Lester said.

"Sure," Kupferman replied. "But do you have to make so much noise doing it?" Lester didn't learn how to talk to Chaim Avigad.

You could get a good pizza in Jerusalem—if you topped it with olives and onions and eggplant and peppers and mushrooms. Sausage and pepperoni were out. Eric missed them. But even a veggie pizza improved when washed down with a Goldstar.

Eric stared at the beer. "I want to drink twelve of these."

"You'd kill yourself." Orly sounded alarmed. Like most Israelis, she drank moderately.

"Nah." He shook his head. "I'd just have a hangover in the morning." After a dozen beers, it would be painful, too, but not lethal. He went on, "And while I was smashed out of my skull, I wouldn't have to think about everything."

"It would still be there when you sobered up. What's the point?" Orly proved she'd never been a serious drinker.

Neither had Eric . . . except, briefly, in the bad time after his first marriage blew up. "The point is, you don't have to worry for a while. That's not always bad."

"If you say so." She thought he was out of his mind. "Besides, why worry? If that kid's the Messiah, it's the most wonderful thing that ever happened, at least since Moses."

"Yeah." Eric finished the beer and waved for another one. He wouldn't drink twelve, but he needed reinforcements. "Wonderful. Maybe I'm too secular for my own good. I'm not ready for the End of Days, if that's what this is."

"If the End of Days is ready for you, big deal," Orly said. "I'm secular, too. I was. If God waves His hand in the sky, I won't pretend it's not there. How dumb is that?"

"Pretty dumb, probably . . . Thanks." That last was to the waitress. He took a pull from the new bottle—something Americans did more often than Israelis. "But—"

"But what?"

"Hell, I don't know. I'm weirded out. I admit it. I never figured I'd be in the middle of . . . this." His wave took in more than the pizza joint.

"You came to Israel because you wanted to dig up stuff about the Bible, not because you wanted to meet the author," Orly said.

"Bingo!" Eric nodded. "You put it better than I could have." They were speaking Hebrew, but she did it in English, too. Some people were natural tennis players. Orly was a natural talker. Eric wished he had the gift.

She gave him a crooked smile. "It's what I asked you before. Even if this isn't why you came here, will you pretend God's not up there waving?"

I sure want to went through Eric's mind. Of course he did. He liked the life he'd been living. He'd figured he would like it even more once he and Orly tied the knot, too. For someone who'd already rolled the dice once and lost, that was a great feeling. Maybe it was selfish of him to put his own desires ahead of those of the Old Testament Deity who'd manifested Himself again after a bimillennial catnap, but . . .

And maybe doing all the things he'd done without thinking twice wasn't smart. The Old Testament God took rules seriously. Which meant . . . "Hey!" Eric said.

"Hey, what?" Orly said. "Is it a joke?"

"No." He shook his head. "Let's get married right away."

She looked at him, then at the Goldstar. "See what happens when you start drinking? You talk silly."

"One beer and a swig isn't *drinking*." Eric set his hand on hers. "I mean it. C'mon—I was gonna get the guts up to ask you soon. I did it now because . . . If we're going to do this stuff, and if God *is* watching, we ought to be married, right?"

"How romantic!" Orly exclaimed. *How sarcastic!* Eric thought. But she didn't get up and stomp off. "You know what?" she said. "That may be a *good* reason to get married, the way things are now."

"Uh-huh." Now Eric nodded. "But I can give you a better one, the real one."

She raised an eyebrow. "Which is?"

"Because I love you."

"That's better," she agreed. "We wouldn't be doing that stuff if we didn't feel that way, would we?" She raised an eyebrow. "*You'd* probably want to, but what do you know? You man, you."

"Babe, sex is a good thing." Eric laughed at himself. Plato and Aristotle and Spinoza needed to watch themselves; a new philosopher was loose. He added, "It's better when you love the other person. Otherwise, you might as well play with yourself."

"I won't tell you you're wrong," Orly said. "We can start arguing *after* we get married."

He grinned. Then the grin slipped. That wasn't so good, not when he was gazing at his beloved. "If we have to take the Old Testament seriously again, we really will have to watch that stuff."

Orly's lip curled. "I'm surprised this Lester Stark hasn't already started braying about it like a jackass," she said.

"He's not as bad as a lot of them," Eric said.

"Oh, joy." She sounded unenthusiastic.

"Well, he isn't." Eric wasn't enthusiastic, either. He did add, "I bet he's at least as tolerant as Kupferman."

"Oh, joy," Orly said again. "Talk about picking your poisons . . ." No, she didn't like the Religious Affairs Minister. "And one of his people has a hold on the kid who can raise the dead."

"That's the kid's uncle, isn't it?" Eric said. "The kid started out ultra-Orthodox, I know."

"Uh-huh. I wonder how he feels now," Orly said.

"Confused," Eric guessed. "Why should he be different? Aside from raising the dead and everything."

"Yeah. Aside from that." Orly clicked her tongue between her teeth. "I'd rather not think about that. If we're going to talk about getting married, we should talk, right?"

"Makes sense," Eric allowed. "Should be simple. We're old enough, we're Jewish, we want to. What's the problem?"

He didn't think there'd be one, which showed what he knew. "Ha!" Orly said. "You're a foreigner, remember? The only way to get married here is through the Marriage Rabbinate."

"Oy!" Eric said.

"You need to bring your passport to their office on Koresh

Street. You need a letter from your community saying you really are a Jew. If you can get it, you need your mother's *ketubah*."

"Oy!" Eric said again, louder. "Her Jewish marriage certificate? I don't think she's got one. She ran off with my father and got married in Vegas."

"They may let you scrape through without it," Orly said. "Then you fill out a form—and pay for it—and go to the chief rabbi's office to get your rabbi approved and a stamp on the form saying he is."

"Marriage by bureaucracy!" Eric said. "Tell me you're making this up, please."

"Who, me? No way," Orly replied. "Once you get that taken care of, you set up a court date—"

"*Oy!*" This time, Eric said it loud enough to make people give him dubious looks. "Why do I need a court date?"

"So you can have two relatives or friends swear you're Jewish. Guys—the court doesn't always recognize women. Sexist idiots. They're as bad as God." She sent a defiant stare heavenwards, as if defying Him to strike her dead. He didn't.

"How do you know so much about this?" Eric asked.

"I found out, in case I ever needed to know," Orly answered demurely. "I could go on—there are another couple of steps."

Eric muttered darkly. "Suppose this is too much hassle? What do people do then?"

"Go to Cyprus," Orly said. "On Cyprus, you have to be breathing and have enough money for fees. Past that, nobody cares."

"How do you feel about it?" Eric asked.

She shrugged. "It seems more official if you do it here. But it's a lot quicker there. I could go either way."

"Let's head for Cyprus and make it legal," Eric said. "We can do it the fancy way when we've got time. How's that sound?"

"Should work," Orly said. "But I think we'd better do the formal ceremony as soon as we can, too."

"In case the world ends?" Eric said with a wry grin.

Orly nodded. "In case the world ends." She wasn't joking.

Chaim liked it on the Temple Mount. He couldn't be alone with his thoughts there or anywhere else. But not many people had been buried up there. He didn't have more and more souls crowding in on him while he was there.

And he'd got some control over the ones he already had. He never would have imagined he could if he hadn't screamed at the Orthodox men rushing him. The ghosts paid attention, too.

He had to scream, literally or mentally, to get them to notice him. Otherwise, they did what they wanted to do. It was like . . . he didn't know what. Uncle Yitzhak had suggested trying to control a restive horse. Chaim didn't want to say yes or no. All he knew about horses was that they weren't kosher.

It reminded him of wrestling with somebody as strong as he was. He and the rest of the ritually pure boys had squabbled. They were boys and they'd grown up together. It was a wonder they hadn't beaten one another's brains out.

When he was strong enough, he could call spirits front and center, and talk with them after a fashion. One remembered stopping a Turkish bullet in 1918. "Bloody 'ell, myte, I didn't expect a sheeny kid'd be the one wot brought me back," the spirit said in English of a sort.

"What *did* you expect?" Chaim asked.

"Jesus, I suppose, or maybe nobody." The dead British soldier laughed at himself. "You ain't neither one."

"Well, no," Chaim said.

"So that's wot I get." The soldier's Cockney accent was so thick, Chaim could barely understand it. "I got my 'ead blowed off, an' when it's Judgment Day you sure ain't Who I expected."

"That's all right," said Chaim. "I didn't expect this to happen, either."

Another ghost or spirit who came up front and center used a Hebrew so archaic it was almost a foreign language to Chaim. An American trying to make out what Chaucer was saying, a modern Greek trying to follow Homer, would have understood the problem. The ancient Jew had as much trouble figuring out the modern world.

"Then this is yet the Kingdom of Judah?" he asked.

"This is Israel," Chaim answered.

"The northern kingdom, the false line, have conquered the true, holy realm?" The ancient Jew sounded horrified.

"No." Chaim was saying that a lot. Nobody understood what was going on. He tried to explain that Israel wasn't a kingdom, and what a democracy was.

"God alloweth this? God hath said it is acceptable unto Him? Without an anointed king, how can you flourish?" The long-dead soul didn't get it.

"These days, just about all countries are democracies. Even the ones that aren't pretend they are," Chaim said.

"Impiety! God will smite them!" The ancient Jew seemed very sure. Chaim couldn't tell him he was nuts. He didn't know that. Everything that had happened lately made him wonder whether the old soul didn't know just what he was talking about.

Chaim felt the dead everywhere he went—and everywhere meant *everywhere*. He got dreadfully constipated the first couple of days after acquiring his supernatural entourage. Then he let nature take its course. It was either that or explode. All these souls had done the same thing when they were alive.

He had to go on eating, too. He went back to that falafel stand in the middle of the Old City. He had soldiers for escorts now, but they didn't drive away any customers. They ate falafel themselves, packing pitas full of salad and the crunchy, greasy balls of deep-fried chickpeas. They were as sloppy as he was.

The soldiers didn't chat up the proprietor's granddaughter. *Don't bother the Messiah's friend.* He had trouble believing he was the Messiah. If he was, orders like that were the first good thing he'd found.

Her name was Shoshanah, which chilled him. Unlike the red heifer, she had a last name, too: Mazar. She was two and a half years older than he was. She wanted to be a doctor. Chaim hadn't thought about what he wanted to be. When you were raised in ritual purity, you didn't have many choices.

"Don't be silly," she told him when he remarked on that. "You've got—what you've got." Her wave encompassed Chaim's ghostly retinue. "What do you need an ordinary job for when you can raise the dead?" She blinked. She had amazingly long eyelashes. "If you can raise the dead, maybe I'd be wasting my time learning to be a doctor."

"I don't think so," Chaim said. "They aren't all the way back."

"They're closer than anybody else can get them," Shoshanah said. "I think that's amazing. I think *you're* amazing."

"Wow," Chaim said. Shoshanah thought he was amazing. He thought she was wonderful because she noticed him. His thinking she was wonderful made her notice him more and think he was more amazing, which made him. . . . Engineers would have called it a feedback loop. Chaim didn't care about anything but a black-eyed girl who sold falafel.

The time difference between Israel and the USA was between seven and ten hours. A call-in radio show that started at six P.M. on the East Coast began at one the next morning in Israel. Stark didn't like night-owl hours, but he didn't want to give up the show, either. Espresso kept him going.

"Here's Melvin from Visalia," his go-between said. "You're talking with Lester Stark, Melvin. Go ahead."

"Reverend Stark?" Melvin seemed unclear on the concept.

"That's me," Lester said—he'd dealt with plenty of people like this. "How are you today, Melvin? What's on your mind?"

"Reverend, where's the Rapture?" Melvin said. "If the Messiah's here, how come all the good Christians didn't get swept up into the air like it says in the Bible?"

"Good question," Lester Stark replied. "It's the question that's troubling me and a lot of other ministers right now."

"What's the answer?" Melvin asked. "Bible's mighty plain about this. I mean, First Thessalonians says what it says."

"Let me quote it, for people in their cars with no Bible handy. This is First Thessalonians, 4:16–17: 'For the Lord himself shall descend from heaven with a shout, with the voice of the archangel, and with the trump of God: And the dead in Christ shall rise first: Then we which are alive *and* remain shall be caught up together with them in the clouds to meet the Lord in the air: And so we shall ever be with the Lord.' "

"I don't see anybody caught up into the clouds," Melvin said. "And that kid doesn't look like he's raising up the dead in Christ. Seems like he's raising anybody who gets near him. So what's going on, anyway?"

"Melvin, anybody who answers that now is going out on a limb," Stark said. "I see several possibilities. One is that the main show hasn't started yet. Maybe the trumpet *will* sound and we *will* go up into the clouds soon."

"Yeah, maybe." Melvin didn't sound as if he believed it.

"Or the coming of the Jewish Messiah may not be the second coming of Jesus Christ," Lester said. "Maybe God has one plan for Jews and another one for Christians."

"Nothing about *that* in the Bible," Melvin said darkly.

"It depends. If you take the Old Testament as applying to Jews and the New Testament to Christians, you can make a case," Lester Stark answered. Nobody would have tried to make that case before all this started happening, but people always viewed Scripture through the lens of history.

"I always believed the New Testament was supposed to sit on top of the Old Testament, not alongside of it, like." No, Melvin wasn't convinced.

"Here's another possibility for you," Lester said. "The Jews may have the right view of things, and we may have the wrong one."

"You don't believe that!" Now Melvin sounded horrified. *You'd better not believe that!* was what he meant.

"I don't," Stark said. "But if it proves true, I will praise the Lord and accept that I didn't understand His ways in fullness."

"*I* won't," Melvin said. Was that stubbornness or anti-Semitism or one from Column A *and* one from Column B? The latter, Stark suspected. His caller went on, "What *do* you believe?"

Lester Stark didn't like coming right out with it, not here in Israel. It enraged local authorities. He answered, "As I've said before, it is possible that this boy's miraculous powers spring from Satan rather than God. I don't know that they do, but it's possible. In that case—"

"The kid's the Antichrist!" Melvin burst out.

Relief filled Stark. He hadn't had to say that himself, on a broadcast the Israelis were bound to be listening to. But shame swamped the relief. Matthew 27:11 sprang to mind. After Jesus was arrested, Pilate asked Him, "Art thou the King of the Jews?"

"Thou sayest," Jesus answered.

Thou sayest, Melvin, Lester thought unhappily.

Melvin wasn't unhappy—oh, no. "Sure makes sense to me, Reverend," he said. "Thanks a lot. I wasn't sure you'd have the guts to say the word, but you did. God bless you! 'Bye!"

I didn't—you did, Stark thought. But it amounted to the same thing. If he was going to say it, he should have said it openly instead of giving hints and letting someone else take the heat.

"Our next caller is Lucille. She lives in North Little Rock," the go-between said. "Go ahead, Lucille."

"Thanks." Unlike Melvin, Lucille got down to business: "If this boy is the Antichrist, what can we do about him? Shouldn't we try and get rid of him before he gets his full strength?"

"If he is—and I'm not saying he is—"

"Cut to the chase, Reverend," Lucille said irreverently.

Lester didn't want to, not when the Israelis could throw him out. "I think Thomas à Kempis was right when he said, 'Man proposes but God disposes.'"

Lucille only sniffed. "A Papist. The real truth is, 'God helps he who helps himself.' How do you take out the Antichrist?"

"I don't, not till I know this boy is he, and I don't know that now." Stark usually admired his flock's initiative. Once in a while, they scared the crap out of him. Lucille planned a campaign against the greatest enemy the world would ever know as if she were figuring out how to get rid of crabgrass in her yard.

If she attacked crabgrass the way she went after the Antichrist, the weeds were in trouble. "Maybe you ought to get hold of the Arabs," she said. "They probably don't like having a Jew maybe Messiah around, either."

"Thank you so much, Lucille," Stark said, which was the cue to get her off the air *right now*. "Who's our next caller?"

"We've got Ray, from Rochester, New York."

"Go ahead, Ray." Lester hoped Ray had both oars in the water.

"When do we see Armageddon?" Ray asked. "When do things start blowing up?" He sounded as if he was looking forward to it.

"Satan and his hosts will try whatever they can to resist the Lord in His righteous wrath," Lester Stark said. "But we still have some other things to go through first, I think."

"We're just about up to 666 years since the Black Death broke out?" Ray said. "That means something, don't you think?"

"I hadn't worried about it up till now," Lester answered, which had to be up there in the understatement-of-the-year race.

"That was a calamity. And if the Antichrist is here, that'd be another calamity," Ray said. "If you've got the number of the beast between 'em—just about—it seems like it ought to be important, you know?"

"Maybe it is. If it turns out to be, God will find a way to tell us. Thanks for your call." That was another kiss-off, though less urgent than the one for Lucille. "Now who's on the line?"

"Next up is Billie Sue. She's calling from Tulsa."

"Hello, Billie Sue," Lester said. "What's on your mind?"

"I think we should do something about the Antichrist, too? Blow him up before it's too late, like?" Billie Sue spoke in bloodthirsty questions. "Don't you think that would save everybody trouble?"

"We don't know he's the Antichrist. I doubt it, even if it's possible," Stark said. "He's a boy. He doesn't shave. He has remarkable power—I don't think anyone would argue with that. And you want to kill him because of what he might be?"

"You can't make an omelette without breaking eggs." Billie Sue figured a cliché dealt with moral obligations. Too many people thought the same way.

"Thanks for your call," Reverend Stark said, and that was that for Billie Sue. "We've got time for one more. Who's next?"

"Here's Henry, in Savannah, Georgia."

"Go ahead, Henry. This is Lester Stark."

"Pleased to talk to you, Reverend. I think I know how come the Rapture hasn't happened."

"What's your theory, Henry?" Lester asked.

"Maybe God hasn't swept up the good people 'cause there's no good people to sweep up. Maybe we've got so far away from what

Jesus taught, we don't deserve to get what First Thessalonians was talking about. Maybe we all have to go through the Tribulation to get sorted out. What do you think?"

"I don't know," Stark said slowly. "That's hard to prove or disprove. I hope you're wrong, but we have to wait and see."

"Reckon you're right, sir. I thank you for your time." Henry left the line without getting booted off.

Mechanically, Reverend Stark closed out the show. He wished he hadn't taken that last call. Thinking the world might be unworthy of Rapture was terrifying. If it was true, it meant he'd failed, and the preachers who'd lived before him, too. *I don't believe it. I won't believe it,* he thought firmly, but not firmly enough. . . .

20

Eric and Orly stood on the Temple Mount, watching Shlomo Kupferman purify earth-moving machinery, cement mixers, and the hard-hatted construction workers who used them. He dipped a hyssop branch in a bowl that held the red heifer's ashes mixed with water from the Pool of Siloam. Then he flipped a few drops onto each man and machine, praying as he did.

"There's something that's never been seen before," Eric remarked: "a ritually pure bulldozer."

It sounded silly, like something from one of Dave Letterman's old Top Tens. When you saw how seriously the rabbi and the hard hats took the ritual, you had second thoughts.

"They're doing the best they can," Orly said. "Even with the Bible and the Talmud, they can't know just how the rituals worked in the First and Second Temples. It's been too long."

"Anybody would think you were an archaeology grad student or something," Eric said. She stuck out her tongue at him.

Once the workers got shpritzed, they went at it. The Temple began supplanting the Tabernacle. Noise, dust, and diesel fumes sullied the holiest site in one religion, which was the third-holiest site in another and an object of watchful attention in a third. Christianity's holiest sites lay inside the Church of the Holy Sepulcher, just a few hundred meters away.

"What gets me is how only Kupferman handles the heifer's ashes," Eric said. "He's the guy who can bind and loose."

"Wrong religion," Orly said.

"You know what I mean."

"Sure." She nodded. "I think he's already purified other rabbis, though. Now they can do purifying on their own."

"They can—uh-huh," Eric said. "But will Kupferman let 'em? He likes power. He likes to grab it and hang on to it."

"So what will you do? Hit him over the head and steal the ashes?" Orly asked.

"Me? I'm the guy who has to prove he's Jewish enough to marry you, remember? Right. Eric Katz, boy Methodist."

Orly laughed. "*I* didn't quote the New Testament a minute ago."

"That's been going on all through the Diaspora. Philo of Alexandria made a good Greek philosopher, only he was a Jew. In Muslim Spain, Jews wrote Arabic."

"And when the Catholics won, Jews *and* Muslims got it in the neck," Orly said, which was also true.

"Whoever's on top gives it to whoever's on the bottom. Jews gave it to Canaanites and Jebusites, Assyrians and Babylonians gave it to the Jews—"

"Greeks and Romans gave it to the Jews," Orly interrupted. "Spaniards gave it to the Jews. Poles and Russians gave it. Germans gave it to the Jews and gave it and gave it."

"And the Jews in modern Israel aren't saints. Ask Munir—and he's had it easy next to the Palestinians." Eric could have said it more strongly. Israel's neighbors had always hated her. The 1948 War of Independence saw bizarre things, like Israeli Air Force pilots flying Messerschmitt 109s (Czech-built postwar versions) against Egyptian B-17s and their Spitfire escorts. But two generations of occupying Palestinian land had proved almost as corrosive for the occupiers as for the occupied.

Orly scowled. "We're on the bottom for 2,500 years, and people want us to be saints if we're on top for twenty-five minutes?"

"I didn't mean that." Eric remembered Shylock. *If you prick us, do we not bleed? if you tickle us, do we not laugh? if you poison us, do we not die? and if you wrong us, shall we not revenge?* That was human nature, boiled down to four questions more painful than the ones from the Haggadah.

"Yes, you did," Orly replied.

They might have had a row if soldiers hadn't come up, looking grim and ready for anything. Instead of snapping at his fiancée, Eric pointed to them. "What's going on?"

"Beats me," she said. "Maybe some VIPs looking around. They don't turn out like this for anybody."

Eric hadn't heard that any foreign dignitaries had come to Israel. The Muslim countries were still screaming about the violation of the Haram al-Sharif. The only thing that stopped them from going to war was what had happened when Iran tried and the endless chaos in Syria.

Western countries also deplored Israel's rebuilding projects. The Arabs and Iranians had oil. Countries didn't want to bite the hand that fueled them. And so . . .

It was a dignitary: Chaim Avigad, maybe the Messiah, maybe the Antichrist, maybe just a kid in way over his head. He looked haunted. Who could blame him, with the ghosts following him like reps from a celestial collection agency? They wouldn't leave him alone till they got what they wanted. By his expression, he didn't know how to give it to them. He didn't even know what it was. To take them up to heaven? How could anyone, even the Messiah, do that?

More soldiers followed him onto the Temple Mount. They fanned out as he walked, Rottweilers with assault rifles.

"Poor guy." Orly sounded so maternal, Eric did a double take. She went on, "I know what he needs."

"What?" Eric didn't think Chaim had any idea what he needed, so how could Orly?

Her suggestion made Eric's eyes cross. Maternal, it wasn't. Eric didn't know whether it would make Chaim Avigad forget the ghosts, horrify them into fleeing, or fascinate them enough so they'd leave him alone.

"Just don't call up Lester Stark," Eric said. "You'd short out half the pacemakers in the States."

"Good," Orly said. "Come on, though. He needs to be happy. He isn't now."

He wasn't. He strode across the Temple Mount like a lost soul himself. The hard hats working on the Temple would have been friendly, but the guards didn't let them get closer.

Before this started, Eric hadn't worried about the Messiah. He'd never once imagined Him as the loneliest guy in town. Judging by Chaim Avigad, that came with the package.

If a girl wanted to do as Orly had in mind, how could she fight through the security? Eric eyed Chaim again. He'd never expected to pity the Messiah, but he did.

Gabriela Sandoval and Brandon Nesbitt had been on the spot when terrorists dirty-bombed Tel Aviv. The other TV, Net, and print reporters from the English-speaking world had to hop planes after the fact. They leaned on the pair who'd been there first.

Now Gabriela watched it happen again. She hadn't imagined a story bigger than Tel Aviv. What could be bigger than a dirty bomb? The end of the world?

Now that you mentioned it, yes.

Everyone who'd flown out after Tel Aviv stopped being a big deal swarmed back. More reporters came along. People from every religious station and network and Web site in the USA came, talking about the Holy Land as if nobody'd ever used the phrase before.

But Gabriela and Lester Stark were the Johnnies-on-the-spot. Things had got more complicated this time around. Stark was an independent contractor, not part of the corporation. He had his own agenda (as if Brandon hadn't had *his*!), and he got difficult if Gabriela tried to rein him in.

She didn't try very hard. If you knew ahead of time you'd lose, why start? Stark headed a bigger enterprise than *Gabriela and Brandon*. He had more money and lawyers. If he got petty, he could blow off what he was doing with Gabriela. He didn't have to bail out, just do an unusable job.

So Gabriela kept quiet about Stark's radio show. His keeping that going had always been in the cards. The interviews with swarms of clean-cut reporters in suits out of the early years of *Mad Men* weren't. They cut into the time he had to work with Gabriela. And the questions those earnest, mostly young, men asked! Not quite how many angels could dance on the head of a pin, but close.

The Antichrist! Gabriela got sick of the Antichrist in a hurry. She finally hunted up the New Testament to see what the born-agains kept yattering about. She hadn't read it for many years. The Gideons didn't leave them in hotel rooms here, but that didn't matter any more. As long as your WiFi worked, you could get whatever you wanted.

The more she read, the weirder it got. "Do you really think everyone will get 666 tattooed on them?" she asked Stark at breakfast. They had the table to themselves; Saul Buchbinder was already arguing with an Israeli bureaucrat, while the minister's wife liked to sleep in.

"People who accept the Antichrist will wear a mark that shows what they've done," Stark answered. "It's in the Scriptures, so it will come true."

"The Scriptures say the world is flat," Gabriela remarked.

"That's different."

"How? Maybe the old rules don't apply any more. Maybe they never did." With coffee in her, Gabriela felt like arguing. It seemed more interesting than what was left of her scrambled eggs.

"It's prophecy," Stark said. "When God talked about the shape of the world before Jesus was born, He did it so people alive then could understand. But when He talked about prophecy, He had to talk about things that would come true. And a bunch of it already has."

"How do you tell the difference between one kind of talking and the other?"

"That's . . . part of what makes Biblical scholarship interesting," he said with a chuckle.

"And how do you know if He did the talking in the Bible?" Gabriela persisted. "If it wasn't just scribes and mystics and people like that?" She'd soaked up a Wikipedia article's worth of knowledge about the Higher Criticism.

"Yes. If." Lester Stark had a charming smile, on TV and in person. "For years, the secular humanists said there was no evidence anything in the Bible was true. Never mind all the archaeological discoveries since they started saying things like that." He understood where she was coming from, all right. "But what about the Ark? What happened to your colleague? How about the Iranian missiles? Or the Iranian President and the Grand Ayatollah? If Chaim Avigad isn't doing something supernatural, what *is* he doing?"

Those were all good questions. Gabriela didn't like feeling on the defensive, but she felt that way now. She poured herself more strong coffee to buy time to think.

While she did, Stark found one more question: "If this is all so ordinary, what are we doing here?"

Making money from our jobs was the first thing that crossed Gabriela's mind. It would have annoyed the preacher, not that he was working for nothing. But that wasn't the biggest reason she kept quiet. In spite of herself, she was nervous God would be listening. And God, she felt sure, didn't like doing something only for the sake of the almighty dollar.

She had to say something. "What are we doing here? The best we can, the same as we would anywhere else."

Stark inclined his head. "Yes, indeed. But if this is the time of the Antichrist, we'll go through Tribulation no matter where we are." Gabriela could hear the capital letter. The minister went on, "Many will yield to evil, and lose their lives and souls because they do."

"You don't have to sound like you look forward to it," Gabriela said.

"I do, if only in that I think it will happen," Stark replied. "I may be one of those sinners. Their fate—which may be mine—saddens me. But that doesn't mean they can dodge it. God said it would come, and I believe in Him and believe Him."

"This all seems very strange to me. Too much happening too fast," Gabriela said. "Like a movie with too many special effects, you know?"

"You mean there are movies these days without too many special effects?" Stark asked, deadpan. Gabriela snorted.

A reporter came up to the televangelist. He treated Gabriela as if she weren't there. She was only a woman, after all. "Can we get your views later this morning, Reverend?" he asked.

Gabriela had never seen him before. He talked like an American, but he sure didn't work for any of the major news services. All the same, he spoke to Lester Stark with easy familiarity.

"Have to be tomorrow afternoon or the day after, Hank." Stark knew him, too. The preacher nodded to Gabriela. "I'm booked solid with Ms. Sandoval and with my own work till then." He remembered she wasn't part of the furniture.

Hank looked nasty, almost ugly, for the moment he needed to pull his face straight. In that half-second, he reminded Gabriela chillingly of Brandon Nesbitt. "Dale will be disappointed," he said.

"I can't give you time I don't have." Stark could say no.

Hank sighed a martyred sigh. "Okay. I'll tell him." *If he cans me, it's your fault.* Gabriela could read between the lines. So could Stark, but he didn't waver. Off went Hank, glum in defeat.

"They'll eat your life if you let them," Stark observed.

"They sure will," Gabriela said, and then, "Did you ever wonder if anybody feels that way about you?"

"Not till I met Shlomo Kupferman," he said with a wry grin. His saving grace, if it was one, was that he didn't take himself too seriously.

"He thinks he has the Messiah on a string," Gabriela said.

"I know," Stark replied. "But who's holding it, and who's held? And what's on the end Kupferman doesn't have?" That put a period to breakfast conversation.

How the man had got through his guards, Jamal Ashrawi didn't know. But he had. "You need to come with me. Now," he said in Egyptian-accented Arabic. "Somebody needs to see you."

Ashrawi was affronted. "Who are you, to order me around?"

"I am somebody who tells you somebody else needs to see you," the stranger said. "I am somebody who tells you you will make your last mistake if you don't come with me right away."

"Ibrahim!" the Grand Mufti called. A bodyguard appeared. Ashrawi pointed to the man who'd invaded his privacy. "Throw him out."

Ibrahim shook his head. "That's not a good idea. You don't know who he comes from."

"Someone who can tell me what to do?" Haji Jamal didn't believe it.

But Ibrahim nodded. "That's right. A bigger fish than you."

There weren't many, not in Palestine and not in the wider Muslim world. "How do you know?" Ashrawi asked.

"You're wasting time," the stranger said. "My friend doesn't like that. He came to Hebron to see you. Keep him waiting, he won't be happy. You won't like it if he's unhappy."

"Boss . . . You better go." Ibrahim sounded urgent.

None of Haji Jamal's guards was a coward. If the stranger could intimidate Ibrahim . . . "All right."

"About time," the nameless man said. "Well, it isn't far."

It was only a couple of blocks from the market square. Everything seemed normal. But wasn't it *too* calm? Wasn't everybody on his best behavior? So it seemed to Jamal Ashrawi. Or maybe his imagination was running away.

They ducked into a doorway. The stranger relaxed—a little. "Israeli patrols won't catch us in the open," he said.

"They haven't caught me yet," Ashrawi said.

The stranger looked through him. "They don't want you the way they want—" He opened a door and finished with one word: "Him."

Ice walked up the Grand Mufti's back. He was in the presence of legend. The handsome man with the gray-streaked black beard nodded. "In the name of God, I welcome you," he said, and his Arabic, unlike his stooge's, had the flavor of Iraq.

"In . . . the name of God," Haji Jamal managed after a pause. He tried again: "I did not look for you here."

That won a smile. "If you had, others might have, too," said the man who called himself a caliph. "Will you drink tea? Will you eat bread and salt?"

"I would be honored!" If the Grand Mufti was being offered hospitality, he hadn't been brought here to die. His host was supposed to be punctilious in such things.

At a nod from the Iraqi, the man who'd collected Haji Jamal

fetched tea, flatbread, and salt. The tea was mint. The bread and salt went back to desert days, and were symbol as well as food.

After the refreshments, Ashrawi asked, "What do you need from me?" He couldn't keep his voice from wobbling.

"You have been harassing the Jews as they rebuilt their Temple."

"Y—Yes." No, the wobble wouldn't go away.

"You have been failing." The Iraqi sounded disgusted. "Time to let people who know what they are doing get on with the job."

"*Inshallah*," Ashrawi said. *If God wills* was always appropriate. Considering what had happened to the Palestinians' attacks—and to the Iranians'—it seemed more so here.

The Iraqi's dark eyebrows came down and together in a frown. "And why would God—the compassionate, the merciful—*not* will it?" he inquired.

"I don't know why God does anything," Haji Jamal said. "But our heavy mortar would not have opened the Golden Gate and let the young Jew fulfill their false prophecy had God not willed it. The other rounds would not have torn the graves so he could pretend to raise the dead."

The ISIS leader looked down his nose at the Grand Mufti. "Some people don't know what they're doing, and don't do it well. Then they blame God for failure."

"I blame no one," Ashrawi said. "I only tell you what happened. If you don't believe me, ask the President of Iran or his chief general or the Grand Ayatollah."

"Iranians. I spit on Iranians. They are still angry God did not give them the Prophet, peace be upon him. They act foolishly—and then, like you, blame God when things go wrong."

Ashrawi could tell he wouldn't listen. "May success bless your men," he said.

"I think it will," his host answered calmly. "Is Tel Aviv radioactive, or not? We didn't do all of that, but we were involved here and there. It shows what can be managed."

"It harmed the Zionists," Haji Jamal said. "But it also enraged them. Without the dirty bomb, they would not have had the will to throw us off the Haram al-Sharif. The United States would not have let them get away with it."

"I spit on the United States, and on the Zionist entity. So does God—you may be sure of that." The Iraqi's eyes gleamed. "We will do what needs doing, I promise. We may need to use some of your men. Is that acceptable, O gracious one?"

What if I say no? Ashrawi wondered. But he could see the answer. *If I say no, I don't leave this room alive.* He had no urge to become a *shahid,* a martyr. He admired such bravery without wanting to imitate it.

And so, after a short pause, he said, "Certainly. I will pray for their success—for your success." He wasn't even lying, though he wondered if it would be as easy as the Iraqi expected.

"May God hearken to you. Watch. You'll see how things should be done." Without giving the Grand Mufti a chance to reply, the Iraqi nodded to his underling. "Take him home."

"Of course." The fellow nodded to Ashrawi. "Come on."

Haji Jamal went with him. They made it back without drawing any attention. The *souq* kept the not quite normal feel Ashrawi had noticed on the way to the Iraqi's door.

Ibrahim breathed a sigh of relief. "Did you talk to—him?" the bodyguard asked, his eyes big and round.

"Yes." Jamal Ashrawi let one word suffice.

"And?"

"And he will do what he will do, and God will do what He will do, and we will see what happens then," Ahsrawi said.

"If anyone can do anything, he's the one," Ibrahim said.

"If anyone can do anything, God is the One," Haji Jamal said. The guard bowed his head.

* * *

Chaim's guards stuck to him tighter than the resurrected souls did. They didn't listen to him even if he screamed. Except at the falafel stand. Then the hard-faced men formed a perimeter around the place, leaving an island of privacy inside their line.

It was what Chaim had. He knew he'd better make the most of it. "Hi," he said to Shoshanah, and then, "I hope I'm not hurting business."

She laughed. "Are you kidding? The soldiers come here when you're not around, and you wouldn't believe what they eat."

"Oh." That didn't overjoy Chaim. "Do they . . . bother you?"

"Not really." Shoshanah spoke with easy assurance. "Besides, they think you can turn them into frogs if they give you any grief." She leaned across the counter. "Can you?"

He started to say, *Don't be silly,* but he didn't. "I don't know," he said slowly. "I never tried anything like that. I never even thought about it till now."

"I bet you could—if you got mad, I mean," Shoshanah said, and then, "You don't get mad much, do you?"

Chaim blinked. "I never thought about that, either. I don't know. I'm just kind of regular, I guess."

"Regular?" She laughed again. "How can you be regular when you're the Messiah?"

"I don't *feel* like the Messiah—mostly, anyhow," Chaim said. "I get sleepy and hungry like anybody else. You guys make great falafels. I get mad like— What are you doing?"

"Getting you some falafels. If you like them, you ought to have them."

He reached into his pants pocket. She waved for him not to bother. "I've got money," he protested.

"Don't worry about it. You think other people don't come here because you do? You're nuts if you do." She handed him the pita and the deep-fried garbanzo balls. "Here. Load your own fixings."

"Thanks. You don't need to do that, though, honest."

"I didn't do it 'cause I needed to. I did it 'cause I wanted to. I never imagined I'd meet anybody like you, let alone that you might like me."

"Might!" Chaim said with his mouth full. Eating a falafel was messy any time. Eating a falafel when the first girl he'd ever really noticed said that . . . The pita started disintegrating a lot faster than usual. Fortunately, he had plenty of napkins. Once he swallowed, he went on, "I think you're wonderful."

"Me?" Shoshanah gaped. "You say you're ordinary. I am."

"No, you're not!" Chaim said fiercely.

"No? Why am I working here till I get drafted?" she said. "I'll worry about school after that. I just want to . . . Right now, I don't know what I want to do. You always did, didn't you?"

That almost made Chaim snarf falafel. He'd never had any notion what he would do if the Temple didn't get rebuilt. He would have been raised ritually pure in a world that had no use for anyone like that. He'd come across an English phrase that summed it up: *all dressed up with no place to go.*

He realized he wasn't as regular as he'd told Shoshanah. Being raised as he was, hardly setting foot on bare ground till he got mad at Kupferman . . . He wondered how weird he really was.

Weird enough to raise the dead. What was weirder than that?

He needed to answer Shoshanah. "I didn't have a clue. I still don't."

"God will tell you." She raised one eyebrow. He thought it was cute. She didn't do much he didn't think was cute, but he hadn't realized that yet. She went on, "I'm not *frum* or anything, but this isn't happening by accident, like. When the time comes, God will tell you."

"I guess." Chaim wasn't a hundred percent convinced. "He didn't tell me what would happen when I ran through the graveyard."

"He didn't need to," Shoshanah said. "He showed you."

"Yeah, but—" Chaim broke off. He couldn't explain what it meant, even to her. He didn't know himself. He had this power, but it almost drove him crazy when he used it. What kind of sense did that make? None he could see.

"Don't worry about it so much," Shoshanah said softly. "If God wants it to be all right, it will be. And if He didn't want it to be all right, why would He do it?"

"I don't know," Chaim said.

"See?" Now she sounded triumphant.

Chaim wasn't so sure. God did what He wanted, for His reasons. If you got in His way, too bad. Chaim shivered, remembering Job's kin.

Once, Yitzhak Avigad had thought he knew what was going on. Now things were happening all around him, and he had no idea how he'd got caught up in them. The Ark, the Temple, his nephew . . . He'd seen a Hebrew production of *Rosencrantz & Guildenstern Are Dead*. Wasn't he stuck in something too much like that?

Matching wits with a human playwright was a fair fight. In God's hands . . . Everything that happened meant something to the Lord. For a mortal to figure out what . . . Yitzhak wasn't sure a miracle would suffice, not any more.

His phone rang. When he was younger, he would have called a phone you carried in your pocket a miracle. The word had a new meaning now. No—it had its old meaning back. A phone was a clever gadget. A miracle was when God showed you Who was in charge instead of expecting you to believe it.

Thou shalt Love the Lord thy God with all thy heart and with all thy soul and with all thy might. The line from the prayer ran through his mind as he obeyed a mortal commandment. *Thou shalt make thy phone shut up.* "Yes?" he said.

"How's Chaim?" his sister-in-law said.

"Fine," Yitzhak answered, "all things considered . . ."

"When can I come to Jerusalem?" Rivka Avigad demanded.

"Nobody's stopping you," Yitzhak said. "It's what? Half an hour from the kibbutz to here? He'll be glad to see you."

"I don't know if I'd be glad to see him," she said. "I just don't know. He scares me. I feel like a duck that hatched a hoopoe."

Yitzhak shook his head. "Not a hoopoe. Hoopoes are *treyf*. Whatever the boy is, you can't call him *treyf*."

"The *goyim* do. Antichrist." She spat the word.

"You start listening to preachers and priests and muftis and ayatollahs, you'll go crazy," Yitzhak said.

"They're already crazy, and they want to crucify my son." Rivka hesitated. "Well, maybe not that."

"Look at the trouble it caused the last time," Yitzhak said dryly.

"Heh," Rivka said. "What are we going to do, Yitzhak?"

"Beats me," he answered. "We have to wait and see what happens and whether God decides to stick his finger in again. I was thinking about that just now."

"I'm not worried about God. God will take care of Chaim," his sister-in-law said. Yitzhak didn't argue. She went on, "I'm worried about all the fanatics. What will they do to him?"

"Nothing God doesn't let them do," Yitzhak said.

"That's . . . true." Rivka sounded happier. "I didn't look at it that way. If God takes care of Chaim, he's safe from those people, isn't he?"

"If God takes care of him, he is," Yitzhak said.

"Thanks. You're a sweetie. *Shalom*." Rivka Avigad hung up.

Yitzhak stuck the phone in a pocket. If Rivka wanted to think he'd given her good news, she could. But the coin had two sides. (*Rosencrantz & Guildenstern* rose in his mind again, and made him uneasy.) If God felt like taking care of Chaim, he would. If He didn't . . .

At least I didn't have to tell her about Shoshanah, Yitzhak thought. Maybe she already knew; everybody in Jerusalem seemed to. But no. If Rivka knew, she would have asked about the girl. Since she hadn't, she didn't.

She would think Chaim was too young—and too holy. She would think he cared about the girl only because her name was Shoshanah. Yitzhak thought that mattered, but he didn't think it was the only thing going on. Projection from a cow to a girl sounded as if it came from Freud or Greek mythology, one.

But Shoshanah seemed like a nice kid. She might end up in more trouble for being friendly to Chaim than he was for hanging out with her. Yitzhak hoped they'd both be okay.

Then he hoped *he* would. And Jerusalem. And *Eretz Yisrael*. While he was at it, he hoped the world would, too.

"Amazing what you can do with reinforced concrete," Eric said.

Shlomo Kupferman nodded. "It really is. And by modern standards the Temple isn't that big a building. So work goes much faster than it would with, say, a skyscraper."

"We weren't thinking of size so much," Orly said. "It looks like the rest of the buildings here. It looks golden, like limestone, not . . . gray."

"Part of that is the stone facing. But you can do almost anything with concrete these days," Kupferman said. Like Eric and Orly, he mixed Hebrew and English almost without noticing. "Making it the color you want? That's nothing." He snapped his fingers. "You can make concrete that floats."

"Can I talk to you about something else?" Eric asked.

"What else is there besides the Temple?" Kupferman sounded surprised. But, seeing the archaeologist was serious, he nodded again. "What's on your mind?"

Eric took Orly's hand. "You know we're getting married?"

"Sure. *Mazel tov*," the rabbi answered.

"We went to Cyprus for the civil ceremony, and that was great. They even took my plastic. But here—we'd do it a lot faster if we could cut the red tape," Eric said. "You know the *megillah* a foreign Jew has to go through before he convinces people here he's Jewish. It takes forever. If you can't speed things up, who can?"

"The system is set up so we don't make mistakes. For you, though, Professor Katz . . ." Kupferman pulled out his phone and punched in a number. He barked at whoever answered, listened for a moment, and barked again. Then he called someone else. He didn't bark this time—he bellowed. The phone disappeared. Kupferman looked pleased. *He enjoys browbeating people,* Eric thought. That wasn't a headline. "Any day after this Sunday," the rabbi said. "It's taken care of. Anyone who gives you more *tsuris,* tell him to talk to me. I'll make him sorry." He sounded as if he wanted to.

"Well!" Eric said.

"Well!" Orly echoed. "Thank you," she added. She sounded as if she'd never expected to say those words to Kupferman.

His sour smile said he knew as much. "My pleasure. This isn't politics. This is religion—and love, I hope."

"Maybe a little," Eric said. Orly made as if to hit him. He ducked more sincerely than she threw the punch. He also touched the brim of his hat to Kupferman. "Thanks very much."

"I already said it's all—" Kupferman pointed toward two bull-dozers rumbling onto the Temple Mount. "Who are those people? We don't need dozers now!" His voice rose to a shout: "Guards! Something's wrong with those bulldozers!"

The hard hats on the bulldozers looked like workmen to Eric. He'd wondered why so many were perched atop the school-bus-yellow diesel snorters, but he hadn't wondered enough to say anything.

Soldiers trotted toward the dozers. The guys on them pulled out AKs and RPGs and started shooting. Some Israeli guards went down. Others returned fire. Facing charging bulldozers, that took nerve.

Eric didn't see what happened next, because Orly knocked him down. "When they start shooting, get flat!" she yelled. She'd been through the IDF mill. She knew what was what, and he didn't. A bullet cracking by where his neck had been a few seconds earlier underlined the message.

Ping! Ping!—metal off metal. The attackers had got the dozer blades up. They were using them against Israeli bullets.

And they were charging the Temple. There was a scene the scribes who set down the Bible had never imagined. Not even St. John the Divine had put berserk bulldozers into Revelation.

Trailing fire, a badly aimed RPG flew past the Temple and off the Temple Mount. It exploded somewhere in the Muslim quarter of the Old City. Eric assumed the attackers were Muslims themselves. They'd just nailed some of their own.

Another RPG blew up a cement mixer. Wet, gooey cement flew. To Eric, it seemed a waste of an expensive round. A terrorist bean-counter would be unhappy with that guy.

A bullet spanged off the paving too close in front of Eric's nose and kicked high enough not to blow his brains out on the ricochet. He broke fingernails trying to claw into the rock.

A bulldozer ran down a couple of Israeli soldiers. They kept shooting, and didn't even try to get out of the way. The machine left red tracks as it ground toward the rising Temple.

What had it been like in the fourth century, when the partly built Temple caught fire in Julian's reign? Was that an accident or Christian arson? To this day, nobody knew. Or was it a miracle, as church historians claimed? Till now, Eric hadn't taken the notion seriously enough to laugh at it. But did God say, *No, it's not time yet,* and stick His finger in? How could you know? How could you know anything for sure these days?

Eric shook his head, though he didn't lift it—he was learning fast. He knew *one* thing. He was scared shitless, almost for real. The pucker factor was mighty, mighty high.

Kupferman groaned. For a second, Eric thought a stray round got him. Then Kupferman said, "The boy! He's coming out!"

That made Eric raise his head enough to see the Temple entrance. There was Chaim Avigad. The kid was ghost-pale and looked even more frightened than Eric felt.

Chaim wasn't alone, or not exactly. He had the Ark with him, his hands on the gold-plated handles. The Ark was floating again, whatever that meant.

The terrorists shouted in triumph. "Now we've got the Jewboy, too!" one yelled. They turned their gunfire on Chaim and the Ark.

Chaim just stood there, hanging on to the Ark for dear life. Eric thought he put his hands on it, not just on the handles. He didn't fall over dead, from that or from the terrorists' fire. All the bullets somehow—or Somehow—missed. As for the ones that headed for the Ark of the Covenant . . .

Later, Eric wondered what slow-motion digitized replays would show. At the time, all he had to go on was what he saw. Lightning flashed from the Ark, back toward everyone who'd fired at it. Men twisted and fell. One bulldozer caught fire. The other exploded with a muffled *whoomp!* that lifted Eric off the ground and then dropped him again, hard.

Diesel engines weren't supposed to blow up like that. Maybe God didn't read the instruction manual. Or maybe He'd written His own.

All of a sudden, it got quiet. Eric looked at his watch. Four minutes had gone by since Kupferman decided he didn't like the looks of the bulldozers. Was that possible? It seemed like four hours, or years.

"Is it over?" somebody asked. Eric needed a second to recognize the voice as his own. It wasn't just because his ears were blasted. His wits were, too.

"I . . . think so." Orly sounded as shellshocked as he felt. She looked around. "None of those assholes is moving any more." The obscenity came out in Arabic.

"Thanks for knocking me down, babe," Eric managed.

She gave him the tag end of a smile. "Any time."

Eric got to his feet. That was when he realized he'd tried to dig without pick, shovel, or trowel. His hands were a bloody mess. He stuck them in the pockets of his jeans.

Then he thought about Kupferman. "You okay?" he asked him.

"Yes." Shlomo Kupferman didn't sound as if he had any doubts. He rose more smoothly than Eric had—but his hands were torn up, too. Kupferman went on, "You have a song in English, don't you, that goes, 'Mine eyes have seen the glory of the coming of the Lord . . . '?"

"Sure. 'The Battle Hymn of the Republic,'" Eric said.

"Whatever the name is." Kupferman sounded impatient with the details. "I don't know what the man who wrote that hymn saw—"

"It was a woman."

Kupferman's formidable, bristly eyebrows flexed down into a frown. "That's not my biggest worry. What we just saw is."

"Well—yeah." Eric looked around for Orly and didn't see her. Then he did: she was giving a wounded soldier first aid. The Temple Mount stank of blood and high explosives and hot metal and burning diesel fuel and burned meat and fear. Some of the fear came from Eric—but not all of it.

And the Ark glittered in the sun, and Chaim Avigad stood there, looking stunned. Eric decided he needed first aid more than the wounded Israeli soldiers. How much of what had happened was his doing, how much the Ark's? Was there any dividing line?

As Eric went over to the kid, he walked past a dead terrorist. The man wasn't just dead. He was scorched and worse: whatever the Ark did to him burned him small, like a steak on the barbecue too long. That burned-meat smell rose from him and his pals. Eric's stomach did a slow lurch.

Chaim Avigad's eyes showed white around the iris, as a scared horse's would have. "Easy," Eric said gently. "It's over."

The kid who'd unwillingly gone into the Messiah business shook his head. "It's never over. It just gets worse." He pointed to the shrunken terrorist Eric had walked by. "I heard him die. I felt him die. I felt them all die, on both sides. Now they're . . . part of the crowd." He gestured.

His entourage of revived souls surrounded him as usual. With the Ark, they reminded Eric not to get too close. The archaeologist didn't know what would happen if he came among them. He didn't want to find out, either.

How can I help him? Eric wondered, seeing he'd bitten off more than he could chew. *How can anybody?*

He asked, "How did you get the Ark out here?"

"It wanted to come," Chaim answered. "I was in the Holy Place—not the Holy of Holies, but the big room in front of that— looking around when the shooting started. I didn't know what to do. But I heard it, like, calling me, so I went in there."

"Uh-*huh*." Eric made himself nod. If you didn't listen to what Chaim was talking about, he sounded like every other teenage boy of his generation.

"When I got there, it was floating. It hadn't done that since it settled down on the rock where it used to be." Chaim could talk about days 3,000 years past as if they were yesterday morning. The Dome of the Rock? An afternoon visitor, gone now. The maybe Messiah went on, "It was, like, floating, so I grabbed it, and it didn't seem heavy or anything, so I brought it out."

"How did you do that?" Eric asked.

"I just did—same way I knew to get it," Chaim said, which wasn't exactly an answer . . . unless, of course, it was. "So I brought it out here, and all that weird stuff happened."

"Yeah. All that weird stuff," Eric agreed tonelessly. "How did all the bullets miss you?"

"Beats me," Chaim Avigad said. "They did, that's all."

"You aren't allowed to go into the Holy of Holies." That wasn't Eric. That was Rabbi Kupferman, who'd come up behind him. The old man's eyes blazed. "No one may go in there but the High Priest alone, and he only on Yom Kippur."

"I did what the Ark told me to do." Kupferman might have sixty years on the boy, but the look Chaim gave back was as unfriendly—and as fierce—as the Religious Affairs Minister's. Chaim went on, "I'll listen to God before I listen to you any old day, *Rabbi*." He turned the title of respect into one near hatred. "I'll listen to anybody before I listen to you. You killed Rosie. You think I forgot?"

Kupferman drew himself up straight. "If I hadn't, you wouldn't have been revealed as the Messiah. You should thank me."

"Thank you?" If Kupferman's eyes had blazed, Chaim's were the inside of a star. Why that gaze didn't vaporize the rabbi, Eric had no idea. Kupferman was made of stern stuff—or maybe he just hadn't figured out what he was messing with. "*Thank* you?" Chaim repeated. "You think I want this? You think I *enjoy* this?"

"If God wants you to have it, you have it," Kupferman returned.

"*Cus ummak!*" Chaim shouted—not a messianic thing to say. "If God wants me to go into the Holy of Holies, who are *you* to say no? You're not the High Priest, even if you play like you are."

For the first time, Kupferman winced. As Religious Affairs Minister, as a senior rabbi, as the man who'd sacrificed the red heifer, he had more of a claim on the high priesthood than anyone else. But Chaim was right. It wasn't his yet.

Sirens wailing, ambulances screeched up the ramp. The paramedics glanced over to the gleaming Ark—how could you help it?—but stuck to business. Eric admired their single-mindedness.

He didn't have much of his own. He realized Chaim had said

something to him, but he had no idea what. "I'm sorry?" he managed.

"I said, will you help me get the Ark back into the Holy of Holies? I brought it out myself, but it's easier with two."

Eric noticed that he didn't ask Kupferman. Kupferman noticed, too, and didn't like it. Eric wasn't sure he did, either. What would happen if he touched those ancient handles? Would he fall over dead, the way Brandon Nesbitt had?

"Okay." Did that come out of his mouth? It did. Only one thing accounted for it: fear of looking like a coward in front of other people. If not for that terror, how could war go on?

"I—" Kupferman started, then stopped. What was he going to say? *I forbid it?* If he tried that, Chaim would give him the horse laugh. Eric extended him credit for being smart enough to see as much. One of the rules archaeologists and historians had was that an order proclaimed time after time was an order everybody was ignoring. You didn't want to issue those orders. They sapped your authority, and you might need it later.

All of which went through Eric's head in maybe half a second. He had time enough to look around before his battered hands closed on the gold-plated *shittim* wood. There was Orly, relieved of first-aid duties by the paramedics. She stared at him. Behind his glasses, his eyes were bound to be enormous, too.

The old gold was cool under his battered hands for a moment, but took on his warmth. *I can feel that. I'm not dead,* he thought.

Then Chaim said, "You have to lift a little." Eric remembered he wasn't doing this only to risk his neck. It had another purpose, too.

"Oh, yeah." How long would he have stood there if Chaim didn't remind him?

He pulled up on the handles. He could feel some weight when he did, but not much. The Ark came up easy as you please. He and Chaim had no trouble carrying it inside the Temple.

The interior walls were still bare concrete. It was like walking through a house before the occupant moved in. *Yeah, just like that,* Eric thought uneasily. Compared to the splendors of the Dome of the Rock, it seemed even plainer than it would have otherwise.

Into the Holy of Holies: a smaller box of hand-laid stone blocks, not concrete. "Are you sure this is okay?" Eric asked.

"No. The bogeyman'll jump out and get you," Chaim said. Eric shut up. There was the stone of the Temple Mount sticking up through the flooring, the way it had in the Dome of the Rock. Chaim pointed at marks on the stone. "It goes right there."

"Mm-hmm," Eric said. Yes, that was where archaeologists thought it had gone in the days of the First Temple. Eric helped Chaim guide it there.

"Let it down," Chaim told him. He did. It settled into place. The rock groaned for a moment. How much weight had settled onto it? An awful lot more than Eric had carried—he was sure of that.

Once he was no longer holding the Ark's handles, he got out as fast as he could. If Chaim wanted to sneer at him, fine. But Chaim didn't hang around, either.

"Wow!" Eric gasped when he got out into the open air again. "Oh, wow!"

Orly took his arm. Was that awe on her face? Eric didn't see awe enough to recognize it. "What was it like?" she asked.

"It wasn't *like* anything," Eric said. "Oh, wow!"

"Like Jacob, you should change your name to Israel." Kupferman sounded serious. "You have wrestled with God and prevailed."

The words from Genesis came closer to what had happened than anything Eric could have come up with. He'd touched a power as much greater than his own as an acetylene torch's was than a moth's, and it let him live. Was that prevailing? "You know something?" he said. "Maybe I will."

He had more trouble prevailing over the IDF medic who swabbed off his cuts and scrapes with bandages soaked in rubbing alcohol. He hissed like a cobra and had all he could do not to howl like a coyote—having the wounds cleaned was worse than getting them in the first place. Of course, he'd been full of adrenaline then; now he felt empty of it and everything else.

That Orly yipped when her turn came made him feel a little better, but not much. "Hush, both of you," the medic said. "Do you want infections?"

"I want it not to hurt," Orly snapped, beating Eric to the punch. "Why couldn't you use something with lidocaine in it?"

"Because this is what I've got left," the medic answered as he swathed their hands with clean gauze. "Thank God the two of you didn't catch anything bad."

"We do," Eric said. Orly nodded. The medic scratched his head. He hadn't come up onto the Temple Mount till after the shooting and the miracles were over. The blood that splashed his tunic and trousers and arms said he'd saved minor hurts like theirs for last.

They went down into the Old City. As soon as they were off the Mount, Orly said, "I'm starved."

"So am I!" Eric exclaimed. Along with adrenaline's ebb, that explained part of the emptiness inside him. *The terror and terrorism diet,* he thought muzzily. How many calories had a brush with death and another with the Lord scoured out of him? Quite a few, by the way he suddenly shook.

"There's a *shawarma* place not far from here," Orly said.

"Lead on!" Eric hoped he didn't sound too much like a hungry wolf when another said it knew of a limping moose somewhere close by.

Lamb sliced from a joint on an upright spit and stuffed into a pita with salad fixings tasted the way the gods on Olympus (who likely weren't nearly so real as the one on the Temple Mount) only wished ambrosia would. Even the smoke from a new customer's cigarette couldn't faze Eric, though he usually hated it as much as most Californians did.

Then he recognized the middle-aged man behind those dark sunglasses. "Haven't seen you in a while, Munir," he said in English. Of the languages they had in common, that one seemed safest.

"Hello. Hello, both of you," Munir al-Nuwayhi said, also in English. "Did I hear you got married? Congratulations if that's right."

"Half right, or maybe a little more," Eric answered.

When Munir quirked an eyebrow, Orly explained, "We went to Cyprus. We haven't had the religious ceremony yet. Bureaucrats!" She turned the last word into a curse.

"Ah." The Israeli Arab nodded. He likely had more, and less happy, acquaintance with the Jewish state's form-fillers and card-filers and rubber-stamp-wielders than she did. "May you be happy together. May your children be many, if that's what you want."

"Thanks," Eric said with his mouth full. Orly, whose mouth was fuller, nodded back at Munir.

The Arab switched to his birthspeech to order, then returned to English: "Were the two of you on the Haram al-Sharif just now? Your hands make me think so."

"Yes. That was—scary." Eric felt the inadequacy of words. *I didn't shit my pants, though,* he thought, not without some pride.

"Those ISIS maniacs—" Orly began.

For a wonder, she did stop when Munir held up the hand with a Marlboro between nicotine-yellowed index and middle fingers. "Are you surprised something like that happened when you took down the mosque and the Dome of the Rock? Are you really?"

"Surprised? No," Eric said before Orly could answer. "But even if the Ark hadn't stopped them, that kind of raid wouldn't have done them any good."

"The Ark?" Munir said, so he didn't know everything that had happened up there.

Eric and Orly took turns filling him in. "What do you think of that?" Orly added after they got to the end.

"I think . . . the world is a much stranger place than I dreamt it was not very long ago," al-Nuwayhi said slowly. The counterman gave him his *shawarma*. He paid, waved away change, and removed the cigarette to bite into it. Eric thought exactly the same thing. Munir went on, "Congratulations on your chance for unexpected archaeological observations, Professor Katz."

"If it wasn't for the honor of the thing, I'd've rather walked," Eric said. Munir raised his eyebrow again. He translated out of slang: "Some things you'd rather not do any which way."

The Israeli Arab bobbed his head; he got that. Then he asked, "You aren't glad the power of God showed itself that way?"

"I'm glad it saved . . . us." Again, Eric adjusted language. *Saved our bacon* would have annoyed both Munir and Orly. "But I wish God stayed out of the world, same as you do."

"Whose God?" Munir and Orly asked the same question at the same time.

"You pays your money and you takes your choice," Eric said. That wasn't standard English, either, but they both followed. He continued, "Staying secular gets harder by the day, doesn't it?"

"Yes," Orly said.

"Oh, yes," Munir agreed. "Fewer and fewer people bother trying, either. That's why . . . things like what happened up on the Haram al-Sharif happen more and more. If you were observant before, you grow more observant now. If you weren't, you start."

"Have *you* started?" Orly was as blunt as any Jewish Israeli.

"Some," Munir said. "The same as the two of you have, unless I'm very wrong."

Eric and Orly looked at each other. Neither tried to deny it. Their faith and the one Munir found himself inclining toward ever more hadn't got on with each other lately, but they couldn't keep from taking it a lot more seriously than they ever had.

Munir lit a new Marlboro while he was still chewing the last bite of his *shawarma*. He took a drag before he wiped his mouth with a paper napkin. "We do the best we can. What else is there to do? But when you measure what we can do against what Allah can do . . ." He didn't go on, or need to.

"*Shalom aleikhem*," Eric said.

"*Aleikum salaam*." Munir went back to English: "And to you also peace. Yes, the two languages are cousins. So are the two peoples. But are any fights worse than fights among kin?"

"The way things look, no," Eric said. Orly's mouth twisted, but she touched Eric's arm in a way that showed she didn't care to quarrel about it.

"You are People of the Book. You are good people. The holy Qur'an does not deny you a hope of heaven," Munir said, and then once more, "*Aleikum salaam*." He raised his hand and the Marlboro in a sort of salute, then walked away from the stand, turned a corner, and disappeared.

"Ibrahim!" Jamal Ashrawi called.

"What do you need, boss?" the bodyguard asked.

"Where is the dog who serves the idiot who bragged of his schemes?" the Grand Mufti demanded.

Ibrahim looked at him. "Careful how you talk, boss. Somebody who doesn't like you so much is liable to hear."

"Should I care?" Haji Jamal was in a temper.

"You want to keep breathing, you better," his bodyguard said.

"Then why do I keep you around?" Ashrawi said.

Ibrahim spread his hands. "We do what we can. You know that—you'd better. But if . . . somebody wants something to happen to you, we may not get lucky. We don't work miracles, you know."

"Neither does that Iraqi maniac," the Grand Mufti said. "He lets the Jews work them with that Ark! Does he wreck the Temple? Ha! Does he get rid of that boy, the one who might be the Antichrist? Ha! Does he hand the Zionist entity a propaganda coup? On a silver platter!"

"You're yelling again, boss," the bodyguard said. "You don't want to yell, especially not about . . . him."

"If he can't stand the truth . . ." Haji Jamal shook his head. "He can't do everything."

"God has judged the people who tried telling him," Ibrahim answered. "He has a bigger organization than you, bigger than anybody but the Americans and God." He named the biggest powers he could think of.

What Ashrawi said about the Americans made what he'd said about the Iraqi sound like love poetry. Ibrahim listened in openmouthed admiration. "Go get his man," the Grand Mufti added. "I want to speak to him."

Ibrahim sighed. "It's your funeral. I hope it's not mine, too. It will be as God wills. There is no God but God, and Muhammad is the Prophet of God." With the *shahadah* fresh on his lips, he went out to beard the bearded Iraqi's henchman.

He came back sooner than the Grand Mufti of Jerusalem had expected. "Well?" Haji Jamal said.

"Call him whatever you want, boss." Ibrahim sounded cheerful— almost giddy. "He's gone."

"What?" Ashrawi could hardly believe his ears.

"Gone," Ibrahim repeated. "He took off for . . . wherever. I heard four different things. Nobody's got any idea."

It made more sense than the Grand Mufti wished it did. He'd been surprised the lord of terrorists and his men came out of their Syrian fastness. The Iraqi must have wanted to supervise this in person. Much good *that* did him. But now he needed to disappear again, because he'd have the Americans and the Zionists hot on his trail.

"All right," Haji Jamal said. "The Iraqi did some great things, but that was long ago, and what did it get him? Life on the run, forever."

"He's still dangerous," the bodyguard said.

Ashrawi nodded, not wanting to quarrel, and went about his

business. He didn't spend all his time in hiding. Right now, the Zionist entity would be too busy chasing the vanished Iraqi to pay attention to him. His bodyguards thought so, too. And so he wandered through Hebron almost as a free man.

It gave him less satisfaction than it might. Hebron wasn't a bad town, but it *was* a town. He missed Jerusalem's brawling life. Even under enemy occupation, Jerusalem was a more vibrant place than Hebron dreamt of being.

He liked that thought, and turned in an alleyway to share it with his guards. Three large, burly men stepped out the back door of an olive oil merchant's shop. Haji Jamal didn't like their looks. He turned around—and found himself facing three more plug-uglies. They moved toward him.

"No!" he said. "In the name of God, the compassionate, the merciful . . ."

"You should be careful when you run your mouth," one said with an Iraqi accent. "You should be, but you're not."

"Now you'll get what's coming to you," added a bruiser behind him. "It's your own fault, too."

They moved in and started beating him. He fought back at first, but an old man against six young ones made bad odds. He sank to the ground and tried to cover his face and privates. He cried out whenever a punch or kick landed.

Someone must have heard him. He was sure of that. Nobody came to see what was going on, though. Did people know who was doing the beating, and know it was worth their lives to interfere? He wondered later. While it was going on, he just hurt.

One goon kicked him in the head three times. "Careful," another warned. "We aren't supposed to kill him."

"Too bad," the first thug said, and kicked him in the ribs instead. Haji Jamal, by then, was too far gone to care. Getting your head treated like a football wasn't good for thought.

He didn't know how the musclemen decided they were through,

but they walked away and left him lying there. His nose wasn't broken. He didn't think he'd lost teeth. But his own bodyguards let this happen to him! What had the Iraqi said that made them back away? Threats to them personally wouldn't have done the trick. They had courage to spare. But if they thought their families would suffer . . .

Something stabbed like an ice pick when he struggled to his feet. The curs had cracked a rib, then. He put a hand on a wall for support. They hadn't stomped his fingers. Thinking about it, that was more luck.

Slowly, limping and wincing, Jamal Ashrawi started back toward his room. He wondered which was worse: the Zionist entity that ruthlessly suppressed everything Palestinian, or the savage Iraqi who punished anyone presuming to disagree with him.

Did it matter? He'd fallen foul of them both.

He came out onto a street with people on it. No one seemed surprised to see him battered and bruised and bleeding. Everyone seemed to have known what would happen if he showed his face outside. *Everyone but me,* he thought.

Ibrahim popped up out of nowhere. "You all right, boss?"

"No thanks to you," Ashrawi said, spitting blood.

"I tried to tell you. You didn't want to listen to me."

Knowing he was right made the Grand Mufti no happier. "You were supposed to keep these things from happening to me."

"We did what we could," Ibrahim answered. "They were going to kill you slow and put it on the Internet, like they do with hostages. We talked them out of that. You ought to thank us."

"I can protect myself from my enemies," Ashrawi snarled, "but God deliver me from my friends."

"That isn't fair," Ibrahim said. "We put our lives on the line to keep you breathing. You might thank us."

"I might, yes." Jamal winced again as that rib stabbed him. Breathing hurt, too. "When I'm sure I want to, maybe I will."

* * *

"I saw it on TV." Shoshanah's eyes couldn't have been wider if Chaim had scored the World Cup-winning goal for the Israeli national team. "You really *did* that?"

"I guess." It seemed unreal to Chaim, too—much of it unreal like a bad dream. "God had a lot to do with it, too."

"Well, sure." That didn't make her any less impressed. "Did He tell you so?" She took it for granted that God might want to talk to him. He wished he could.

"It doesn't work that way," he said. "I kind of knew I was supposed to get the Ark out of there. After that, stuff just—happened. I thought they were going to shoot me."

"Wow!" Shoshanah breathed. Chaim admired the breathing. Who would have known anything so ordinary could be so beautiful? She went on, "You saved the Temple."

"I guess," Chaim repeated. "Just luck I was even there." Was anything "just luck" these days? Had anything ever been "just luck"? The more he thought about it, the more he doubted it.

By the way Shoshanah tossed her head, she doubted it was just luck, too. She asked, "How did those"—she said something incandescent that was part Arabic, part Russian—"get onto the Temple Mount in the first place?"

"They jumped the guys who were going to take the bulldozers up there. Some of them spoke Hebrew, so they fooled the real workers," Chaim answered. "I don't know how they got past the soldiers so they *could* jump the dozer crews. I heard this from Army guys, you know, and they don't want to admit they screwed up."

"Army guys," Shoshanah said scornfully, as if she knew more about them than she wanted to. Even before all this started, they would have come to the falafel stand, and she was pretty enough that they were bound to hit on her.

Chaim hadn't thought much about soldiers till lately. Being ritually pure would have kept him from getting drafted when he turned eighteen. Many ultra-Orthodox refused military service. The government mostly let them get away with it.

"I heard all the shooting," Shoshanah said, "but I didn't think you might be there till I saw you on TV. Then . . . I don't know what I thought then. I'm glad you're okay."

"Wow." Nobody'd ever said anything like that to Chaim before. Bashfully, he went on, "You want to know something? I'm glad I'm okay, too. I was *so* scared."

"Why? God would've made sure you'd be fine," Shoshanah said.

"If He wanted to, sure. If He decided he needed to do something else . . ." Chaim thought about Job's unlucky relatives one more time. They'd got in God's way, and He'd run over them like that bulldozer squashing Israeli soldiers. No—it was worse. The soldiers might have dodged, or the bulldozer might have broken down. Nobody dodged God.

"He wouldn't do that." Shoshanah sounded very sure.

"Ha!" Chaim said. If you looked at the Bible, God was about being mighty. So many prayers began, *Blessed art Thou, O Lord our God, King of the Universe. . . .* Not Prime Minister or President. King. A king did what he wanted. If his subjects didn't like it, tough luck.

The way Shoshanah looked at him said she wanted to argue. But how was she going to argue with somebody who knew from experience? You couldn't. Instead, she asked, "What will you do now?"

"Beats me," Chaim said. "I feel like a football, you know? Somebody'll kick me, and I'll go wherever I roll."

"No!" Now she sounded mad. "You're your own person, no matter what. If you weren't, I wouldn't like you the way I do."

That was as thought-provoking as the feeling he ought to run into the Holy of Holies and grab the Ark. All he said was, "I hope so. I wonder how much I've got to do with what's going on, though.

I bet the prophets didn't always want to be prophets, either. They did it anyhow. If God grabs hold of you . . ."

She came around the counter and put her arms around him. "What happens if I grab hold of you?" she said. Then she kissed him.

There were video games where the lights flashed on and off when you won. That was what Chaim felt like. He'd got pecks on the cheek from his mother, but those had nothing to do with this. They might be called kisses, but so what? This was a *kiss*.

All the ghosts howled at the same time. Some, the kids, didn't know what Chaim was doing. He didn't, either, but he learned more with every astonished thud of his heart. Some who'd died as adults cried out in horror. Others felt the same delight Chaim did.

"What do you think of that?" Shoshanah asked from a distance of maybe two centimeters. She was almost as tall as he was; he could see gold flecks in the dark brown of her irises.

"Can we do it again?" Chaim blurted.

She laughed—not at him, or he would have been crushed. "Sure," she said. He noticed more this time: how she molded herself against him, how soft she was, and how warm. He felt himself getting hotter by the second, especially in one place. Would that gross her out? It didn't seem to.

When the kiss ended, he didn't want to let her go. "Thank you," he said—he'd always been raised to be polite.

This time, she did laugh at him, but not in a mean way. "Don't be silly," she said. "It takes two."

"I guess," he said. Did that mean she enjoyed it, too? He sure hoped so. If she did, maybe she'd kiss him some more.

"You're funny. You know that?" she said.

"I guess," he said one more time. But funny was *way* better than he'd felt with all the shooting at the Temple.

22

Out of the blue, Gabriela Sandoval remembered her first game of D&D. She'd been an eighth-grader; the session was at a middle-school friend's house. The DM was a nerdy high-school sophomore named Elias Valencia. These days, he was a senior VP at Google. Nerdiness had a way of wearing off, or at least paying off, as you grew up.

That wasn't why she remembered the game, though. She remembered what he'd said just before they started: "The way this works is, I'm God and you're not. If I tell you Saturday Night Fever's broken out, take off your chain mail and boogie."

In the studio roughing out what they'd do when they went on-camera, she didn't talk about D&D with Lester Stark. Stark was liable to think it sprang from Satan. But she had Saturday Night Fever, bad. "Do you know what this is?" she said.

Stark poured some bottled water into a plastic cup—a whistle-wetter—before shaking his head. "Tell me."

"It's the biggest story in the history of the world, that's what it is!"

The televangelist sipped from the cup. Then he shook his head again. "I don't think so."

"How can you say that?" Gabriela had trouble believing her ears. "Are you out of your mind?"

"Well, you never know." Stark's dry sense of humor didn't fit her mental picture of how a fundie should sound.

"So why isn't it, then, if you're so damn smart?" Gabriela tried not to swear around the reverend, but she slipped this time.

It didn't faze him. "Because it's bigger than that."

She stared. "What *could* be?" Her whistle-wetter was coffee in an insulated plastic cup. She drank some, wishing it had cognac or Irish whiskey in it.

Stark still didn't bat an eye. "The biggest, the *last,* story in the history of the universe. They don't call these the Last Days for nothing, you know."

"I guess not." Gabriela flinched from thinking of things like that. If God, the God Who could say *I'm God and you're not* so emphatically, was showing His hand for the first time in all these years, *something* big was cooking. But you went day by day as best you could. You figured tomorrow would be like today, because today was like yesterday. Sometimes you got a surprise.

How big a surprise could God give you if He felt like it?

"You see what I mean." Stark didn't make it a question.

"Maybe I do." Gabriela thought she had a good poker face. None of the TV execs she dealt with could read her, and those people had dorsal fins and peered through sniper scopes. But the preacher from Alabama saw straight through her, down to the fear she didn't want to show herself, let alone anyone else.

"Is your soul ready for divine judgment?" Stark asked.

No, Gabriela hadn't worried about her soul till lately. In the industry, a soul could be a professional liability. She knew dying was likely to be messy and painful, although, like most people, she thought about it as little as she could. But death? She'd figured death was like going under anesthesia and never coming out. Oblivion.

What if she was wrong? What if she'd have to answer eternally for everything she did here? Yeah. What if? She *really* wished that coffee were spiked.

"Who can say?" she answered after a pause.

Stark beamed, which startled her. "Not being sure is a sign you're on the right road," he said. "Have you thought about accepting Jesus Christ as your personal savior?"

"Not really. When I thought about it at all, I figured the Pope had a private line upstairs, if you know what I mean." With a crooked grin, Gabriela added, "And right now, it looks like the Messiah's a Jewish kid with nothing but peach fuzz. Do *you* think of talking with Rabbi Kupferman about converting?"

"All the time," he answered, which left her without a comeback. People didn't admit such things—except Stark did. He went on, "I still haven't decided which side Chaim's playing for. When I make up my mind . . . I'll do whatever I do."

"You think he's the Antichrist, and Jesus will come along later?" Gabriela said. "Even now?"

"I think he could be."

"You went to a seminary, not law school."

"You mean you never heard of canon law?" Sure enough, Stark could take it and dish it out. He grew serious again. "It still seems an open question. It's in God's hands—and Satan's."

Gabriela was used to people in the business going on about God. So many of them did it so often. Some of the ones who didn't were Scientologists. She wondered what *they* thought of all this.

But those God-shouters hardly ever gave Satan equal time. Satan wasn't a big deal among her associates. Folks assumed they were heading straight up to the Pearly Gates. Nobody'd worried about the Opposition since the Stones song way back when.

The TV business mirrored America. In Puritan days, hellfire

and damnation were staples of the religious diet. No more. Hell now was like sex in Victorian days. If you didn't think about it, it would go away.

Unless it didn't.

Gabriela admired Stark for looking the Devil in the eye and puckering up to spit therein. That he thought he had to, though, terrified her. So did everything else that had happened lately. Once you'd been scared like this a few times—fright oddly different from the one when the dirty bomb knocked her sideways—how much did one more round matter? As long as it didn't make you keel over on the spot, not much.

"We haven't heard from all the precincts, either," she said.

"What do you mean?" Stark asked.

"Christians have a notion of what will happen when everything hits the fan. Jews do, too." Gabriela pointed east. "So do the Muslims."

"Oh. Yes." Now the minister looked uncomfortable. He'd talk about Christianity and Judaism till the cows came home—as the red heifer had. He had much less to say about Islam. Now he went on, "I don't believe they have a true religion or Muhammad was a true prophet. And I don't believe we need to worry about their view of the End of Days."

Gabriela thought he had more in common with Kupferman than he realized, remembering the Religious Affairs Minister's *dumb-ass camel driver* crack. "Over a billion Muslims would think you should be dunked in boiling butter for saying things like that," she returned. "Suppose they aren't so wrong after all? Then what?"

As he had before, Stark said, "We see how it plays out, that's all. What else can we do?" He sounded more harassed than usual. Gabriela felt proud of herself. She *could* make him antsy if she worked at it. Almost plaintively, he went on, "Aren't things complicated enough?"

"I think so," Gabriela said. "I guess you do, too. But does God?"

She got the last word. Only later, as they went through a smoother version of their latest argument for the cameras, did she wonder if she wanted it.

Jamal Ashrawi healed more slowly than he wished he would. He wasn't so young as he had been. A doctor bound his chest in suffocatingly tight bandages to immobilize the broken ribs. "Take it easy while things get better," the man advised.

"What choice have I got?" the Grand Mufti asked. "I'm too wrecked to go anywhere in a hurry."

"Yes," the doctor said. The diploma behind him came from the University of California at San Francisco. Haji Jamal despised the United States. But a U.S.-trained doctor, he judged, was more likely to know his stuff than one who'd studied in Cairo or Beirut or Teheran.

The West knew more about the things of this world than Muslims did. Christians and Jews would go to hell when they died. But when his body was afflicted here and now, such knowledge suddenly seemed much more valuable.

"Do you need more pain pills?" the doctor asked.

"Please." Ashrawi tried not to seem too eager. The Qur'an did not forbid them. He liked the way they cut his aches and the slow, dreamy feeling they gave him. If it was like the feeling you got from wine, he understood how hard it was for the Prophet to ban alcohol.

"Wait one moment." The doctor had a safe in a back room there, and kept his medicines inside. He returned with the pills. In the West, they would have sat in a plastic bottle with a cap that was hard to take off. Here, he handed them to the Grand Mufti, who dry-swallowed one and put the rest in a pocket.

"Thank you," Ashrawi said.

"You took a battering," the physician said. "I'm glad you're better. More and you would have been in God's hands, not mine."

"While they were beating me, I knew I was in God's hands," Haji Jamal replied. He'd also been in the Iraqi's hands. Had the man wanted him dead, he would have died—and his bodyguards might have joined the killers afterwards. Ashrawi didn't care for the irony.

The doctor nodded gravely. "I understand. Thanks to God, you are recovering now. Praises to the compassionate, the merciful."

"Just so," Jamal Ashrawi agreed. The suffering he'd gone through reminded him of his years.

"Now that you have the pills, I have done all I can do for you today," the doctor said. "I hope you will excuse me, but other patients are waiting."

"It's all right." The Grand Mufti could be magnanimous. He'd taken one of the marvelous pills, and he had more. He didn't need the doctor now. "I will visit you again in a couple of weeks." *Sooner if I run out of pills,* he thought.

"I am at your service," the other man said. And what did that mean? That the doctor knew how much he liked the painkillers? As long as the man kept giving them to him, what difference did it make?

Ashrawi had just left the office when his phone rang. "Yes?" he said.

"May God's blessings visit themselves upon you and yours." The speaker's voice was cultured, intelligent, and Iranian.

"What is the latest in your part of the world?" Haji Jamal asked cautiously. Not much news came from Iran since the missile attack on Israel failed and the Mossad mounted its swift retribution. Ashrawi kept trying to believe that.

"I have great news," the man said. A government functionary? An ayatollah? Often, in Iran, there was no difference.

"Tell me!" Haji Jamal exclaimed, as if he were astonished. It was all he could do not to laugh. Why else would the man call?

"An official announcement will come soon, but you deserve to know ahead of time because of your struggle against the Zionist entity," the Iranian said.

The pain pills slowed Ashrawi's thoughts, but didn't seem to blur them. "An official announcement of what?" he inquired.

"Of the fact that the Mahdi has come among men in the holy city of Qom," the Iranian answered. "Together with the returned prophet Jesus, peace be unto Him, the Mahdi will sweep the Jews away. All the rocks and trees will proclaim that they have Jews hiding behind them waiting to be killed."

"Not *all* trees." Haji Jamal was proud, too—of his own learning. "The *gharqad*—the boxthorn—is said by Bukhari and Muslim to be a Jewish plant, one that will shelter the wretches even in those times."

"I have not heard that before. I shall pass it along to those who can judge its truthfulness," the Iranian said. Ashrawi fumed despite the pill. The man had his nerve, to doubt him. The Iranian went on, "Never mind the *gharqad* for now. The Mahdi!"

"Yes, so you said," the Grand Mufti answered. "I have one piece of advice for you, one you won't want to hear."

"But you are going to tell me whether I want to or not, aren't you?" the Iranian said.

"I am, because you need to listen to me," Haji Jamal said. "Be careful before you proclaim the Mahdi to the world. If you are wrong, God will make you sorry. He will make you and your countrymen look like fools, and the man you have declared the Mahdi will not live long." How much would the Iranians care? No more than Palestinian outfits that routinely used suicide bombers.

"Have no fear on that. God is with us here. He has made the signs plain enough. The Mahdi will come to Palestine to slay the Antichrist the Jews have raised up," the Iranian said.

"May it be so." Ashrawi left it there. Maybe the man was right, and things would go as he said. Or maybe he was talking nonsense.

He was an Iranian and a Shiite, after all. In fact . . . "Why are you telling me this?"

"So you can preach the Mahdi's coming, and the Jews' downfall," the Iranian replied. "Let pious Palestinians know what lies ahead. Tell them not to despair. God is on our side. He always has been, and always will be."

Go ahead. Preach. And when the "Mahdi" turns out to be a crop-headed Iranian taxi driver with drool running down his chin, you can look like an idiot along with everybody else in your country. If the Mahdi *did* appear, the reborn twelfth descendant of Ali, if the Shiites were right . . . If that happened, and if the Grand Mufti didn't acknowledge the Mahdi when he had the chance, who would take him seriously again?

"Preach," the Iranian said once more.

"Have no fear. I will," Ashrawi told him. The Iranian rang off. The Grand Mufti hadn't said what he would preach. A good thing, too; he had no idea.

The rabbi frowned as he examined the paperwork. "This is all irregular," he said at last.

"Yup," Eric agreed. Orly looked proud as she nodded. Eric went on, "It's legit, though. Marry us, please."

"I've never seen so many formalities waived." The rabbi plucked at his gray beard. Conservative and Reform Judaism went nowhere in Israel; here, if you weren't secular, you were Orthodox. Orthodox rabbis held a monopoly on marriages.

Eric played his trump card: "If you think anything's wrong, call Rabbi Kupferman and ask him."

"That . . . probably won't be necessary." The rabbi didn't want to have thing one to do with Kupferman. In his shoes, Eric wouldn't have, either. Kupferman was Trouble with a capital T.

Orly gave him a sweetly predatory smile. "Then marry us." She didn't add, *And quit fucking around,* but she might as well have.

"I suppose I'd better," the poor man said. "Who knows what would happen to me if I didn't?" Eric thought he was talking about Orly, not Kupferman.

Now that she'd got what she wanted, she stood demurely by Eric and held his hand while the rabbi went through the service. Eric understood only bits and pieces. It was chanted, and the language was archaic. An Israeli fluent in modern English would have had trouble with Spenser, too.

He did make his proper responses. And he stomped a glass when the rabbi wrapped it in a towel and put it by his foot. That symbolized the destruction of the Temple. Once the rebuilding was finished, would it vanish from the ceremony? He didn't know, but thinking about it was interesting.

He also knew enough to put the plain gold band on Orly's index finger, not her ring finger. She could move it later. "I pronounce you man and wife," the rabbi said.

They kissed. Eric figured Orly would leave the rabbi dead on the floor if he tried to stop them.

"Congratulations," the man said when they broke apart. "Yes, *mazel tov.*" The second time, he sounded as if he meant it.

"Thank you," Eric said.

"What will you do now?" the rabbi asked. Kupferman would have known better than to come out with a question like that.

Because this fellow didn't, Eric and Orly both laughed. The rabbi turned a shocking—and, no doubt, a shocked—pink. "I think we'll do some of that, yes," Eric said.

"It's one of the reasons people get married," Orly said.

The rabbi went pinker yet. Eric hadn't thought he could. "It shouldn't be the only reason," he managed.

"I didn't say it was," Orly answered sharply. "I happen to love him." She took Eric's hand.

"Me, too," Eric said. He wondered if they'd laugh at him for saying he loved himself, but they understood what he meant.

"Let me try again," the rabbi said. "Where will you go for your honeymoon?"

"Oh, a long way off," Orly said.

"The Sheraton Plaza," Eric agreed. Kupferman or somebody had pulled strings to get them a luxury suite for a couple of days—and nights. Then they'd head back to the cramped apartment. Neither said anything about that.

"With so many places to choose from . . ." the fellow began.

"We're archaeologists," Eric said. "Everything that's going on is going on here."

"Ah. I knew I'd seen you before," the rabbi said. "You were in the crew that found the Ark. Do you know how jealous I am?"

Eric squeezed Orly's hand. "I'm sure you can find yourself a nice girl, too." He enjoyed being difficult.

"I'm married, and that isn't what I meant." The rabbi seemed to buy a clue. "As you know perfectly well."

"Who, me?" Eric denied everything.

He and Orly took a cab to the hotel. By his looks and accent, the driver had come from Russia not long before. He showed a fine command of Arabic invective, though, as well as *mat*. The traffic made bad language as necessary as a spare tire.

"Here," he said, screeching to a stop in front of the Sheraton. "Twenty shekels." He was very plain about the money.

Eric tipped him five shekels, which made him happier as he zoomed away. A warm-brown bird with a crest tipped with black and with boldly striped black and white wings and back flew off, path as darting and erratic as a butterfly's. "Hoopoe!" Eric exclaimed in English. "How do you say *hoopoe* in Hebrew?"

"*Dukhifat,*" Orly answered, so he learned a new word.

The desk clerk gave them a fishy look when they checked in with no luggage. But their reservation was in order, so they got their key cards. Up they went. After Eric opened the door, he grabbed Orly, picked her up, and carried her over the threshold. She squawked: "Be careful! You'll hurt yourself!"

She wasn't much smaller or lighter than he. But some things needed doing. When they went inside, they found champagne sitting in an ice bucket by the bed. "How about that?" Eric opened the card attached to the bottle. "It's from Yoram."

"French stuff, too, not the swill we make here," Orly noted. "That was sweet. Expensive, but sweet."

"Sure was." Eric nodded toward the bed. "And now, doubly official Mrs. Katz . . ."

"If you get any hornier than you already are, I'll throw you out the window," Orly said.

"Long way down," Eric said.

"Mm—I suppose so," Orly said. "So all right—shall we try the champagne?"

"We'd better," he answered. Everything went fine. Eric made the second ceremony official the same way he had with the first one over on Cyprus.

After a while, even wedding-day eagerness flagged. "Wow," he said lazily. "Happy wedding day!"

"It is," Orly agreed.

"Wow," he said again, and then, "After a while, we can call room service."

"Okay," she said, and reached for him in a tentative way.

He felt tentative, too, or something like that. "John Henry the Steel-Driving Man would need a rest right now."

"Then we'll rest." Orly grabbed the TV remote instead.

Eric snorted. "Boy, the romance wears off in a hurry."

"Hush." She turned on CNN. Like most Israelis, she was a news junky. And, for a wonder, CNN was actually showing news. Ratings was a god more pitiless and fierce than Jehovah.

"In Teheran," a female talking head said, "Iranian authorities have unveiled a young man who they claim is the Mahdi, the revived twelfth descendant of Ali, who was the prophet Muhammad's son-in-law. In Muslim beliefs, the Mahdi and Jesus—who is a prophet in Islam, but not the Son of God—will lead their faithful to victory in the final days of the world."

"Cheesy," Orly said. "We find the kid who may be the Messiah, so they trot out the Mahdi. I don't know if it's funny or pitiful."

"Yeah," Eric said. The image cut to a feed from Iranian TV. Two mullahs were leading the kid to a lectern in front of a huge portrait of Ayatollah Khomeini. The dead ayatollah's stern visage was meant to dominate proceedings.

Somehow, it didn't. Eric had got a good look at Chaim Avigad when the ISIS guys attacked the Temple. The kid had been scared to death, but he'd also had a direct connection to Something. It wired him, as if he'd stuck a wet finger in an electric socket.

This Iranian kid looked the same way. He had big, doelike black eyes that made you forget the rest of his face—and Khomeini, too. He was older than Chaim, old enough to grow a beard, but it was soft and thin. "God has called me to do this," the subtitles said for him. "It was not my idea, but God must be obeyed."

"Yeah, right. Tell me another one," Orly jeered.

"I don't know." Eric heard his own worry. "He's got the same spooked look Chaim does." That was a good word. If you went up against God, you were out of your weight.

"God has chosen you to show the Jews what liars they are— right?" Even in subtitles, the guy interviewing the so-called Mahdi sounded like a son of a bitch. Orly flipped him off.

"God has chosen me to do His will," the Iranian kid said.

"He has chosen you to punish the wicked Jews." Again, the interviewer's voice admitted no possible doubt.

CNN cut away. Eric wished they would have stayed; things were getting interesting. "Another anti-Semitic asshole," Orly said.

"I don't like to argue with a beautiful naked woman, especially one I'm married to . . ." Eric said.

"Then don't," Orly told him. "How can anybody take those Shiite yahoos seriously?"

Wasn't that the Jewish equivalent of the Iranian's going on about wicked Jews and impious liars? It sure seemed that way to Eric. But Orly would *so* not want to hear that. He said, "The fellow who was talking with the kid has his head wedged. But the kid . . . ? I don't know. If God can land on one boy with both feet, why can't He land on two?"

"What's next?" Orly wasn't buying it. "Some guy from Mountain Flats, Arkansas, who says he's the second coming of Jesus? Will you believe him, too, when he gets on TV?"

"Before all this started, I wouldn't," Eric answered. "Now? Who knows? If he can heal the sick and raise the dead"—*and make the little girls talk out of their heads*: a line from an old song—"maybe he's genuine. Who knows anything any more except the Guy Upstairs?"

"This is all getting too bizarre to stand. What are we supposed to do, anyway?" Orly said.

"Order more champagne?" Eric suggested.

"At room-service prices?" Orly said. "Did you rob a bank when I wasn't looking, or has God driven you out of your mind?"

"Yes." Eric called room service and talked to a nice young lady who seemed eager to take his order . . . and money. Then he turned back to Orly. "We should put something on—for a little while, anyway."

"Spoilsport." She threw on a robe. Eric got into another one.

A guy from room service knocked on the door a minute and a half later. He wasn't an Israeli; Eric guessed he came from India. Like developed countries all over, Israel had trouble filling a lot of low-level jobs with its own people. Relentless Israeli autonomy made service jobs extra tough.

Eric handed him a U.S. five-dollar bill to make him disappear. The door had just closed when Orly got rid of the robe. "Trying to give him a bigger thrill than the tip?" Eric asked.

"Who, me?" She sounded no more innocent than she had to. Then they got back to honeymooning.

Why Eric didn't roll over and go to sleep right afterwards, he couldn't have said. He'd always hated doing anything he was supposed to do. Had his parents wanted him to be a Biblical archaeologist, he probably would have sold shoes.

Orly started quietly snoring next to him. She had a smile on her face, which was nice. Champagne gave him a fine buzz. So did honeymooning. They went well together. This was a *lot* more fun than the quickie on Cyprus. Eric wondered why he hadn't proposed sooner. Once bitten, twice shy—that summed it up.

He turned CNN on again, softly, so he wouldn't bother Mrs. Katz. *How about that?* he thought. He did some smiling of his own.

The news network was still showing news. He hoped they wouldn't get in trouble. A Congressman had been caught on tape soliciting a bribe. He swore he was innocent. There'd been a coup in an African country whose name the newsman couldn't pronounce. Something was making flying fish in the central Pacific die. And . . . "The self-proclaimed Mahdi in Iran says he wants to go to Jerusalem," the newsman said. "More after these messages . . ."

23

"Hello, Jethro." The Reverend Lester Stark tried to muster enthusiasm for his call-in show. Callers and listeners deserved it. If you started mailing it in, everybody would notice, and then you were in trouble. "What's on your mind?"

"Well, I want to know more about this Mahdi thing that's been all over Twittter and Instagram lately. What kind of a Moslem superstition is it?" Jethro was calling from Alexandria, Louisiana. His accent said he hadn't moved there recently.

"I don't like it when Muslims call our beliefs superstitions. I don't want to pin that label on theirs, either," Stark said. He'd done that while talking with Gabriela, but he wouldn't with millions listening. Hypocrisy? Maybe.

"There's a difference," Jethro said. "Christians believe what's true, and Moslems don't. It's simple, isn't it?"

Lester Stark suspected Jethro was simple. He said no such thing. He just answered the question: "Muslims believe in the Mahdi the way Christians believe in the Second Coming. The Mahdi is the rightly guided one—they say—who will lead Islam to victory in a last battle."

"If that's not superstition, what is it?" Jethro said.

Religion, Stark thought. A cynical man, or a secular man, might say the two were the same. Recent events could make such a man think twice, though. "It's what more than a billion people believe as strongly as you believe in the New Testament."

"But I'm right," Jethro insisted.

"Thanks for your call." Stark disconnected him. Then he went on, "Now, believing in the Mahdi has been more a Shiite thing than a Sunni one, but more Sunnis lean that way these days. I don't want to get into the differences between Sunnis and Shiites—that's too complicated for this show. Think of them as being like the differences between Catholics and Protestants. The Sunnis say they're more traditional. They say the Shiites are making it up as they go along. The Shiites say the Sunnis are just plain wrong."

That might get him a B on a Western Civ exam. He punched a button. "Our next caller is Jane, from Duluth, Minnesota. Go ahead, Jane."

"Thank you, Reverend," the woman said. "How come this Mahdi is such a baby? He would hardly shave if he shaved at all."

Lester smiled. "I understood you. If you believe the Iranians, the answer is that the twelfth descendant of Ali, Muhammad al-Muntazar—the Expected One—was still young when he disappeared in Samarra in 878. So he'd be young now that he's, uh, returned."

"What's he going to do now that he's come back?" Jane said.

"He wants to come to Israel and meet with the boy here who the Jews think is the Messiah," Stark answered.

"What'll happen if he does?"

"They used to call that the sixty-four-dollar question," Stark said. "I don't know. Anybody who says he does is lying or talking through his hat, if you want my opinion."

"Will the Israelis let him come?" Jane persisted.

"I don't know that, either, and I've got sources in high places in the Israeli government." Stark wasn't lying, but Shlomo Kupferman wouldn't talk about this. That miffed him, but he couldn't do anything about it. "We'll see how things play out."

"Can I ask you one more question?"

"Quick."

"Do you think this Mahdi is genuine?"

"I have no idea. The mullahs might put up somebody just to get their prestige back. I don't believe God would like them to do that, but God can speak for Himself, as He's made plain. If someone who isn't genuine bumps up against Chaim Avigad, he's liable to be sorry."

"I bet you're right. Thank you, Reverend."

"Thank *you*. Our next caller is . . . Betty, from Oklahoma. Hello, Betty."

"Hello. Don't you think people who aren't Christians will go to hell, like the Bible says on account of they won't be washed in the blood of the Lamb and accept Jesus Christ?"

Thanks a lot, Betty, Stark thought. There was a question with dynamite in it. If he said yes, the Israelis might yank him off the air. If he said no, listeners back in the States would he angry. And if he hedged, didn't he anger God?

He did the best he could: "I believe that, yes. You need to believe in Christ to be saved. What God wants done in this world . . . I think He will make clear very soon now. Then everyone, of whatever religion, will have his or her faith tested."

"*I* won't," Betty said smugly. "I know what I believe, and I know it's true." She hung up.

"God has already given us surprises. He may have more," Stark warned. He wondered if she was still listening. Or had she got her licks in and then gone back to . . . *To disapproving,* the minister thought. *And she's good at it.*

He got through the show. The Israelis didn't pull the plug on him. Betty's question ate at him after the show was over. That didn't happen every day. Usually, he walked away once the calls stopped coming.

"How *will* it all turn out?" he asked his wife back in their hotel room.

"We'll see," Rhonda said. "We're lucky—we're alive *to* see."

"With the resurrection of the dead, so will everyone else." Lester grinned crookedly. "And it's liable to get crowded, too."

"If God can bring the dead back to life, He can find a way to deal with that," Rhonda said. Lester laughed and kissed her. Still, he wasn't sure which would be the bigger miracle.

Yitzhak Avigad watched the Temple rise. Every time he went onto the Temple Mount, it was closer to finished. It wouldn't be a modernized reconstruction of the Second Temple, but it came closer to that than to anything else.

Most of the scars from the ISIS attack were gone. Some remained, at Shlomo Kupferman's orders. "Let the world see that this Temple, like the others, was established through adversity," he declared. "Let God also know why the blemishes remain."

God could figure that out with no help from Kupferman. So it seemed to Yitzhak, anyhow. The world wouldn't give a damn. The world was still pissed at Israel for disassembling the Dome of the Rock. The world could . . .

But even Yitzhak had to admit the world had a point in one way. The Temple would be massive, imposing, impressive. It would be God's home on earth. The Dome of the Rock was beautiful.

When the Arabs got over their snit, they could restore the beauty somewhere else. Then they could spend the next thousand years grumbling in their coffeehouses about how the Israelis had dispossessed them. Arabs were like that.

So were Jews. Would Israel have come back to life if any people less stubborn tried to revive it? Yitzhak didn't think so. When two stubborn peoples banged heads, they struck sparks.

Then again, the Arabs might not have so long to grumble. That his nephew could be the Messiah had never crossed Yitzhak's mind. But Chaim seemed to be. And the End of Days seemed to be rolling down on the world like a runaway freight.

This alleged Iranian Mahdi . . . Yitzhak didn't believe it. To him, the Iranians opened their mouths only to lie. That they might think the same about Israelis . . . proved to him they were anti-Semitic bastards.

An engineering crew was taking down the causeway that had spanned the valley between the Temple Mount and the Mount of Olives. There were more soldiers guarding the work crew than men in it. Tanks poked cannon snouts this way and that. Helicopters darted overhead: dragonflies of death.

Terrorists should have realized that messing with anything connected with the Temple wasn't smart. Anybody who did didn't know terrorists—so Yitzhak was convinced. The IDF agreed. He would have been astonished if it hadn't.

More Israeli soldiers came onto the Temple Mount. Yitzhak wondered if they were Chaim's guards. His nephew's life had turned upside down since he started raising the dead. It would have been worse if Chaim weren't so good at putting his foot down. Nobody in Israel seemed anxious to push him, not when eighty-three percent of the people (according to the latest poll) thought he was the Messiah.

But these soldiers were only guarding the U.S. Vice President. He had his own security men, too, in off-the-rack suits and worried looks. Yitzhak moved away. The security folks would have moved him anyway; they were determined to keep a perimeter around their man.

How much did perimeters matter, when the End of Days might

be coming? But the security weenies, Israeli and American, didn't think that way. The Vice President had always needed protection. He always would. World without end, amen.

Signs said the world wasn't without end, though. There are more things in heaven and earth, Mr. Vice President, than are dreamt of in your foreign policy. Yitzhak shook his head. Maybe the world wasn't going nuts when he started mangling *Hamlet* to himself, but he was.

Following the Vice President came photographers and reporters. The Veep wouldn't have known he was here if they weren't along to tell him so. An Israeli soldier spoke to a buddy in Hebrew: "He wanted to see the Ark. We had to tell him no."

"I bet we did!" The second soldier laughed. They didn't seem much older than Chaim to Yitzhak, though they had five years on him.

If they'd used English, the American reporters would have been all over them. Refusing the Vice President anything came close to secular sacrilege. But when secular sacrilege met the religious kind, it lost. Jews had excluded gentiles from the holy precinct for forever, when they could get away with it.

Pompey walked into the Holy of Holies in the first century BCE, and walked out amazed that it was empty. The Ark was gone by then, of course. Pompey might not have been so lucky in Jerusalem had he disturbed it. Or he might—who could guess God's will? But the Third Temple had an outer courtyard where gentiles were permitted, as Herod's Temple had had before. That was as far as the Vice President got.

They set up a lectern for him there. He stood behind it and spoke in commonplaces. Yitzhak half listened as the phrases boomed out: ". . . this impressive building . . ." ". . . fulfillment of an ancient dream . . ." ". . . marking a new era . . ." ". . . memorable achievement . . ."

He wasn't wrong, just dull. If he weren't dull, he might have ended up President. Then someone else in an expensive suit would have stood there sweating and mouthing clichés.

When the Vice President finished, a reporter called, "What do you think about the Arabs who were dispossessed from the Temple Mount when Israel rebuilt the Temple?"

The Vice President did a hell of an impression of a deaf man. A flack said, "No questions today." Away the almost-great man went, handlers and guards holding others at bay.

A tale told by an idiot, full of sound and fury, signifying nothing. A chill ran through Yitzhak. He didn't have to change a word to make that bit of *Macbeth* fit too well.

CNN was getting scary. The new Grand Ayatollah looked out of the TV at Eric. He yakked in Farsi. Eric could read it with a dictionary and patience, but didn't speak it. A translator gave an English voiceover: "We invite the government of the Zionist entity to send a plane to Teheran to bring the Mahdi to Jerusalem so he may confront the so-called Messiah. Or, if the Zionist entity will permit it, we will fly him there. Any precautions the Zionists wish, including inspections or their own pilot, we accept. There is no God but God, and Muhammad is the Prophet of God, and Ali is the Friend of God."

A pretty, blow-dried CNN newsreader replaced the gray-bearded, turbaned ayatollah. What she had to say seemed anticlimactic: "No immediate comment from the Israeli government."

"What do you think?" Eric asked Orly. They were back at their apartment after the too-brief honeymoon. The air conditioner was on the fritz. It whined and delivered half as much cool air as it should have.

"They never said anything like *that* before," she answered. "They must think their kid is something."

"I guess," Eric said. CNN cut away to a tape of the young man who claimed to be the Mahdi. Again, his eyes struck Eric: terrified and terrifying at the same time. Eric didn't know what he was, but he was something out of the ordinary.

Orly had her own question: "How many Mahdis have there been?"

"Lots," Eric said. "It's such a handy-dandy title, anybody who wants to give his uprising some class calls himself the Mahdi." The one people in the West remembered was the guy in the Sudan who'd given the British fits late in the nineteenth century. Kipling and Churchill and the movie *Khartoum* gave him a dose of immortality. But he wasn't the only man who claimed the rank—or the most recent.

"So why take this one seriously, then?" Orly said.

Because of his eyes. But Eric couldn't say that. He tried something else instead: "Because the times are messed up, and nothing, including the Second Coming, would surprise me any more."

To his amazement and dismay, Orly burst into tears. "Why did you have to say something like that?" she demanded.

He took her in his arms. She didn't push him away. She just clung to him. "What was I supposed to say?" he asked in honest distress.

"Something that made me feel better, not made me worry more."

"Sorry. I thought you wanted a straight answer."

"I did." Orly hiccuped. "But I wanted something that made me feel better, too."

"Oh," Eric said again. She was asking him for a miracle bigger than anything the Ark or Chaim Avigad had doled out till now. Telling her so appeared hazardous to his marital health.

CNN switched to the disgraced, imprisoned founder of a company that went belly-up and left employees and stock owners holding the bag. He had colon cancer, and needed surgery. That struck Eric as fair punishment for an asshole. One more thing he didn't say—he wasn't sure Orly would get the joke.

Then she made it herself. Eric almost dropped his teeth. He squeezed her till she squeaked. "What was that for?" she asked.

"Because I love you," he said. "Because you're nuts the same way I am."

"Good. That will make things last." Orly paused. Her smile melted. "If anything lasts, I mean."

"Yeah. If." Eric probably wasn't winning any Mister Grin competitions, either. How long had it been since people talked seriously about the end of the world? Hundreds of years (unless you were a Millerite, anyway). They talked about it and talked about it, and it didn't happen, and they mostly decided it wouldn't, so why worry?

Except it looked more and more as if it would anyhow. What were people supposed to do about that?

"You know what?" he said. "I'm scared out of my mind."

"Good." Now she squeezed him. "You aren't the only one."

"What are you going to do?" Shoshanah asked, her eyes wide.

"I don't know," Chaim answered. "Get a falafel? I'm hungry."

She started to fix him one. "Doesn't God tell you?"

"It doesn't work like that," Chaim said. "I wish it did. It'd be a lot simpler."

"How *does* it work?" She handed him the pita and the balls of deep-fried chickpeas.

He stuffed in salad and took a bite. Part of the fun of eating a falafel was getting it into you without making a mess. Israelis quickly developed the knack. You could tell a tourist by what he wore on the front of his shirt. The bite gave Chaim time to think—and to notice one (or several) of his ghosts remembering how falafel tasted. How did you explain something that happened without words?

"Sometimes I get feelings, you know? It's not God telling me or anything—I'll just have an idea about what I ought to do." He paused for another bite. "Most of the time I've got to figure it out like anybody else."

"You're doing a good job," Shoshanah said. "Who knows what would've happened to the Temple if you weren't there?"

"Yeah, who knows?" Chaim had had his childhood messed up because of the Temple. Only now that he'd started walking wherever he wanted did he realize how messed up it was. He'd started to suspect that the Temple was only a means toward what God had in mind, not His end purpose. Which made all his years up on stilts and away from grass and dirt seem even more pointless.

Shoshanah said, "You're smart, too. You've got all the answers."

"Answers?" he said. "I don't have all the *questions*. I've got these ghosts in my head—and you. You're the good part."

Swarthy and suntanned, she turned red anyhow. "Me? I'm nobody. Don't be dumb."

"You're the best thing that ever happened to me."

"You're the Messiah. You can't say stuff like that." Shoshanah sounded angry.

"I'm still me," he said. "The other stuff—it happened 'cause God wanted it to. I had nothing to do with it. But I found you by myself." Chaim paused. "I think so, anyway."

She laughed shrilly. "You better believe it, hon. God's got better things to do than lead you to Grandpa's falafel stand. Yeah, just a few—million."

To Chaim, the *hon* was more important than all the rest. He suspected Shoshanah was wrong. God kept track of *everything*—that made Him God. Chaim had trouble believing he'd stopped at this falafel stand by accident. He had trouble believing there was any such thing as an accident. But he didn't argue with Shoshanah.

He finished the falafel and wiped grease off with his napkins. Then he said, "I've got to go. Somebody I need to see."

"Somebody important, I bet," she said without rancor.

"*You're* important. This is just—stuff." Chaim made a face.

She blushed again. When he leaned across the counter toward her, she leaned toward him. When God made kissing possible, He knew what He was doing. Other possibilities . . . The Song of Solomon was in the Bible, too.

He didn't want to leave. He wondered whether what he wanted had anything to do with anything. The Israeli soldiers grinned when he rejoined them. "She's cute," one of the guys in khaki said.

"Yeah!" Chaim agreed. Their grins got wider.

He went onto the Temple Mount. Kupferman was there, a hard hat doing duty for a *kippah*. He eyed Chaim with a curious expression: half resentful, half respectful. He might be Religious Affairs Minister, but he couldn't tell Chaim what to do. The other way 'round, in fact. No wonder the resentment got in there.

"Yes? What is it?" he asked, as cautiously as he had in him.

Chaim said, "That Iranian who says he's the Mahdi . . ."

"Oh. Him." Shlomo Kupferman's lips curled under his thick white mustache. "What about him?"

"Let him come here."

"What?" Kupferman's eyebrows leaped. "He's a fake, a propaganda tool. *As phony as a three-dollar bill,* they say in America."

"Let him come anyway," Chaim said. "He needs to. I don't know how I know, but I know."

"We don't want anything to do with the ayatollahs." Kupferman sharpened. "Or will you show him up for the fraud he is? Making fools of the mullahs is always worth doing."

"Think whatever you want." Chaim didn't want an argument, and he'd known he'd get one. Kupferman couldn't do anything without one. "Just get him here."

That was the wrong way to handle Kupferman. He bristled. "Are you telling me what to do?" *You punk kid* lay under the words.

Chaim looked at him. "Yes. You tell the other people you need to tell. Make it happen, that's all. It has to happen."

"Says who? You or God?" Kupferman demanded.

"You think *I* care about some guy in Iran?" Chaim said. "This is all part of . . . whatever it's part of."

Kupferman pondered. "What will happen when this—this Shiite comes to *Eretz Yisrael*?"

"I don't know," Chaim said. "Something important."

"You're out of your mind," Kupferman muttered. He gnawed at his mustache. Chaim thought that was gross. As if Kupferman cared what he thought! But the rabbi *did* care about the bigger stuff. Kupferman scowled at him. "I wouldn't do this for the President of the United States, you hear me?"

"Okay." Chaim thought the American President was a jerk, but he yielded a little because he knew he'd won. "You'll do it for God, won't you?"

"For God," Kupferman agreed. "It had better be for God."

Jamal Ashrawi'd never imagined his body could turn so many different colors. With those purples and reds and yellows, he looked like a sunset. But sunsets didn't hurt every time they moved, or even if they didn't.

There were rumors something had happened to the Iraqi on his way back to wherever he went after the attack on the Temple failed. Some said his plane crashed. Some said his car smashed. Some said he just vanished. Haji Jamal couldn't find out if any of the rumors was true. He hoped they all were.

He winced whenever Ibrahim came to see him. He didn't know if the bodyguard had another affiliation now. He didn't dare try to find out, either. Such situations made life . . . complicated.

"Boss, something's on Al Jazeera you should see," Ibrahim said.

That seemed safe enough. Getting to his feet hurt less than it had a few days earlier. He was making . . . some progress.

A senior Israeli military officer looked out of the TV. The Zionists wore boring uniforms: none of the gold and glitter Arab generals loved. Gold and glitter had nothing to do with how an army fought. Too many Middle East wars proved that.

In excellent Arabic, the Zionist said, "We agree to the Grand Ayatollah's proposal. We will send an airplane to Teheran to bring the young man called the Mahdi to Israel. Then we will see what God has in mind for him, for the Messiah, and for the world."

Ashrawi stared. "They agree? Just like that?" He could hardly believe his ears.

"He says so." Suspicion clotted Ibrahim's voice. "Maybe something will happen before this plane lands at Ben Gurion."

"Maybe," Haji Jamal said. "But would the Zionists risk infuriating the Muslim world like that?"

"Satan drives them," Ibrahim said. "Who can guess?"

He had a point. Then Al Jazeera switched to a feed from Iran. The Grand Ayatollah spoke in Farsi with an Arabic translation on the crawl. "We have reached a temporary accord with the Zionists, so that the Mahdi may go to Jerusalem and fulfill his destiny. May God and Muhammad and Ali—peace be unto them—ensure that the result is successful."

"Shiites," the Grand Mufti muttered. They were full of dissimulation. It was part of their creed, and had been for centuries. They believed it proper to pretend to be what they weren't to avoid persecution.

A commentator replaced the Grand Ayatollah. "Both Israel and Iran have appealed to the United States to help with security and intelligence measures. The Americans are said to have agreed. Such cooperation is also extremely unusual," he said.

"Madness!" Haji Jamal exclaimed.

"When the End of Days draws near, can you expect anything else?" Ibrahim said.

The commentator went on, "Perhaps the Last Days *are* approaching. Will the prophet Jesus—peace be unto him—come down from heaven to make it all plain?"

The Grand Mufti's jaw dropped. He might have expected that from Iranian TV, or from the Hezbollah's station. But Al Jazeera was almost as secular as CNN.

He switched channels. His English would do. CNN had a good-looking woman reading the news. Ibrahim leered at her shamelessly uncovered hair. So did Haji Jamal, but not so openly.

She was also talking about the arrangements between the Zionists and the Shiites. "Washington hopes this will bring a new era of cooperation in the Middle East," she chirped.

Ibrahim could follow English, too. He suggested what Washington could do with its hopes. Then he suggested what the pretty newscaster could do to him. "Hush," Ashrawi told him. "I want to hear what else she says."

He wondered if the bodyguard would suggest what he could do to himself. But Ibrahim only grunted.

"Some ministers also wonder what this meeting may mean," the woman said. "Here is a statement Lester Stark issued from Jerusalem, where he is observing the building of the Third Temple."

Haji Jamal hated what the Zionists were doing to the Haram al-Sharif. When Stark appeared, he looked more like an executive than like the Christian ministers the Grand Mufti was used to. Ashrawi remembered seeing him on TV before.

"Surely we are close to the Last Days, to the prophecies given in Revelation." Stark's English had an accent slightly different from the newscaster's. But he didn't talk fast, so Ashrawi could follow. "We have waited so long for the times the Bible talks about, but now they seem to be here."

Another preacher back in the United States said the same thing in different words. "The Christians can see it," Haji Jamal said. "The

Jews can see it, and God, the compassionate, the merciful, despises the Jews."

"Well, who doesn't?" Ibrahim said.

CNN put on a priest who taught at an American university. He was more cautious than the other Christians. "I don't think we've had such an amazing sequence of events, events so difficult to explain by natural causes, since Jesus Christ walked the Holy Land two thousand years ago," he said.

"He is too stupid to know about Muhammad, peace be unto him," Ibrahim jeered.

The Grand Mufti shook his head. "He's not stupid. He knows about God's Prophet, but doesn't accept him. Rejection is worse than ignorance."

When the American news channel started talking to a rabbi, Jamal Ashrawi turned it off. He didn't need any more blather from Jews.

"But they don't know how the End of Days will turn out. I want to hear them wailing when God punishes them for turning away from the Seal of Prophets," Ibrahim said.

"Every man and woman will be a Muslim," Ashrawi said dreamily. "Every pig will be slaughtered. The Christians who think Jesus is the Son of God will laugh out of the other side of their mouths."

"Out of the other side of their heads," Ibrahim said. "The holy Qur'an doesn't say Kalashnikovs will be used in the last battles against the misbelievers. But it doesn't tell us they won't, either." He always had his AK with him.

"Just so," Ashrawi agreed. But not all misbelievers were Christians and Jews. Would God spare the Shiites? Would He spare a coward who failed to protect the Grand Mufti? Haji Jamal hoped not.

24

Gabriela did her best to get permission to bring a crew to Ben Gurion Airport to film the alleged Mahdi's arrival. After a couple of midlevel functionaries told her she couldn't, she called Shlomo Kupferman. As he had before, he answered the call himself. But, when he heard what she wanted, he said, "No. That's just not possible. *Shalom.*" She found herself without a connection.

She didn't give up. She asked Lester Stark to phone the Religious Affairs Minister. Stark did. The conversation didn't last long. He put the phone back in his pocket, shaking his head. "He won't let us," he reported.

"I already knew that," Gabriela said. "Would he tell you why?"

"Not really." The preacher sounded unhappy. "I've seen him more gracious—let me put it like that. He doesn't care for the idea that this Iranian is coming."

She still didn't give up. Saul Buchbinder knew Kupferman, too. The producer called willingly—more than willingly, because he wanted exclusive footage as much as Gabriela did. But he also struck out. "The old *mamzer* knows more Yiddish than I thought," he said. "He told me to *geh kak afen yam*."

"To what?" It meant nothing to Gabriela.

"To go take a crap on the ocean," Buchbinder translated. "To get lost, it means."

"I guess it would," she said. She sat down with the producer and Stark. "What *is* Kupferman's problem, anyway?" she grumbled. "He's the Religious Affairs Minister. If he wanted the so-called Mahdi to stay away, the fellow'd never leave Teheran." She said *so-called* whenever she talked about the Iranian, even when she wasn't in front of a camera. Like Big Brother, the Israelis were watching her. Listening to her, too. Not saying *so-called* might make her seem to buy into the line the ayatollahs were putting out.

Stark shrugged. "My guess is, somebody's pushing him. And he's better at doing the pushing than getting pushed."

"Plenty of guys who push a lot are like that." Buchbinder sounded as if he spoke from experience.

What he said matched what Gabriela had seen. Still . . . "He's a big wheel here," she said. "Who can put the screws to him like that?"

"Maybe the Prime Minister, though I wouldn't think so, not for this," Stark said. "Or maybe the so-called Messiah."

Sure as hell, he could be dangerous. Gabriela thought he'd made a shrewd guess, though. "Have you made up your mind yet about what you think of him?" she asked.

"No. I just don't know enough." The televangelist's voice was troubled. "I'm sure he's not the Second Coming of Jesus Christ. I'm also sure he has supernatural powers. How he gets them . . . I'm not sure of."

He didn't insist Chaim Avigad was the Antichrist. He still thought it was possible. Buchbinder couldn't resist needling him: "If Chaim *is* the Messiah, doesn't that turn the whole New Testament into hooey?"

"It may, but I don't think it will," Stark said. "Too much of what's happened lately comes too close to prophecy to let me."

"Prophecy, sure, but whose?" Gabriela said. "Jewish? Christian? Muslim? Maybe you pay your money and you take your choice."

"I'm not worried about money," Stark said. *Really? Then why did you dicker so hard?* she wondered. But the preacher went on, "When souls are at stake, what difference does money make?"

"It will to some people," Buchbinder predicted. He must have realized how that might sound coming from him, for he quickly added, "They won't all be Jews, either."

"I didn't think they would," Stark said. "You know that."

"Yeah, yeah." Saul waved it aside.

Gabriela listened to the byplay with amusement she didn't show. Lester Stark wasn't anti-Semitic in the usual sense. He didn't think Jews were wicked. He just thought they were waiting for the wrong bus.

For his part, Buchbinder wasn't observant in the usual sense, but he was passionately Jewish. Listening to someone who was sure everything his ancestors had believed for the past 2,000 years was nonsense had to grate on him. Maybe it was better to be hated than dismissed.

Or maybe not. Some of the stuff ISIS and Hezbollah put out would gag a serial killer. And Iran financed Hezbollah. God only knew what game the ayatollahs were playing.

One more phrase liable to be exactly true these days.

Since Gabriela couldn't film the arrival of the plane from Teheran herself, she watched on the Israeli feed she was using. It was an El Al plane, so it looked like many that landed at Ben Gurion—the Israelis didn't trust an Iranian jet in their airspace. But few incoming airliners had F-15s flying top cover.

Touchdown was smooth. She breathed a sigh of relief as the plane stopped. What would the mullahs have done had anything gone wrong? Whatever they could, she was sure.

No jetway here. No hike to baggage claim and customs. They wheeled stairs to the airliner. A squat, probably armored, limo rolled down the runway and stopped nearby.

Several people got out. Gabriela looked for Chaim Avigad, but didn't see him. The woman doing the English voiceover said, "Chaim Avigad will meet the so-called Mahdi on the Temple Mount. He declined to come to Ben Gurion International, saying he did not wish to disturb the spirits of more dead persons at this time. Acting for him is his uncle, Yitzhak Avigad."

The camera focused on the guy in the least expensive suit. Once reminded who he was, Gabriela recognized him. He looked uncomfortable. They all did, but the dignitaries had practice with awkward public situations. Yitzhak stuffed his hands in his pockets and bounced on the balls of his feet.

A security guard went up the stairs to the El Al plane. The man did something Gabriela had never imagined she'd see: he knocked on the door. It didn't open till he did.

The first man out was another guard. This fellow carried an Uzi. Behind him came the—maybe so-called—Mahdi. Muhammad, called al-Muntazar—the Expected One—looked and dressed like a revolutionary Iranian. He was slim and swarthy and long-faced. He wore black trousers and jacket, and a shirt open at the neck.

He looked around in wide-eyed wonder. "He has never left Iran before," the newswoman said. "He won't have to clear customs, either. He doesn't know how lucky he is."

Gabriela laughed, though the Israeli woman wasn't joking. She wished she could hear what was going on out there. Instead, she was stuck watching. She knew what an indignity that was.

Yitzhak thought Muhammad al-Muntazar looked even younger in person than in his pictures. An older Iranian in robe and turban—handler, interpreter, or maybe both—followed him. One Israeli bigwig standing on the tarmac was fluent in Farsi—he'd been born in Teheran. Yitzhak wasn't, but he assumed Muhammad also understood Arabic.

He decided to find out, saying, "In the name of God, welcome to Israel."

And the kid answered, "In the name of God, I thank you." He spoke classical Arabic with a mushy Farsi accent. "You will be the Jewish Messiah's uncle."

"That's right." Yitzhak wondered how he knew. Had he been briefed? Or did he just . . . know? His eyes suggested the latter. Seeing those eyes, Yitzhak wondered about the *so-called* tag. They were half exalted, half terrified: the eyes of someone who'd seen much too much of something great and terrible. They looked a lot like Chaim's, in other words.

Introductions followed. The Israeli who spoke Farsi did the honors for his country's VIPs. Muhammad presented the older Iranian as Ayatollah Ali Bakhtiar. "He can also translate," he said.

"How many Iranians speak Hebrew?" Yitzhak asked in his own language.

"Not many, but I am one." Bakhtiar's accent was thick, but no worse than those of plenty of Israelis. Switching languages, he went on, "I also use English." He switched again: "Or Arabic, like you."

"You are a scholar," Yitzhak said politely.

"Your nephew's not here?" Ali Bakhtiar didn't want to call Chaim the Messiah, no matter what Muhammad al-Muntazar said.

"No. He's back at the Temple Mount." Yitzhak stuck to Hebrew, and to a name Muslims disliked.

The Iranian ayatollah didn't say anything except, "Then let us go there, and see what happens then."

"Is that what you want?" Yitzhak asked Muhammad al-Muntazar. Then, realizing the kid wouldn't have followed his conversation with Bakhtiar, he added, "To go straight to the Haram al-Sharif?" When he spoke Arabic, he used its name for the place.

"Yes," Muhammad answered. "That is what I came for."

Most of the Israelis knew enough Arabic to get by. When your neighbors spoke the same tongue, you picked up some. The Prime Minister opened the limo door with his own hands. "Then let's go," he said.

They'd cleared the highway between the airport and Jerusalem. Yitzhak had no idea how, but they had. *Maybe Chaim asked,* he thought uneasily. God might listen to his nephew.

Several limos, all looking just like this one, wove in and out among escorting motorcycles. That would make it harder for somebody with an RPG to blast the right one. Yitzhak hoped so, anyhow.

The limo was the quietest car he'd ever been in. All the same, he heard helicopters whirring overhead. Israel was taking no chances on letting anything happen to the Expected One.

Muhammad al-Muntazar didn't say much. He peered out through the limo's tinted windows. What was he thinking? Nobody had the nerve to disturb him. Yitzhak knew *he* didn't.

Traffic made everybody slow as the motorcade got into Jerusalem. Maybe not even God could clear all the cars there. Whether He could or not, He didn't choose to.

When Muhammad murmured in Farsi, Yitzhak eyed Ali Bakhtiar. "He says, 'This is the place,'" the older Iranian said.

Yitzhak nodded. For better *and* worse, Jerusalem had been the place for 3,000 years now.

Into the Old City. Soldiers were everywhere. If ISIS had stolen uniforms, the way they'd got hard hats before . . .

Nobody started shooting. The soldiers *were* soldiers. The limos drove to the Western Wall. Some Orthodox Jews, rejecting the new Temple, kept praying there and sticking written prayers into the cracks between Herod's huge stones.

Troops kept the praying men away from the cars. The limos went up the ramp that led to the Temple Mount. Muhammad al-

Muntazar sucked in his breath when he got his first look at the Temple.

Ayatollah Ali Bakhtiar flared his nostrils. "You tore down the Dome of the Rock for *that*?" he said. "You should be ashamed."

"When we want art criticism, we will ask for it," the Prime Minister said. "And we didn't tear it down. We took it apart so it could go up somewhere else. That's more respect than Muslims ever gave our monuments."

"Enough, both of you, please," Muhammad said in Arabic. He wasn't supposed to know Hebrew. Maybe he was good at reading tone. Or maybe God was giving him the gift of tongues.

The limo stopped. The others already had, to form a perimeter around it. Terrorists would want to shoot the Prime Minister. And some Israelis, Yitzhak admitted to himself, wouldn't mind taking out Muhammad al-Muntazar.

"Well," the Mahdi said, and opened the door. He got out first. The other dignitaries and Yitzhak followed.

Soldiers, a TV crew, a radio crew, and still photographers had also gone up onto the Temple Mount. Muhammad paid no attention to them. His eyes were on a small figure standing alone in the Court of the Gentiles. Tears blurred Yitzhak's sight for a moment. His nephew wasn't quite man-tall yet. Did it matter? In the ways that mattered, Chaim was a lot bigger than any other man alive, even without his half-visible cloud of ghosts.

"I will go to him," Muhammad al-Muntazar said, as if someone had told him he couldn't. He hurried toward Chaim.

Ali Bakhtiar started after him. Muhammad said something in Farsi. The ayatollah answered. Muhammad said something else. Bakhtiar's shoulders sagged. Muhammad went on alone.

"Muhammad told him to stay here. He asked how Muhammad would speak to the Messiah," said the Israeli who spoke Farsi. "Muhammad told him God would let them talk. What do you say to that?"

"I don't know. What *do* you say to that?" Yitzhak returned.

Ali Bakhtiar said. "You don't. You let the Mahdi do as he thinks he must—no matter how foolish it is."

Yitzhak pointed to Chaim. "A lot of things my nephew's done lately make me feel the same way." He hadn't expected to sympathize with an ayatollah, but he did. Things were out of their hands now. Whatever would happen, it was with the kids.

And God.

Chaim watched Muhammad al-Muntazar walk across the Temple Mount toward him. He envied the Iranian's beard, even if it was thin. His own cheeks yielded only fuzz. It was slightly darker than it had been a year earlier, but it wasn't whiskers.

He wondered if he'd been wrong when he browbeat Kupferman into letting Muhammad come here. He'd been so sure something important would happen . . . but maybe not. He knew he was nothing but a human being. He had feelings about what God wanted, but he didn't *know*. How could you *know* God? God was too big for that.

That's what I should have told Shoshanah, Chaim thought. He didn't know *her* as well as he wanted to, either, and she was a girl. (He almost thought *just a girl*, but Shoshanah wasn't *just* to him.) If you couldn't know another person that way, could you know God?

Maybe the Mahdi would tell him.

Standing there and letting Muhammad al-Muntazar come to him might be rude. He walked toward the Iranian and held out his hand. "Peace be unto you," he said.

"And to you also peace." Muhammad took Chaim's hand.

What language were they using? Chaim didn't wonder till afterwards. They understood each other—he knew that. What else mattered?

"So," he said. "He's chosen you, too."

The Mahdi nodded. "He has. I'm supposed to hate you, you know. Even the rocks and the trees are supposed to cry out against Jews when the Last Battle comes."

"We don't love Muslims, either, or Iranians," Chaim said. "But how can I hate you? I never had a brother, and now I do."

Muhammad al-Muntazar gave him a wry grin. "Misery loves company, right?"

"Right!" Chaim exclaimed. "This is wonderful, what God did with us—did to us—but it's miserable, too, and He has to know it. We'll never be ordinary again." He thought about Job once more, and everything that had happened to him so God could make a point. Did Muhammad al-Muntazar know about Job? Chaim asked him.

"Yes. The Qur'an speaks of him. He was a great prophet. Satan afflicted him, but he stayed fast to God and was rewarded in the end," the Iranian said.

"He got wealth. He got a new family. But all the people who died to test him stayed dead," Chaim said.

"Did they? The Qu'ran says his people were restored to him," Muhammad said. "Still, I don't know if that means his dead kinfolk were brought back to life or if he got new ones."

"The Bible says he got new ones. And the ones who died scare me," Chaim said. "They have for a while now. God worried about Job and took care of him. But what about the others? What did they do to deserve to die like that?"

"Maybe they were sinners," Muhammad said uncertainly.

"Nothing in the Bible says so," Chaim answered. "Does anything in the Qur'an?" The Mahdi shook his head. Chaim went on, "God does what He wants to people, and what they want doesn't count."

"Do you want to escape God's will?" Muhammad sounded shocked.

"Don't be silly. I can't. God will do whatever He wants to do. But it's liable to be hard on a lot of people."

"Before I got here, I thought it would be hard on Jews and Christians, not on Muslims," Muhammad al-Muntazar said. "Now . . . I don't know."

"I don't, either. We have to wait and see." Something else occurred to Chaim. "God is good at waiting and seeing. The Ark waited 2,600 years before He let anybody see it again. Do you want a look at it?"

"Is that all right?" Muhammad asked. "Don't you Jews keep people who aren't Jews away from it?"

"Sure, but that doesn't count with you. If God didn't want you to, He wouldn't have let you get this far. C'mon." As Chaim led the Mahdi into the Temple, he wondered whether Rabbi Kupferman would have a stroke by the time they came out. Chaim had broken the rules, going into the Holy of Holies to get the Ark when ISIS attacked the Temple. Now he was breaking them again. It wasn't that he didn't care: more that he thought he had to break them to do the right thing.

"I've seen photos of the Dome of the Rock," Muhammad remarked as they walked through an opening in the Soreg—a stone partition a little more than a meter high (three cubits high, Kupferman insisted on saying) that surrounded the sanctuary. "My keeper is right. That building is more beautiful than this one."

"Your keeper?" Chaim echoed.

"Ayatollah Bakhtiar. He is clever and pious, so he thinks he can take care of me." Muhammad sniffed. "Only God has that right."

Chaim hid a grin. The ayatollah sounded like Shlomo Kupferman. "I know what you mean," he said. They strolled through the Women's Court, the Men's Court, and the Levites' Court. In the Priests' Court, in front of the Temple itself, stood the altar. "Pretty soon we'll start sacrificing again."

"You don't sound happy about it," Muhammad said.

"I'm not," Chaim admitted. "After what they did to Rosie . . ." He explained about the red heifer. But then he added, "If that hadn't happened, would I have found I can raise the dead? It's God again, doing what He wants."

"Yes, that has to be a miracle," the Mahdi agreed. By now, Chaim had his raised ghosts under enough control that they often weren't obvious to most people around him. Some could still tell they were there. Chaim wasn't surprised Muhammad al-Muntazar, also touched by God, would sense them. The Iranian went on, "Before I got here, I would have guessed it was Satan's miracle."

"And now?" Chaim asked tartly.

"Now I have seen you and talked to you." Muhammad touched a forefinger to his forehead: an odd little salute. "Now I know better."

"Okay. I wondered about you," Chaim said. "I wondered if you were a phony."

As he had, the Mahdi asked, "And now?"

"Now I know better, too," Chaim agreed. "God did this to both of us. We've got to make the best of it—if we can."

They went up the stairs and into the Holy Place. The gold menorah and the gold-covered table for showbread already stood there, taken from the museum in the Old City. Tall, narrow sunbeams lanced through the south-facing windows. Despite them, the Holy Place remained gloomy.

Two golden cherubim ornamented the first curtain hanging between the Holy Place and the Holy of Holies. Chaim parted it and stepped through, Muhammad following. The inner curtain was similarly adorned. "Ready?" Chaim's voice dropped to a whisper.

"Yes." Muhammad's was no louder.

Chaim passed through the inner curtain. Again, Muhammad was only a pace behind him. The Holy of Holies should have been pitch-black. No windows pierced the walls. The two thick hangings between the Holy of Holies and the brighter Holy Place outside should have soaked up the light that tried to get through.

But the Ark shone with no light on it. Chaim wondered if it had done that before the archaeologists found it. He supposed he could ask Kupferman. Then he shook his head. He could ask one of the archaeologists. Maybe the American with the cute girlfriend who was also an archaeologist. No, she was his wife now.

Muhammad al-Muntazar slowly nodded. "It is a thing of God, and from God. I wondered about that, too. The Black Stone in the Ka'aba in Mecca must be like it."

"I don't know. I won't argue with you, though." Chaim hadn't thought anything about Islam was true. The further this went, the more complicated everything looked.

He wondered if that was what growing up was all about.

The Mahdi sounded shy as he asked, "May I . . . touch it?" Chaim needed a second before he knew where he'd heard that longing before: in his own mouth, when he was talking with Shoshanah.

This was more dangerous than a girl was for a shy boy. "Don't ask me. Ask God," Chaim said. "The Ark killed a man who didn't believe what it could do. If God doesn't want you to touch it, it will kill you, too."

Muhammad dropped to his knees and touched his forehead to the floor of the Holy of Holies. Jews didn't pray that way. But wasn't what your heart held more important than how you showed it? Chaim thought so. Would God?

After a minute or so, the Mahdi got to his feet. His face was calm, even exalted. "I will do it," he declared. "If I die, it is God's will. Tell Ali Bakhtiar I said so."

That made Chaim gulp. What would happen if he came out alive and Muhammad didn't? Nothing good. The Iranians would hit the ceiling in fourteen places. They might start throwing rockets again. If they didn't, their Hezbollah stooges in Lebanon would.

"There is no God but God," Muhammad al-Muntazar said. He touched the Ark of the Covenant as reverently, as gently, as Chaim touched Shoshanah. The Mahdi turned back to Chaim with a broad, relieved smile on his face. "I live!"

"The Lord our God, the Lord is one," Chaim said. As Muhammad had left out the Muslim part of the *shahada*, so he left out the Jewish part of the *Shma*. It seemed . . . right. He didn't realize he would do it till he already had.

He really wanted to talk to Muhammad about girls. The Mahdi was older. He had to be more experienced. But the Holy of Holies was the wrong place, and this was the wrong time. Too bad.

"Maybe we better get back," he said instead.

"Probably a good idea," Muhammad agreed. "Those are the TV pictures Iran is waiting to see."

"Who isn't?" Chaim answered, and Muhammad nodded.

When they got out where the cameras could see them again, they turned toward each other. They smiled and clasped hands once more. *If this photo isn't everywhere in the world tonight, I'll be surprised,* Chaim thought. But he didn't expect to be—and he wasn't.

Eric's ring tone was the *Dragnet* theme. Orly's came from an Israeli hip-hop track. This call, the night after the Messiah met the Mahdi, was his. *Dum-da-dum-dum! Dum-da-dum-dum-dummm!* He grabbed the phone off the nightstand. "Eric Katz."

"Eric, it's Yoram. You home?"

"Yoram! What's up?" Eric hoped he sounded as pleased as he was. Yoram Louvish had fallen off the map lately.

He didn't answer any of Eric's questions. Instead, he asked, "You home?" again.

"We sure are. Both of us," Eric said.

"Can I come over?" the Israeli archaeologist asked. "Never can tell who listens to phones."

Yoram wants to come by, Eric mouthed to Orly. When she nodded, he said, "Sure. Give us fifteen minutes to straighten up."

"See you then," Yoram said, and the line went dead.

"What does he want?" Orly asked.

"Don't know. He didn't want to say on the phone," Eric answered. Not that you couldn't tap a phone. But Yoram Louvish was about as far from an enemy of Israel as you could get. If he thought somebody was listening in . . .

"Has he gone 'round the bend?" Orly asked, which summed up what Eric was thinking.

He shrugged. "Beats me. We'll both find out."

The straightening was halfhearted. Orly had never heard of Martha Stewart, and Eric couldn't stand her. Books and papers made up most of the mess—and the décor. Where mess stopped and décor started wasn't obvious.

Yoram knocked fifteen minutes later on the dot. He shook hands with Eric and hugged Orly and kissed her on the cheek. "Haven't thrown him out yet?" he said.

"He has entertainment value," Orly answered.

Eric didn't know whether to be annoyed or proud. "Can I get you a beer?" he asked Yoram.

"Oh, God, yes!" the archaeologist said, as if he'd been wandering through the desert the past forty years. Eric took out three Goldstars. He and Orly sipped theirs. Yoram half-emptied his. That wasn't his usual style.

"Can you tell us what's on your mind now?" Eric asked.

Yoram looked at the beer left in the bottle as if he'd never seen anything so interesting. In a low voice, he said, "I wish they'd never started rebuilding the Temple."

Whatever Eric had thought he might hear, that wasn't it. The glance he sent Orly went past bemused to astonished. "You *were* all for it," he blurted.

"I know. Funny, eh?" Yoram smiled a small, sweet, sad smile. "Only goes to show you should be careful what you wish for. Because you might get it."

"What's that mean?" Orly asked, blunt as usual.

Yoram finished the Goldstar. The way he stared at the dead soldier made Eric bring him another one. Yoram sketched a salute as he swigged. Then he said, "They'll start sacrificing at the Temple any day now. It'll be back in business."

"I know. I don't like that, either," Eric said. "A lot of people won't like it when they see how many animals die and how much blood gets splashed around. We'll have to worry about PETA along with Hezbollah and ISIS."

"PETA?" Orly asked.

"People for the Ethical Treatment of Animals," Eric explained.

"Jokes," Yoram Louvish said. "I come over here with worries, and he makes jokes."

"I wasn't kidding," Eric said. "Some of them are terrorists, too. They've caused trouble in the States, raiding labs and like that. I'd be amazed if they don't have a branch here."

"Okay, you weren't joking." Yoram drank more beer. "But I'm not worrying about these PETA people or ISIS and Hezbollah, either. Not even about Iran."

"For God's sake, who are you worrying about, then?" Orly asked.

"You said it," Yoram answered.

Orly and Eric spoke together: "Huh?"

"God." Yoram looked up through the cottage-cheese ceiling.

"That's—" Eric started to tell Yoram it was silly. However much he wanted to, he couldn't.

"You see," Yoram said. "All this has happened so God can do . . . whatever He'll do. When Kupferman offers the first lamb on the altar in front of the Temple . . . What happens then?"

"Why are you telling us? Why not Kupferman?" Orly asked, which struck Eric as a good question.

And Yoram Louvish had a damn good answer: "Because Shlomo doesn't want to listen to me. If God chars him off the altar, he'll be happy. He thinks he will, anyway."

Eric nodded. Kupferman looked forward to the end of the world with the same passion as any Christian or Muslim fundamentalist. What surprised the American was that Yoram didn't. Eric asked why not.

"Because I like it here," Yoram said. "I'm just not ready for that kind of change."

"But if that change is ready for you . . . ?" Orly said.

Louvish gave her a crooked grin. "I know. I helped start all this, and now I don't want to see how it ends. Funny, huh? So how come I'm not laughing?" He stood. "Thanks for letting me bend your ears."

"It's okay," Eric said. Instead of heading for the door, Yoram went into the john. *Vitamin P,* Eric thought.

"Boy, he's got it bad," Orly said in a low voice.

"You aren't kidding," Eric agreed. "Too late to worry now, you know?"

His wife's expression spoke loudly, and what it said was, *You American.* She spelled it out: "It's never too late to worry."

"I guess not," Eric said, the other choice being a fight he didn't want. "I—" He broke off because the toilet flushed.

Yoram came out. "Trying to decide how *meshuggeh* I am?" he asked. "Believe me, I hope they chase me with a butterfly net."

Eric *was* an American, and tried to deny everything. Orly said, "If you talk crazy, why shouldn't we think you are?"

"I have one excuse—if I'm right, I'm not crazy." He left before either of them could say anything more.

They looked at each other. "Oy," Eric said.

Orly snorted. She didn't like Yiddish. (*Meshuggeh* was Hebrew, too.) Few Israelis did. It reminded them of the ghettos they'd escaped. (It reminded Eric of his parents talking about things they didn't want him to understand.) She said, "It'll be all right. If the Messiah and the Mahdi can get together without trying to knife each other, Yoram's worrying about nothing."

"*Alevai*," Eric said. That was also Hebrew borrowed by Yiddish. It meant, *May it be so*. But Yoram was bound to be right about one thing. God would do what *He* wanted, not what His people did.

25

The priests wore spotless white robes. They closed them with red sashes, each tied on the left. Their headgear reminded Chaim of a turban, except that it was open on top, while the ends of the cloth strip fell down to their shoulders.

They undoubtedly thought they looked holy. Chaim Avigad thought they looked silly. He didn't know what Muhammad al-Muntazar thought. The Mahdi stood waiting while he wrangled with the priests.

"He can't come in here," a man in white said. "No gentile can come into the holy places reserved for Jews."

"You idiot!" Chaim shouted. One cool thing about being the Messiah was that he *could* yell at grown-ups. Gray streaked the priest's beard, but he turned pale. Chaim went on, "Were you out to lunch the other day? He went into the Holy of Holies with me! Not just the Holy Place, the Holy of Holies. He touched the Ark, and God let him live. You say I can't bring him in here? Who do you think you are?"

"I—" The priest gulped. "I'm trying to do what's proper."

"You're not very good at it," Chaim said. "Move, before something horrible happens." He gestured. "C'mon, Muhammad."

"I'm coming." Among the white-robed priests, the Mahdi might have been an ink blot with shoes. But they parted before him and Chaim like the Red Sea parting before Moses.

TV cameras followed the newcomers. Learned commentators were probably picking apart what Chaim told the priest. If Jews were good at anything, it was splitting hairs. Christians and Muslims would be listening, too. In the days of Herod's Temple, news took weeks or months to go from one end of the Roman Empire to the other. Now the world seemed to know about things five minutes before they happened.

"Don't you get sick of being watched?" Chaim asked Muhammad.

"Oh, a little," the Mahdi answered. They both laughed.

There was the altar, and the ramp leading up to it. Atop it stood Shlomo Kupferman. Now he wore High Priest's regalia, which he hadn't when he sacrificed Rosie. That didn't make Chaim like him any better.

They didn't sacrifice animals up there. They had a place just north of it where that was done. It had two dozen metal rings to hold down the lambs or goats or oxen while their throats were cut, eight stone columns, and eight marble tables. The columns had hooks to hang the carcasses on and let them bleed out; the tables were for rinsing the organs that would go into the fire.

A chorus of Levites chanted prayers as priests led four lambs from a chamber where they'd been inspected for blemishes. "This reminds me of the butcher's shop back home," Muhammad said. "We sacrifice, too—a goat after we make the *hajj* to Mecca."

He wasn't mocking the ceremony, then. That made Chaim feel better. The lambs went willingly. They didn't know they needed to fear. Nothing stank of blood—yet. Tomorrow's animals might not be so complacent.

Sacrificers eased the lambs into the rings, which they lowered to restrain the animals. The men cut the lambs' throats at the same time. Blood drowned the lambs' startled bleats. This was going out around the world. Chaim wondered what people thought. If they couldn't stomach it, why weren't they vegetarians?

The priests caught the spurting blood in gold and silver *mizrakim*. Two men used their fingers to sprinkle it against the sides of the altar; two others poured it out at the base. Shlomo Kupferman looked down in satisfaction. "We come into our own once more!" he said. "These rituals have not been carried out for almost two thousand years, but we revive them."

"What does he say?" Muhammad whispered.

Chaim told him. He used the same Hebrew words Rabbi Kupferman had. But the Mahdi understood him. God had given them the gift of following each other. What they were supposed to do with it . . . Chaim didn't know yet. God had His purposes: Chaim was sure of that.

Six priests carried the washed and dried legs and innards of each lamb up to the altar. As they cast the flesh onto the fire burning atop it, Kupferman took his text from the eighth chapter of I Kings. Chaim echoed the words for Muhammad: "'Lord God of Israel, there is no God like Thee, in heaven above or on earth beneath, Who keepest covenant and mercy with Thy servants that walk before Thee with all their heart: Who hast kept with Thy servant David that which Thou promisedst him: Thou spakest also with Thy mouth, and hast fulfilled it with Thine hand, as it is this day.

"'Hearken Thou to the supplication of Thy servant, and of Thy people Israel, when they shall pray toward this place, and hear Thou in heaven Thy dwelling place, and when Thou hearest, forgive.'"

Kupferman paused to arrange the offering on the burning logs with a golden poker. Chaim whispered, "This is how King Solomon prayed when he sacrificed at the First Temple for the first time."

"Ah, Solomon." Muhammad nodded. "God gave it to him to bind winds and demons—so the holy Qur'an says."

He too spoke in a low voice, but drew Shlomo Kupferman's formidable glare. Chaim surprised himself by smiling back at him. He might be tough, but was he tough enough to outdo the Messiah and the Mahdi? *I don't think so!* went through Chaim's mind.

For a second, he wondered if that smile would make Kupferman blow a gasket. But the High Priest seemed to remember that he had a ceremony to get through. He looked away from Chaim and toward Muhammad. The Mahdi nodded with grave courtesy. *He doesn't know Kupferman yet,* Chaim thought.

Perhaps spurred by that nod, Shlomo Kupferman returned courtesy for courtesy. When he resumed his prayer, he went further into I Kings 8 than he might have intended at first: "'Moreover concerning a stranger, that is not of Thy people Israel, but cometh out of a far country for Thy name's sake—'"

"Well done! Well said! Truly the hand of God must lie behind it!" Muhammad exclaimed when Chaim gave him Kupferman's words.

The rabbi continued: "'(For they shall hear of Thy great name, and of Thy strong hand, and of Thy stretched out arm;) when he shall come and pray toward this house; Hear Thou in heaven Thy dwelling place, and do according to all that the stranger calleth to Thee for: that all people of the earth may know Thy name, to fear Thee, as do Thy people Israel; and that they may know that this house, which I have builded, is called by Thy name.'"

Muhammad's somber features glowed. "Your Bible has fewer false places in it than I thought. For we Muslims do fear God, even as Jews do. Christians, too—I suppose. And we prayed here when it was the Dome of the Rock. Truly God speaks to all."

"Yes," Chaim said. *And so does Kupferman, and it must be harder for him than it is for God*. But if Kupferman made the effort, couldn't God do the same?

No sooner had Chaim thought of that than a thin line of fire came down from the sky and engulfed the sacrifice.

Whenever the Israeli TV camera near the altar panned across Muhammad al-Muntazar's face, Gabriela had to remind herself not to mutter under her breath. Sitting beside her in the studio, Lester Stark fumed enough to set off the smoke detectors.

It wasn't that they lacked permission to use the Israeli feed. They had it. But a Muslim had gone into a part of the Temple that was supposed to be for Jews alone. Why couldn't a Christian like, say, Reverend Stark do the same?

Gabriela had had it out with Shlomo Kupferman in an unpleasant phone conversation the night before. "Listen, Ms. Sandoval," Kupferman said, "the Iranian has the Messiah on his side. If Jesus comes down from heaven and tells me to let Lester in, I'll do it. If the Messiah tells me to, I will. Till then, I'm hanging on to as much of the traditional arrangement as I can."

She had no comeback for that. She didn't even try to get Stark or Saul Buchbinder to change the Religious Affairs Minister's mind. Both Jesus and Chaim Avigad failed to come through. Stark swallowed his pride with a show of grace. He was doing commentary for millions of Christians in the USA, Canada, England, Australia, New Zealand, and wherever else Christian people understood English.

The camera showed the lambs getting their throats cut and priests gathering the blood so they could sprinkle it on the altar. "What exactly are we seeing here, Reverend Stark?" Gabriela asked, lobbing him a softball.

"It's called blood sacrifice," he said. "In a way, I respect the Israelis for not flinching from it. That's quite remarkable, really. With these offerings, Judaism comes back to its ancient roots, and it comes back to them with the two young men called the Messiah and the Mahdi watching. That they're friends, not mortal enemies, may be the most hopeful sign from the past few days."

Priests carried the disjointed lamb carcasses up the ramp to the top of the altar. Gabriela wondered what city folks in the States made of genuine gore. The blood and guts on TV dramas and video games was fake—you wouldn't be able to stomach it if it were real. Most violence and mayhem got edited out of TV news these days. But the lambs *had* had their throats cut, even if it didn't go to the States live and in color. That *was* their blood sprinkling the altar. What did the priests' fingers feel like, all sticky with it? If you hadn't grown up on a farm, you wouldn't know.

Onto the fire went the lamb pieces. Kupferman stirred them with a gold tool from the Reconstruction Alliance's museum. It looked like Fort Knox's fireplace poker. Glancing down at notes on her iPhone, Gabriela said, "No one's worn the High Priest's regalia since the first century. Caiaphas would have worn it when Jesus talked with him."

"That's right." Stark nodded. "A lot of what we're seeing here today is what our Lord would have seen before the Crucifixion."

Kupferman preached in Hebrew, and Biblical Hebrew at that. Gabriela knew a few polite phrases of the modern language, no more. Stark read Hebrew well, but had trouble following it when spoken. Fortunately, the Israelis had e-mailed them a summary. Their press office was almost as efficient as their military.

Stark used the King James version with his audience. "Some of them will have different translations, but that's all right," he'd told Gabriela before the ceremony began. "Even people who don't use the King James respect it."

"They should," she'd said. "It's a miracle."

"Excuse me?"

She'd felt proud she'd confused him. "The only great work of literature ever produced by a committee," she'd explained.

"Oh." He'd laughed more than she expected. "You've got something there, all right."

"And it's in the public domain, too, so you don't need to worry about copyright."

He'd rolled his eyes. "You've got something there, too."

But the Religious Affairs Minister went deeper into I Kings than the press office thought he would. Gabriela was relieved that, with the English in front of him, Stark got the drift. "Generous of Rabbi Kupferman to include the Iranian in his prayers," he said.

"Why did he do that?" she asked.

By the way the televangelist shrugged, it had surprised him. "Fear of the boy the rabbi calls the Messiah? Or simply fear of God?"

"Either or both could do it," Gabriela agreed.

Then fire from heaven took the sacrifice. Staring at it in her own wonder and fear, Gabriela stopped wondering why Shlomo Kupferman did things.

After a moment, she glanced over at Reverend Stark. He'd talked about God his whole adult life, but he was no more ready for a genuine, no-shit miracle than she or anyone else was. The gobsmacked expression on his face, as if he'd just been whacked in the kisser by a big salmon, said so louder than words.

Words . . . Saul Buchbinder's voice from the control room was loud in her earpiece, and no doubt in Stark's as well: "C'mon, you guys! You've got to talk through this!"

"The only thing that occurs to me right now is a call Jack Buck made when I was a little girl watching baseball on TV," Gabriela said slowly. "Ozzie Smith hit a walkoff homer, and he said, 'I don't believe what I just saw! I don't *believe* what I just saw!' But the home run was real, and so was . . . this."

Lester Stark also got his motor started. "God seems to have accepted the offering the Jews made to him from the altar at the Temple. Unless I'm totally wrong, we've just witnessed a miracle unknown since Biblical times."

"Good! That's good!" Buchbinder was all enthusiasm and all business. "Keep going! Look at Kupferman's *punim*!"

That had to mean *face*. Zero Mostel would have been jealous at how the Religious Affairs Minister's eyes bugged out. "By the way Rabbi Kupferman looks, he didn't begin to expect that God would receive the sacrifice like this," Stark said, picking his words with care.

"He looks . . . the way people look when they see a miracle. The way Reverend Stark and I look here in the studio right now," Gabriela said. "I don't think English or any other language has words strong enough to describe it." Again, because words were all she had to work with, she tried them anyhow: "Have you seen how a cat puffs out its fur and bottlebrushes its tail when you slam a door and scare it? I'm all over goosebumps, and if my hair isn't standing on end I can't tell you why not."

"I wasn't going to admit it, but I'm the same way," Stark said.

The Israeli camera went to Muhammad al-Muntazar and Chaim Avigad. "Muhammad looks as amazed as Shlomo Kupferman," Gabriela said. "The rabbi's astonished this is happening at all. I'd say Muhammad is at least as astonished it's happening in a Jewish place of worship. That adds another layer to his surprise."

"Chaim Avigad looks surprised, too, but perhaps less than either the rabbi or the Iranian," Stark put in. "Miracles wouldn't be miracles if we took them for granted. But, unless I'm reading him wrong, he might almost be asking the Lord, 'What next?'"

"I'd guess you may well be right," Gabriela said. "And even if you're imagining what's going on inside Chaim's head, none of us imagined the fire that came down from the clear sky."

"No. Will secularists claim it was a laser beam from a drone or a high-flying plane or even from a satellite in space?" Stark asked. "If they do claim such things, will anyone listen?"

"The next question is, if God took a hand in things here, where will He reach out next?" Gabriela said.

"Only God knows, which has never been more literally true," Stark replied.

"I think you're right," Gabriela said. And, as soon as they were off the air, she sent her ex a text, something she hadn't done more than a handful of times since he walked out on her. *Start sending Heather to church. Now. Don't screw around,* she wrote. After a moment, she added, *Or we'll all regret it forever.* She nodded and hit SEND.

Jamal Ashrawi monitored Israeli TV. It told him how the Zionist entity wanted to be perceived, which was useful. Sometimes it told him things the Zionists didn't want outsiders to see. Then it was priceless.

He'd done everything he could to keep the Zionists from building the Temple. Others had done everything *they* could, too. The bruises had faded from Haji Jamal's body, but the mortification would never leave his soul.

Neither would the mortification of failure. Everything his friends tried came to nothing. So did everything the Iraqi tried. The Grand Mufti took somber satisfaction in that.

Ashrawi and Ibrahim sat on a shabby sofa, watching the Jew in the ceremonial garb wait for other oddly dressed priests to bring the cut-up pieces of the sacrificial lambs. "See how they stole the idea of sacrifice from us," the bodyguard said.

"They're Jews. What do they do but steal?" Jamal Ashrawi said.

"And look at the so-called Mahdi," Ibrahim jeered. "By God, Haji Jamal, Iranians are a useless breed."

"I won't argue." The Grand Mufti lit a cigarette. Ibrahim looked wistful. Ashrawi set the pack of Winstons on the sofa. Ibrahim took a smoke.

They watched as the chunks of lamb went into the fire on the altar. The old Jew in the glitzy breastplate stirred them with his golden poker—and more fire came from heaven.

"What crap!" Ibrahim exclaimed. "Get Al Jazeera—see if they edit out the special effects."

Haji Jamal was already reaching for the remote. But Al Jazeera carried the same feed. "Jewish and Christian announcers claim this is God's fire accepting the sacrifice," a scared-looking commentator said. "No eyewitness has claimed anything different."

"It's crap," Ibrahim said. "You can see better trick photography at the movies."

"Yes." Haji Jamal's heart wasn't in it. Some Christians were almost as upset with the Zionists as Muslims were. If they said this wasn't a special effect, it probably wasn't.

Ibrahim started to say something else. Before he could, another guard stuck his head into the room and told him, "Somebody's at the door for you."

"Oh, yeah?" Ibrahim rose. "Is she pretty?" He laughed raucously. Kalashnikov slung, he lumbered after the other guard.

Ashrawi flipped from Al Jazeera to the Hezbollah channel to Fox to CNN to the Israeli broadcast to the BBC. Nobody was saying anything but that it looked as if God was accepting the Jews' sacrifice. Not even the Hezbollah man could deny that, though he tried.

Then Haji Jamal heard a burst of gunfire that came from much closer than the Haram al-Sharif. A minute later, the guard who'd summoned Ibrahim came in with a wiry little guy with a big mustache who carried a Galil. "He's dead, Abdallah?" the Grand Mufti inquired.

"He's dead, Haji Jamal," the wiry guy answered.

"Then you've got his job," Ashrawi said. "I don't need people with divided loyalties." Ibrahim had let the Iraqi's thugs thump him. If he figured he could get away with that, he was stupider than Ashrawi thought. Haji Jamal nodded to the guard who'd summoned Ibrahim. "You're number two now, Umar."

"Gotcha, boss," Umar said.

Umar would watch Abdallah. Abdallah would keep an eye on Umar, too. Haji Jamal would keep poking through Umar's connections. If he found any he didn't like, Umar would have an accident.

Abdallah jerked the Galil's muzzle toward the screen. "What's going on here?" he asked. Ashrawi told him. The new chief bodyguard whistled softly. "Never a dull moment, is there? Do you think God could really be on the Jews' side?"

"I hope not!" Haji Jamal exclaimed. That was a horrible idea.

Abdallah must have thought the same thing. "If He is . . ." The bodyguard hesitated, then said, "If He is, the Intifada goes on—against Him."

"No!" Ashrawi shook his head. "Who is at war with God? Who is doomed to lose everything at the End of Days? Who, Abdallah?"

"Satan," the guard said unwillingly.

The Grand Mufti nodded. "Yes, Satan. If you're against God, you're for Satan. You spend eternity in hell. Do you want that?"

Again, Abdallah considered. "I don't know," he said. "If God is for the Jews, then He doesn't know what He's doing."

"Be careful what you say," Haji Jamal warned. "God . . . seems to listen more closely than He used to."

"He knows what's in my heart. Whether I say it doesn't matter," Abdallah said.

"Muhammad is the Prophet of God," Ashrawi said, and Abdallah nodded. The new chief guard's name meant *Servant of God,* but he wanted to be rebellious. Haji Jamal prayed it wouldn't come to that.

* * *

Eric wondered how to put his soul in order. He hadn't worried about it before times got strange. He'd always figured a soul was low maintenance—what else came with a lifetime guarantee from the Manufacturer? But maybe even a soul needed a tuneup and new hoses every million miles or forty years, whichever came first.

Orly gave him a very peculiar look when he put it that way. "Are all Americans nuts, or is it just you?" she asked.

"I think this is just me," he answered, not without pride.

"You're probably right." His wife went on, "And we could use help."

"I'm glad you said 'we,' " Eric observed.

"Oh, I'm messed up, too. I don't pretend I'm not," Orly said.

"You know what's sad?"

"Tell me."

"We didn't say, 'Let's go to the synagogue. That'll fix everything.' "

Orly nodded. "And we didn't say, 'Let's get purified with the red heifer's ashes and sacrifice at the Temple. *That* will fix everything.' That isn't what ails us." She cocked her head to one side. "What *does* ail us?"

By the way she said it, she didn't think Eric would answer. But he did: "The modern world. We're too used to thinking for ourselves and looking at evidence. We're too used to looking *for* evidence. We're not used to letting God take care of things, or of us. It doesn't come natural, the way it would have two thousand years ago."

Orly weighed that—and the way she weighed it would have been alien to the men who wrote the Bible, or to the prophet Muhammad. And, having weighed it, she nodded again. "I think you're right."

"You know what else?" Eric said.

"What?"

"Millions of secular Jews are in the same boat, and secular Muslims, and secular Christians. And you know what else besides that?"

"No, but you're going to tell me, aren't you?" Orly said.

Eric nodded. "The boat's liable to be the *Titanic,* with an iceberg off the starboard bow."

She poked him in the ribs. He poked her, too. She squawked. She knew all kinds of dirty-fighting moves he didn't, but she was ticklish and he wasn't. If they'd been out to maim each other, she would have smashed him. In a friendlier game . . .

Soon, the game got friendlier still. Eric stopped worrying about his soul. His body was in excellent shape. It had to be, to give him so much pleasure. And he and Orly weren't even sinning, not when they were married. That made him feel smugly happy for a little while . . . till he remembered all the times they'd done it before they were married, and all the times he'd done it with other women who weren't married to him, and the times he'd done it with women married to other men. What did God think of *that*?

Nothing good, probably. "We are so messed up," he said.

"We're nowhere near that well off," Orly said. "Only I don't know what we can do to make anything better."

"We can pray. Except I'm no damn good at it," Eric said.

"Neither am I. I never got the habit."

"That's what it is," Eric agreed. "If you do it all the time, you get used to it. I'd just feel silly. Even now, I'd still feel silly." He laughed, not that it was funny. "I'm a modern man, and I still wonder if I'm what God had in mind all those years ago."

"If you're not, He's stuck with you—and with me, too."

"Uh-huh." Eric laughed again, this time with an edge in his voice. " 'All those years ago,' " he echoed. "How many years? Just a few thousand, looks like. Jesus!"

"You *are* an American," Orly said. "No Israeli would go 'Jesus!'

like that. And we haven't heard anything from Him. Maybe the Christians have been full of shit all along."

"Nothing would surprise me any more. Except you." Eric kissed her. "You surprise me all the time. But I like it."

"You'd better." Orly laughed. "We're both scared a lot, but not at the same time. That's good. We prop each other up."

"Sure," Eric said. But if they propped each other up and God knocked them both over, how much good was the propping? That seemed to be one more thing he didn't want to think about.

"That's going to be checkmate," Chaim said. He liked playing chess with Muhammad. The Mahdi was better, but not so much that Chaim had no chance.

Muhammad didn't get mad when he lost, which was also good. "It's a Farsi word," he said. "Two, in fact. *Shah mat*—the king is dead." He chuckled ruefully. "Mine sure was."

"You got me the two times before that," Chaim pointed out. His phone rang. He grabbed it. *"Shalom?"*

"Shalom, Chaim." Rabbi Kupferman's voice always sounded funny when he talked to Chaim. Kupferman wanted to treat him like a kid, but understood he couldn't. The Religious Affairs Minister didn't like it for beans. "Would you come to the Temple, please? We have a new gold menorah in the Holy Place, and we would like your blessing for it."

What do you mean, we? Kupferman would have been happier if Chaim stayed away from the Temple. Then it would have belonged to the rabbi. That stuck out all over him, like a hedgehog's spines. But his priests had a different idea, and he couldn't ignore them no matter how much he might want to.

Chaim wasn't wild about going back himself. He might have said no to piss him off, but the route from the flat where he was staying in Jerusalem to the Temple went past Shoshanah's falafel stand. "I'll be there in forty-five minutes, okay?" he said.

"Why not sooner?" Rabbi Kupferman asked. Then he muttered, "That girl . . . All right. It will do."

"And I'll bring Muhammad along," Chaim added. "We just finished a game of chess."

"God doesn't seem to mind," Kupferman replied. By the way he said it, God needed to listen to him before He let a Shiite set foot where only Jews should go. He sighed. "Since God doesn't mind, I don't . . . too much. *Shalom.*"

"You like annoying him, don't you?" Muhammad said dryly. "I'm that way with Ali Bakhtiar. Religious bureaucrats."

"Yeah!" Chaim said. "That's what they are!"

Somebody knocked on the door. Chaim looked out through the peephole. But it was one of his bodyguards. He opened the door. "You're going to the Temple?" the soldier asked.

"That's right. How did you know? . . . Oh." Chaim felt foolish. Of course Kupferman could get hold of the guards. That was only sensible, even if it left Chaim with no privacy.

IDF men, Galils at the ready, fanned out around him and Muhammad. He assumed people he couldn't see also watched them. He wouldn't have been surprised if they watched him while he was in there, too. Maybe the toilet and shower were off-limits, maybe not.

Nobody seemed surprised when he stopped at the falafel stand. Shoshanah beamed at him. "Hi, Chaim." She nodded to Muhammad, who'd been there before, too. "*Salaam,*" she said—she knew more Arabic than Chaim did.

"*Salaam,*" Muhammad returned—Arabic was a foreign language for him, too. He grinned at Chaim. "I like her—you found a good one."

"Thanks. I think so, too." Chaim was glad Muhammad hadn't

tried to move in on him. Shoshanah was closer to the Mahdi's age than to his. He feared he was a boy next to the Iranian.

"Can I get you guys anything?" she asked, first in Hebrew, then in Arabic.

"I just stopped to say hello. We're on our way to the Temple," Chaim said.

"Oh. Well—hello." She winked at him.

"You're crazy," he told her.

She gave half a curtsy. "I try." She came out from behind the counter. "Like for instance—" She hugged him. He kissed her.

Muhammad turned his back and watched a sparrow hopping on the ground. Shows of affection freaked him out. So did the women in short dresses and tight pants and with uncovered arms and uncovered hair. He was as antsy about that as any of the ultra-Orthodox here. He never said anything about it, though. He looked the other way. He was as polite as a cat.

At last, Chaim broke the clinch. "We have to get there," he said.

"Okay. I'm glad you stopped." Shoshanah went back. *She'd make a good rabbi's wife,* Chaim thought. He wondered if she would make *him* a good wife. He decided it was too soon to worry about things like that.

Muhammad stopped bird-watching. They went on toward the Temple Mount. Muhammad surprised Chaim by saying, "That wouldn't happen in Iran in public."

"I guess not," Chaim said.

"But it's not—nasty, the way we make it out to be." Muhammad sounded surprised, too. "It's just—different, you know?"

"Some people here get upset about it, too," Chaim said.

Up the ramp to the flat top of the Temple Mount. Over to the Temple. Gold-plated spikes on the roof gleamed in the sun. They were there to keep birds from hopping around and fouling the holy building. That was one of Herod's innovations, reproduced 2,000 years later.

Chaim glanced from the roof to the heavens. He saw Muhammad doing the same thing. Fire hadn't come down since the first sacrifice. He wondered why they were both jumpy now. Something in the air? In their spirits?

There was Uncle Yitzhak, outside the Holy Place. Chaim waved. His uncle waved back. Had he thought this would happen when they went to inspect the red heifer? Had anybody?

And there was Kupferman, talking with some archaeologists. Chaim recognized the American and the Israeli woman he'd married. She was pretty, even if she had to be close to thirty.

Kupferman spotted him and Muhammad. He didn't miss much. He had the High Priest's regalia on again. The gold and semiprecious stones of the breastplate flashed as he turned toward them and beckoned them forward.

TV cameras followed them. They tracked Chaim as he stopped, too. Half a step later, Muhammad did the same thing. Chaim's mouth dropped open. If Muhammad's didn't, Chaim had no idea why not.

Trailing clouds of glory—they couldn't be anything else—Jesus descended from the heavens toward the Temple.

26

Eric had always had mixed feelings about the Temple. It struck him as a religious Disneyland—a theme park dedicated to God. How relevant that was to the twenty-first century was a different story . . . for him, anyway.

Not for the priests who carried out the rituals. They were sure they knew what they were doing. They might even have been right. The Old Testament and Talmud explained the rituals in minute detail. They didn't always explain *why* the rituals were required. Talmudic scholars said God knew His reasons for the rituals of the red heifer, but they didn't.

From the way things were working out, it looked like He did.

You could also learn from a religious Disneyland. Civil War reenactors taught historians things about moving and ordering men they couldn't learn from books. Making stone tools helped anthropologists. If you wanted to *see* how Herod's Temple worked, checking out the new edition couldn't hurt.

Not that it was *just* like Herod's Temple. By the time of Christ, the Ark was long gone. Herod's Holy of Holies was empty. Not this one. Rules for the Ark went back to the First Temple.

Well, that was, or could be, interesting, too.

The priests worked hard to be authentic. At a place like Williamsburg, you got a sanitized, denatured version of the real thing. What vacationers would visit a place that smelled like the genuine colonial Williamsburg?

Sacrifices here were as gory as the originals. Those smells lingered. So did the bleats and moans of dying animals. Eric had heard that the Israeli SPCA tried to get an injunction to stop the killings. After fire came down from the heavens, the animal-rights people couldn't find a judge who'd give them one. Who wanted to take chances with the Guy Upstairs, now that He was back from vacation?

Thoughts like that rose in Eric's mind all the time. For better and worse, he *was* a modern man, with millions like him. What God would do with—or to—such a cross-grained throng was another interesting question. It was *the* interesting question.

Watching a menorah getting consecrated promised to be interesting, and also not bloody. Smoke from the morning *tamid* offering was already rising when he and Orly got to the Temple, but he couldn't do anything about that.

In English, he whispered, "You know what the smell of the sacrifice reminds me of?"

"A barbecue joint," she whispered back, also in English. "Me, too. And you know something else?"

"What?" he said.

"Almost as many people here know English as Hebrew."

"Yeah, yeah." But using English made Eric feel less blasphemous. Speaking the language of the Old Testament didn't mean you *had* to be serious about God—but it helped.

He saw Chaim Avigad and Muhammad al-Muntazar come into

the square just outside the Holy Place. He'd left Orly behind by then; she had to stay in the Women's Court. She didn't like that; neither did most Israeli women. Nobody listened to them, which was the fate of most women through most of history.

Eric could legally go anywhere except inside the Holy of Holies—and, thanks to Chaim, he'd gone there. Being a Katz, a cohen, a priest, had advantages.

The seven-branched menorah stood near the altar on a prosaic wheeled cart. With the cart, it was taller than Eric. It gleamed. You saw something that big, you didn't think it could be solid gold. But it was. Nothing but the best for God. And, with the restoration of the Temple, getting gold out of people was a lot easier than it had been.

TV cameras watched the menorah. Eric wondered if their crews were cohanim or Levites, depending on placement. He wouldn't have been surprised. Not much surprised him any more.

So he told himself, till he saw people looking away from the gold candelabra and into the air. *Up in the sky! It's a bird! It's a plane! It's* . . . It wasn't anything nearly so trivial as Superman.

"Oh, Jesus!" Eric muttered. A heartbeat later, he realized that should have been a vocative—*O Jesus!*—and not the mild oath it almost always was.

Who else would be descending from heaven with no visible means of support? *Yeah, Who?* Eric's mind gibbered. In case the sight of a man—or a Man—coming down as if on an invisible escalator wasn't enough, glory streamed from Jesus.

Glory looked more like the Northern Lights than anything else Eric could think of. But the Northern Lights didn't show up at Jerusalem's latitude. And they didn't show up in broad daylight.

Jesus stared down at the city where He'd preached and died. His face was preternaturally—or supernaturally—calm. Eric wondered whether He'd float to the Temple or to the Church of the Holy Sepulcher. *The lady or the tiger?* he thought wildly. He wasn't in very good shape.

He glanced at Shlomo Kupferman. The rabbi's face was anything but calm. A handful of words summed up *his* expression: *give me a fucking break.* All this time, Jews had died for saying Jesus wasn't the Son of God. But here He was. If that wasn't a miracle putting him up in the air there, Industrial Light & Magic was behind it. Eric didn't think special effects could match what was going on.

Chaim Avigad and Muhammad al-Muntazar watched Jesus descend with identical awed anticipation. They didn't think He was a special effect. If they didn't, Eric didn't. If He wasn't, though, the whole world might bust loose any minute now.

Messiah. Mahdi. Son of God (or maybe only—only!—prophet). Together again for the first time. *I really am losing it,* Eric thought.

It was going to be the Temple, unless Jesus adjusted His flight plan at the last minute. That wasn't impossible. Nothing was impossible these days. Nothing at all.

That might have been the scariest thought he'd ever had.

Robe fluttering around Him, Jesus dropped into the courtyard outside the Holy Place. His face, long, lean, and bearded, wasn't like the ones on Byzantine mosaics—He looked too Jewish—but they came closer than the Western Christs Eric had seen.

The courtyard had been crowded, but nobody wanted to get near Jesus. He said something. It wasn't Hebrew. To Eric's surprise, he understood it anyway: Aramaic, close cousin to Hebrew *and* Arabic.

"I have returned."

That was what He said. *You and General MacArthur,* Eric thought wildly. But MacArthur needed only three years to get back to the Philippines. Jesus had been away a little longer than that.

* * *

Jesus gestured. The glory streamed out from him again. It enveloped Chaim and Muhammad al-Muntazar. Yitzhak Avigad stared at his nephew through the pearly light surrounding him. Chaim looked amazed, but not unhappy or pained. The same was true for Muhammad, not that Yitzhak cared so much. If Jesus did anything to Chaim . . .

Jesus gestured. This time, it meant *Come here.* Chaim and Muhammad both came. Nobody else, not even Shlomo Kupferman, dared move. Yitzhak wanted to yell *No!* at the top of his lungs. For his nephew to go to—that . . .

He kept quiet. He'd seen hell in combat, but he couldn't open his mouth in the face of what plainly came from heaven. And Chaim wouldn't have listened to him if he yelled. To Yitzhak, the kid was too young to have to make choices like that. But God had other ideas. How old was David when he went out to face Goliath? Not old enough, his father would have said. David did what he had to do, though.

Chaim would, too. Whatever it turned out to be. And whatever it cost.

"Ladies and gentlemen, this is the most amazing moment in the history of the world," Lester Stark said, staring at the monitors that brought images of the Second Coming from the Temple. "Prophecy is fulfilled! Jesus *has* come again!"

"Are you relieved to be able to say that, Reverend?" Gabriela Sandoval asked.

He glanced over at her in something close to resentment. Didn't she have any spiritual sense at all? Evidently not—she just sounded like a reporter doing her job. And she did it well enough to get an honest answer out of him: "To tell you the truth, I am. For all my faith, I had doubts. I wondered if this day would ever come, but here it is!"

What will the Jews say now, when they've denied Jesus' divinity for the past two thousand years? He didn't say that out loud, no matter how much he wanted to. But what occurred to him first was *Oops!*

"Don't you wish we could see this with our own eyes, not just on TV?" Gabriela said.

She did find questions that cut to the heart of things. "I sure do," Stark replied. "But we aren't Jews, and so we aren't allowed to come close enough to the central Temple precincts to do ourselves any good."

"Like most of Jerusalem, like almost all of Israel, like everyone else in the world, all we can do is watch and wonder," she said. Her mouth twisted in a wry smile. "And try to explain a bit to our audience."

"Try, yes. Chaim Avigad vouched for Muhammad al-Muntazar, which is why the Muslims have a presence in the Temple. I thought it was unfair that Christians didn't. But there's Jesus Himself, standing in the courtyard. Things do even out," Stark said.

Jesus made a come-hither gesture. Slowly, Chaim Avigad and Muhammad al-Muntazar walked toward him. *Suffer the little children to come unto me,* Stark thought. But Chaim was not a little child, Muhammad a young man. Thinking of a quotation didn't make it fit.

"What will happen when the Messiah and the Mahdi meet the . . . the Son of God?" Gabriela needed an effort, but she said it.

"I have no idea. We'll all find out together."

"Do you wish you could be out there with them?"

Of course I do! Stark almost screamed it—Gabriela's questions could cut deep. What he did say was, "Yes, but this is about what God wishes. What can I do about it?"

He knew the answer to that: nothing. If he regretted it for the rest of his days—and maybe for all eternity as well—that was also part of God's plan . . . wasn't it?

* * *

When Jesus descended on the Temple, Jamal Ashrawi hoped it was to scourge the Zionists for everything they'd done to the Palestinians, to all the Muslims around them. "Our day is come at last!" he said. "The prophet will give us the victory that is rightly ours!"

"*Inshallah*," Abdallah said. His new bodyguard was a man of few words. He didn't go on and on, the way Ibrahim had. That let Haji Jamal talk more.

"Of course God will be willing!" he exclaimed. "When was God ever unwilling to punish those people?" Abdallah only grunted.

But when Jesus showed no sign of blasting the Temple or smiting Jerusalem in a way that would make the dirty bomb look like a blessing, Haji Jamal's suspicions leaped to life again. "Maybe it's not Jesus at all," he said. "Maybe it's trick photography. If the movies can do it . . ."

Abdallah grunted again. "I don't think so," he said.

The Grand Mufti almost called him a fool. But Ashrawi was shrewd. If you insulted your chief bodyguard, bad things would happen to you. Abdallah would be sorry afterwards. He'd say he was, anyhow. *Much good that would do me*, Haji Jamal thought.

"There is no God but God, and Muhammad is the Prophet of God!" Abdallah murmured. He didn't think he was watching special effects. Haji Jamal didn't, either.

He wondered why none of the accounts of the End of Days had the Prophet returning from heaven. The Mahdi took his place. That the Mahdi should be an Iranian, a Shiite, infuriated the Grand Mufti. He kept hoping the ayatollahs were lying.

But the Jewish so-called Messiah accepted Muhammad al-Muntazar. Jesus seemed to, as well. The prophet (not the Son of God, as the Qur'an made plain in the suras called The Table Spread and Repentance) gestured to the Mahdi—and to the Messiah, too. So Jesus also accepted the Jew!

They both came toward Jesus. The Grand Mufti fumed. *He* was the chief Muslim prelate of Jerusalem. Why wasn't Jesus summoning *him*?

"The Jews will be sorry for what they've done to me," he growled. His bodyguard sent him a curious look.

Chaim Avigad's heart pounded. He'd never expected Jesus to appear. Who would have?—who that was Jewish, anyhow? He'd never expected to meet the Mahdi, either. And he'd really never expected to like him. But he had, and he did. If Jesus was coming down from the heavens, what could anybody, even the Messiah, do about it?

Not much.

He could, and did, watch in awe as Jesus descended. A vagrant was somebody without visible means of support. By that standard, Jesus was a vagrant. He flew through the air, as if God had repealed the law of gravity just for Him. Chances were God had.

Chaim wanted to reach out for the iridescent, opalescent glory streaming from Jesus. He did, to discover it was insubstantial. He could see it, but he couldn't feel it or touch it.

Next to him, Muhammad al-Muntazar was doing the same thing. When Chaim's eyes met his, Muhammad gave back a sheepish grin. Did he feel he'd been caught acting like a baby playing with something shiny? Chaim had, too.

Jesus came down in the courtyard close by the Holy Place. "I have returned," He said. His words sounded something like Hebrew, but they weren't. *Aramaic?* Chaim wondered. It didn't matter, not to him. He understood Jesus whether he knew His language or not, the same way he understood Muhammad. God . . . provided.

Rabbi Kupferman stood on the altar in the High Priest's fancy regalia. His eyes looked ready to bug out of his head. Chaim had upstaged him by becoming the Messiah after Kupferman sacrificed Rosie. Now here he was, presiding over another sacrifice, in the middle of the Second Coming. *Does that make you feel three centi-meters tall? Something ought to, don't you think?* Chaim wasn't sorry to see Kupferman learn humility.

The rabbi wasn't the only one behaving as if he couldn't believe his eyes. No one in the Python sketch—which Chaim had seen a dozen times, with Hebrew subtitles—expected the Spanish Inquisition. No one here expected the Second Coming.

And what people didn't expect, they feared and hated. Chaim saw that on lots of faces. *Get used to it. Get over it,* he thought. *What choice do you have?*

Jesus gestured to Chaim and Muhammad al-Muntazar. Chaim looked at Muhammad. The Mahdi was looking back at him, as if asking what he wanted to do. No one had ever done that with him before. It made him feel grown up: much more so than saying *Today I am a man* at his bar mitzvah when he plainly wasn't. Some-body was looking for *his* judgment. Pride warmed him.

He only wished they had more choice. If Jesus called you, you had to see what He wanted. Chaim took the first step toward Him. Muhammad al-Muntazar followed a fraction of a second later.

"Welcome," Jesus said when they came to him. He set His right hand on Chaim's shoulder. The hand felt like . . . a hand. Chaim didn't know what he expected it to feel like, but not that, somehow. Jesus nodded to him. "My elder brother." He put His left hand on Muhammad's shoulder and nodded to *him.* "My younger brother."

For a second, Chaim thought that was nuts. Jesus was eons older than he was. Muhammad was older than he was, too. But then Chaim's head started working again—or maybe the knowledge came straight from God through Jesus' hand. Who could guess?

But Judaism was older than Christianity, while Islam was younger. That had to be what Jesus meant. *Parables,* Chaim thought. *Jesus talks in parables. Riddles, like.* He'd heard that. He'd never dreamt it would matter to him.

The American archaeologist probably knew more about how

Jesus worked. Not because he was an archaeologist. Because he was an American. Jews there—Muslims, too—had to live in a country where Christianity was bigger. They couldn't help soaking up stuff about Jesus.

Chaim was getting *his* education now, straight from the source. "You two will understand . . . some of what I am, what I've been through," Jesus said. "Some burdens are too large to lay on a man, but there are times when you have to bear them anyway."

"Yes," Chaim said, as Muhammad whispered, "Oh, yes."

"I never knew anyone before who could grasp even part of it—except God, of course," Jesus said. "I never knew a man who could grasp it, I should say. God is . . . different."

"Why—? Why did You come back now?" Chaim asked.

"Because it was time," Jesus answered. "Because the End Times, the time for the last battles against evil, may be at hand."

"Which side is evil?" That was Muhammad al-Muntazar, also stumbling over his words.

"By their works shall you know them," Jesus said—a response that was liable to cause more trouble than none at all.

"What . . . do you want with us?" Chaim asked.

Jesus' eyes met his. "Is it not written: 'Then we which are alive and remain shall be caught up together with them in the clouds to meet the Lord; and so we shall ever be with the Lord'?"

"Not in my Scripture," Chaim said stubbornly.

"Not in mine, either," Muhammad agreed.

"Your Scripture is true, in its way," Jesus said to Chaim. He turned to Muhammad. "And so is yours. And so is that other one."

That's impossible. They can't all be true at once, Chaim thought. But a lot of impossible things had happened lately. If Jesus said God had arranged things this way, Chaim couldn't tell Him He was out of His tree.

Muhammad al-Muntazar had something else on his mind. "Where is the prophet Muhammad, peace be unto him?" he asked.

"He is with God and with the other prophets, and peace has come to him," Jesus replied.

"Why didn't he come to earth?" the Mahdi persisted.

"God did not will that he should," Jesus said, and Muhammad bowed his head. When you got an answer like that, and got it from Someone like this, what could you do but accept it?

Which brought Chaim to a question of his own: "What are You going to do with us?"

"Why, what I told you before," Jesus said.

"Huh?" As soon as Chaim made the uncouth noise, he realized you probably weren't supposed to say *Huh?* to Jesus.

To his relief, Jesus smiled, which made Him seem a little less awe-inspiring. "What is written in that Scripture neither one of you cares for," He said.

Chaim's jaw dropped. "You're gonna take *us* up into heaven?" he blurted.

"That is why I have come," Jesus said.

"Truly there is no God but God," Muhammad said in a low voice.

"The Lord is one," Chaim agreed. But if the Lord was one, what was Jesus doing here? Was He just—just!—a prophet? Was He man and God at the same time, the way the Christians said? Or was God using Him as a projection and mouthpiece? Christians would probably figure that was heresy, but Chaim didn't care. Jesus said everything in all the Scriptures was true, but it looked to Chaim as if everything in all of them was partly wrong, too. Everybody would have to get used to that.

Or else everybody would have to start fighting about it. Wasn't that part of what the End Times were all about?

"Do we have a choice about this?" he asked slowly.

"You always have a choice." Jesus' voice was deep and serious. "You can choose to obey God, or you can choose to disobey Him. And you will bear forever what springs from your choice now."

When He said *forever,* he didn't mean *for the rest of your life.* He meant *forever.* And He *did* mean it, too.

Chaim sighed. "We'd better do it that way, then. I wanted to find out more about Shoshanah, but . . ."

"Don't fret," Muhammad said. "Heaven also has its pleasures: virgins and wine and honey and feasting."

Heaven didn't have those things as far as Jews were concerned. The Jewish afterlife was murky. But if everything in all the Scriptures was true—who could know what that meant? He'd have to find out. And if heaven was the way Christians or Muslims said it was, maybe he *would* see Shoshanah one of these days. Next to *forever,* what was *for the rest of your life*? Not much.

"The time has come," Jesus said. "Are you ready? Have you made your choice?"

"Yes." The Mahdi didn't hesitate.

"Yes." Chaim did, but he chose the same way.

Next thing he knew, he was rising. There was the Temple Mount laid out below him. There was Jerusalem. There was Israel. There was the Middle East. There was the world. His ghosts came with him . . . trailed after him . . . something like that. They weren't gone, anyhow, the way he'd almost hoped they would be. He knew a moment's wonder: the world seemed round and flat at the same time. That should have been impossible, but it wasn't.

Then, instead of looking down, Chaim looked around and up. He should have been in outer space, choking for lack of air, but, again, he wasn't. He was . . . somewhere else. Except for the cherubim on the Ark, he'd never seen an angel before.

As for Him Who made the angels . . . In that first instant, Chaim knew he'd made the right choice.

Aramaic, Hebrew, Farsi . . . Lester Stark read the first two, but didn't speak them well. He knew none of the third language Jesus, the

Messiah, and the Mahdi used among themselves. They all understood one another, as the Israeli and Iranian had from the start.
But, while broadcasting live, Stark didn't know what they were saying. That was a handicap.

He wished he had an Israeli or American Jewish scholar and an
Iranian beside him. Instead, he had Gabriela Sandoval. She was
pleasant to look at. She was bright. She'd shown herself a more than
capable reporter. A linguist and Biblical scholar she was not.

That American archaeologist—Eric Katz, that was his name—on
the team that found the Ark, he would have been perfect. Or an
Iranian Jew who could follow all three of them . . . *Wish for the stars
while you're at it,* Stark thought.

Saul Buchbinder would start yelling in his ear again if he didn't
say something soon. He came out with, "They're talking to one
another in what seems a friendly fashion"—a masterpiece of analy-
sis if ever there was one.

"Have any idea what they're saying, Reverend?" Gabriela asked.

Regretfully, he shook his head. "Someone will—someone does,
I'm sure—but it isn't me."

Jesus proved Himself a man of the Middle East as well as the
Son of God (Lester was damned if he'd believe Jesus was only a
prophet [*Or maybe I'm damned if I believe anything else*—a depressing thought]): He talked with His hands. So did the Messiah
and the Mahdi. They might have been haggling over a brass lamp,
only they weren't.

Jesus looked up to the heavens. Chaim pointed west. At the
Temple? At something in Jerusalem? At the Mediterranean? Toward the United States? Stark had no way to know.

Then Jesus seemed to ask a couple of questions. The Mahdi answered first, with one word. The Messiah said, "*Ken.*"

"I don't know much spoken Hebrew, but I know that means
yes," Stark said.

"By Muhammad al-Muntazar's face, he said the same thing," Gabriela added. "But what did they agree to?"

She and Stark found out a moment later. "They're . . . rising into the air, Jesus and Chaim and Muhammad," the televangelist said. "They are rising into the clouds to meet the Lord in the air, as is written." He'd been preaching from First Thessalonians for years.

But he'd always thought the Rapture would come to everybody good, everybody worthy, just ahead of the Last Days. Jesus was returning to the heavens with only the Messiah and the Mahdi. What did that mean?

"What does this mean?" Stark asked his audience. Many of them, he knew, sat in front of their TVs with Bibles open, trying to work things out for themselves. He went on, "This doesn't seem to fit the Premillenarianism I've long espoused."

"Can you explain Premillenarianism for people who haven't long espoused it?" Gabriela asked.

"Briefly, that the Rapture would take place before the Last Days," he said.

As he spoke, Jesus and Chaim Avigad and Muhammad al-Muntazar rose and dwindled. There were no clouds in the enameled dome of the sky except the clouds of glory emanating from Jesus. Did that mean this wasn't what First Thessalonians had in mind? Stark thought it unlikely, but how could you be sure? Was prophecy detailed enough to include a weather forecast a couple of thousand years in advance?

Then something else occurred to him. "Perhaps Premillenarianism is less . . . damaged than I thought at first," he said. "Perhaps Jesus *has* taken up into the heavens the people God reckons worthy—the *only* people He reckons worthy."

"Just two of them?" Gabriela pounced, as well she might. "Neither one Christian? What would that mean?"

"I don't know right now," Stark admitted. "Maybe the smartest

thing we can do is watch the monitors and see what we can learn."
And keep our big traps shut, he thought.

"One thing we've learned, wouldn't you agree?" Gabriela said.
"If Chaim Avigad, the Messiah, is going up toward heaven with
Jesus, he pretty definitely isn't the Antichrist."

"Er—yes," Stark replied. "That does seem plain."

"So does something else," Gabriela went on. "If the three of
them are going up to heaven together, doesn't that mean all the
Abrahamic religions—Judaism, Christianity, and Islam—are acceptable in God's eyes? What else *can* it mean?"

Lester Stark took a deep, reluctant breath. He wanted to say that
only Christianity—that only his particular brand of Christianity,
not Catholicism or Orthodoxy, definitely not something bizarre
like Mormonism—was the one true faith. He wanted to, but he was
watching the same thing she was, the same thing much of the world
was. He was watching . . . and God was listening. No one could
doubt that now.

"I don't see how it can mean anything different," was what came
out of his mouth. "I don't see how anyone of good will can imagine
it means anything different."

The Son of God, the Messiah, and the Mahdi flickered, first
once, then again and again. Then they were gone, though Stark
didn't think they'd risen too high for cameras to pick them up.
Maybe heaven wasn't a mile beyond the moon after all. Maybe you
had to peel back a corner of space-time to find it.

Or maybe I don't understand what's going on, Stark thought.
That seemed all too probable. As if plucking the thought from his
head, Gabriela said, "Isn't it Saint Paul who talks about seeing
through a glass, darkly? That's a lot of what we're doing now."

"It certainly is," Stark agreed. "When we die, when we see
clearly, we'll know everything we have to wonder about here."

"What *do* we know about this extraordinary day?" she asked.

"First and most important, that God *is* immanent in the universe. No one can deny that any more. And, as you said, that He approves of—no, that He loves—all three Abrahamic religions," Stark answered. "And we still must believe the Last Days *are* upon us. History is ending. Eternity lies ahead. In heaven? Or hell? The choice is ours." He looked straight out at all the people on the other side of the screen. "The choice is—yours."

27

"Whoa!" Eric Katz breathed as Jesus and Chaim Avigad and Muhammad al-Muntazar rose toward the heavens. Rose toward heaven? He wouldn't have been surprised. By now, he was willing to believe that amazement had been burnt out of him—and from a good part of the human race.

Everybody else outside the Holy Place looked as poleaxed as he did. Even Shlomo Kupferman might have taken a two-by-four between the eyes. He stood atop the altar, his eyes aimed upwards, his beard spilling over the High Priest's bejeweled breastplate.

Eric had to bite down on the inside of his cheek to keep from guffawing. Kupferman's pose and clothes and anxious demeanor reminded the archaeologist of Sumerian statuettes of stone and terracotta. Those figurines always looked worried. The Sumerians seemed convinced their gods were out to get them. Since they lived in a region with no defenses to speak of, and their main natural resource (not counting oil, and they wouldn't have) was mud, they might not have been wrong, either.

Kupferman had that *What are You going to do to me now, God?* look, too. All things considered, he'd earned it.

"Should we go on, sir?" a lesser priest asked.

The Religious Affairs Minister needed a distinct effort to call his mind back to mundane affairs. He shook himself, like a dog coming out of cold water. "Yes," he said in a voice that sounded as much like his usual tones as Roseanne sounded like Beyoncé. "We should do that."

Business as usual. That was what people like him were good for. In Herod's Temple, Caiaphas had probably been the same way. And when business as usual flew out the window—or up into the heavens—people like that got a bad press. It had happened before. It would again.

Yitzhak Avigad was staring into the heavens, too. He kept looking up even after he stood. He also looked like somebody who'd just taken a flounder in the face. He'd been brushed by a miracle that meant he'd never see his nephew again.

Eric went over to Yitzhak. "You okay?" he asked—not the most profound question, but maybe one that would get the other man talking.

Like Kupferman, Chaim's uncle seemed to come back from a long way off. "He's gone," he said.

"Yeah." Eric nodded. "But you know how we say somebody who dies is going to a better place? Chaim isn't dying, but he's going to a better place anyway. Most of the time, we just say that. Now you know it's true."

Yitzhak Avigad also nodded. "Yes, I know it. That doesn't mean I like it." He whistled: a low note of wonder. "This started when we went to the States to check out the red heifer."

"Do you think so?" Eric said. "Isn't it more likely that it started when God said, 'Let there be light,' and there was light?"

"You can say that about anything," Yitzhak said.

"You sure can," Eric agreed. Later, he would worry about whether free will was anything more than a figment of predestined man's imagination—a figment man was predestined to have. He went on, "Don't you think God paid special attention to this part of the plan, though?"

"I suppose so," Yitzhak said, most unwillingly.

"Chaim's in good company," Eric said. "Who got taken up bodily into heaven before? Elijah, Jesus . . . and Muhammad, I guess."

"Every word is true, and it does me no good," Yitzhak answered. "I have to tell my sister-in-law why she'll never see her son again."

"Because God wanted him," Eric said. Most of the time, such phrases felt like the consolation Job's comforters might have given. Here it was nothing but the truth.

"Rivka wants him, too. God's got him. She doesn't, and she won't," Yitzhak said.

"Who would?" Eric replied. Behind him, a sheep's bleat subsided into gurgles after a priest cut its throat.

"And the other thing I've got to do is tell Shoshanah Mazar—that girl at the falafel stand—she won't see Chaim again, either," Yitzhak said. "That'll be almost as hard as telling his mother. If—" He broke off, shaking his head.

"If what?" Eric asked.

"Never mind." Yitzhak's voice was a slammed door.

Eric didn't push it. He recognized finality when he heard it. Even if Yitzhak didn't cough up answers, Eric could imagine his own. If Shoshanah had gone to bed with Chaim, maybe he wouldn't have been holy enough to get carried up into heaven. If Chaim's mother had raised him a different way . . .

But Eric shook his head. Maybe Chaim Avigad wouldn't have ended up the Messiah if something like that happened. It would have been some other pious Israeli kid. And what difference would that make? A different pious family would mourn and exult at the same time. It would matter to them, not to the world.

And with God manifesting Himself in worldly affairs, who could guess what a realistic policy was now or would be five years from now . . . besides living the best life you could, anyway? God only knew—which held too much truth for comfort.

Eric glanced up at Shlomo Kupferman. He wanted to ask Kupferman what it had been like for him, too. But the would-be High Priest was intent on finishing the sacrifices. Kupferman seemed *very* intent on that, to the exclusion of everything else. He reminded Eric not so much of the Pharisee passing on the other side of the road but of an ostrich with its head in the sand.

Ostriches didn't really do that, of course. Even if they did, they wouldn't have been appropriate birds to think of while thinking of Kupferman up there on the altar. Like hoopoes—in that if in no other way beyond birditude—ostriches weren't sacrifices acceptable in God's eyes.

Nu? So what? Eric might have sounded like a Borscht Belt comic inside his head, but he had the feeling he was touching truth, and ritual purity be damned.

Shlomo Kupferman didn't want to acknowledge that Jesus had just made His Second Coming. He didn't want to acknowledge that Jesus had headed back to heaven with a Jew and a Muslim, either. For the rabbi, it'd be business as usual at the Temple, nothing else.

That wouldn't fly. Eric was sure it wouldn't—and that Kupferman intended to roll with it anyhow. Kupferman would be sorry. You commonly were when you wouldn't face the obvious.

Eric was also sure Kupferman wouldn't listen to him. Kupferman hadn't got the Temple rebuilt by listening to other people. But couldn't any story have a goddamn happy ending?

Jamal Ashrawi watched Jesus ascend with the Jew called the Messiah and the Iranian youth called the Mahdi. The Grand Mufti didn't like believing either was what he claimed to be, or that Jesus was what He seemed to be.

But the other choice seemed to be believing Jesus was a Zionist actor and everything He was doing, special effects. With everything else that had happened, the Grand Mufti couldn't.

Abdallah sat beside him on the shabby sofa in the hideout, also watching intently. "Isn't it strange that a Jew can go up into heaven, Haji?" the bodyguard asked. "Tell me how that can happen."

"You do me too much honor." After that moment of modesty, Ashrawi went on, "It is possible. In the Qur'an, it is written not *all* Jews will go to hell—only most of them."

"I suppose so," Abdallah said. "But that little punk? And a Shiite? If they're in heaven, I'd be happier in hell. The company's better."

He'd said such things before. Haji Jamal had no idea he was reinventing a joke Christians had been making for a hundred years. "Be careful what you say!" Haji Jamal exclaimed. "There is no God but God. Do you want Him to give you what you say would make you happier?"

The bodyguard thought it over. "No, I guess not."

"An eternity in hell . . ." Ashrawi shuddered. He'd always believed, but sometimes belief felt stronger, sometimes weaker. His was very strong now. Whose wasn't? How many sinners who laughed and said *There is no God* were vowing to mend their ways now? Tens of millions? Ashrawi was sure of it. Not just Muslims, either, but Christians and Jews with them.

Jesus and the Messiah and the Mahdi winked out. They vanished from the screen, though they hadn't risen so high that the cameras on the Haram al-Sharif couldn't follow them. Was *that* a special effect? Ashrawi didn't think so. He thought God had taken them to heaven—wherever heaven really was.

"They're gone! What now?" Abdallah sounded astonished. So did the CNN announcer. The Grand Mufti ignored her. She was a

Western woman. But his new head bodyguard needed some answer.

Haji Jamal had trouble giving him one. He was astonished, too—how could anyone not be? The Dome of the Rock had stood atop the Haram al-Sharif for more than 1,300 years. In all that time, there was no sign Jesus would come back to it, or anywhere else. After the Jews tore down the Dome of the Rock and built their Temple in its place, Jesus showed up. Where was the purpose in that?

Slowly, he replied, "What now? I'll tell you what. We have to make the best of it. If God accepts the People of the Book, we need to do the same. It will take some getting used to, but we must. Can you doubt that?"

"No! By God, no!" Abdallah said.

"*By God,* yes," Ashrawi said. "Now we are in God's camp or in Satan's. If Islam is true"—he paused, then went on—"and Christianity and the Jews' faith with it, we must stay in God's camp. Is it not so?"

The chief bodyguard nodded. "It is."

"All right, then," Haji Jamal said. "Our enemies are also God's enemies. Maybe, at the End of Days, you or I will slaughter the last pig."

"May it be so, *inshallah.*" Abdallah's eyes glowed.

"God *is* willing," the Grand Mufti said. "Would He have given us these miracles if He weren't? Now it's up to us to go on with His plan and see how it plays out. Can we do that?"

"I'm sure we can!" the bodyguard said.

"Good," Haji Jamal said. "So am I."

Rivka Avigad glared at her brother-in-law, her eyes wild. "Why didn't you do something?" she said. "Why didn't you stop him?"

Yitzhak Avigad had known this would be bad. He hadn't known

it would be *so* bad. But how could you get angry at a mother whose only son had just vanished off the earth, even if he'd gone straight to heaven in the company of Jesus? You couldn't.

"What was I supposed to do, Rivka?" he asked, as gently as he could. "Shoot him? That might have stopped him from going to Jesus—if I had a gun."

"Don't be ridiculous." Chaim's mother tossed her head. "I didn't mean shoot him. I meant stop him."

"How?" Yitzhak had to hang on to his temper. Rivka hadn't seen the look on Chaim's face when Jesus descended. (She hadn't seen the same look on Muhammad al-Muntazar's face, either. But he was just an Iranian, not her baby.) "What should I have done?"

"I don't know. You were only a few meters away." She threw the fact in his face. "Something!"

"I'll tell you what I could have done," Yitzhak said. Rivka leaned toward him. The apartment at Kibbutz Nair Tamid had never seemed so cramped. Yitzhak went on, "When we went to the States to look at the red heifer—"

"Yes?" She seemed ready to tear a response from him.

"I should have stopped at a hamburger stand and bought him a bacon double cheeseburger," Yitzhak said. Rivka gaped. He nodded. "That might have done it. As long as he stayed ritually pure, though . . . this was going to happen."

"We went to so much trouble. He had to put up with so much, and do without so much—" Rivka started to cry.

"I was one of the people who kept him from having it," Yitzhak said. "We believed in what we were doing. So did he."

"I never would have started if I'd known it would lead to—this," his sister-in-law said. "I wanted him to be happy and *frum* and maybe a priest after the Temple got rebuilt. That would have been wonderful. I didn't dream he'd turn into the Messiah and—and go away forever." More tears slid down her cheeks.

Yitzhak wondered if Mary said things like that when Jesus started His career. You always wanted your children to be special. But who wanted—or expected—a son *that* special? But Jesus had called Chaim—or more likely the Jews through Chaim—his elder brethren. And, through Muhammad al-Muntazar, he'd called Muslims his younger brethren. Once the videos were fully translated, there was no doubt of that. If God or the Son of God or a prophet or whatever Jesus truly was had said such things, how could you not take them seriously? You couldn't.

Yitzhak didn't try to tell Rivka any of that. Too much, too soon. He did say, "You don't know what'll happen. You do things and hope for the best and see how they turn out. The only One Who knows what's going to happen is God."

"Much good that does me." She didn't hide her bitterness.

"It does what He wants it to do," Yitzhak said. "I don't think we've got anything to do with it, unless He decides to listen to prayers."

"If He listened to prayers, I'd have Chaim back," Rivka said. "He won't listen to anybody or anything."

"Be careful what you say." Yitzhak felt he should whisper. But what was the point? God heard him any which way.

"Do you think it makes any difference?" Rivka replied. "He knows it's true." She tapped her forehead with a finger. "And it's here, too." That finger tapped the smooth curve above her heart. "If He doesn't like it, He'll do whatever He does. Like I care one way or the other."

"But—" Yitzhak wanted to say she had a better chance of heaven if she acted the way God wanted her to. Seeing Chaim in the next world didn't mean so much to her, though. How could it?

"But nothing," Rivka said. "I'm a good Jew. We all are here. And then God goes and does this to *me*? He's got a lot of nerve."

Yitzhak remembered Chaim's dissatisfaction with the Book of

Job. Rivka was dissatisfied with it, too, in her own way. Not for her was Job's unquestioning submission. If God did something she didn't like, He'd hear about it from her. Maybe that was the difference between the Iron Age and modern humanity. Maybe it was just the difference between Job and Rivka Avigad.

All Yitzhak could say was, "I'm sorry," one more time. "I loved him like my own son—you know that."

"Uh-huh. I do." His sister-in-law nodded. "You've been more like a father to him than Tzvi was, that's for sure."

"Yeah." Yitzhak's mouth tightened. After the divorce, his brother hadn't wanted thing one to do with Rivka or Chaim. He'd never get the chance now.

She shook her head, not at him but at fate. "I know he's gone to a better place." Her mouth twisted. "How many million people have said that? But I really do know. I saw it happen. Knowing doesn't help."

"I found that out, too," Yitzhak said. "He isn't coming back, and we'll miss him the rest of our lives."

"He isn't coming back," Chaim's mother repeated. "As long as we're here, he might as well be dead. That's what makes it so hard. I keep thinking he'll ask me a silly question or want some ice cream or . . . or *something*."

"Me, too." Yitzhak hesitated again, this time for a different reason. He went ahead anyhow: "One of these days—whenever you want—once things straighten out a little—"

"If they ever do," Rivka broke in.

"Yeah," Yitzhak agreed. "If they ever do, can we talk about you and me—the two of us—one of these days?"

He wondered if he'd botched it. He feared he had—it sounded like a botch to him. He also wondered if he'd startle her too much for her to take him seriously. The worst thing she could tell him was no. How was he worse off?

How? he asked himself. *Easy. Then you'll* know *she isn't interested instead of just wondering. That's no good.*

He realized she wasn't startled. Which meant *he* wasn't as good at keeping things to himself as he'd thought he was. Oh, well.

"You could have asked me any time the past ten years," she said. That wasn't exactly true. He'd been married to Sarah part of the time, and getting over losing her after that. Still . . . He *had* wasted too much time. Rivka went on, "You never know how things will go, but we can find out. How's that sound?"

"As good as anything can right now," Yitzhak answered. How good was that? Rivka had said it—they could find out.

This is the way the world ends/ Not with a bang but with breakfast, Gabriela thought. Eliot wouldn't have approved. *Well, T. S., Eliot* went through her head—a joke she'd first made in high school. And she knew some things old Thomas Stearns hadn't. It looked as if the world *might* end, some time in the not too indefinite future. Meanwhile, she got hungry.

So did Lester Stark and Saul Buchbinder, who shared the table with her. Rhonda Stark went right on sleeping late, Second Coming or no Second Coming. Gabriela admired her sangfroid without being able to match it.

"How do we end this? Why doesn't God have better writers?" Buchbinder grumbled. "Jesus takes the Messiah and the Mahdi up to heaven. So? Who wins? Who loses? Which side were we supposed to be on?"

Gabriela thought those were all terrific questions, even if she could answer none of them. She felt like a cat trying to figure out how and why people did things. Any guess she made would look too much like a cat's in God's eyes.

Reverend Stark buttered a roll and put cream in his coffee. *Fid-*

dling with his food buys him time to think, she realized. "We're likely in the Last Days," he said after a sip from his cup. "God hasn't intervened so openly in the world since the Crucifixion . . . or since he gave Muhammad the Qur'an." He might be a cat, but he was an analytical cat—a variety Eliot never wrote about.

"You don't like saying that, do you?" Gabriela asked.

"No, but what choice do I have after everything that's happened?"

"Good for you!" Admiring his integrity, she air-clapped. "Plenty of people wouldn't change no matter what happened."

Buchbinder said, "It's funny. I'm not the most observant Jew ever, y'know, but I always figured Christianity and Islam were to Judaism like Windows is to the Mac OS. They're clunky ways to get to what oughta be simple and neat. Now I find out they all come from the same software firm! Sheesh!"

"I can tell you what some of the problem is." Stark managed a wry grin. "Humility. I have to keep reminding myself—humility. I don't know it all. Boy, did I get my nose rubbed in that."

In his own way, he was admitting to being a cat. "You aren't the only one," Gabriela said.

"That's a different part of the problem," he said.

"Now you've lost me," she told him.

Saul Buchbinder nodded. "Me, too."

"Look at it like this," Stark said with a commanding gesture that reminded Gabriela she was sitting across the table from a preacher cat. It was impressive and intimidating at the same time . . . if you were a cat yourself, anyhow. He went on, "Before, we thought the Second Coming would settle things."

"Maybe *you* did," Saul gibed.

"It settled one thing, anyway," Gabriela said. "God's there, all right." She wouldn't have bet on that before this started. She just hoped God would forgive her her trespasses when her celestial credit card came due—or, depending on how you looked at things,

forgive her for clawing the couch and pissing on the rug. Deliberately not looking up at—through—the ceiling, she added, "This is
sending all the scientists back to the drawing board."

"More to it than that," Stark said. "God's there—but when Jesus
came and took the Messiah back with Him, God didn't tell anybody what the right way to believe was."

"I thought that meant all three were fine," Gabriela said. "I still
think so."

"Many people do." Stark's courtesy never failed him. "Maybe
they're right. But some Jews will say, 'We rebuilt the Temple. That's
why this happened.' Some Christians will say, 'The Son of God's
more important than the Mahdi or the Messiah.' And some Muslims will say, 'It's the way the Qur'an said it would be.'"

"People like that should just shut up," she remarked.

"Maybe." No, Stark seldom came right out and disagreed. But
he had his own ideas. "Remember, though—if they're right, the
Tribulation's coming. We're already seen a lot of prophecy come
true."

"Oy! My aching back!" Saul put in. Except for the *Oy!*, Gabriela
was thinking the same thing.

"*My aching back* is right," Stark said. "God's alive and well. He's
watching us. So what we do had better please Him if we know
what's good for us."

"Always a big if," Gabriela said. The lyrics from *Santa Claus Is
Coming to Town* chimed in her head. But there was a huge difference between presents or no presents and heaven or hell. A *huge*
difference. "If all the, the Abrahamic religions are all right in God's
eyes, the way it looks, isn't everybody at least trying hard to get
along the most important thing right now?"

"It sure is," the preacher said. "We've already been trying that
for two thousand years, but don't you think we've got extra reason
to now?"

"My aching back!" Buchbinder repeated.

"Tribulation," Stark said solemnly. "We may find out who's right and who's wrong. Prophecy makes that plain."

"Or we may find out the details don't matter and trying is what counts," Gabriela said. "That's what 'elder brother' and 'younger brother' meant to me."

"Believe me, I hope—I pray—you're right," the preacher said.

Gabriela refilled her empty cup. She added cream and sugar to the steaming coffee, then caught the waiter's eye. He hustled over. He was short and thin, medium brown, with wavy black hair. That and the singsong way he said, "Yes, ma'am?" made her pretty sure he came from India.

"Bring me a shot of rum," she told him. "A double, in fact."

"Ma'am?" His eyebrows jumped. It wasn't even half past eight yet. Israelis scorned lushes, and the waiter must have picked up the locals' attitude if he didn't have it to begin with. Stark seemed startled she was drinking so early, too.

She just looked at the brown man. He shrugged, went away . . . and came back with the rum.

She poured it into the coffee. It almost made the cup run over—almost, but not quite. When she drank the corrected brew, it warmed the cold spot in her belly. "You believe Tribulation's coming anyway?" she said to Stark. It was a question, and then again it wasn't.

He nodded. "Yes. I do."

He might not hesitate. Years in the industry had taught Gabriela that coming right out and saying yes could be as bad as saying no. She answered, "I'm hoping not." Even so, she felt like another. But one, even a stiff one, was medicinal. If one wasn't enough, all the rum in the world wouldn't be. But Gabriela also hoped she wouldn't need it.

* * *

After a big earthquake, aftershocks went on for days, months, even years. Eric remembered the 1994 Northridge quake. Right after it, people walked on eggs, amazed at what had happened and afraid something worse would. It hadn't then, but . . .

Jerusalem had that feeling now. What was coming next? Eric wasn't anxious to find out. Some people seemed to be. They thought they already knew. Eric didn't know whether to be more afraid that they were right or wrong.

He didn't want Armageddon. He wanted a normal life. He wanted to publish what he'd unearthed, and to find out what being married to Orly was like. The bit he'd known so far was great. Maybe one of these days . . . kids?

Did you want to raise kids in the Last Days, if these were the Last Days? If you didn't, wouldn't the other side win by default? Eric thought so, even if it wasn't clear who the other side was.

Signs seemed moderately promising. A large Israeli medical mission went into the West Bank, and neither Fatah nor Hamas fighters opened up on it. The seventeen different sides in the Syrian civil war had stopped shooting at one another for the moment, and the Iranians, the Turks, and the Russians were pulling troops out of what was left of the country. Even Albanians and Serbs in Kosovo were trying to get along. Maybe none of that would last, but you never could tell these days. Maybe it would, too.

He was walking through the Old City when somebody called, "Professor Katz!" in English.

He turned. "Hello, Barb," he said. "Haven't seen you for a while. I didn't know you were still in Israel."

"Where else would I go?" Barb Taylor answered. "Aren't these wonderful times to be alive in? I saw the Second Coming! On TV, but I did. If that doesn't make me one of the luckiest people in the world, I don't know what would. And I know God loves me. That's all I need."

"Are you sure?" Eric asked.

"I'm not worried about it," Barb declared. He must have given her a look, because she nodded and said it again: "I'm *not*. I'm heading for heaven. I was sure before, but I'm really sure now, know what I mean?"

"I guess," Eric mumbled. God *was* there. Some people, like Barb, had believed already. Adjusting came easier for them. Eric couldn't help believing now. If somebody hit you over the head, you believed in baseball bats. That didn't make you like it. He still *wanted* to be a secular humanist.

Barb Taylor beamed. She *was* a sweet-natured person, dim but sweet. "I'm sure you're going to heaven, too!" she said, as if that were his fondest wish.

It should have been. He realized as much. Making himself conform to the new reality wasn't easy. "You sure?" he asked with a lopsided grin. "I'm just a Jew, after all."

"God loves everybody." Barb spoke with absolute conviction. "Look at what Jesus told the Messiah and the Mahdi."

Eric didn't laugh. But he didn't let that pass, either. "Tell it to Brandon Nesbitt," he said. "Tell it to the President of Iran."

She waved her hand. "God loves everybody." If she said it often enough, she might make it true. She added, "All three of them went to heaven together. You were there when they did. I saw you on TV, too."

"Yeah, I was there," Eric allowed. "Scared the crap out of me. I don't think it's as simple as you make it out to be."

"We wouldn't be here if we weren't working out God's plan—all of us," Barb said. "He knows what He's doing."

That's what I'm afraid of, Eric thought. Somewhere, the pans on the scales of his cosmic balance swung a little. Maybe not literally. Maybe just in God's mind. *Thou art weighed in the balances, and art found wanting.* So much for *God loves everybody*.

But Barb beamed at him. "It'll be all right. God's peace and happiness last for eternity."

"I hope you're right." Eric wondered if he meant it. *Weighed in the balances. Found wanting . . . Stop that!*

She fluttered her fingers in a gesture that looked more California than New England. "I am. God will take care of it. Now I've gotta run. See you." Away she went, plump and dowdy and . . . saved?

How could you know? Even with God in the picture, you still had to do the best you knew how to do. Eric glanced east, toward the Temple Mount. But the answer wasn't there. The answer, if there was one, lay inside him. It always had.

HARRY TURTLEDOVE is the award-winning author of the alternate-history works *The Man with the Iron Heart*, *The Guns of the South*, and *How Few Remain* (winner of the Sidewise Award for Best Novel); the Hot War books (*Bombs Away*, *Fallout*, and *Armistice*); the War That Came Early novels: *Hitler's War*, *West and East*, *The Big Switch*, *Coup d'Etat*, *Two Fronts*, and *Last Orders*; the Worldwar saga: *In the Balance*, *Tilting the Balance*, *Upsetting the Balance*, and *Striking the Balance*; the Colonization books: *Second Contact*, *Down to Earth*, and *Aftershocks*; the Great War epics: *American Front*, *Walk in Hell*, and *Breakthroughs*; the American Empire novels: *Blood and Iron*, *The Center Cannot Hold*, and *Victorious Opposition*; and the Settling Accounts series: *Return Engagement*, *Drive to the East*, *The Grapple*, and *In at the Death*. Turtledove is married to fellow novelist Laura Frankos. They have three daughters—Alison, Rachel, and Rebecca—and two granddaughters, Cordelia Turtledove Katayanagi and Phoebe Quinn Turtledove Katayanagi.